MINE TO HOLD

PROTECTION SERIES BOOK 5

KENNEDY L. MITCHELL

ABOUT THE AUTHOR

Kennedy L. Mitchell lives outside Dallas with her husband, son and two very large goldendoodles. She began writing in 2016 after a fight with her husband (You can read the fight almost verbatim in Falling for the Chance) and has no plans of stopping.

She would love to hear from you via any of the platforms below or her website www.kennedylmitchell.com You can also stay up to date on future releases through her newsletter or by joining her Facebook readers group - Kennedy's Book Boyfriend Support Group.

Thank you for reading.

Cover Design: Bookin It Designs

Editing: Hot Tree Editing

Proofreading: All Encompassing Books

❀ Created with Vellum

PROLOGUE

With a quick flick of his wrist, the turn signal activated as he slowed, approaching the four-way stop just two blocks from his home. Double-checking both ways, he sped up, turning the wheel down the quiet, family-oriented suburban street. The massive brick homes passed slowly as he stuck to the speed limit, knowing a child or ball could appear in the street at any moment, more worried about the hassle it would be if he hit either, rather than injuring someone. Perfectly manicured lawns, not a single stray brown leaf littering the dormant grass, and large mature trees were the norm in this part of the greater Nashville, Tennessee, area.

He eased the BMW 7 Series into the long driveway that circled around the front of his home. After cutting the engine, he allowed himself a moment to breathe and take in the surroundings, ensuring nothing was amiss. Across from him, on the lawn next door, two teenage boys tossed a football back and forth while a younger girl energetically played with a set of dolls on the long front porch.

Though they'd just moved in, he hadn't taken the time to get to know any of his new neighbors, had no interest in knowing anything about them as long as they didn't pry into his business. The house on the other side of him sat dormant, a black matte wooden For Sale sign staked in the grass by the curb broadcasting to the world that it was empty of occupants.

His lip curled at the thought of all the cars and irregular traffic that would come with the house being on the market. It wasn't ideal. More eyes to study his every move, though he was smart enough to never physically tie his side business to his home for anyone to suspect him of the illegal activity. Stretching across the console, he wrapped his thin fingers around the handle of his hefty briefcase, stuffed full of files from the office and his work laptop, and pushed open the driver door.

As he emerged, the two boys paused their game for a split second, watching with curiosity in their gazes as he stalked up the light-lined walkway. Even though they'd only been here a short while, there was no doubt everyone stayed clear of him, probably sensing he was a little off. Good thing they didn't know exactly how true their gut instincts were.

Though assuming he was only a "little" off was a gross under-statement.

Three years ago, he had the foresight to alter his life in order to appear more... normal to the curious eye. This helped others from studying him too closely, allowed her to play buffer between him and the rest of the world. The lack of people interaction was the reason he chose the profession that he coincidently was very good at. After growing up away from society with only his family for company, working alone was exactly what he needed.

Inserting the correct key into the deadbolt, he gave it a hard twist and shouldered the door open, slamming it shut the moment he was inside.

"That you, honey?" a soft feminine voice called from the direction of the kitchen.

He ground his teeth to keep from lashing out. That term of endearment was like sandpaper scraping against this skin. His so-called wife knew he hated it yet still forced the issue, trying her best to make their marriage somewhat warm.

After depositing the laptop bag along the entry table, avoiding the overflowing vase of fresh flowers and stack of mail, he strode down the long hall toward the kitchen.

"Hey," she said over her shoulder as she stirred something in a large pot. His stomach rumbled, reminding him he'd skipped lunch to run a more pressing errand. "You're home late."

"Couldn't be helped. Emergency at work." He watched as her shoulders fell in visible disappointment. Fuck. He needed to make nice before she made his life a living hell, nagging him like he knew she would. Careful to keep from touching a single inch of exposed skin, he placed what he hoped was a comforting hand on her shoulder and gave it a tentative squeeze. "I'm sorry. I should've called."

But you don't matter was what he wanted to tack on at the end.

Because in the grand scheme of his life, she was just another puppet.

"I left a stack of invitations that came today on the entry table," she told him. "Let me know which ones you want to attend and I'll RSVP. I can't believe we actually got invited to the Parkers' annual holiday party."

A genuine smile pulled at his lips. *Good.* His plan was all coming together.

"Dinner will be ready in ten minutes," she said, shooting a half smile over her shoulder. "You want to take a quick shower first?"

It was odd that she knew his routine, how he liked things done and in what order, yet he couldn't even tell someone if she liked coffee or tea. Those details slipped through the cracks with her, but not with the other women in his life. Not the ones he watched with rapt attention without them knowing, studying their comings and goings before passing the information off. Their lives were meticulously documented, watched, and categorized to ensure they were the right ones. The ones who would be worth the investment.

Without another word, he slipped his hand from her shoulder and turned, leaving her standing over the stove watching him go. The heels of his thousand-dollar shoes clipped along the polished wooden stairs as he headed up to the third floor instead of the bedroom.

His personal floor.

The wife had the lower two floors, could do whatever she pleased there, but not on the third.

After unlocking the deadbolts to his home office—justifying the additional security because of the files he brought home—he slipped inside, closing the door quietly behind him and engaging the locks. The soft leather of the rolling chair molded around him as he settled in the seat. Two quick clicks of the mouse instantly activated the four large monitors, which were carefully placed to not face the door or window.

He entered the first thirteen-symbol password, which prompted for another ten-symbol password before his self-built security system approved. From the outside, according to anything that was documented on the hard drive, this computer setup was a home hub for his business, but hidden online, in the deepest recesses of the dark web where most were too afraid or unskilled to breech, that was where his real money and pleasure was created.

After a series of three additional security checkpoints, all four monitors flickered from the boring spreadsheets and lines of code, going black before blinking to life with new visuals on the screens.

Two played a live feed from various points in a bar where he'd hacked into their own security feed instead of resorting to installing his own cameras. Another screen showed an empty lobby of an apartment building where he could monitor the comings and goings of his special puppet.

Dragging the keyboard closer, he entered a line of code and hit Enter, changing the last screen from some woman across the country making dinner inside her apartment to a local, empty apartment. This video feed was why his stomach growled, why lunch wasn't even a thought when he'd raced across town to install the three cameras while his special puppet was at her weekly therapy visit, none the wiser that he had broken into her home.

Clicking to the next video feed, the one aimed toward the door, he waited, knowing she'd be rushing home soon enough, not wanting to miss a single second of watching her live her life unaware of his prying eyes.

Noting that he had a few minutes, he swiveled the chair toward the other screen and clicked a few keys. A single bed wedged in the corner with a lone naked woman chained on top appeared.

He cocked his head to the side, studying the way she lay there, no fight left.

Pity. Those first few days, she fought tooth and nail to get free, which he knew raked in the most money. Though after two weeks of him directing, every ounce of torture taking her to the brink and back, it wasn't surprising that she was at the end of her shelf life.

With a sigh, he pulled up the chat room he'd created for this puppet's term, the location changing constantly to stay under the FBI's radar, and typed tonight's choices for his viewers to bid on.

$100,000 per vote.

The option with the most votes wins.

Live results - two days. Link provided then.

Option one: Studded paddle with plug.

Option two: Blood play.

Option three: Snuff.

After hitting Enter, he leaned back and interlaced his fingers behind his head. Barely thirty seconds had passed before votes began trickling in. A smile twitched at the corner of his lips, with option three already showing to be the favorite. He knew it would. Anytime he offered that option, the sick fuckers who watched his live streams chose it. Considering this was puppet number forty-seven, he knew without a doubt that option number three would win.

Which meant he needed to plan her exit, clean up, and select a new puppet from the half-dozen potentials.

As if sensing his needs, his special puppet raced through the front door of her apartment building, blonde ponytail swaying with the quick movement. He flicked the video feed to watch her bound up the stairs, full tits bouncing with every jump, making his dick twitch. Those were new. Last time he had her, she was still just a child, a too-thin perfect ballerina. Now her hips had rounded, stomach not nearly as flat. Even with the changes, she was still perfect, everything he'd imagined the few years they'd been apart.

Assuming what would come next, he quickly unbuckled his belt in anticipation, slipping his boxer briefs low enough to pull out his half-mast cock. The moment she burst through her door, his heart rate kicked up. This was the first time he'd seen inside her apartment, gotten this close to the only one who mattered.

Tinley Harper.

Chest rising and falling with his heavy pants, he clicked to the camera in her bathroom. Unblinking, he watched as she stripped off her clothes, tossing them to an enormous pile in the corner.

Naked.

Gloriously naked just for him.

Squeezing his now rock-hard cock, he pumped his hands, breath catching as he tugged harder and harder while watching her rub soap all over her body through the glass door of the shower.

Soon she would be his again.

And this time he would be prepared, ready to keep her his and his alone.

She was his first obsession, the strongest though not the last. A flash of anger had him tugging his hand faster, remembering his past mistakes that led her to leaving him too soon, before he was done with her.

By Christmas, his special puppet would be his once again.

And only his.

For the rest of her life—however long he deemed that would be.

1

BRYSON

Tuesday, December 4th

The tight breath I'd held a little too long burned in my lungs, desperate for release, as I softly closed the door, careful to not make a sound as it snicked shut. Releasing the death grip around the egg-shaped doorknob, I silently whispered a quick prayer that this time my precious, never-tired daughter stayed in her crib. I waited, ear pressed to the painted wood door for any hint of movement. Only when thirty seconds of silence radiated from the nursery did I release my breath and turn, tiptoeing down the stairs toward the living room.

Halfway down, I gripped the rail to keep from stumbling, scraping my other calloused palm down my weary face as I attempted to repel the wave of fatigue.

Holy hell, I was exhausted.

Beyond exhausted.

Being a single, working parent was not for the faint of heart. Or old fuckers like me. Being almost forty was tiring enough. Add in a job that never stopped and I was fucked.

Entering the living room, I bent, lower back protesting as I gathered the scattered assortment of stuffed animals my sweet two-year-old, Victoria, flung around the room earlier in the day. Cleaning up was redundant considering she'd just throw them around again tomorrow, but I needed the distraction to avoid the elephant in the room.

Oh hell, she'd whip my ass if she heard that thought. Just the image of my elderly, still spunky-as-hell mother chasing me around the room with a wooden spoon made my lips twitch upward in a haphazard smirk.

"You look terrible," she said from where she sat in the armchair by the front bay windows.

"Thanks, Mom," I grumbled, not feeling the irritation I tried to push into my tone. She meant well, always did, even if she had a blunt way of going about it.

"You'll make yourself sick working as hard as you do and not resting when you get home." I raised my brows at the pink stuffed bear in my hands and rolled my eyes, too respectful of my mother to actually point that look her way as she spoke. "You need a break."

I didn't stop the incredulous huff that rattled in my chest.

Mumbling something under her breath, she went back to stitching the hole in Victoria's favorite shirt. Why she loved that *My Little Pony* shirt as much as she did, I had no fucking clue, but letting her wear it day in and day out made my life easier. Her repetitive clothing choice was not worth the battle.

"I'm a single dad," I said as I collapsed on the couch. The weight of the last few months crashed over me, making my head fall against the back. "And an overworked federal agent who can't seem to hold down a damn nanny no matter what I pay."

The last one was at least honest with me, saying she couldn't work for me because of my crazy schedule and demands.

Demands.

My grip on the teddy bear tightened to the point of stitches popping along the seams.

I didn't see how asking for updates throughout the day, for the nanny's attention to never deviate from Victoria, to allow me to track their movements, and occasional drone surveillance while they were at the park was deemed as demanding.

They called it controlling.

I wanted to strangle them for being so damn naïve. Didn't they know the horrors this world did to sweet children, unsuspecting women? No, they didn't because I worked my ass off daily to keep those fuckers who got off on hurting others out of their nightmares and six feet below ground like they deserved to be. My job was to preserve the innocence of this world, yet these nannies were leaving because of the excessive time it took to keep everyone safe.

At the weight of Mom's stare, I rolled my head along the couch to face her.

Eyes narrowed, lips pursed, I internally cringed, wondering where this conversation was headed.

"How long has it been since you had a day off?" she asked.

"I have PTO coming up for Christmas—"

"I'm talking about from life, son. Don't be dense."

"Is there such a thing?"

"People do it all the time. Get away for the weekend to recharge, get laid—"

"Mom," I exclaimed, and sat up straight. Throwing the teddy bear into the toy basket, I closed my eyes.

"Don't you 'Mom' me. You're an adult. I'm an adult. We can talk about sex."

"No, we cannot." Not with her. For more reasons than her being my mother. I knew this topic was sensitive because of my bastard of a father.

"You need to find someone who can help you, and you won't find her stuck in this house watching *Mickey Mouse Clubhouse* on your days off."

Twisting on the couch, I laid an arm along the back. "I had someone, a wife, and now—" Her string of grumbled words lit a fire of annoyance deep in my gut. She'd only become vocal about her dislike for my late wife after the accident. "I'm not dating just to find Victoria a mother."

"What about finding someone for you? You deserve to be happy, Bryson." My rising irritation vanished at her soft tone. She really meant well. "And I know it's been a while since you have been. Even before the accident." She arched a challenging brow, daring me to say otherwise.

I swallowed hard. I wanted to say she was wrong, to defend the life Heather and I lived before she was taken in the car accident, but I couldn't. Because she was right. Two years was a long time to gain perspective on a relationship you'd once thought was perfect. Two years to look back at all the lonely nights I'd had during our years together. I hadn't noticed it then, fully in love with Heather with all my heart, but now—thanks to my mother's direct comments—the imperfections AND the coldness in our marriage had slowly become apparent.

"I adored my wife," I stated. "No marriage is perfect."

Mom huffed. "Yes, you adored her, but what did she give you in return, huh? You gave that woman everything, and all she wanted was more hours in the day so she could be at that damn hospital with her patients."

I cringed, hating the old scars she opened with the truth in her words. "She was helping people, Mom. I understood that."

"And you didn't work day in and day out with the FBI? How was her work at that psych hospital more important than you, than your needs and hers?" She hitched her chin toward the stairs that led to Victoria's nursery.

"It was different," I said defensively. "Mom, can we not do this tonight? I'm fucking exhausted and just want to go to bed."

"Listen, I know you don't enjoy hearing all this, but it's time. It's time for you to realize you deserve better than being stuck grieving a woman who wasn't that great to you and never a mother to that sweet baby upstairs." Again, couldn't disagree with her there. As excited as Heather was to have a baby, she sure changed her tune the moment she realized how much work an infant was. I would've been lost those first few months if it weren't for Mom helping every spare minute she could. "I swear, the minute she pushed Victoria out, she tossed her in your arms and left for work."

"Now you're just being dramatic." I chuckled.

Mom crossed her arms over her chest. "She never *really* wanted a baby, just the idea of one." Sadness swelled in my chest at her words. "And in the end, she didn't even want this. Everything you did to give her the best life you could provide."

"I loved her," I said, hating the crack in my voice. My heart was still raw from losing Heather, even though the words and opinions Mom spouted rang true. I'd overlooked so much in my blind love and devotion to my wife. Now looking back, I felt somewhat foolish knowing everyone else saw it but me. "She was the mother of my child, my wife."

Mom's features softened. "I know, Bryson. I know you loved her. That's you, son. When you love, you love with all that big heart of yours, which you know I love about you. But just because we love someone and do everything we can to make them love us back, doesn't mean they will."

Heavy silence filled the living room. She was right, but that didn't mean I felt the loss any less.

Sighing, I surveyed the room, taking in the early fifties, small, cottage-style home, handpicked decorations, and warm feel. This house, which now felt like a home, was all me. Heather had wanted something bigger, less of a home and more something to show off, just like she was raised. Unlike me.

The shrill ring of my cell phone had me groaning, just knowing it had something to do with work. The couch groaned as I shifted forward to swipe the ringing phone off the coffee table, silencing it as I pulled it close to keep the noise from waking Victoria.

When I checked my screen, my best friend's name, Tallon Harper, flashed across.

Unease at seeing him calling this late made my gut roll. Not because of how I felt about the jackass but because of his younger sister, Tinley. Ten years ago, his name flashed across my cell phone much like tonight, with me unsuspecting about the devastation headed my way, the call setting off a chain of events that will forever haunt me.

After swiping my thumb across the screen, I pressed the smooth glass against my ear.

"What's wrong?" I said in way of greeting. He knew to expect that type of response from me these days. After Tinley's abduction and Heather's accident, my paranoia at receiving another life-altering call had escalated to concerning levels.

My pulse raced at the silence that followed.

"Tallon," I snapped. "What the hell is going on? What is it?"

"Calm your man boobs." Fucker. I hadn't had man boobs since puberty. The prick knew that too. I cut a side-eyed glare at Mom, the reason Tallon even knew I was a chubby kid since we didn't meet until college. I knew better than to introduce those two. "Everything is okay."

Though the way he said that last word signaled the opposite.

"What's going on?"

"Fuck, you're tense. Not everything is about to go wrong, dude. You know what you need?" *Oh fuck, I know where this is going.* "You need to get laid."

I groaned and dragged a hand along my scruff-covered jaw. "What's up with everyone butting into my sex life?"

"Or lack thereof," Mom said from across the room.

"That your mom?" Tallon asked. "Tell her I said hi and thanks for the banana bread."

I turned toward Mom and threw a hand in the air. "You sent him your famous banana bread? I didn't get any," I groused.

"He's my favorite," she said with a single shoulder shrug, smiling.

"I gave you a grandchild," I huffed. "And I'm your actual son."

"You should listen to us and get laid." I waved her comment off before she could say anything else to distract me from the jackass on the other end of the line as he continued. "Though this time use a condom. I'm already draining all my extra funds on spoiling that adorable niece of mine."

All my irritation at him and Mom diminished. He really did his best at spoiling Victoria, even though he lived a state away and was always traveling the country for the FBI. "You still in LA working on that case?"

"Yeah." My attention snagged on the tired sigh he tacked on the end. "These cases are challenging, to say the least. Which is why I'm calling."

Shoving off the couch, I stood and strode over to the fireplace, the dwindling flames warming my lower legs, and leaned a shoulder against the stone mantel. "You need help? I could request to be put on the task force, but you know I can't travel."

For the last eighteen months, Tallon's task force had focused on identifying an elusive, sick fucker who'd tortured, raped, and murdered women all across the country. Thirty-two victims and counting. The analysts at Quantico were working to tie other unsolved murders to this unsub, but they were hampered by the way he constantly changed cities and states. Before the local police could put together that they had a serial killer on their hands, this unsub was already gone, hunting in a new city.

"No, though I appreciate the offer. You'd be a tremendous help even just working from Louisville. It's.... I need a favor," Tallon said, clearing his throat, heightening my anticipation. "I'll be out here another week, maybe ten days, wrapping up a few loose ends." He paused.

"Okay," I drawled. It wasn't like Tallon to beat around the bush. This had to be some favor. "What do you need, man? You know you can count on me."

"I know, which is why I'm asking. I need you in Nashville. As soon as possible. Fuck, tonight if you could swing it."

I furrowed my brows, staring into the glowing embers of the fire. "Why? Tinley okay?" My heart raced at the thought that she wasn't. Though she was ten years younger, she'd always held a special place in my heart, driving an insistent need to protect her.

"Yes, she's fine. For now." I swallowed hard, gripping the edge of the mantel to keep me from running to the truck and driving to Nashville. "The local police contacted me about a murder victim they have, and, well, I'm worried about her being there alone, without me or someone else to keep a watchful eye on her."

"Why?"

"It's the nature of the murder that has me calling and asking such a huge-ass favor. I know you have a job and Victoria, but... the victim's body showed signs of prolonged captivity. I don't know the details, just that a local detective reached out knowing I'm working on cases that have a similar MO. As soon as I'm done here in LA, I'll head home to review evidence and see if it's the unsub we're tracking. But even if it's not... I don't like the idea of her being there alone with some sick fuck so close."

"You think it's him?" I didn't need to elaborate. We both knew who I referred to. Ten years later and his baby sister's abduction was still fresh in both our minds. Though she didn't go through torture like the victims of the unsub Tallon was investigating, the prolonged captivity rang true to that sick fuck's MO.

"I don't know. I need to focus on these cases here and I can't, not with Tin there unprotected. And don't ask why this is different. I just have this gut feeling she's in danger. I can't ignore my instincts on this, not with her."

My mind whirled at all the things I'd have to move around to accommodate his request. "Fuck, Tallon. I want to help, but...." I slid my gaze up the stairs like I could see to the nursery. "Another nanny just quit, and—"

"I'll take Victoria." I snapped my attention to Mom, who had put down the needle and thread, staring at me with rapt attention, clearly following along with the conversation. "She can come stay with me, or I can stay here. Perfect time for that life break we discussed."

I opened my mouth to tell her no, then shut it when her eyes narrowed in annoyance.

"How long do you need?" I asked into the phone, already knowing I would go with Mom willing to watch Victoria. Not only was it my best friend asking for a favor, but it was Tinley's safety too.

Plus, the idea of spending time with Tinley again made my pulse race, which was new. Heat rose to my cheeks as a mental picture of her from the last time I saw her six months ago, when I'd been in town for a briefing at the local FBI office, flashed in my mind. Tall, thick, long blonde hair, petite features, and wide, almost clear blue eyes. Eyes that held distrust, fear, and a lot of anger—a far cry from the sweet, submissive ballet prodigy I met all those years ago.

"Five days maybe, a week tops. And don't worry about finding a place to stay. You can take my room."

My brows shot up over my forehead at that tidbit of information. Damn, when was the last time he and I caught up? "Your room?"

"Yeah, well, she needed help with making rent. You know how hard it's been for her to hold down a job, so I offered to split a space. We moved into a two-bedroom apartment a few months ago. I was relieved as hell when she finally agreed. The places she's lived in the past few years were shady as fuck."

"I'm guessing your headstrong sister doesn't know you're also doing it for your peace of mind."

"Hell no. You know Tin. She's determined to move on from her past, to not let what happened ten years ago affect her life now. So if we tell her I asked you to babysit her, she'll punch you in the balls before you can even walk through the door."

I grimaced. "You want me to lie to her about why I'm there?" My gut churned at the thought.

"Not lie, per se, just stretch the truth a little. You need a vacation from your hectic life. Hell, maybe find some random pussy and get laid." I growled at his comment, but he ignored me. "We can tell her you're there for a brief vacation and don't want to pay for a hotel room, and since I won't be there, I offered my room. She won't say no to that. She trusts you as much as she does me. Plus, it's really my call. The last few months I've covered the entire rent payment to help. She's been strapped for cash more than usual lately."

I swallowed hard. "You think she's slipping again?" She didn't look like she'd been drinking the last time I saw her. The opposite, in fact. She looked good. *Too* good. I shook my head at that thought. Nothing good would come of allowing that sliver of interest to bloom. She was ten years younger than me, my best friend's little sister, and I was still grieving.

Wasn't I? Or had the grief simply faded as the exhaustion of being a single working dad engulfed my every cell? Now wasn't the time to unpack that mindfuck. Though the idea of having someone to share my life with, a partner in all this, did light a flicker of interest in my heart. Interest that had long been snuffed out.

"No. She's too stubborn to fall back into that destructive cycle. Hell, the girl doesn't even take an Advil these days. Now she's into some natural oil shit she found online to help with aches and pains."

Essential oils, if I had to guess. Though I wouldn't admit I knew exactly what he was referring to out loud. If I did, Tallon would no doubt fly from LA, kick my ass, and forcefully take away my man card if he knew I used that same shit to help Victoria sleep through the night. The mix of lavender and peppermint being diffused in her room right now was a godsend.

No one needed to know this softer side of me except Mom and Vic. Especially not my asshole best friend.

"Good. I don't think you could watch her go through that again." Or me. Watching her struggle through rehab, then acclimating back to normal daily life, had ripped me to shreds. Though Tinley was a fighter, not afraid to put in the work. Always had been. "I don't like the idea of lying to her, T. If she finds out, she'll never trust me again."

And I'd rather show Tallon all the tiny bottles of natural oils in my collection than lose Tinley's trust.

"It'll be fine. You're not lying. Squeeze in a Tinder hookup or two while you're there to validate the misdirection. Oh, and there's my mom and Rich's Christmas parties."

Turning toward the kitchen, I stopped by the small beverage cart and grabbed the first bottle of bourbon I could find. Not bothering with a glass, I popped off the top and took a deep swig.

"Parties, as in plural? How many this year?"

Tallon and Tinley's mother and stepfather's Christmas parties were audacious and boring as fuck. I went to one years ago as Tallon's guest and hated every second.

"While you're there? Only one."

"No."

"It's for Tin, I swear."

Fucker knew the way to get me to say yes. Tallon knew I had a soft spot for his sister. Though that soft spot had shifted from brotherly love to piqued interest. Another thing I would not be telling my best friend if I wanted to keep my balls attached to my body.

"You know things have been rocky between Mom and Tin since we found her," he continued. "It's getting worse, and I swear if I leave them alone together, one of them will end up dead."

My lip curled in a snarl. With the self-defense moves I taught Tinley a couple years back, my bet was on her surviving the encounter and not that bitch mother of theirs.

"You'll be there for moral support. I'll even buy you a tux."

"I don't need your money," I grunted. Though I sure as hell had little extra cash lying around to spend a few thousand on the type of tux I'd need to purchase to fit in at the event.

"If you'd lay off the IPAs, you could fit into mine."

"Why are we friends again?"

"Because no one else would put up with your grumpy ass. So yes or no? If you don't want to go, then I'll ask one of my local agent buddies—"

Jealousy I had no right to feel roared in my gut. I tightened my hand around the liquor bottle until my knuckles turned white.

"I'll do it. But I need at least twenty-four hours to figure shit out at work and here. We just wrapped up a case, so it shouldn't be an issue for me to leave for a while." An idea jumped to the forefront of my mind. "And send me the notes on the case in Nashville. I worked with some badass BSU agents a few months ago who taught me a few things. Maybe I can determine if this victim can be tied to your unsub before you even get to Tennessee."

"Great idea. But your priority is Tinley. Make sure she stays safe without letting her know you're there for her."

"Right."

"And don't tell her the details of the case. It might set her recovery back."

Not the recovery from prescription painkillers and alcohol. No, Tallon meant mentally. Which was another way she'd changed when I saw her six months ago. She was stronger, lighter in a way I couldn't describe.

"Got it. I'll let you know when it's all set."

"Cool. I'll call Tin and give her a heads-up after I hear from you."

After catching up on all things not Tinley and murder, we exchanged clipped goodbyes, and I disconnected the call. Staring into the smoldering fire, I pressed the smooth edge of the bottle to my lips as I ran through a mental checklist of everything I needed to handle before packing up a week's worth of clothes and hitting the road.

A week in close quarters with my best friend's little sister, who, in the last year, had shifted from the sweet teenager I'd always seen her as to a beautiful, independent woman, without Tallon there to remind me of my place.

Terrible decision or not, I was headed to Nashville. I just had to hope my willpower was strong enough to keep those lines from getting blurred.

This seemed like a train wreck waiting to happen.

But with Tinley's safety on the line, I couldn't bring myself to not go, no matter the consequences.

2

TINLEY

Wednesday, December 5th

Muscles straining, I stretched a little farther, reaching for the highest shelf, fingertips grazing over the edge of the cardboard box in the supply closet. Needing a little more height, I pushed up to my tiptoes, enduring the pain blooming through my disfigured feet like I'd done for years as a pointe ballerina.

"Here." Startled, I fell forward against the shelf. "Let me help you with reaching that," the manager's familiar deep voice said from directly behind me.

Muscles tensed, heart now lodged in my throat from his unannounced approach in the small closet crammed full of supplies for the bar, I lowered to flat feet and twisted around. I sucked in a breath when my nose almost brushed his. Too fucking close. The edge of a steel shelf dug into my upper back as I shuffled back to put additional space between me and the bar manager.

With a smirk on his boyish face, he reached high over my shoulder, eyes never leaving my narrowed ones. I didn't move. Couldn't. I was frozen from panic, something that hadn't happened in months.

What the fuck is wrong with me?

Darting my gaze from side to side, I took a small opening to escape, forcing my body to move, slipping beneath his outstretched arm. Only when a few precious feet of personal space were reclaimed between us was I able to focus on slowing my racing heart.

"If you could spare the time to come back here yourself, why did you ask me to do it?" I asked now that my brain was back to functioning order. My jaw tightened as I stared him down, more annoyed with myself and my body's reaction than with him. I'd done so well the last year, growing stronger physically and mentally so these incidences were no longer a daily occurrence.

"You've been gone for ten minutes, Tinley." With a grunt, he pulled the heavy box down and set it on the ground between us. Squatting low, he whipped a knife from somewhere and sliced through the clear packaging tape, keeping the flaps closed. "We need these cocktail napkins now, not by close."

I cursed myself. How long had I stood outside the supply closet, stuck in the doorway, unable to venture into the darkness? I wasn't sure what it was about this closet in particular that triggered memories I'd spent ten years pushing to the back of my mind, but whatever it was always kept me from entering without a little personal pep talk. Maybe it was the too-small light bulb that did little to dispel the darkness, or the confined space and single exit.

"Sorry." I sighed, reining in my embarrassment. Bending forward, I grabbed several thick stacks of cocktail napkins, piling them high against my chest to carry as many as possible. "Thanks for your help. I'll take these out there."

He stood tall and placed both hands on his hips.

I swallowed hard now, realizing that in my hasty need for escape from his closeness, I put him between me and the only exit, which was now blocked by his wide stance. He wasn't a big guy, lankier like me, but it took little to fill the area. Blood pounded in my ears as I stared past him to the open door.

I had to get out of there.

"Listen, I've been meaning to talk to you." Having no clue I was about to melt down into a full panic attack, he shifted on his feet and ran a hand over his short black hair, taking all the time in the world to spit out whatever he needed to say. Frozen in place, I just blinked, focusing on my breathing to keep from passing out. Now *that* would be embarrassing. "Can you work a few extra shifts this month? With Christmas around the corner, we need all hands on deck."

"Yeah, Jase," I rasped, juggling the stack of napkins when a bunch fell. "Just put me on the schedule and I'll make it work. But I'll still need my Tuesday and every other Thursday afternoons as unavailable."

"That when your boyfriend's home?"

Was it just me, or was that a lace of intrigue in his tone?

"No," I said instead of lying. "Just a standing date with my therapist."

His eyes widened. Yep. Nothing scared off men like telling them you were batshit crazy and needed biweekly therapy or you'd be back in the looney bin.

I tapped the side of my head with a single finger. "Have to get all these crazy voices out of my head before I do what they tell me to."

"And what's that?" he asked with a wince, stepping back toward the door.

"Cut off every male's dick within reach."

His jaw slackened before his features pulled into a wince. I cocked a single brow in his direction and took a step forward, which made him retreat into the brightly lit hall. Eager to get out of the small space, I continued to press him until he stumbled, slamming against the wall opposite the supply closet. Hurrying past him, I focused on the swinging door that led to the fully packed bar, the pounding music already vibrating along my skin and ears, and evening out my breathing.

Damn, I need to get my crazy under control.

Sneaking behind the bar, I maneuvered around the bartenders who weren't dancing along the bar top to one of the many songs that played just for them. One girl at the end of the bar turned, pointing her booty-short-clad ass at the crowd. Catching my attention, she rolled her eyes in annoyance as she continued to move through the choreographed dance before plastering that fake smile back on as she turned to face the rowdy crowd once more.

Shaking my head, I filled the plastic containers, keeping out of everyone's way like the good barback I was. Well, until I wasn't. This was my sixth job this year. It had nothing to do with my work ethic or timelines. More my attitude.

Anger issues, some might call it.

Snapping at customers, pushing them off stools, and dropping drinks in their laps was frowned upon everywhere, even if the asshole deserved it. But I couldn't stop myself when the right—or wrong—situation presented itself. An overwhelming need to protect engulfed me when I saw a woman in need of someone stepping in, which pushed me to do things that got me fired if the asshole male complained or made a scene.

Which was almost every time. Most men didn't enjoy being put in their place by someone they saw as beneath them.

Head down, focused on keeping the bar stocked to make the bartenders' lives easier, the rest of the shift flew by. When last call rolled around, I wasn't sure I could stand another second on my throbbing feet. A sheen of sweat coated my skin, and I was beyond hungry. A hot glass, just out of the dishwasher, heated my fingertips as I unloaded the crate of clean dishes beneath the bar when one of the female bartender's stern voices snagged my attention.

"It's just a show," she said to the massive man leaning against the bar. I rolled my eyes. I knew his type. We all did. Jackass meathead who thought every woman on the planet should find him attractive in his way too small T-shirt that actually made him look ridiculous. "None of what you saw tonight was meant just for you."

"Come on, sugar," he said, pressing his ribs a little harder against the other side of the bar to get closer to her. "I know you were doing it just for me. I saw that look in your eye."

"And what look is that?" she asked with a huff before turning her attention back to her closing duties.

"That you want my cock more than your next breath."

My back straightened as heated anger flowed through my veins, chasing away the toll of the hard night's work. Watching the two of them, I knew what would happen before he made his move. I started to warn her, but he was faster. A massive hand lashed across the bar, grabbing her forearm in what looked like a bruising grip.

"Hey," she shouted, all annoyance gone, only surprise and fear on her face.

"You want this," he said, grabbing his crotch with his free hand. "Don't deny it."

That was it.

"Holy hell, you're delusional." Both their heads snapped my way. "She's saying no because she knows men like you have a baby turtle's head for a pecker," I said, turning to lean an elbow along the bar. My long rose gold ponytail swept over my slim shoulders as I tilted my head, considering him. Taking a section, I twisted it around a finger. "You should lay off the steroids there, Hulk Hogan. I hear it gives you ass-ne, plus the pecker shrinkage. Which you and I both know you can't afford." I flicked my gaze to where his hand still gripped his crotch.

The idiot blinked. It took him a full five seconds to comprehend what I said, but I knew the moment it all clicked. His features pinched, and his face reddened.

"What the fuck did you say to me?" With a shove, he released the bartender, making her stumble backward.

She shot me a worried glance before hurrying away, no doubt to get security before this asshole could release the rage clearly coursing through him.

What could I say? I was good at getting under people's skin.

Call it my toxic trait number fifty-three.

Yes, I had a lot.

"Oh, so you're hard of hearing too," I said while inspecting my black nails. "Damn, guy, do you have any redeeming qualities?" I lifted a shoulder and turned back to my work. "You should go. And don't fucking touch her again."

The troll of a man snarled as he stalked closer, a vein on his orange-tinted face bulging along his forehead. I had half a mind to ask him where he got his spray tan done so I could never, ever visit the same place.

"And I'm assuming a bitch like you is gonna stop me?" With a sneer, he gave me a once-over.

To piss him off further, I held up both hands in a double one-finger salute.

"Nope," I said, popping the *P*. "He is." I tilted my head toward the even more massive man stalking our way, though his smile made him seem less intimidating than the roid-rage fucker still glaring daggers my way. Unlike Hulky here, I knew this man—who was part of our regular security team and was clearly amused that I'd found myself in this type of situation yet again—knew how to fight and use his heavy bulk to keep me safe, not do harm.

With a roar, the Hulk Hogan wannabe lunged, arms extended across the bar, hands grabbing for my shoulders. I took a casual step back, putting myself just a few inches out of his reach. A sweep of potent body spray-saturated air wafted up my nose, making it wrinkle in disgust. The next second, Hulky's face slammed into the bar, both arms wrenched behind his back.

"Making friends again, Tinley?" The security guard smirked and shook his head as he pressed more of his weight on top of the bellowing drunk idiot. "Come on, asshole. There's a holding tank somewhere downtown with your name on it."

"I'll fucking kill you," the man roared as he was jerked off the bar, his wild, bloodshot eyes finding mine. "I'll be back. We're not done, cunt."

For the first time since the altercation began, a snap of icy fear laced through my veins.

"I'll be back. We're not done."

Those words, those too-familiar words, haunted my days and nights. Ten years ago, another man said those same words, promising to return for me. For several seconds, I watched as the drunk was practically dragged toward the exit, another security guard coming in to help while on the phone with the police. I tried to focus on the here and now, like my therapist had coached me.

"Hey." I snapped my head to the left, relaxing when I found the bartender from earlier. She chewed on the edge of her nail, looking everywhere but at me. "Thank you. Again."

I lifted a shoulder, the movement stiff as terrible memories continued to hold a part of me captive.

What the fuck is wrong with me tonight? This was twice in one night that I'd slipped back into those memories.

"No sweat," I said, clearing my throat, hoping to make it sound stronger than I felt. "It's always easier to react when you're not the one in the middle of the confrontation."

"Well, me and the girls would like to take you out and buy you a shot or something." Excitement filled her features. "You've helped almost all of us in one way or another the past few months."

"Thanks, but I actually don't drink."

"Dinner, then, or breakfast at this point? There's a diner down the street—"

"Another time, maybe?" Even though I knew I wouldn't follow through, just like I hadn't the previous times the others had asked. "I'm beat."

She nodded. "It was busy tonight. I feel disgusting from a beer that was spilled down my front." She flicked a quick look down my ripped black jeans and white Doc Martens, then back up to my loose black V-neck T-shirt. "You ever considered bartending? You have the perfect body for dancing."

My returning smile was strained.

Yeah, I knew my body was meant for dancing. It was all I did for the first sixteen years of my life. Every minute in a studio of some kind, practicing form and working on my endurance. Though that was then. Now...

Now I danced for no one.

Not even myself, despite how much I missed the way dancing chased away reality, providing a bubble of peace that was just for me.

"I should finish up," I said instead, trying to keep the bite from my words. She didn't deserve my anger. It wasn't her who fucked me up for the rest of my life.

Turning away from her confused look, I went back to stocking the bar as fast as possible, determined to get out of there before someone else could stop for small talk.

Wiping down the bar, I thought back to the night's events. Something was off, a wrong feeling in the air. Small things were making me remember, triggering feelings I'd fought to overcome. If I were honest with myself, it wasn't just tonight. This "off" feeling started a few weeks ago when it felt like eyes were on me all the damn time. I hated being watched, the paranoia of someone staring without me knowing making me jumpy and constantly on edge. I couldn't pinpoint why or where the feeling was coming from, but it didn't go away even when I got home, which used to be my only reprieve from, hell, everything.

It was close to 3:00 a.m. when I finally tugged on my black leather jacket and pushed out the back door that led to the alley. Making my way to the main street, I stood under a bright streetlamp and pulled a pack of cigarettes and my phone from my tiny backpack purse. While calling a car with one hand, I nimbly tugged a cigarette from the hard pack with the other. The filter brushed along my red lips as I studied the screen, frowning when the estimated wait time popped up.

"That shit will kill you."

I froze yet again, but for a totally different reason than all the other times that night. I knew that voice. It sent a flurry of butterflies to take flight in my lower belly, but it was out of place.

Tugging the unlit cigarette free, I spun on my heels. Shock rolled through me, though a smile still pulled at the corners of my lips at finding my lifelong crush standing just a few feet away, looking as hot as ever.

Bryson Bennett.

Swoon.

I pointed the cigarette at him and arched a brow. "So will that beer gut of yours."

Which was a lie, but I had trouble coming up with another comeback as I took in the sight of him. Bryson was as fit and sexy as ever, which said a lot since I'd known him since he and Tallon roomed together in college. I sucked in a shaky breath as I gave him a slow once-over.

Dark jeans hugged thick thighs that I'd always wondered what would feel like beneath my palm, his normal well-worn Red Wing boots, and a soft-shell North Face jacket that concealed the hard, defined chest that I knew lurked beneath. His hazel eyes sparkled beneath the lamplight, the corner of his perfect lips twitching upward in a calm smile.

I pressed a fist to my stomach to stop the fluttering. My crush on the older man, my brother's best friend, was embarrassing and pure torture considering he'd never even looked at me the way I longed for, never hugged too long or brushed a lingering touch along my skin. No, Bryson Bennett was the man who I wanted desperately but who would never want me back.

And why would he?

I was damaged, broken, and he was amazing.

"Good to see you, Tinley."

My responding shiver at hearing my name on his lips had nothing to do with the cold winter night. His eyes narrowed at the slight movement.

"You cold?" I shook my head. He pursed his lips, clearly not liking my answer. "My car is in the pay-by-the-hour lot a block over. Come on, I'll drive you home."

I melted. Okay, maybe not literally, but inside, I totally did. Somehow, his protective smothering soothed the layers of thorns and ice I kept around me. I started toward him when a burst of high-pitched giggles and laughter filtered through the air.

My stomach dropped as the five young, beautiful, and way less damaged female bartenders shuffled out of the alley onto the street. They pulled up short seeing me, their alarmed gazes going from me to Bryson.

I knew the moment they took in his enormous frame, handsome face, and commanding presence. I swear one of the girls' knees gave out. I rolled my eyes at their dramatics as they batted their lashes at him.

"Who's your friend, Tinley?" one bartender asked as she stepped away from the group and closer to Bryson. She fanned out her long coat, allowing a peek at the tiny outfit she wore beneath.

Bryson, though, he didn't even give them a side glance, those intense eyes of his locked on me. A look I couldn't figure out flicked across his features before vanishing, making me wonder if I'd imagined it.

"This is Bryson Bennett," I said after clearing the anger clogging my throat. Waving a hand between them, I fought to keep my smile in place. "The girls I work with. Girls, this is Bryson."

"Bryson," the eager bartender said in a soft, breathy voice. My shoulders tensed, my hand curling around my phone in a tight grip to keep me from throwing it at her head. "Love it. We're going to the diner down the street. You two want to join us?"

My lips parted, ready to tell them to back the fuck off. He was my unrequited love, damnit. Even if I had no right to feel possessive about him, I still did.

"Thanks for the offer," Bryson said before I could say anything. My heart sank, shoulders sagging. "But I'm taking Tinley home. It's been a long day, and I'm beat." He tilted his head in the direction he'd said his car waited, those hazel eyes locked on me. "You ready?"

I nodded and stepped toward him. "See you guys tomorrow," I said as I passed the clearly disappointed group of women. The moment I was close, he pulled me into a side hug, draping a heavy arm over my shoulders. It only took a few steps before my mind caught up to the surprising chain of events. "So, as nice as it is to see you, want to tell me what's going on and why you're here outside my work at 3:00 a.m.?"

Please say here to fuck me senseless.

Please say here to fuck me senseless.

"Didn't your brother call you?"

Hmm. That response wasn't promising on the fucking-me-senseless hope. I chewed on the corner of my lower lip as I checked my missed call log. Five from Tallon, plus one voice mail.

"It seems that he did." Pressing the voice mail icon, I hit the speaker button as we continued to walk down the downtown Nashville streets.

"Hey, Tin, it's your brother." I snorted at that. He was such an old man sometimes, forgetting that I knew exactly who was calling because duh, his number and name were in my phone. He always acted older than his thirty-seven years. "Listen, I have a favor to ask. Bryson needs a little R&R, and, well, I offered our place." The toe of my boot hit the sidewalk, causing me to stumble. If it weren't for Bryson's hold on my shoulder, I would've face-planted. "He's planning to stay for a few days, maybe a week, depending on a few things. I told him he could stay in my room since I won't be back for a while yet. Just make sure the fridge is stocked and the place is picked up. You know him, he's super easy. Oh, and maybe you could introduce him to some of your friends. The fucker needs to get laid."

I sucked in a sharp breath, the frosty night air slicing through my lungs like razor blades while the hand on my shoulder tightened almost to the point of pain.

"I'm going to kill that dick," Bryson hissed.

I tried to smile through the pain in my heart at the thought of Bryson with someone else.

"So you're staying with me. Alone," I said, avoiding the idea of setting him up with my nonexistent friends. For the first time in a long time, I was thankful for my reclusive nature and poor attitude. If I didn't have any friends, that meant I didn't have anyone to set him up with, which meant there would be no sex for Bryson.

Selfish, sure.

Maybe that was another one of my toxic traits.

But the thought of his attention on someone else, that protected and safe feeling his sheer presence offered me directed on someone else, made my heart feel heavy. Beyond sad, like there wasn't enough air in my lungs.

Bryson stopped and turned, placing a hand on each of my slim shoulders. I tipped my face up to his. Thankfully, my tall height kept me from having to strain to search his gaze.

"If that makes you uncomfortable, I can get a hotel."

"No," I rushed out. Closing my eyes, I tried to rein in the roller-coaster emotions racing through me, jumbling my thoughts. "I don't mind you being there with me. It's fine."

"You sure? You seem"—he tilted his head to the side as he searched my face—"tense. Maybe you should have that cigarette after all."

I couldn't help my smile. "Yeah, I'm sure. Now come on. We need to find a store that's open. I have nothing to eat at the apartment."

"Or...."

"Or?"

"I know of one place that's your favorite and open at all hours."

He was too easy to fall for. Not even the boys—and I meant boys, not men—I'd dated in the past remembered my favorite indulgence. Yet here was this man who shouldn't care but did, because that was Bryson Bennett. Always had been, even to that ice queen of a wife of his who never deserved an ounce of his love.

"Krispy Kreme sounds amazing," I responded honestly. "And I know the closest one."

"And probably know every night manager and staff member."

I shot him a wink and grabbed his elbow, tugging him into a fast walk.

Bryson and donuts.

Just the things I needed to shake off the feeling of unease that had permeated every second of my life these last couple weeks. While he was close, nothing could hurt me.

Physically, at least. My heart, well, that was a whole other issue.

One I'd dwell on after he was gone.

A week with Bryson and only Bryson.

Not sure if this would be heaven or hell for me.

But I was excited to find out.

3

TINLEY

A curse whispered past my lips the moment I pushed open the apartment door, every light in the place already on, just like I left it. The living room was a mess—clothes, blankets, bras, and.... My eyes widened as sheer horror filled me. Turning on my heels, I slammed the door in Bryson's surprised face before he could get a step inside.

"Fuck, fuck, fuck," I whisper-yelled as I ran toward the rose-shaped sex toy lying on top of the coffee table. Wrapping my hand around the small device, I drew my arm back and chucked it as hard as I could into my bedroom, only relaxing when it thumped to the floor.

Twisting like the frantic crazy person I was, I scanned the room for anything else that would literally kill me from embarrassment if found by Bryson. Fingers tangled in my long hair, I turned for the door just as a soft knock echoed through the apartment.

A mix of confusion and humor lined his features when I pulled the door open and motioned for him to come inside.

"Everything okay?" he asked. "You almost made me drop the goods here."

He held up the two boxes of glazed treats. In the other hand, he carried a stuffed duffel, a hanging clothes bag draped over his arm.

"So, old people still have quick reflexes," I joked as he passed. "Good to know for future reference."

"I'm not old," he grumbled, a hint of annoyance in his tone.

Surely, he didn't believe me. Thirty-seven was not old, even though our age gap was a running joke between the three of us. They'd make fun of technology, and I'd offer to get them a paper menu and run out to the car to get their readers. It was funny, though it didn't seem to have the same lightness as it had held years prior.

I furrowed my brow, watching as he tossed the two bags onto the couch and meandered toward the kitchen.

"Love the new place," he said, taking in the large apartment. After setting the boxes on the granite island, he began opening cabinets until he found the one with the plates and pulled out two. "How long have y'all been here?"

"Just a couple months. It's a big step up from my last place." I watched in awe as he set a plate and paper towel in front of where I sat on a metal barstool. "Thanks, but you didn't have to do that. You're my guest, remember?"

"And I'm invading your space. It's the least I can do." A waft of yummy goodness moved through the apartment when he opened the box and twisted it around to face me, inching it closer with a single finger. "Plus, I'm used to moving nonstop with Victoria."

"How is that little cutie?" His daughter was adorable. Thankfully, she inherited all of Bryson's personality and heart, and none of his late wife's.

"Hell on wheels, but I wouldn't want it any other way." His words and soft, adoring smile had a gentle sigh passing my parted lips. Great, I was swooning. Literally swooning.

I needed a distraction from his square, scruff-covered jaw and full, kissable lips with faint smile lines curving around them. His nose was slightly crooked from a critical hit during a football game in college, but somehow it made him look more handsome—ruggedly handsome.

"What?" he said, noticing my overly long stare.

Right. Shit, I was awkward as fuck around him. With other men, I was all sass and confidence, but not Bryson. No, of course I turned back into fifteen-year-old me who couldn't form coherent sentences the moment he stepped into the room.

Smiling, I snagged a donut from the box and shoved the whole thing between my lips.

His hazel eyes widened, and he shook his head, clearly amused. "Which one is Tallon's room? I'll put my stuff away. I'm sure you're beat and ready to get to bed."

"Get to bed." I really wish he wouldn't say things like that. All I wanted was to respond with a *Yes, please.* Which was clearly not his intent but more of a statement considering it was almost four.

"The door on the left. I'll grab you fresh sheets and help you make the bed." Wrapping my lips around one finger, then another, I sucked off the leftover icing as I followed close behind him, making sure Bryson didn't accidentally venture into my room. While he set his things down, I shuffled past for the bathroom, where Tallon kept his clean linens. "His bathroom is bigger than mine, which I'm constantly jealous of, but at least we each have our own."

After grabbing a fresh set of sheets that were perfectly folded—my crazy OCD brother even ironed his sheets before folding them—I went back to the bedroom, finding Bryson staring out the floor-to-ceiling windows.

"Beautiful view, right?" When he said nothing in response, I began stripping the bed. "So, Tallon's voice mail said you need some R&R." I swallowed, unable to voice the other thing Tallon mentioned Bryson needed. "What were you hoping to do while you're here?"

Still no response.

Okay... this is odd. Bryson was the fun one, lighthearted, the opposite of my grump-o-lump brother.

"Everything all right?" I asked as I tugged a pillowcase off a firm pillow. "You're acting strange."

Turning, he scrubbed a hand over his jaw. "Are you dancing?"

My stomach dropped. "What?"

"At the bar. Are you a dancer? I know what type of place that is, and I need to know if you're dancing or not."

I swallowed, not sure how to read the intensity pouring off him. It felt like more than overprotective brotherly love; it felt possessive.

It felt outstanding.

"No," I whispered, now hugging the pillow to my chest. "I'm a barback, which... wait, how did you even know where to find me?"

He visibly relaxed, his features morphing back to the same old Bryson I'd always known.

I wasn't sure how to feel about that shift.

"Your brother. When I showed up, you weren't here, so I called him to find out where I could find you. The bar was the first place I checked. I got there right as you guys closed. One of the security guys told me you were still inside, but he wouldn't let me in." His brows slowly rose up his forehead. "Said you were a trouble target and couldn't risk letting me in to see you. What's that about?"

I bit my lower lip to hide my smile. "Interesting. I don't have a clue."

"Liar," he said, his smile so wide that faint lines burst from the corners of his eyes.

"It's just...." I blew out a breath and went back to stripping the bed, this time with Bryson's help. "You know how since... everything, I've been a little overprotective when I see someone in trouble?"

"You mean do I know how you toss yourself headfirst into a confrontation that you probably should mind your own business about? Yes, I know what you're talking about. It's why I gave you those self-defense lessons, remember?"

Oh, I remembered. Remembered every touch and the way he'd mold his body around my own to correct my stance. My heart rate kicked up as my core clenched at the memory.

"Well, that's what they're referring to. At that type of bar, there's always some asshole who thinks he has a right to treat the girls like they're nothing more than a piece of flesh."

"Tinley...."

I dropped my side of the fitted sheet and held up both hands in surrender. "I never do it intending to finish the fight, I swear."

He groaned and tipped his face toward the ceiling. "That does not make me feel better."

"The security there is solid. Those guys look after me."

"I'm sure they do," he grumbled, morphing back to grumpy-pants Bryson. Catching himself, he closed his eyes and inhaled deep through his nose. "Do you like it? The job, I mean."

"It's a job. Pays the bills until I figure out what I want to do with the rest of my life. Plus it's the only industry that doesn't bat an eye at my sporadic work history. It's not fun, but it does the job."

"What do you mean?"

"Keeps money in my account and my mind and hands busy. The grueling work and long hours are nice. I can't sit too long or I think."

He laughed. Playfully, I grabbed the still-folded flat sheet and threw it at his face, which he, of course, caught midair. "And thinking is a bad thing?" he asked.

"When your thoughts are as dark as mine are, yeah."

His carefree smile fell.

Shit.

I knew not to go there.

Desperate to redirect this conversation, I cleared my throat and motioned for him to fluff out the sheet I'd just thrown at him. Thankfully, he picked up on the hint, even if his features said he wasn't happy about it.

"Anything in particular you want to do while you're here?" I asked. "I'm sorry to report that I don't have any friends to set you up with." *Or any friends at all.* "I can show you around during the day, but my boss asked me to pick up extra shifts because of the holiday craziness."

"Nothing like forced family time to drive people to the bars."

"There is so much truth in that statement, it's not funny."

He shot me a smile. "Honestly, I don't have any plans. I was just hoping to lie low. Are you sure your boyfriend won't mind me staying here?"

Boyfriend?

I cocked my head to the side, staring with a blank expression.

His cheeks turned pink. "You mentioned someone the last time I was here."

"Oh," I said, realization hitting me. "Huh, excellent memory." Bryson's shoulders visibly relaxed. "No, I'm not dating anyone. In fact, I don't even remember the person I was referring to. That's how inconsequential that guy was." I snorted and fluffed the top sheet, flapping it out to spread it evenly across the king-size bed. "Not that any of them have been."

"Oh?" he asked, keeping his face turned downward as he shoved the edge of the sheet beneath the mattress.

"What about you? Have you started dating again?" It had been over two years since Heather had passed, yet I hadn't heard Tallon mention anything about Bryson being ready to move on until tonight.

Please say no. Save my heart and say no.

"No." I blew out a heavy breath, rewarding me with a confused look from Bryson. "Between work and Victoria, I barely have time to sleep. Honestly, I just started feeling ready to even think about dating again. But...."

"But what?" I rolled the navy comforter over the freshly made bed and tossed two pillows toward the headboard before perching on the side, curling a leg onto the mattress.

"A lot has changed since I was last out there, you know." The mattress jolted with his weight as he sat on the other side, mirroring my position. My heart rate kicked up being this close to him, on a bed —alone. "Heather and I met through work, so even back then, I wasn't actively searching for someone. It all seems impersonal now."

"If the end goal is sex, that doesn't need to be personal, right?"

"I don't think I could just meet someone one second and then fu... sleep with them the next knowing we'd never see each other again. Even before Heather, I wasn't that guy."

"I know," I said, smiling at his widening eyes. "You've been friends with Tallon for a while, Bry. You forget how close the three of us used to be."

Before her.

He sucked in a breath. "You haven't called me that in a while."

I lifted a slim shoulder and turned my attention to my twisting fingers. "Heather"—I flinched saying her name, as if it could summon her from the grave—"wasn't a fan of me being as close to you as we were."

"What? Why the hell not?"

Oh sweet, naïve Bryson.

"She'd give me a look that said she didn't like it when I called you that, so I just stopped. I didn't want to cause any friction between you two, you know?"

"Why didn't you say anything if she was making you feel uncomfortable?" His brows dipped, and his lips turned down.

I always knew he had no clue she was a bitch behind his back or that I harbored a massive crush on him from the moment we met. But she knew my innocent little heart was crushing on her man. Oh, she saw right through me with that brilliant brain of hers. I felt terrible not being able to turn off my feelings for the married man who starred in all my fantasies of a happy future, but I couldn't. Even though I tried. I stayed away from them, stopped coming over when he and Heather would visit Tallon.

I tried. I really tried.

Though seeing him there across the bed from me, looking as good as ever, I realized there was never any hope of me losing these feelings for someone who made me feel good. Not just the butterflies or heat between my thighs that flared with his long looks. No, this man made me feel good about myself. Not damaged or broken or used. Bryson had always given me the confidence to push through the bullshit I was fed to believe.

In Bryson's eyes, I was Tinley Harper, twenty-seven-year-old goof who loved Krispy Kreme donuts, was obsessed with nineties Gwen Stefani, and was afraid of the dark for more reasons than anyone, even he, knew. To everyone other than Bryson and Tallon, I was Tinley Harper, failed rising ballet star, emotionally damaged, physically beautiful—if you didn't count my mangled feet—and constant train wreck who needed to be bailed out by her superstar brother on a monthly basis.

Okay, maybe that last one was what I thought about myself since it had become a trend this last year. But when most of my money went to the damn therapist who cost almost a full week's pay each session, I needed his monetary help and unwavering support. Because I wasn't giving her up. For the first time since my abduction and everything that followed, I was getting better. Accepting myself, flaws and all.

Well, doing better besides the recent bout of flaring paranoia.

I definitely needed to put that on the agenda to discuss during our next session.

"I'm sorry she made you feel that way," Bryson said, voice low. "You avoiding me the last few years now makes sense."

"Well, that and you're terrible company," I teased.

A small smile erased the frown. "Ditto, kid."

Call me crazy—hell, most did—but a sliver of a thrill rolled through me at hearing him call me that. It used to annoy the hell out of me. It was a pointed mention at our age difference and why he'd never want me because of my age. Though tonight, on this bed, that new odd look in his eyes made that word feel different.

Shit. Do I have a daddy fetish?

"So, no boyfriend," Bryson mused.

"Nope," I whispered. "Well, there is this one guy." I swallowed against a dry throat. "But he doesn't know I'm into him."

"Why not just tell him? Look at you, kid. He'd be a fool to not be fucking ecstatic that you're into him." His gaze traced over my long rose gold hair. He reached across the bed and grabbed a few strands, giving it a soft tug.

Fuck.

Oh fucking hell.

Pure lust flared in my gut. I wanted him to grab more, tug harder.

"What's up with the hair color, by the way?"

"You don't like it?"

"Didn't say that," he said with a shake of his head. "Just... it's new.

Or old, maybe, considering I haven't seen you in a while. Which, by the way, I'm glad Tallon offered this place up to stay. It's good to see you. I didn't know how much I needed this until now."

"This?"

He inhaled a deep breath, his solid barrel chest puffing out. "Easy."

I nodded, completely understanding what he meant, because somehow he took the words right out of my mouth. For the first time in too long, the moment I heard his voice, I felt at ease.

Safe.

Protected.

"It was change my hair color or cut bangs."

"Huh?" His nose scrunched in confusion.

I huffed out a laugh and waved him off. "It's a girl thing. I needed a change, and this was way less of a commitment than bangs, which are always a terrible idea when you're staring at yourself in the bathroom mirror wanting to change the tragic track your life is on."

"And bangs could do that?"

"Most definitely, but so can hair color. Hence this." I twirled a shiny lock around a single finger. "It's one of those wash-in colors and will fade, but taking control of my look made me feel powerful in a way. I've always had the same long boring hair—"

"It's not boring. It's classic," he cut in with a bit of bite to his tone.

Oh, how I missed that. Bryson was the only one who wouldn't let any of my self-deprecating digs slide. Or anyone else's.

"I could never cut it or color it when I was younger, then never had the courage to do it after everything. I felt like after I got home from the hospital, there was so much change from my future being derailed that I didn't need more. But now I'm realizing I did need that change, the shift in direction, then as much as ever. Now I'm finally at a place where I can without worrying what others will think."

His grin grew until a wide yawn that he covered with a fist interrupted it.

"I'm sure you're beat," I said in a rush as I pushed off the bed. "I'll see you in the morning." I grimaced, thinking about the limited amount of food in the apartment. "You'll need to DoorDash break-fast, though. I have absolutely nothing edible in the fridge."

"Then what have you been eating?"

I turned at the door to face where Bryson now stood, thick arms crossed over his chest.

I sighed and slouched against the doorframe.

Swooned. I swooned yet again.

"I mostly eat out."

"If all I find in that kitchen is Froot Loops, yogurt, and chocolate milk, you and I are going to have words, kid."

"Then don't look," I replied with a grin. "And don't go acting like you'll do anything. You're just a big teddy bear." I gestured toward his massive frame and then gun resting on his hip. "This doesn't intimi-date me, remember?"

Bryson stood taller, somehow taking up more space in the small room than just moments before. One menacing step, then another as he drew closer, a look I couldn't read on his stern features, but still I held my ground.

"Maybe I've changed," he said, stopping directly in front of me. I angled my face upward, eyes searching his. "Maybe you should be scared of the extent I'll go to make sure you're taken care of."

"I can take care of myself," I murmured.

"Never said you couldn't. Doesn't mean I'll stop. Now, go to bed, kid. This old man needs his beauty sleep."

It would be so easy to close the distance. To press my lips to his.

Fulfilling a longtime fantasy which hopefully would be followed by him taking control and continuing to take until we both had our fill of one another.

His eyes sparkled as he tugged his bottom lip inward, teeth sinking down in a sexy, feral way.

A bolt of surprise shot through me.

Did he feel the same?

This look was new. It felt oddly like the same interest and desire swirling inside me, tying me up in knots.

Before I could question it, Bryson stepped back, putting space back between us. Disappointment had my heart sinking. He cleared his throat and looked toward the bathroom.

"I should shower." *Wait, was that an invitation? I swear I've seen this exact scene in a porno before.* "Good night, kid."

Right. This isn't a porno.

"Good night." The urge to tack "daddy" at the end was almost too strong to stop. Instead, I turned on my heel and hurried to my bedroom.

Only once my door was closed, my back pressed against the cheap wood, did I allow the grin to spread, bunching my cheeks to a point that no doubt made me look maniacal.

There was definitely something there.

And I now had a week to uncover what that something was.

4

BRYSON

Thursday, December 6th

At 6:30 a.m. on the dot, my lids peeled open, heavy from the too-little sleep I'd gotten.

"Fuck." I rolled over, blinking away the haze covering my vision. Staring at the ceiling, I gave myself a second to reacclimate myself to where I was.

Victoria at home with Mom.

A week alone with my best friend's younger sister.

The little sister who'd somehow morphed from a beautiful girl into a stunning, strong woman over the past year. Who made me want to press her against the wall and capture her lips with my own. I groaned as my already stiff cock hardened further.

Fucked. I was truly fucked, but I couldn't bring myself to stop this train wreck from happening. Hopefully she didn't pick up on the fact that I was rock-hard from the moment her nearly clear blue eyes met mine last night.

Pressing two fingers to my closed lids, I attempted to massage away all my inappropriate thoughts. Last night proved something else, something I didn't realize I'd missed. I'd missed her, missed the ease that always came with our conversations and jokes. The way she needed someone watching out for her, even if she denied it with her every breath. I'd missed everything about the strange friendship that had grown with Tinley over the years, yet after last night and the feelings she invoked by her just being her, I knew our friendship would never be the same.

As of last night, my mind caught up to what my body and heart had told me for months.

I was ready to move on. To put the past grief behind me and step into the next phase of my life.

I'd always miss Heather. No matter what others thought of her, she'd always have a tight grip around a sliver of my heart, always be a part of my memories. But it was time to put the rest of my heart back to use, to love again and make fresh memories.

For me.

Not for Mom or Vic or anyone else, but to move on for me.

As much as my body wanted to move on with the beauty in the next room, I had to remind myself that it wasn't possible. Not only would Tallon rip off my balls and feed them to me with a fork and steak knife, but Tinley would never want who I was now.

A single father.

A widower.

A man closer to forty than thirty, ten years her senior.

Finding a woman who would take me as I was, Victoria and all, would be difficult but not impossible.

Maybe I should try out those dating apps just to move on.

A rush of anger-fueled heat raced through my veins at the thought of the fucker she'd mentioned last night. The man she wanted but was clueless that she was into him.

Idiot. If she ever opened up and told me the asshole's name, I'd smack him so hard upside the head that he'd have a concussion. How could someone not know, not be waiting on her every word, hoping she'd be interested?

Kicking out of the sheets, I sat up and twisted along the mattress, stomping my feet to the cool, fake wood floor. Interlacing my fingers,

I stretched them high over my head. My stiff muscles tugged and burned, back cracking as I twisted to the left, then right. I fell back on the bed and it shifted, the frame's legs scraping along the floor. Scrubbing a hand over my face, I draped a forearm over my eyes, wishing like hell I didn't have a dumb internal alarm clock that forced me out of bed no later than half past six every day.

My ears perked at a soft knock that filled the bedroom. Before I could process what was about to happen and the fact that I was buck naked, my fully hard dick resting on my stomach, the door opened, flooding the room with bright light from the rest of the apartment.

I blamed it on my still half-asleep brain, but I didn't move an inch until a squeak of surprise rang in my ears. Bolting straight up, I grabbed the sheet I'd kicked off minutes earlier and tugged it across my lap, though the bulge only made my hard cock obvious.

"I'm so sorry. I heard something strange. It's just.... I mean.... Dick."

"Fucking hell," I groaned, embarrassment heating my skin. I forced myself to twist toward the door. Tinley stood a couple feet in the room, her eyes wide, hand covering her gaping mouth. My gaze slipped lower, taking in her long naked legs, tiny ass-hugging underwear, and white tank top that made it clear she was not wearing a bra by the way her hard nipples poked through the ribbed material. "Tinley," I said on a half growl, half groan, unable to stop staring at the clear outline of her pussy.

"It happens to everyone," she said in a rush, a hand slipping down to grip around her neck. Fuck, she was not helping my dick situation. "I mean, morning wood is a common thing."

For some unknown reason, jealousy seeped through my embarrassment and growing desire for the leggy beauty. How the hell did she know about morning wood? My fingers curled into tight fists, pulling the sheet tighter around my lap.

"Though I don't think that thing is," she said, followed by a high-pitched giggle. "Oh shit. I'm sorry." Covering her face, she turned quickly but didn't make it all the way around before she ran off, blind.

I was off the bed before the thud of her slamming into the corner of the doorframe filled the air. Her responding yelp of pain felt like a knife to the heart. Not giving two shits about my naked ass, I strode closer and gripped her shoulders to steady her as she staggered backward.

Ramming her ass right into my cock.

I grunted at the feel of her tight ass pressing against the sensitive head. Pushing her out to arm's length, I kept her facing away from me so she wouldn't see me restraining myself, which was no doubt written clearly across my face.

"Are you okay?" I gritted out. But she didn't respond with words, only a whimper. "Tinley." With a huff, I gave up any sense of propriety and twisted her around to face me, only to curse at the sight of blood seeping through the fingers clutched around her nose. "Damnit."

Carefully, I guided her toward the bathroom to assess the damage. Once inside, I slammed the toilet lid down and helped her sit on top before turning to rummage through the linen closet. Not giving two shits about messing up the perfect stacks of towels, I took two and turned only to pause at her wide, tear-filled eyes tracking my every move.

"Here." Crouching in front of the toilet, I adjusted her hands, placing a washcloth over her nose, then moved one of her hands back to keep it in place. "Hold it as tight as you can without causing pain." Shifting to kneel, I flung out the larger towel I'd grabbed and tied it around my waist to hide my dangling junk. The first glance of blood cut through the desire, which meant every time I moved, my cock slapped between my thighs.

No one wanted to see that shit.

"I think I'm dying." Her words were barely audible through the hand towel.

"It's not that bad."

"From sheer embarrassment. That's a thing, right?" Somehow, despite the shit show the last five minutes had been, I smiled. "My gravestone will read 'Here lies Tinley Harper, who died from massive dick trauma.'"

I couldn't help it. I burst out laughing, tossing my head back as my entire body shook.

Tinley's eyes widened, clearly realizing what she had just said, and then she squeezed them shut. "That is not what I meant. I meant your big dick shocked me, and... I ran. Fucking hell. Right about now, I'm wishing I never vowed to stay sober."

That dried up all humor from the room.

I shook my head. "Shit, I didn't think of the pain. What do you have here that you can take, or should I take you to the hospital?"

Her free hand lashed out and wrapped around the back of my neck, preventing me from standing.

"No. No hospital. I can manage the pain. As long as it's not broken, we should be good."

"Are you sure?"

"I didn't practice pointe hours a day, my toes screaming and bleeding, without having a high pain tolerance. Plus, I'm a girl."

Her fingers flexed, tightening and loosening against my neck, sending flares of heat everywhere our skin touched.

"What does that have to do with anything?" I wanted to demand that she not bring up the fact that she was a woman since I was doing everything I could to not stare at the sweet curves of her pussy or her perfect nipples that were pointing right at me, begging me to take a nibble.

The towel around my waist shifted as my cock twitched.

"It means I have a higher pain tolerance than you." Her eyes twinkled. "Okay, I'm going to remove the washcloth. If the damage is critical, do not curse or grimace. That reaction will not, I repeat, will *not* go over well. In fact, it will make this whole situation worse than it is, if that's even a possibility. Assess the situation, then give me a game plan on what we need to do next."

I felt my brows rise.

Her shoulder rose in a simple shrug. "We dealt with injuries a lot in dance."

"Who knew dancing was such a dangerous sport?" Reaching up, I cupped a hand over her own as gently as I could. For half a second, my mind wandered to how massive my hand was compared to her thin dainty fingers. "Okay, let's do this."

"Heads up. If I pass out, just lay me flat on the floor and keep my legs above my head. I'll be fine as long as I don't choke on my blood as it seeps—"

"What the hell did they do to you in that damn dance company?" I snapped, suddenly enraged at how much she knew about taking care of various injuries.

Instead of replying, she removed the washcloth, ending the conversation.

Keeping my features neutral, I gave her normally cute little nose a thorough once-over.

"Looks straight to me, no bends or divots. You must have hit it in just the right spot to make it bleed but not cause damage."

A thin stream of blood continued to slip from her nose. Covering it with the blood-soaked cloth, I stood, knees popping with the quick movement. The sound of water from the faucet filled the awkward silence as I soaked another washcloth.

"Here," I whispered as I switched out cloths, tossing the other into the tub to deal with later. "You need to put ice on it. What are the odds you have frozen peas in the freezer?"

"Slim to none, Bry. Slim to none."

"Assumed as much. Come on. We need to get some clothes on you."

"And you," she muttered, quickly avoiding my gaze.

Helping her stand, I kept a steady hand on her as we emerged into the bedroom. Digging through my duffel, I pulled out a pair of gym shorts, slipping them on beneath the towel to keep my cock hidden in an effort to not scare her again. I left the towel on the floor, and we shuffled side by side to her room.

After insisting she sit on the bed, I followed her directions around the room, collecting a pair of sweats from a drawer and a zippered hoodie from the closet. I pursed my lips at her sock-covered feet, the tops stained with a few drops of crimson. Rummaging through the drawers, I selected a warm-looking pair of socks with rubber dots on the bottom.

Something on the floor caught my eye. Bending forward, I picked up the rubber flower-looking thing and held it up close to my face.

"What's this?" I asked.

Sheer horror filled what features I could see.

"Drop that now," she basically screamed.

Like it was literally on fire, I turned my hand over and allowed the small thing to fall back to the floor.

"Thanks," she whispered with a relieved sigh.

I shrugged off her odd reaction and moved around the bed to help her get changed. With the same gentleness I used when dressing Victoria, I helped one of Tinley's arms through one sleeve and then moved to the other, zipping the front of the hoodie up all the way to her neck. She chuckled, but it dried up the moment I slipped the soft cotton pants leg over one foot, then the other.

I swallowed hard, inching the sweatpants up her toned legs, the tips of my fingers brushing along her soft skin until I hit the edge of the bed.

"I need you to stand up," I rasped, knowing the moment she did, her pussy would be right at face level.

"Okay," she said with a forced breath.

I glanced up, watching her full breasts rise and fall in quick succession.

I bit back a groan when, just as I expected, her sweet-smelling mound was level with my lips. It would be easy to lean forward, closing the small distance to nip at the panty-covered goodness.

"Bry." Her tone held a high-pitched quality, almost like a whine.

Shaking out the lust fog, remembering she was injured and most likely confused by my hesitation, I pulled the pants up over her hips, pulling out the edge of the hoodie to cover the waistband. After switching out the socks for a clean pair, I stood abruptly and turned for the door.

"I'll get you some ice."

Not waiting for a response, I hurried from the room toward the kitchen, only releasing my held breath when I wrapped my fingers around the edge of the counter. Closing my eyes, I inhaled deep through my nose and exhaled slowly to soothe my thrumming blood that was desperately trying to collect below my waist once again.

It took a few unsuccessful attempts, but in the last drawer, I found what I was looking for. Filling the small plastic baggie with ice, I wrapped it in a dish towel and turned.

"The hell?" I cursed, finding Tinley now perched on the stool. "Sorry, took me a second to find a bag to put the ice inside."

The smeared blood was gone around her face, though she still held a cloth beneath her slightly swollen nose. Thankfully, it really didn't look too bad. The hands that were covering her face when she hit the wall protected her from worse damage.

"We need to talk about this," she said, her eyes on the granite in front of where she sat. The next second, she rolled her shoulders back and met my gaze, her ice-blue eyes solid with resolve. "We're both adults here."

"We really don't," I said on a groan. If she asked why I acted so strangely in her room, I wasn't sure what I would say.

"We do. My therapist says getting everything out in the open helps my healing. It's when I keep my thoughts and feelings bottled up that I try to find a destructive outlet. So." She dropped the rag to the island and clasped her hands together. "I saw your penis."

I flinched like she'd attempted to kick me in the nuts.

This was not the conversation I wanted to have at fucking 7:00 a.m., but if she needed it, fine.

"I'm sorry I called it massive—"

"Tinley," I pleaded.

"It's perfectly proportionate."

"Your choice of words is making it worse."

She gnawed on the corner of her lower lip. "I didn't want you to feel bad about the word massive."

"Could any guy feel bad about their dick being called massive?"

"What if it gave you a complex, and you avoided sex for the rest of your life because you thought no one would want your monster cock?"

"Please, please, let's stop talking about my dick."

"I thought I heard a noise and that you were in trouble. That's why I came into your room, or Tallon's room." We both flinched at the mention of his name. Oh, he would be pissed at just about everything that had happened this morning. "And I'm sorry you had to see my vibrator."

My breathing halted. Frozen. I was fucking frozen.

Did she just say vibrator? Oh, the swell of visions that invoked. Yet...

"I saw nothing like that, Tinley."

She nodded, keeping her steady gaze on me. "You did. That rose thing. It's a clit sucker."

I couldn't. Nope. I was so fucking beyond my restraint when it came to this woman and her casual way of talking about monster cocks, vibrators, and clits. Did she really expect me to stand here, in nothing but a pair of gym shorts, doing nothing to hide what her words did to me?

Tossing the bag of ice to the island, I held both hands up in surrender.

"I'm going to take a shower," I called over my shoulder, already on the move so she didn't see the way my shorts tented.

"We're not done talking—"

"We sure as fucking are, kid. We sure as fucking are."

Closing the bathroom door, I tugged the thin shorts over my hips, stepping out of them and directly into the shower. I turned the knob and braced my palms along the white subway-tiled wall as icy spray sputtered from the showerhead.

"So, are we good?" Tinley's shouted voice filled the bathroom from what sounded like the next room.

I huffed out a laugh.

Good?

I was so far from fucking good it was laughable. I was dying by a thousand cuts, and she asked if we were good. When her every breath and look and word made me want her more.

Want a woman I'd never have.

"Yeah," I yelled to ensure she didn't step foot in the bathroom. If she did, I wasn't sure I'd have the restraint to not pull her inside with me. "We're good, kid. I'll be out in a few."

I could almost hear her thinking from the living room. Despite it all, I smiled.

"Great," she shouted a few seconds later. "You want to go get breakfast? My treat for being a perv and accidentally seeing your penis."

What terrible thing did I do in a past life to deserve this?

"Yes to breakfast and no to you paying. Now, can I please shower?"

"Oh, yeah, right. I'll do the same. Alone, I mean. Not together. I'm not suggesting we shower together."

Fucking hell. This woman will be the death of me.

"Right, you're showering now. I'll just... see you in a few."

Outstanding. With that vision of us showering together now, I had to either dig up memories of decaying dead bodies or rub one out. She deserved better than for me to envision her while I stroked myself, or for me to picture some faceless woman.

Dead bodies it was.

Good thing that with my past cases, I had plenty of content to pull from.

5

TINLEY

Head tipped back, I released a cackle at the story Bryson was telling, not giving two thoughts to the insistent throb along the bridge of my nose. After hands down the most embarrassing morning—scratch that, the most embarrassing *moment* of my entire life—things were back to normal between us. Though I was almost positive that I would never be normal again after seeing the size of his stiff cock. Holy hell, I did not know the real deal came in that kind of size.

"And that was the last time I saw your brother drunk," Bryson said with a smile of his own as he took a sip of crappy coffee.

That reminded me to make a mental note to stop by the store on the way home and buy more coffee grounds. I tossed the last almost full bag last week when the taste seemed off, and had been living on cheap coffee from the gas station down the street since.

The hairs on the back of my neck stood on end, tugging my attention from across the cracked and stained table to out the window of the twenty-four-hour breakfast food restaurant. Scanning the streets, I searched for what was making me feel off, but nothing unusual stood out. A few high-end cars and a white panel van with an electric company logo plastered along the side were parked along the opposite side of the street, while several downtown workers hurried along the sidewalk, no doubt ready to get out of the cold.

"You see something?"

"Hmm?" I said as I dragged my attention back across the table. Bryson's light brown brows were furrowed as he searched my face.

"I asked if you saw something. You went all quiet and got a lost look staring out the window, like you were looking for something or someone."

I chewed on the corner of my lip, debating if I should tell him how I'd felt more paranoid than normal lately and like there were eyes on me even at home, which was absurd. It made me sound crazy, and that was the last thing I wanted him to think about me. He'd never treated me differently after everything ten years ago, and I sure as hell didn't want him to start now.

"I think...," I started, trying to get my wording right. "It's been ten years, you know. Ten years on December 22. I think I'm feeling a little off because of that."

"Off how?" he asked, moving his empty plate aside to press both thick forearms onto the tabletop. "What's going on, kid?"

I bit my lip to slow my grin. Fuck, that nickname in his deep, gravelly, commanding voice. It did so many things to me.

"I've just been feeling more paranoid than normal lately. I'm sure it's nothing."

"I wouldn't be so sure," he muttered.

"What do you mean?" I asked, sitting up straight, alarm now coursing through my veins.

"You have good instincts, Tinley. You've been through hell and back, survived, and now live a full life." Eh, full was a gross exaggeration—unlike me calling his dick massive—but I'd allow it for now. "That hones a person's ability to pick up on subtleties others can't."

"Like a superpower."

"Sure," he said, fighting a smile that quickly turned somber. "Do you feel in danger?"

"Not with you here," I said honestly. I should tell him how I felt, how I'd always felt. But what would it accomplish? Either it would push our closeness, this amazing friendship, away or make him pity me. The broken girl who thought she had a chance with a man like him.

"Well, that comment absolutely makes up for you calling my cock proportionate."

"Oh my gawd," I groaned, and went to cover my face, but a firm grip on my wrist stopped me.

"You'll hurt your nose again."

He swept his thumb along the underside of my wrist, which I left bare this morning in my hurry to leave the awkward cloud that hung in the apartment. I watched as his thumb lifted and lowered as it brushed over the prominent thick scars. The scar tissue had faded to white after a couple years, but the thick, raised reminder would always be there.

His gentle touch, the upcoming anniversary, and the heavy paranoia had a memory of him flickering to the forefront of my mind. A memory I cherished, the only one from those dark days after they found me.

"Do you remember what you said when you saw me in the hospital?" I murmured, staring transfixed at his sweeping thumb.

His grip tightened, drawing my unfocused gaze up to his.

"It was something like 'Hey, kid. The cafeteria has Krispy Kreme donuts.'"

I nodded as hot tears gathered behind my eyes. "Why?" I croaked around the unshed tears clogging my throat. "It was so"—I blew out a breath—"normal. Tallon was treating me like I was made of glass and couldn't stay in the room longer than a few seconds. My mom, well, she made her feelings known the moment I finally saw her the day they released me." The sharp stab of abandonment seared through my heart just as sharply now as it did then. "No one knew how to treat the saved, bloodied, traumatized girl, and then there was you."

"I'm sorry if it made—"

"Sorry?" I huffed. "Sorry? Bry, you saved me from a complete mental breakdown with those words. With your normal tone and casual look, I found a sliver of hope that I was still normal."

"How have I never known this?" he asked. Shifting his hold, he gripped my hand.

"I was lost for a long time. Things were bad at home when I told Mom and Rich I had no plans to still attend the American Ballet School like I planned. My future was unknown. The pain and fear drove me to pills, alcohol, sex." His grip tightened, almost cutting off the blood supply to my fingers. "But you stayed the same, no matter my ups or downs. Always treated me like I was more than what happened to me, more than my vices to help me fade away, to block it all out."

"You are, Tinley. You are so much more than you even give yourself credit for."

"My whole life was planned. I was going to be someone." I shook my head when he tried to speak up. "Be someone that everyone else wanted me to be. Did you know I stopped enjoying dancing when I was in middle school? Then in high school, I hated it. I hated it because that was all people saw me for."

"No, I didn't know that." He glanced down at his free hand that had curled into a fist. "It was my mom."

"Huh?"

His lips twitched in a hesitant smile. "You asked how I knew what you needed that day in the hospital and every day after. Because of my mom."

"The same mom who sends me banana bread even though I've never met her?" I asked, squirming in my seat. This was the deepest conversation we'd ever had. Something was shifting between us in this moment in a cheap diner that still smelled of all the cigarettes that were smoked throughout the years.

"Seriously?" he grumbled. "I swear that woman and I are going to have words when I see her next. Sending all the good stuff to my friends and not me."

"Sorry," I said, hiding my smile behind my water glass. "Didn't know it was a sore subject."

Blowing out a breath, he looked to the ceiling and scrubbed a hand over his face.

"So, your mom," I encouraged.

"I can't believe we're doing this in a Waffle House."

"Doing what?"

"I was nine," he said. Seeing the tension in his body, I flipped our hands around so now I was holding his, squeezing softly for comfort. "I heard something and got up to investigate. My parents' room wasn't far from my own." Dread tightened my gut, making the waffle and gallon of syrup I'd inhaled churn inside. "There are many people out there who believe a man has a right to his wife's body, whether or not she's willing. It's an ancient church mentality."

"Bry," I whispered.

"But what I witnessed that night was my dad raping my mother. There are no other words for it. She was doing her best to stay quiet, which I'm guessing was for my sake, but I saw her tears, witnessed her pain, her fear as my dad took what he thought was rightfully his as her husband. I was frozen, unsure of what was going on or what to do. In that moment of confusion, her eyes met mine, and that earlier fear turned to terror. I ran. I'm ashamed to admit I ran back to my room and hid under the covers, crying. At the time, I thought I was crying for my mom, but now I realize—"

"You were crying for you. You lost something seeing that," I whispered. "An innocence."

"And respect for my dad. But not my mom. I stayed up all night pulling my shit together and planning how I would act the next day around her, around him."

"You two lovebirds done?" I whipped my face to the older server's weathered face. "I'll leave the bill for ya here. Pay up front. Have a great day, ya hear? And be careful. I hear a storm is headed our way."

"Thanks." Bryson swiped the ticket from the cracked linoleum table and shuffled out of the booth. Reaching out, he helped me, guiding me to the register with a palm firmly placed in the center of my lower back.

I chewed on the inside of my cheek as I watched him pay. His smile was strained, muscles tense, though he treated the cashier with respect and kindness. Outside, the winter wind sliced across my cheeks, blowing my loose hair over my eyes.

"And how did you?" I asked. Leaning a hip against the cold metal of his black truck, I tugged the edges of my black leather jacket tighter to keep out the chill. "How did you treat your mom the next morning? I can't imagine how she felt knowing you saw her at her weakest."

Resting one arm atop the open door, he tucked his other hand into the front pocket of his jeans.

"When I made myself leave my room the next morning for school, I found her in the kitchen. The moment her worried eyes met mine, I saw her shame and embarrassment. In that moment, I hated my father to the point that I wished I was strong enough to kill him myself. When she looked away from me, I walked up to her, grabbed her trembling hand, and waited for her to look at me."

"And what did you say?" I whispered, too afraid to break the intensity of the moment.

"When she looked at me, I smiled and said, 'Good morning, Mom. What's for breakfast?'"

I couldn't help it. I burst out laughing. It was so simple, so casual, and oh so perfect.

"And every morning after that. It turned into our routine, despite me knowing what happened most nights. I wanted her to know that what happened to her did not define her in my eyes or my heart. She was not a victim to me but still my mother, still an amazing woman, still the same woman I idolized. What he did to her did not change the way I saw her. It only changed the way I saw him."

The metal edge dug into my hip as I used it for leverage to lunge forward before wrapping my arms around his neck. Pulling him lower, I hugged Bryson with the same ferocity he used in saying those words.

Pressing my face to the hot skin of his neck, I savored the feel, inhaling his musky, masculine scent. I sighed as his arms wrapped around my back, squeezing me tighter against his firm body.

It was official.

I loved this man.

Body. Mind. Soul.

And nothing between us would ever be the same.

"COME ON, it'll be good for you. We can't sit on the couch watching *Friends* all day."

"Now that just sounds like a challenge," I grumbled while dragging my feet down the hall. Bryson shoved open the stairwell door and held it open, gesturing with a sweep of his hand for me to go first. "I'm telling you, since I gave up my dancing days, I'm not much of a workout girl. I'm still living the dream life of being in my twenties."

"What does that have to do with anything?"

With a steadying hand on the rail, I jogged down the flight of stairs with Bryson at my side. "Oh, I forget, it's been a while for you." I shot him a pity-filled look, earning me a long, thick middle finger shoved in my face. "It means I'm still living the life of eating what I want when I want and not gaining a single pound. Hell, this little jog down the stairs just worked off a couple pounds."

"Ah, to be young," he grumbled in return.

"Come on, there has to be something good about being old?" Using my butt, I shoved against the metal bar across the door, releasing the lock. Smiling like a fool, I gestured for him to go first this time.

He stopped in front of me, the toes of his tennis shoes nearly tapping my own. "Yeah, I guess there is one thing that's good." His low voice did crazy things to my belly.

"And what's that?" Oh shit, I was breathless. The man made me breathless with just a husky tone. I was so fucked. And not in the good way.

"Early bedtimes, of course," he said with a grin and wagged his brows. "Well, it would be if I didn't have a daughter who refused to sleep."

Inside the apartment complex's state-of-the-art gym, Bryson headed for the row of treadmills. He pointed to the one beside him.

"We'll warm up for fifteen minutes. Then we can do a refresher course on those self-defense lessons I gave you."

Um, yes, please. If he would've started with that bit of information, I wouldn't have dragged my feet. Sure, the refresher would be good for me, but more than that, his body would be against mine. Even if he didn't want me that way, I'd take all the physical contact I could get from him.

Did that make me lame?

Great. Toxic trait number fifty-four: will store a certain man's hard body pressed against hers for her own spank bank.

"Sounds good." Finger on the up arrow, I held it down until the belt beneath my feet moved, pushing me to a fast walk. "You work out every day?"

"Try to, but it doesn't always happen."

"Not that you need it." I immediately cringed. "I just meant that, from what I saw this morning, you look good. You know, for your age." *Holy hell, stop talking, Tinley.* "For any age, I mean. You're hot."

Taking his eyes off the overhead TV, he shot me a wink. "Thanks, kid."

The sound of his feet hitting the treadmill filled the silence until he spoke up again.

"You're different," he said between breaths. "In a good way. More forward, that's for sure. I don't remember you being so...."

"Blunt?"

"Open."

I pressed the button again, increasing my speed, forcing myself to do the awkward arm pumps. "That's my therapist's idea. She said if I let it all out, get what I'm thinking out of my head, then it won't stick in there and fester. Like this morning. I talked about it, got it out on the table, and now I'm not in my room hiding under the covers to avoid you all day until I go to work later."

"It's smart, and I enjoy knowing what you're thinking. It's refreshing, honestly."

I preened at his offhanded compliment. "I wish Tallon was around enough to see it," I said, more to myself than Bryson, though I knew he heard me. "He's gone so much, and I know he just expects me to fuck up again."

"He does not," Bryson defended.

"It's okay. I know he does." I chewed on the corner of my lip. "I just wish he didn't, that he could see this time is different."

"I can tell. Does my opinion trump your brother's?"

I laughed. "They're more equal."

"Want me to kick his ass?"

That time my laugh was loud. "No, but I'll keep that in mind for when he pisses me off."

"Which will be the next time you two talk."

So he knew things were strained between Tallon and me. Interesting. Tallon had clearly opened up to him about it, and I wasn't sure how I felt about that. At least he saw there was a growing rift between us, one that started after the abduction. I was a fuckup, there was no doubt about it, but it would be nice to have my brother believe in my recovery. Though he had no reason to, considering the last few times had failed and I'd slipped back into those self-destructive habits.

The beeping of Bryson's treadmill pulled me out of my head. Slowing to a walk, he interlaced his fingers behind his head, chest rising and falling with his deep breaths.

"Ready?" he asked, climbing off the treadmill. Gripping the hem of his T-shirt, he wiped the beads of sweat from his face, giving me a peep show of his washboard abs and neatly trimmed happy trail, which really should have been an ecstatic trail considering I knew what he was packing beneath those shorts.

"Yep. I'm ready to kick your ass," I said with a grin, averting my eyes from his stomach. "You're going down."

I was halfway to the blue mats laid out in the gym's corner when Bryson moved in behind me, wrapping an arm around my throat. I froze, but not for the reason he no doubt suspected. Every inch of his body pressed against me, thick thigh wedged between mine. I swallowed down a desperate whimper.

The arm around my throat flexed, making it difficult to sip down air, but it turned me on, making my core throb. When his lips brushed against the shell of my ear, there was no holding back my shiver.

"You sure about that, kid? Think you can take me down?"

"Yes," I whispered, voice too full of the desire coursing through me.

"Then break out of my hold."

Um, I'll pass. Thank you, though.

When I didn't make a move, he laughed, hot breath fanning along my neck, making goose bumps sprout in its wake.

"That's what I thought." I stumbled backward when he stepped away, nearly falling on my ass if it weren't for him catching me by the shoulders. "Come on, kid. Let's do this."

Giving myself a second, I watched him walk away, doing my best to not stare at his ass.

He'd held me for less than thirty seconds, yet my panties were wet, and my heart was racing. How would I survive a full self-defense lesson with his hands all over me, full focus on my every move?

A mischievous smile pulled at my cheeks.

If this killed me... what a way to go.

6

TINLEY

Saturday, December 8th

"Are you sure?" Bryson asked for the hundredth time, checking over my shoulder toward the empty bar.

"Yes," I groaned in fake frustration, because I actually loved his obsessing. It made me feel all warm and tingly inside, unlike when Tallon or any other male tried, which left me feeling suffocated and controlled. "We went through this last night, remember? The security here is awesome. They all know me by name and keep an eye out for my... intervention moments." His lips pressed into a thin line. "Go do whatever you want to do. I get off at eleven."

He ran a hand over his short dirty-blond hair. "I need to stop by the local FBI office to grab some files your brother wanted me to look over. I'll be back around ten thirty to pick you up."

Before I turned, I shot him a smile. "I had fun doing nothing with you today."

Understatement of the year. It was more than fun; it was perfection. Lounging on the couch all day, binge-watching *Friends*, eating snacks—healthy ones Bryson forced me to buy at the store—

laughing and talking. Perfection in its purest form because it was nothing and everything at the same time.

"Me too. Next season tomorrow?"

My smile widened, bunching my cheeks until they hurt. "Sounds perfect to me." Shoving his shoulder, I pointed toward the front doors. "Now go. I'll be fine. Go enjoy your quiet time without my annoying ass."

"Your ass is anything but annoying," he grumbled under his breath.

I stopped my backward retreat toward the bar. "What was that?"

"See you at ten fifteen."

Smiling from ear to ear at his overprotective antics, I turned and skipped across the room to clock in for my shift. The door to the back swung open, the security guy from the other night coming through with a tight look on his face.

"What's with you?" I asked, holding the door open while I waited for his response.

He glanced behind him as if checking to see if anyone else was listening. I inched closer when he leaned forward, ready to hear the juicy gossip I was expecting.

"That big fucker from two nights ago, the one who came after you. My buddy down at the station just called me. They found the guy dead about a block away from the station."

"What?" I gasped, my hand coming up to cover my open mouth.

"Yeah, they don't know what happened, but apparently it was gruesome. His...." The man's features pinched. "His junk was cut off and his throat slashed. He apparently walked out of the station, hungover as hell, and that was it. My friend called me asking if I knew of anything that happened at the bar with someone who would want him dead like that."

"Oh shit."

"I said nothing about you. That guy had almost two hundred pounds on you, Tinley. You couldn't have done what he said happened to that guy."

He was right, but it still felt too close to home. A guy who threatened me was now dead. That couldn't be a coincidence, right? But of course, this guy wouldn't see any correlation because he didn't know the threat that hung around my neck like a noose waiting to tighten at any moment.

"Anyway, my buddy mentioned a detective might pop by in the next few days to question us since we were the last ones who saw him. They think their best chance of finding the sick bastard who did that is here."

"Okay, wow. Yeah, I'll be on the lookout. Thanks for the heads-up."

In a daze, I punched in for the shift and made my way back to the bar to get started.

Totally a coincidence.

Right?

The hours flew by, and before I knew it, my shift was over. As I set the last of the clean glasses out, someone nudged my side.

"Hey, some guy is looking for you," one bartender yelled over the music. "He's at the end of the bar. Said he was with the police and flashed a badge of some kind." She shot me a concerned look before sliding a full pint to the waiting customer. "You in some kind of trouble?"

I shook my head, not trusting my voice. With a strained smile, I wiped my hands over my short black shorts and down my black fishnet-covered thighs, then turned in the direction she showed. Sure enough, a man—a good-looking man—had his intense focus lasered on me. When he caught me looking, the seriousness lifted from his features. I raised a single finger in the air, telling him I'd be with him in a minute.

Checking my phone, I found three texts from Bryson.

Bry: Still working on this case with another agent. You cool if they come over to keep going over some stuff?

Bry: Outside. I'll wait for you here by the front doors.

Bry: See you soon.

Grabbing my stuff, I maneuvered my way through the packed crowd, as it always was on a Saturday night, toward the man still waiting.

"You the detective?" I yelled at his back.

He turned, not even jumping, as if he was already aware of my approach. "Yep. I just have a few questions for you." He winced and pointed to the ceiling. "If you're off work, think we could go somewhere less chaotic to talk?"

"Oh, I can't. I'm meeting my boyfriend." Yeah, totally called Bryson that to someone else before clearing the title or even the hint of intimate feelings with him. But, I mean, it sounded good on my lips.

A slight tightness pulled around his eyes as they narrowed, turning more menacing. I stepped back at the sudden shift in his demeanor.

"It's only a few questions. Maybe I could take you to him or wait with you outside."

I held up my phone. "He just texted, letting me know he's already here and waiting by the door." Someone bumped into me, sending me staggering to the side. "How about you give me a time and I can come down to the station? I don't know much, but I'll tell you all I can."

His lips pulled back in a forced smile. Clearly, he wasn't excited about that prospect, but I didn't care. Who conducted an interview regarding a murder at a bar anyway?

"Yes, that would work better, wouldn't it? I'll call you to set something up. I'll see you to the door."

Tossing back the last of his drink, he stood and pressed up against me, angling us toward the back door. I moved a few steps before I came to my senses that I meant the front door, not the back employee door.

"Front door," I yelled, and pointed the opposite direction we were headed.

He continued toward the back. Digging the heels of my Doc

Martens into the floor, I held my ground as he tried to push me forward. Then suddenly the pressure on my back was gone.

"I forgot to pay. I'll call to schedule."

I whipped around, parting my lips to give him my cell number, but he was gone. Scanning the crowd, I glimpsed his floppy dark brown hair as he weaved between the mass of bodies.

Odd guy.

"Hey." A heavy hand landed on my shoulder.

Spinning around, I bunched my fists, ready to strike. My heart raced with my fight-or-flight soaring from that unusual exchange with the detective and the feeling of menace he radiated.

"Whoa there, kid."

Tipping my face up, I slumped in relief when the dim overhead lights highlighted a familiar face. Bryson grabbed both my shoulders as I leaned forward, pressing my forehead to the center of his chest.

"Everything okay?" he asked, his lips brushing along the shell of my ear.

"Yeah. Let's get out of here."

He narrowed his eyes, clearly not believing the lie, but shifted to press a hand to my lower back, guiding me toward the doors instead of commenting. As we weaved through obnoxious, rowdy customers, I cast a quick glance over my shoulder at the feeling of someone watching.

Outside, I took in a lungful of the chilly night air, loving the way it felt, almost cleansing from the body odor and sweat that I'd inhaled all night.

"You sure everything's okay?" Brows pinched, he scanned my face. "I won't give you hell about smoking if you need one."

"Nah, I'm good," I said, already feeling relaxed with him by my side. "Just tired, I guess."

"Shit, I didn't think about that. I'll call Agent Burton to say tonight won't work after all to keep going over the case notes. Maybe I can go tomorrow to get the rest of the files—"

I gripped his forearm and tugged him to a stop. "No, it's fine.

Swear. If this keeps you from having to work tomorrow, tonight is fine. Though I'm starving, so dinner will need to happen first."

With a clipped nod, he continued down the sidewalk, hovering close to my side. "Already have dinner covered. Agent Burton will pick up some food for all of us. We haven't eaten yet either. I wanted to wait for you. I just have to let her know what we want."

I pulled up short, making him stop and turn. His hand went to the gun resting on his hip while his gaze scanned the surrounding area. "Her? As in, Agent Burton is a woman."

"What? Oh yeah," he said, relaxing his tense stance. "That a problem?"

"Nope," I said, popping the *P*. "No problem at all."

Fuck this day and its roller-coaster emotions.

7

TINLEY

O h, it was a problem. Like "the doomsday clock should be moved up" type of problem.

All shift I'd planned how the night would go. How our amazing day would continue to an amazing night. I'd worked through what to say, how to tell him how I felt. How I'd always felt about him. The last two days had changed something between us, almost as if he felt the same attraction to me as I did him. I thought those soft, long looks and casual touches meant something.

In my daydreaming while at work, I imagined him saying he wanted me too, then carrying me to the bedroom to fuck me senseless, though I'd be okay with a wall or couch. That would be his call. I was generous like that.

But now? Well, disappointment was stabbing me in the heart like a thousand ice picks.

Because this current situation was most definitely *not* in my daydream.

I glared across the living room from my perch on a kitchen barstool, fuming as I watched them be all fucking over each other on the couch. Okay, maybe that was a slight exaggeration. They were sitting close on the couch. Too close in my opinion.

And of course, Agent Burton was beyond beautiful, which made all this that much worse. Every high-pitched giggle that echoed through the apartment set me even more on edge. Plus, she'd sneak in a way to touch him every chance she got. A playful shove to the shoulder, a hand on the forearm as she leaned closer to whisper a detail they didn't want me to hear.

That was the biggest blow. When Bryson actually suggested I go hang out in my room.

To leave them alone so they could fuck in private.

Okay, again, slight exaggeration, but hell, how could I not take it to the extreme?

Why else would he not want me around? Sure, the case and things they were discussing were confidential, but it had to be more than that, right? Why else would he try to send me to my room like a kid?

Grumbling under my breath, I shoved another spoonful of Froot Loops between my lips.

"Did you say something?" Bryson asked, turning to face me, the move making him lay an arm along the back of the couch to twist. It was now situated right behind the evil agent trying to seduce my self-declared boyfriend.

Bryson's eyes narrowed at the bowl in my hand. I shot him a saccharine smile, knowing he wasn't a fan of me eating this shit rather than the healthy crap Agent Boyfriend Stealer brought over.

"Is that all you're going to eat?"

"Yes, Dad," I said with an eye roll. "I'm suddenly not feeling that great."

Agent Burton turned, putting their faces too close together for my liking. I shoved another spoonful into my mouth to keep from hissing at her.

"Maybe you should go lie down," she said with a hopeful glint to her eyes.

I narrowed mine. "I'm good."

That smile turned sharp. "Love your look, by the way. I loved the nineties too. It's cute that you're bringing that style back." Pretty sure the word cute was supposed to be a slam. "Did you have to dig through your mom's closet to find all that? You can't be a day over twenty."

Oh sweet, sweet evil agent. Two can play that game.

And side note, I'd always win.

"Oh, thank you. I can give you my skin regimen since you look days past forty."

"Tinley," Bryson said with shock and a hint of laughter in his voice.

"Whatever," I said, hopping off the stool. Taking the bowl to the sink, I rinsed it out and shoved it into the dishwasher. "You two have fun."

Bryson stood, his face pinched in what looked to be more confusion than anger.

Oh, he was sweet. Did he not know the two women in the room were on the verge of a catfight over his delectable ass? I didn't blame him. No, I blamed her. Okay, maybe I blamed him a little. I mean, how did he not see that shit? How did he not see me, see how I hung on to his every word and how my eyes turned to hearts any time I looked his way?

How. Did. He. Not. See. Me?

Stomping through the living room, ignoring the gruesome pictures splayed out on the coffee table, I shot Miss Thinks She's Fucking Clever an evil glance that promised death before slamming my bedroom door shut.

Pacing my room, I ran a hand through my hair, messing it up at the roots. My grumbled string of curses and plans of murder were cut short when a knock sounded at my door before it opened a few inches. Hope raised my spirits only to be dashed when Miss Knows She's Beautiful poked her head into the small space.

"You okay?" she asked. Sneaking a glance behind her, she opened the door wider and stepped inside my room. Crossing her arms, she dropped the fake sweet mask she wore out there with Bryson. "Stop being a brat."

"Excuse me?" I said, jaw dropping.

"I can see it. He can see it. There's no missing the cute little crush you have on Bryson." That was a lie, right? "Stop thinking you have a chance with someone like him."

"Someone like him?"

"Listen, you won't understand this until you're older." Oh, I hated her so much. "But men like Bryson are scarce. I've had my eye on him for months since he visited our office, and I won't let you ruin this chance I have with him. Clearly he wants me too or he wouldn't have asked me over."

I shook my head. She didn't know Bryson if she really thought that. I had zero doubt that Bryson invited her over to truly work, not get their fuck on. "If we're going by the whole 'I saw him first' thing, then I win. I've known him for years."

She huffed. "Yeah, and where has that gotten you? He sees you for the little girl you are. Leave men like him to women who can handle him."

What was up with all the bitches being attracted to Bryson? First his late wife and now this ho.

"What are you doing?"

Miss I Probably Kill Puppies For Fun whirled around, a smile now covering the earlier constipated frown.

Maybe she needed to poop.

"Hey," she said to Bryson, her tone much higher than it was seconds ago. "I just wanted to check on Agent Harper's little sister since she said she wasn't feeling well. Do you think we need to take her to the children's hospital?"

I barked a laugh and threw my hands up in the air. "You've got to be kidding me."

"Tinley?" Bryson shouldered past Miss I Need a Suppository.

I balled both hands into tight fists at my sides as rage and hurt raced through me. Maybe she was right and he'd never see me that way. Those odd looks the past forty-eight hours were me dreaming. I would always be the little sister in his eyes, not a woman to love.

I needed a drink. Or dick.

Or both.

They were my crutch, the destructive behaviors I fell into when I kept the emotional shit going on inside me buried deep. Even though I'd been doing so well, on a positive path for so long, I couldn't bring myself to care. All I wanted was this ache in my heart to go away.

"I'm actually feeling much better," I said through gritted teeth. Pulling my phone from the back pocket of my black shorts, I tapped on the screen. "I'm going out."

"Out? Out where?" Bryson took a step closer, reaching for my phone.

I turned, keeping it out of his reach. "Not sure. It's not even midnight yet. I'm sure I can find someone free."

"No, you're not going out. You're staying here where it's safe." The bite in Bryson's tone had me typing faster.

"Yes, I am," I snapped, still staring at my phone so he wouldn't see the tears collecting. "Let's see, Tinder or Bumble."

"Bumble," Miss Now Overly Helpful called. "Those guys are always looking for an easy lay."

"Perfect," I hissed.

"Put the fucking phone down." At the tremor in Bryson's voice, I glanced over my shoulder only to freeze. Face flushed, eyes narrowed, he looked on the verge of exploding. My heart skipped as a thrill-filled zing coursed through my body. "You're not going anywhere."

"And who's going to stop me?"

Bryson stood taller and crossed his arms over his chest. "Selena." Oh right, that was her real name. I liked mine better. "I think it's time for you to go."

"But we're—"

"Leave the files. I'll bring them back to the office when I'm done."

"Bryson," she whined, grabbing his bicep. "Don't let her ruin the night."

My lip tugged up in a snarl at seeing her hands on him.

"We're done working. I need to have a few words with Miss Harper here"—oh, why did the way he said my name sound deliciously foreboding?—"regarding my expectations for her behavior and tone when speaking to those of authority."

Yes. Authority. He could have authority over me.

I had no clue what that even meant, but yes.

Heat sizzled beneath my skin, making clammy sweat slick my palms and the back of my neck.

But no, I was mad at him. Wasn't I? Could I be both turned on and mad?

Yes. Yes, I could.

Snagging my purse off the dresser, I slung the tiny backpack over one shoulder. Hitting them both with my bony-ass shoulder, I stormed out of the room. When he let me pass without resistance, a wave of disappointment cooled my anger, making the threat of tears come back with a vengeance.

He was going to let me go.

Just like that.

The ho was right. He didn't feel that way about me. Didn't feel as possessive of my body as I did his. It was all in my head, like so many other things.

The cool metal of the doorknob bit into my hot palm as I gave it a hard twist.

One inch.

That was as far as the door opened, a sliver of the abandoned hallway coming into view before it was slammed shut by the large palm sealed to the middle of the dark wood. My palm slipped as I yanked, putting all my weight into getting it back open, but the door remained sealed.

That should've scared me. With my past, I should've freaked the fuck out, screaming for anyone to hear. But I wasn't. Not with him. Never with Bryson.

He wasn't the monster who haunted my nightmares and memories.

He was the slayer, capable of chasing away the ever-present darkness that lurked at the edges of my mind.

A shiver ran down my spine when sizzling skin sealed around the back of my neck. My eyelids fluttered, an almost whimper passing my lips when that grip tightened. I followed the tug without resistance.

"Thank you for your help tonight, Agent Burton. I'll be in touch if I find anything of interest in the notes and files."

"Call me," she almost begged. "And not just for work, Bryson. I'm available, always for you."

"Get the fuck out of my apartment," I seethed. My body trembled with the restraint to not launch myself at her and wring her neck.

"This toddler-like tantrum won't change anything," she said at the door, angry gaze locked on me.

Like a feral cat possessive over the fish's head it dug out of the dumpster, I sprang forward, hands outstretched, ready to claw her pretty brown eyes out. The hold on my neck yanked me back, pulling me just out of reach of the now wide-eyed agent.

"Out," Bryson yelled.

The slam of the door echoed around the apartment. Chest heaving, I struggled to get my breathing under control, the anger and exhilaration making it hard to calm down.

One second I was staring at the closed door; the next the room spun. A gasp caught in my throat when my back crashed against the door. Two hands smacked on either side of my head, making the wood vibrate against my back, effectively boxing me in.

I stared at his chest, not wanting to look up just yet.

"What the hell was that about?" he said, the words clipped.

"Nothing," I said, my voice sounding just as strained as his.

His responding laugh held no humor. "Obviously, since you're acting like a damn brat."

Oh helllllllll no.

Brat? Well, hell, maybe I was, but that still didn't give him the right to say it out loud. Didn't he know anything about women? How in the hell did this guy survive marriage with this little understanding of what words to use and not to use—ever?

Fixing my face to hide all signs of hurt, I tilted my face up to his. To his credit, he didn't flinch, even though I was trying to kill him with my glare.

"How did it go *working*?" I hissed.

"Fine. What the fuck, kid? You're acting crazy right now."

"Crazy?" He winced at the high pitch in my trembling voice. "Crazy. *I'm* the one acting crazy when that *bitch* walked into my apartment and basically dry-humped you on the couch with me sitting right there?"

His brows pulled together, a deep line forming between them. I fisted my hands to keep from reaching up and smoothing the wrinkled skin. "Dry-hump...? What the hell are you talking about?"

"Why did y'all need privacy?"

His head tilted to the side. "Because of the details of the case. I didn't want you to have to hear all that."

I crossed both arms over my chest. His eyes briefly dipped to where my boobs pressed against the tight material of my black tank.

"I'm a big girl, Bryson. You don't have to protect me from that stuff."

"Oh, I'm well aware of how grown up you are, kid." *Wait. Is that heat or anger in his quiet tone?* "And yes, you need me to protect you, and whether you like it or not, I always will."

"Do you want to fuck her?"

"What?" he exclaimed. "Who?"

"Miss I Want All Up In Bryson's Pants."

"Who the hell...? Selena?"

"Selena," I mocked.

"Tinley," he grumbled. "Just tell me what the hell is going on. I'm so fucking lost right now. Just tell me. Tell me what you want from me."

"You," I shouted, tossing my arms out to the side. "You, you fucking idiot. I want *you*."

And the exact opposite of how I wanted him to react happened. Sheer horror, as in just walked up on a mutilated body, washed over his face.

Shoving off the door, he put several feet of space between us. He held out both hands and shook his head.

"You don't mean that."

"Right, because you know how I feel. How I've always felt."

"No. You're just emotional."

"Emotional?" He had a death wish. How did I never see this before?

"Not that. I mean... fuck." Running a hand through his hair, he turned to pace a short track. "You're confused."

"First emotional and now confused. Do you really take me to be some girl who doesn't understand what this is?"

"And what's that?" he croaked.

Dropping my head, I allowed my long hair to shield me as the tears I'd held at bay finally broke free.

"Nothing, Bryson. Nothing, it seems. Fuck, unrequited love is a bitch. The books don't make it sound as painful as it feels."

He paused, his Red Wing boots almost toe-to-toe with my black Doc Martens. "You're in pain?"

"Yes."

"Because of me?"

Knowing full well tears soaked my cheeks, I tilted my face up to his. "Because I want you, and you don't feel the same."

There. I said it.

It wasn't nearly as horrifying as I expected it would be. It felt right. Now the ball was in his court.

"You don't mean that. It's been an amazing two days, but...." Reaching out, he cupped my cheeks, swiping each new tear with a delicate brush of his thumbs. "It's the proximity, the approach of the anniversary."

"It's not," I cried.

"It has to be, Tinley. It has to be. You don't want someone like me."

I shook my head. "Someone like you? Bry, you're amazing."

A wash of sadness overtook his face. "I'm a single dad. I'm ten years older than you, kid. You don't want someone like me. The baggage that comes with being with me."

"I do. You're more than what you just listed. You're kind, funny—"

"I'm not."

"Let me show you," I whispered. "I think you feel the same way, but maybe you're just scared of what all this means. Things are different between us now. I'm not just Tallon's little sister. I'm a woman. A woman standing in front of the guy she's always crushed on, hoping he feels the same pull. The connection I've never felt with anyone but you."

"How long?" he asked.

"Long enough to know this"—I reached out, pressing a hand to his chest—"is what I want. And you, the real you, Bry, is everything."

His sad eyes searched mine. Leaning forward, he pressed a kiss to my forehead. "This is... a lot to process." I laughed at the honesty in his strained voice. "The last ten minutes have been...."

"A roller coaster." I shook my head, his hands falling to his side. Stepping forward, I wrapped my arms around his sides and squeezed. "You act surprised."

"I am. You went from—"

"Careful," I warned.

"A wide range of emotions in a very short amount of time."

"You were married, right? Surely my behavior doesn't come as a shock. Most women are easily excitable."

When he didn't respond, I eased back, pressing my chin to his sternum. Being in his arms felt right.

Bryson stared at the door, at my back, his jaw working back and forth.

"Give it tonight," he said. "Give me tonight. Then we'll talk. There's some stuff you deserve to know before... ah hell, before all my self-restraint crumbles. Stuff that might change your mind about all this. It's not just me I have to consider, Tinley."

"You're restraining yourself?" I asked with hope in my soft voice. I'd dive into the other things he said later. Right now, I wanted to focus on the important words. "From me."

Hooded hazel eyes met mine. My lungs froze at the pure lust shining behind them.

"Since the moment I saw you standing on the sidewalk two nights ago. Seeing you was like a punch to my heart, slamming it back to life after months, hell, maybe even years of disuse."

"Wow," I breathed.

"So yes, I'm holding myself back. If I were a good man, I'd leave right now and never come back so you could find someone who deserved you. But not even the reaper himself could make me leave you, Tinley. But we'll give ourselves tonight. I need you to make sure what you feel won't change once we're together. I'm not sure if I could handle you walking away once I have you. I don't do flings. I don't do casual fucks. So if you see me as a goal, something that once you've gotten it—"

Pushing up to my tiptoes, I slammed my lips to his, which parted on a desperate groan. An arm wrapped around my back, sealing me tighter to his hard body. Holding on to his neck, I wrapped both legs around his waist.

"Holy fuck, kid. You're killing me," he said against my lips, making no attempt to pull back. The door pressed to my back, pushing my front against him. My hard nipples brushed along the lace of my bra, making me shiver. Flexing, I tightened my legs, pressing my needy center against the obvious bulge contained beneath his jeans. "Not. Helping."

This was really happening. My heart soared, knowing everything was out on the table and he didn't push me away. Instead, I was in his arms, shamelessly rubbing against him.

"What I feel won't go away, Bry. Trust me. Trust me to not hurt you. To not hurt us both."

A mood-killing ring cut through the apartment. The strain on his face shifted to annoyance as he reached into his pocket and scowled at the phone. Turning the screen toward me, I groaned at Tallon's name flashing. "It's like he knew."

"Fucking cockblock, that brother of mine."

Bryson's barked laugh vibrated through my body, sending a ripple of pleasure to my core. "You know, if we do this, you and me, we'll have to tell him. I won't sneak around with you."

I nodded, a soft, lovesick sigh brushing against my lips. Of course Bryson wouldn't want me to be his dirty little secret, even if us being together might strain his and Tallon's friendship. Another reason to love the big teddy bear of a man.

"But I'll do it," I said, planting a soft kiss to his slightly swollen lips. "He's your best friend but my brother. And *when*, not *if* we do this, Bryson. I will convince you we're happening."

"No convincing needed. I just... fuck. He's calling again. I need to get this."

Unlatching my legs, I slowly slid down until the balls of both feet touched the floor.

"Well, if you reconsider this whole 'need a night' thing, come to my room. I have grand plans to use a few of my toys to unwind this tension from that kiss."

His jaw went slack.

With a quick peck to his cheek, I gave the other side a firm pat and started for my room.

Was I playing dirty?

Well, yes.

Now to wait. Good thing I had enough lust thrumming through my system to outlast even the best battery.

8

BRYSON

"What?" I snapped the second I pressed the screen against my ear.

"Whoa, that's some greeting. I see you haven't gotten laid yet or you'd be in a more chill mood." All frustration at his timing vanished at the clear exhaustion in his voice, though he tried to hide it with the jabbing comment. "I got the text earlier that you were meeting up with the agent covering the murder there in Nashville. Just wanted a quick update."

"We went over the files—"

"It was the hot one, right? Agent Burton is who was assigned the case. I hope you took advantage of that woman's clear lady boner for you. She hasn't stopped asking me about you since you two met a while back. Are you seeing her again, sans clothes and a murder file?"

My mouth opened and closed as I struggled with what to say next. How in the hell did Tallon and Tinley see Agent Burton's attraction to me, yet I was completely in the dark until Tinley enlightened me?

"There are a lot of similarities to this murder case and the cases you're investigating," I said instead of responding to his question about seeing her again. With a cautious glance toward Tinley's door, I moved to the kitchen and lowered my voice to keep her from hearing the case details. "Extensive torture, signs of captivity—for weeks, considering when her missing person report was filed—and then there was the similar cause of death."

"Throat slashed with a jagged instrument."

I nodded and ran a hand over my eyes. "No hesitation marks, signaling this wasn't his first time."

"What about the personality of the victim? Does it fit in line with the others? Attentive, customer-facing job, kind to everyone they encountered, never met a stranger...."

"Not sure yet. They didn't know the right questions to ask the victim's family and friends."

"I did that on purpose. Didn't want some incompetent agent or detective asking leading questions that could mess with the results. We need to know with no suggestive wording if the female victim's personality matches the profile our killer targets."

"Smart," I mused.

"Don't sound so surprised."

"I can talk to the family and friends when Tinley is at work one day."

"Speaking of my sister, how is the brat? Hopefully not giving you too much trouble." I released a humorless laugh. If he only knew. "That bad, huh?" Tallon said after a sharp whistle when I didn't immediately respond. "Listen, she's... still healing, you know. Take it easy on her when she's in one of her moods. She's just so fragile and innocent."

I pulled the phone away to stare at it. Was he talking about the same little sister who had just pounced on me, kissed me, then taunted me with the visual of her playing with her toys while waiting for me?

Toys.

As in plural.

I twisted, looking toward her bedroom once again. What was she doing now? Was she planning to use that flower toy or maybe something larger to fuck herself with? I squeezed my eyes shut as all the blood in my veins rushed to my cock. Reaching down, I gave it a hard squeeze over my jeans and adjusted myself to a less uncomfortable position.

"Hey, you still there, B?"

"Yeah," I responded, voice tight with arousal. "She's fine. Though she isn't as fragile as you make her out to be. She's strong, T. Better than I've seen her in a while."

"She's my sister," he responded slowly. "I think I know her better than you." Somehow I didn't believe that, not anymore. "This new therapist is doing wonders, but I'm waiting...." He sighed heavily. "Something will mess up her recovery, and then we'll be back at square one."

"That's fucked-up, T," I nearly growled in annoyance. "You're expecting her to fail."

"Maybe, sure. But I'm the one who picks her up every time. I'm the one who has to watch all the hard work she put in get sucked down the fucking drain because something triggered her. I know my little sister."

I gritted my teeth. I wanted to yell at my idiot friend, but I knew his negativity toward her recovery was out of self-preservation than anything to do with her. It killed him each time she relapsed when he'd gotten his hopes up that she was finally back. Plus, I knew he carried the burden of her abduction because he wasn't there to protect her, that he couldn't find her. It wasn't until the fucker left Tinley on some couple's front steps half dead that we found her.

I hinted at him seeking therapy too over the years, but each time he shrugged it off, saying he wasn't the one who needed it.

Three weeks. For three weeks, his baby sister was missing. Three of him searching, of sleepless nights, worrying until only sedatives would calm him down. He didn't share Tinley's trauma, but he had his own he needed to deal with.

"With the captivity piece with these victims, do you think it's the same unsub who took Tinley? The extent of torture and the cause of death make it drastically different. She didn't...."

I couldn't finish the words.

There were many details of her time as a captive that neither I nor anyone else was aware of. The type of torture the new murder victim's body showed was brutal, with daily abuse, where the notes from Tinley's physical exam showed no such markings of physical trauma. In fact, the rape kit showed zero signs of sexual assault. Though that empty look in her eyes when she finally woke up signaled terrible things had happened, not that she told anyone.

For six months after the abduction, she refused to talk.

I wasn't sure if she ever shared exactly what happened during those three weeks with Tallon or the detectives assigned to her case.

"I know," Tallon said with a sigh. "But there's something about it that makes me think it's somehow connected. Maybe he realized he needed the thrill of the kill or, like we've tossed back and forth, that Tin was special to him. Why else would he have gotten her help before she died from the infection? Maybe he's just using these women because he sees them as disposable."

"That's a stretch."

"Either way, we have a string of murders across the country. Someone is doing this to these women, and I sure as hell will catch the bastard so we don't keep adding names to the list."

"You're good at your job, T. You're doing all you can."

"If I were," he said, frustration clear in his voice, "then this fucker would be behind bars." He took a deep breath and exhaled loudly. "Listen, I gotta go. Tell Tin hey for me. Oh, and if you need a drink, I keep the alcohol in the cabinet above the fridge. It's locked, but the key is in the bedside table drawer underneath the box of condoms."

"Why is it locked?" I fisted my free hand, pressing it to the top of the granite. What the fuck was he doing keeping things locked?

"Don't get pissed at me. It was her idea. Ask her. I'll talk to you when I know more about the time frame here in LA. I'm still thinking another day or two here. Oh, and have fun tomorrow night."

I racked my brain, trying to figure out what he was referring to. "What's tomorrow night?"

"The holiday party, remember? Just keep Tin from strangling Mom or impaling her on an ice sculpture."

A chuckle rumbled in my chest. Based on what I saw tonight, if Tinley was pissed off, Tallon's worries of physical violence from her weren't that far of a stretch. "I'll do my best."

I tapped the rounded edge of the phone against my opposite palm after he disconnected the call, thinking over everything he said. Was the new murder here and the ones Tallon's task force were investigating somehow connected to Tinley's abduction ten years ago? If they were, why did he let her go and kill all the other women?

The soft hum of vibrations had all thoughts vanishing. I whipped my head around, eyes glued on Tinley's open bedroom door. Dropping the phone, I gripped the edge of the counter, my knuckles turning white. Dipping my head, I squeezed both lids shut and inhaled deep through my nose, blowing it out between tight lips.

Tallon did not know how tempting his little sister was. She wasn't weak and fragile; she was strong and beautiful, and a damn tease.

A soft moan rolled through the apartment.

Fuck.

I should walk away. Cover my ears, march into Tallon's bedroom, and close the door behind me. If I were a good man, a worthy best friend, I would. But the spitfire woman who knew how to seduce a man to his knees with just her words brought out the not-so-gentleman in me. She brought out the desire-driven madman who craved to devour her whole, consume every gasp and pant that crossed her lips because of me.

The depraved side she enticed with a simple kiss, the side that said fuck our age gap, the responsibilities at home, and my best friend's opinion, was winning. Because I wanted her. Wanted her with every ounce of blood thrumming through me, every breath I wanted to give her, if that made her mine. It was a losing battle. One I was tired of fighting, even though it had only been two days in close proximity with the little vixen.

Straightening to full height, I rolled my neck, hooded gaze zeroed in on her open doorway.

I could do this.

I could be the standup fucking man Mom raised and walk past her door to give us the time tonight to consider what we wanted and how it would change everything.

Even if my cock hated the idea of waiting. It wanted her now, not tomorrow.

Though she'd *invited* me to join her, in a way. So ignoring that gracious offer would be rude. And who wanted to be rude to a sexy-as-hell woman who literally wrapped her legs around you and forced her tongue down your throat to tell you she'd been in love with you for years?

Not this guy.

I was halfway to the room when it hit me.

Oh shit.

I was the guy. The fucker I wanted to backhand across the skull because he was an idiot to not see she was into him. I was said idiot.

But now that I knew, what would I do about it?

Stopping at the threshold to her bedroom, I stood frozen at the sight of her sprawled out on the bed. Like the rest of the apartment, every light was on, giving me a full view of the writhing beauty partly covered with a thin white sheet, a flawless nipple peeking out, teeth sunk into her lower lip, eyes squeezed shut. I followed the arm hidden beneath the sheet to where her hand moved between her spread legs.

A pained groan caught in my throat.

I'd never seen anything so erotic, so beautiful. With zero hesitation, no abashment, she chased her own pleasure with the lights on, highlighting her every move and twitch.

"You're welcome to join." My gaze slid back up her body, stopping on her hooded ice-blue eyes staring at me.

I smirked and crossed both arms across my chest. "Looks like you've got the situation handled."

Her lids fluttered shut as she arched off the bed, a soft moan filling the room.

"Fucking hell," I groaned. This was torture. Beautiful torture.

"Still sure about wanting time to think?" she asked breathlessly.

"Not so much," I muttered. "But if I step foot in this room, I don't trust myself to not take this further than what we're ready for."

"So honorable."

"I wouldn't say that. I'm about to come in my fucking jeans watching you play with your pussy."

She smiled. "Do you want me to stop?"

"Do you want to?"

"No," she whined. "Oh, fuck." A full-body shudder had the entire bed shaking. Mouth open, features pinched in pleasure, she called out my name.

My feet moved before I could stop. The rug muffled the thump when my knees slammed to the floor. Fingers tangled in her hair, I leaned against the edge of the bed and slammed my lips to hers. If she was surprised by the sudden attack, she didn't show it, quickly responding by curling a hand around the back of my head and pulling me closer.

"You're amazing," I muttered against her lips before devouring her mouth the way I wanted to consume her entire body. "I should ask 'Why me?'"

"Because it's always been you, Bry. In my heart, it's only been you."

Pulling back, I searched her face, looking for any hint of regret or hesitation.

"Touch me," she whispered. "Help me ease what you started."

When she put it that way, how could I say no?

After a sharp tug, I released her hair to skim my hand down her body, heart thundering in my chest from the feel of her soft skin beneath my fingers. Palming her full breast, I squeezed and brushed the pad of my thumb over the tight nub.

"Harder," she ordered, gaze locked on my hand. "I... I can't do soft." I wanted to ask, but a flash of insecurity behind her pleading eyes had me swallowing the question.

Squeezing harder, I pinched and rolled the tip of her stiff nipple between two fingers, savoring the wash of pure ecstasy that overcame her face.

"Yes," she encouraged. "Just like that."

Slanting closer, I flicked the tip with my tongue, then blew a steady stream of air over it that made her curse. Desperate to feel all of her amazing body, I eased my grip on her breast, sucking her nipple hard and biting on the tip as I trailed my fingertips down her taut stomach. Her breath hitched as I lazily caressed a single finger along her slit, only to groan as I continued lower. Palm pressed to the inside of her knee, I drew it closer to the edge, fully opening her pussy.

I couldn't stop. Which was good, since I was fairly certain only a heart attack could stop my wandering fingers. Fisting the top sheet, I flung it to the opposite side of the bed, exposing her bare pussy, though the view was blocked by the damn toy.

"Move it," I demanded. Her stomach muscles flexed as her hips bucked off the bed and a whine reached my ears. "Now, Tinley." A shuddered breath blew past my parted lips when she obeyed. "That's a good girl."

"Bry," she whimpered. "Touch me."

A sharp grin tugged at my lips. Shaking my head at her bossy words, I trailed the tips of two fingers up her inner thigh, loving the goose bumps that erupted in their wake.

"You're a hell of a woman, Tinley," I stated in awe of her. "I've never known anyone like you."

"And you never will."

Cupping her mound, I slipped a single finger down, parting her wet slit. Back and forth I teased her entrance, gliding the tip of my finger in before moving back up to circle her swollen nub. Encircling her wrist in a tight hold, I guided the hand still death-gripping the sex toy back to where she had it. The moment it pressed to her clit, a sharp cry passed her parted lips, her hips flexed, and those long, lean legs trembled. An arm hooked beneath her knee, I held her open and watched as two of my thick fingers disappeared inside her core.

"Fuck yes," she cried, her free hand grappling to wrap around my wrist. Her fingers slipped down to intertwine with mine, adding two additional fingers thrusting into her pussy.

A snarl crept out when she attempted to take control and set a quick pace.

Inferno-level heat burned beneath my skin, and sweat beaded and slipped along my temples as I slowed to enjoy each thrust, watching our combined fingers disappear inside her tight pussy. I held back a grunt when my painfully hard cock twitched inside my jeans, desperate for a feel of her glorious body. Not breaking the rhythm, I shifted to dip a hand beneath the waistband of my jeans, desperate to ease the throb, but her voice made me pause.

"Wait," she panted. "Hold out your hand."

I did as instructed, wondering what in the hell she planned. Withdrawing our fingers, she wiped the slick liquid along my awaiting palm and smirked.

"Fuck," I groaned. Her arousal glistened in the bright light, tempting me to have a taste.

"Now you're good. Hurry, though," she whimpered, sealing her eyes back shut. "I'm close."

"Yes, ma'am."

The second my slick hand enveloped my dick, I thrust into the tight fist. Fingers in her pussy, fucking my fist coated with her juices, completely gone in the richest lust I'd ever felt, I exploded in my jeans half a second after her own cry of pleasure echoed around the room.

The toy soared across the bed, rolling off and landing on the floor. Golden-pink hair stuck to her forehead, Tinley pressed an elbow to the mattress to wrap a hand around the back of my head, tugging my lips to hers. Our heavy pants merged as our tongues danced, chasing the remnants of our orgasms through the other.

Hot damn.

It was official. There was nothing to consider in wanting Tinley.

Only how to make her mine.

Possibly forever.

If she'd still have me after I told her why I was really there.

THE SENSATION of something being off pulled me awake earlier than usual the following morning. A slow recognition of the bed shifting, or maybe the weighted presence of someone in the room.

Heels of both palms to my eyes, I rubbed the sleep away and blinked, squinting past the bright stream of light that cut through the still-dark room. Pressing up to both elbows, I literally jolted back, the back of my head slamming against the leather headboard.

"The fuck?" I croaked at the silhouette of Tinley perched at the end of my bed. "What the hell are you doing in here, Tinley?"

"Couldn't sleep. You ready for that talk?" With her face cloaked in shadows, I squinted to get a read on her expression.

"What?" I said, yanking the sheet up to cover my bare chest. Sure, she'd already seen me naked, but after last night, I felt exposed. I'd fucking exploded in my pants right in front of her like a teenager, for God's sake.

"Last night, you said you needed a night to think things over. It's the next day, and here I am, ready to talk and get things moving forward."

I slid my gaze to the windows and rubbed at my face, trying to make my brain speed up. "How long have you been sitting there?"

"Just a few minutes."

"You realize how creepy this is, right?"

"Or...." She tilted her head to the side, her hair slipping over her bare shoulder with the movement. "Okay, yeah, totally creepy, but I couldn't sleep, so here I am."

I narrowed my eyes, watching her hands chafe up and down her arms.

"Why not?"

She blew out a heavy breath, sending a few strands of hair

floating upward. "I don't know. It felt lonely after you left to come in here. I just... I don't know, felt vulnerable."

The sliver of annoyance at being woken up in the most startling way possible faded at her honest admission. Heaving a sigh, I raised the sheet and tilted my head toward the other side of the bed. With a happy squeal, she crawled closer and maneuvered beneath the sheet. Internally, I said a prayer of thanks for the foresight to slip on boxer briefs before bed. The thin fabric barrier would hopefully keep my overly enthusiastic cock away from her until everything was out in the open.

Wiggling down the bed, she draped an arm over my waist and rested her head on my ribs.

I closed my eyes and bit my tongue. Her mouth was way too close to where I desperately wanted it.

"Usually I can just leave, you know?" she said, squeezing herself tighter against my side. "I've always been able to love them and leave them once I got what I wanted out of the deal. I shouldn't have been surprised that it was different with you. It was like this hollow place had been carved in my chest that was left empty the moment you left."

Wrapping an arm around her, I gave a comforting squeeze and kissed the top of her head. I should be honest and tell her I felt the same. That the small distance between us was almost too much for me to get even an hour of sleep. Which was shocking considering the ball-draining orgasm I gave myself at her bedside, then another afterward in the shower while cleaning up before bed.

"So, did you think while you slept all alone in here?" she asked.

I cringed at the hopefulness in her soft tone. But I had to tell her. Before things went further between us than they already had, she deserved the truth.

"Yeah. Yeah, I did," I said.

"And?"

"And you deserve the truth."

Her hair slid along my bare skin as she shifted to tilt her face up to mine. "And what's that?"

"That I lied about my reasons for being here." Her body locked up, muscles tensing against my side. Fuck, I would lose her before I truly had her. "I'm here because Tallon asked me to come."

My heart cracked, sorrow and pain leaking from the gaps when she pushed off me and shifted across the bed.

And just like that, the hint of happiness I'd felt since arriving snuffed out, leaving a cold hollowness I was all too familiar with in its place.

9

TINLEY

Sunday, December 9th

After putting some distance between us, I curled both knees to my chest and pressed my cheek on top, staring out the floor-to-ceiling windows. Bright morning sun rays cut through the sky, highlighting the tall buildings littering the view.

"Explain what that means."

The mattress jolted as he moved along the bed, though the space between us was still cold, meaning he didn't shift closer. That might hurt more than his declaration of only being here because of Tallon.

"It means he called me Wednesday, asking me to drop everything to watch over you until he could wrap things up in LA."

"Why?" I asked, confusion clouding my brain. I was hurt too, but more confused. No way what we shared last night was fake. So what did that mean? That I was a convenient body that he used to sate his needs? Though that didn't fit, because he was reluctant to engage. Hell, I'd tempted him in every way and he still tried to be strong. Any other man would've dropped their pants and fucked my desperate self the moment I said sex toy. "I deserve to know," I gritted out, sensing his hesitancy.

"You have to believe me. I didn't expect this... expect you."

I huffed. "You knew where you'd be staying, Bry. Not sure how you can say you didn't expect me."

A heavy hand cupped my shoulder. Turning my head, I pressed the opposite cheek to my knees and stared into his pleading hazel eyes.

"Fine, I didn't expect what seeing you again would do to me. Tallon asked me to come here because he's worried about you—"

"Fucking Tallon. I swear he's just waiting for me to fuck up again. I'm doing better," I hissed.

"No, Tinley, he's worried about your safety because of a local murder."

I huffed and rolled my eyes. "That makes zero sense, Bry. There are murders that happen around me all the damn time. I live in a big city with big-city crime."

His features hardened, making my stomach clench with worry. "The victim's body displayed marks of prolonged captivity. Slices on her wrists where restraints had cut into her skin, almost to the bone."

I swallowed hard. Releasing one shin, I ran a fingertip over the raised scar along the opposite wrist.

"You said body. The.... He didn't kill me, Bry. So why would Tallon be so overprotective about this recent case?"

Bryson's features grew somber. "You know why."

"Because of what he said," I murmured.

"I'll be back. We're not done."

He nodded, even though I hadn't said it out loud. It was the one piece of information I'd shared with Tallon, who apparently told Bryson.

"So yeah, he's overly cautious when it comes to you. Tallon indicated he had a gut feeling that you were in danger, and I said yes. The moment he mentioned you, I said yes. I dropped everything, took time off work and left Vic with my mom, and drove down in the dead of night to get to you."

"That makes me feel *slightly* better," I admitted. Gnawing on the corner of my lip, I studied the comforter. "Am I in danger, Bry? Be honest with me."

His responding sigh told me everything I needed to know. "I don't know. Maybe. If I could pinpoint a direct threat, I'd take you out of this city before you could say vibrating flower."

My cheeks bunched, sliding over the smooth material of the comforter covering my knees as my smile grew.

So he was here because I might be in danger. Fine, not ideal, but it brought him to me, so I couldn't be that angry. Though now that we were in this deep conversation, I needed to know one more thing before I jumped in with both feet.

"Is it real for you?" I asked, tipping my face up to search his. "What I feel for you is real, Bryson. The realist thing I've ever felt, but I need to know if you feel the same or at least have the potential, the desire to feel the same. That I'm not just something that's convenient for you to play with—"

Hot skin wrapped around my ankles beneath the comforter. In one wide grip, Bryson pulled me down the bed, forcing my back to drop against the soft surface. Careful to keep his full weight off me, he hovered close and slipped a hand beneath my neck, tipping my face up to meet his with the press of his thumb beneath my chin.

"First, you're not a 'something.' Never say that shit around me again." I swallowed hard, mouth suddenly dry, and nodded as much as I could with his firm hold. "Second, yes, this... whatever is developing between us *is* real. I don't know where it will go, or what will happen next, but I do know I want to find out. But you'll need to be patient with me."

I sucked in a sharp breath. Damn, was I pushing him before he was ready? "Are you not ready to move on—"

He shook his head. "No, it's not that. It was because things were cold between Heather and me for a while before her death. What I'm trying to say is I haven't...." He blew out a breath. "I'm out of practice on the emotional piece of relationships."

"Okay," I whispered, licking my lips. "That's okay, because I haven't had an emotionally intimate relationship, maybe ever, so we can be patient with the other together."

Bryson reached up and tucked a rogue piece of pinkish hair behind my ear. "And don't forget, I'll leave in a few days," he offered. "I'll need to go back to my job, my daughter, all of which is in Louisville. I don't want you thinking I can stay here in Nashville with you, even if I wanted to. I have to go back."

"I know."

"Do you, though? Do you want to start something that could end next week? Not because we want it to but because it has to?"

I tilted my head. "Is this what you stayed up last night thinking about?"

He nodded. "That and telling you the reason I was here. The real reason."

My lips tugged on a sad smile. "Bry, when you've lived a life like mine, you take every good opportunity when it presents itself and don't question the timing or the what-ifs of the future. That's exactly what I want to do now, with this. To give us a shot, a chance to explore if this between us could be more than just a childhood crush, more than physical attraction. If the time comes for you to leave and you're ready to say goodbye, then I'll accept that. What I won't accept is you holding yourself back from trying because you fear the future."

"I'm not scared," he grumbled above me.

I smirked at the pout in his tone. "It's okay to be scared of something like this, Bry. Hell, I am too, though that's buried beneath my desperate need to have my way with your naked body."

"You can't say shit like that," he groaned, leaning forward to press his forehead to mine.

"Just stop thinking about the what-ifs. If you're into me, and I'm into you, let's give it a chance. Give ourselves a chance at happiness, even if it's just for a little while."

"That's the problem. I'm not sure that once I have you, have all of you and know what it's like to have this light finally back in my life, that I'll be able to walk away. I'm a possessive man, Tinley."

"If you didn't notice with the slightly crazy scene last night, I am too."

Fine lines sprang from the corners of his eyes with a growing grin. "With my baggage, plus the distance and age gap... what happens when you finally realize you deserve someone who can give you the world and I'm not that man?"

"What happens if everything works out and we realize we're each other's lobsters?"

He furrowed his brow, clearly confused. "I'm not even going to ask."

"It's the equivalent of two people who are meant to be together forever. Despite the odds, they always find their way back to each other. What if this works and we get to be happy for the rest of our lives? You forget that I'm already aware of all this baggage you're talking about. And frankly, you lumping that sweet child into that term is fucking rude. Any woman would welcome that little girl into their heart. You're a package. There is no thinking of you as a separate entity. It's either you *and* Victoria or nothing."

My heart clenched at the hitch of his breath. "You really mean that?"

"I wouldn't say it if I didn't. And besides, it's not like I'm asking for a marriage proposal or for you to promise that your dick is my dick for the rest of your life."

The mattress shifted when he pushed away to roll onto his back, tossing an arm over his eyes. Lying on my side, I wedged both hands beneath my cheek, studying his profile. The scruff had grown out to a short beard that stressed his jawline and somehow made him more attractive than before. It fit him, a little rugged yet not. My gaze dipped to his bare chest and arms, studying the lines of black ink. I trailed a finger along his bicep, following the various shapes and designs.

"You've added more ink," I mused. "I don't remember you having half sleeves on both arms."

Arm still draped over his eyes, he bobbed his head with a clipped nod. "I've slowly added more over the past few years. Though this one asshole agent I worked with several months back had a shit ton, even on his hands and fingers."

The image of a fully tatted Bryson flashed in my mind, making my stomach flip. "Oh, that sounds hot."

Bryson's arm lifted high enough for him to shoot me a side-eyed glare. "Anyway, he got me in the mood to add even more. I've debated completing the sleeve. Someone suggested various things Victoria plays with and likes at each stage as she grows for the new design, so the memories are literally written on my skin."

Could this man be any more adorable? There was something creepy to me about putting someone's face on your body, but this was beyond cute.

"I think that's a great idea."

He shrugged, the sheet slipping a little farther down his defined chest. My teeth sank into my lower lip as I fought to not touch him. "It is, except her current obsessions are stuffed teddy bears and a *My Little Pony* T-shirt. I swear I can't get her to wear anything else these days."

"Sounds like she has good taste. *My Little Pony* was the shit back in the day. And don't begrudge a girl for wearing the same thing over and over. We have our favorites that make us feel pretty or are just comfortable even on fat days."

"Fat days?"

Elbow pressed into the mattress, I balanced my cheek on my knuckles. "Okay. I'm really questioning if you and Heather were actually married. You seem kind of... oblivious to women's ups, downs, and crazy."

Running a hand over his beard-covered cheeks, he studied the ceiling. "In the short time I've been here, I've realized a few... oddities about Heather and our marriage."

"And what's that?"

"One thing I loved about Heather early on was her lack of drama. She told you what she wanted, we talked through our shit instead of fighting, never got overly emotional about anything, that sort of thing." I cringed. That was not me. At all. "And I loved all that about her, but with her being so analytical, emotionless most of the time... looking back, it seems cold now after being here with you."

"Thanks?" I said, tilting my head to the side, debating if that was a slam or a compliment.

His responding deep chuckle filled the small bedroom. "You're emotion personified, Tinley, and that's not a bad thing, just a fact. And I did not know how much I missed that. Missed the passion that comes with the highs and lows. The urge to strangle someone one second and then—"

"Strangle them while you fuck them senseless the next?"

"Fucking hell, woman." He turned his smiling face my way, and I grinned at the amusement flickering in his hazel eyes. "You don't hold back, do you?" Pushing up, he mirrored me and licked his lips. "So, we agree."

"On what?" I asked, my heart rate ratcheting higher. "On the whole strangling thing? Yes."

He groaned and looked to the ceiling like it might save him from me and my bluntness. "That we're on the same page with our expectations if we do this."

My head bobbed with my nod, cheek slipping on my knuckles with the slight movement.

"Good." Closing the distance, Bryson pressed his soft lips to mine. Butterflies erupted in my lower belly as heat swelled between my thighs. "Now." A hand snaked around my waist. With zero warning, a wide palm smacked against my nearly bare ass. The slap hadn't even faded from the room before he shuffled off the bed to stand. "I need coffee and breakfast. Want to help?"

I rubbed at the stinging skin, lower lip pressed out in a pout. "Or we could stay in bed," I said, and circled a finger at his very stiff erection. "And have coffee and breakfast after we take care of that situation."

Amusement lit his features as he shook his head and stepped farther away from the bed, well out of my reach.

"As amazing as that sounds, I need food and so do you. Then we'll figure out something fun to do in the city before the party tonight."

I groaned and fell to my back with a dramatic huff. "Do we have to go?"

"Tallon made it sound like it, yes."

"Just because he's still on Mom's good side," I grumbled.

"And you're not?"

Shifting my face away so he didn't see the flash of wounded pain, I shook my head. "No. We haven't been for a while. Though I've only recently taken a stand against Mom... being her. You'll see what I mean tonight. Without Tallon around to distract you, I know you'll notice her carefully placed jabs and snide comments."

Twisting to face him, I forced a smile; it morphed into a frown as he tugged a pair of light gray sweatpants over his thick thighs and covered himself.

"I don't like the sound of that at all."

My shoulders rose and fell in a small shrug. Picking at the edge of the comforter, I avoided his pointed look. "It's subtle, but you are hyperaware when I or someone else even thinks a negative thought about me." That made me smile like it always did. "I used to think she treated me differently than Tallon because she wanted more for me, that she pushed me hard so I could achieve my dreams. But after...." I shook my head, sending loose strands of hair to slip over my shoulders. Lip between my teeth, I chewed on the edge and pulled both knees to my chest. I blew out a breath, making a few rogue pink hairs go flying. "I want someone to know the truth. Would you be open to going with me Tuesday to my therapy appointment?"

He stalked around the bed, the mattress dipping under his weight when he perched on the edge. A single finger pressed beneath my chin, tilting my face upward.

"If that's what you want, of course I will, Tinley. But don't do that for me, if that's what you're thinking. There's nothing about your past that could scare me away."

I really wanted to believe him, but he didn't know the details of my sordid past. No one did except those who actively took part in tarnishing my childhood.

"You coming with me is for me. It will feel good to get the stuff I've buried out in the open to someone other than my therapist. It's cleansing, but I need to do it with her present. I know she'll keep me from stripping myself too deep emotionally."

He beamed down at me, a crooked grin that made my heart so damn full it almost hurt.

"You're amazing, Tinley Harper. Never forget that. I'm in awe of you, your strength, and your dedication to the healing you need." He interlaced our fingers and gave a firm squeeze. "I don't know if it was a blessing or a curse that I didn't see you like this sooner, but I sure am fucking glad it happened now."

"Me too," I whispered. "I'm glad you finally see me."

When he looked back up, there was a glint of determination behind his eyes.

"And I will never not see you for the beautiful, strong woman you are for as long as I'm living." Gripping the covers, he yanked them off, causing cold air to waft over my toasty legs. "Now come on, let's get some breakfast. Eggs, bacon, toast, and coffee sound good?"

My smirk grew into a smile as I allowed him to pull me off the bed, trotting behind him as he led me into the living room. I started to tell him I'd rather have his sausage, but a knock on the front door had us both freezing.

"You expecting anyone?" he asked, tugging me closer and putting himself between me and the door.

I mean, really, could he get any sexier? Ready to throw himself in front of an unknown threat all for me. And it wasn't because of this new budding relationship. No, this was Bryson being Bryson. He'd always protected me, even when I fought him and Tallon tooth and nail, insisting I could do it all on my own.

Spoiler alert: I couldn't.

Damn. There was another toxic trait for the books.

"No," I said, glancing at the clock on the microwave. Seven in the morning. What in the hell did someone want this early? "I'll go check—"

Before I could even get an inch around his bulky frame, he turned and leveled a hard stare my way. "The hell you are. You're practically naked."

Another knock had his shoulders tensing.

"Again, life of a dancer. I'm so used to prancing around in next to nothing—"

"Not helping," he said, the words distorted because of his tightly clenched jaw. "Please go put some clothes on. No one gets to see that pretty pussy but me."

Eyes wide, I glanced down at my boy-short-clad mound. Damn, he was intense, and the way he said "pussy" sent a shiver of anticipation down my spine.

When I turned to dutifully obey, I only got a single step away before a loud smack rattled through the apartment and a stinging pain flared along my right butt cheek. Jaw slack, I whirled around, pressing both hands to where he'd spanked me.

"What the hell?" I demanded. "I was going!"

"That's for the back talk."

My mouth opened and closed several times before words formed. "Dominant much?" I wanted it to be snarky, but my voice was breathless and full of the desire coursing through me.

"Oh, kid, you have no idea. Now go." He pointed toward my bedroom. "I'll answer the door. Do not come out until I tell you."

I so wanted to make a comment about him sending me to my room like a punished child, but another forceful knock sent me scurrying away. The moment I closed my bedroom door, I pressed my ear against the cheap wood only to be disappointed when I couldn't hear anything.

A surprised squeal escaped when the door opened, sending me leaping backward to keep it from hitting my face. I stumbled, catching myself on the wall before I could crash to the floor. An annoyed scowl pinched my face as I glared at my sock-covered feet. I used to be graceful, could leap and bound across a stage without faltering. Now everything was different without the couple of toes they'd removed to save my feet.

Anger simmered in my chest at the unfairness of my life. Sure, I still had both feet, could walk after lots of therapy, but I wasn't the same. Parts of my body I used to rely on, that I had set my future on needing, were simply gone. Gone because of *him* and those too-small toe shoes he'd forced my feet into for me to dance for his sick enjoyment. He made me dance while he hid in the shadows, watching—always watching. Nausea churned my stomach as that awful high-pitched noise he'd made while jacking off while I danced echoed in my brain.

"Tinley." Bryson's booming, panicked voice snapped my face up to his, eyes blinking as I dragged myself back to the present.

I shook my head, hoping that would clear the remaining memories away. "Huh?"

A deep line formed between his brows. Unable to stop myself, I ran the pad of my thumb along his skin, soothing the stress lines from his face.

His wide eyes flicked between mine. "You just went, I don't know, vacant is the best way to describe it, and wouldn't snap out of it. Where did you go?"

I forced a smile, hoping to ease his concern. "There are still things that make me remember what he did to me, the aftereffects of those three weeks, which always comes with a wave of rage followed by sadness and shame, ending with me eating my weight in Oreos and chocolate milk." I poked a finger at my soft belly. "Hence why I've put on weight this last year. Though I have to admit, I love how some settled in my boobs."

Bryson just stared down with worry instead of focusing on where I cupped my full breasts. With a sigh, I dropped my hands.

"I'm fine," I said, surprising myself. "Really. I... I usually get lost in this whirlpool of thoughts and memories, but you just stopped it." I tilted my head, my grin turning genuine. "Look at that, Bry. You even protect me from myself."

"Always. Now come see what the guy dropped off. It's a gift of some kind."

"Gift?" Tugging on some super-soft joggers and an off-the-shoulder No Doubt concert T-shirt, I hurried to the living room. "What the hell is that?"

A large white box with a pale pink ribbon tied around the top sat on the coffee table. Approaching it like it was a bomb, I circled it once before sitting on the edge of the couch and poking the hard cardboard side.

"Wonder what's inside," I mused. The delicate ribbon whispered through itself with a gentle tug before falling to the glass top. It rustled as I pulled the lid free. Tugging it closer, I unfolded the gold tissue paper. "What the hell?"

Pinching the edge of the soft silver material, I stood, pulling the beautiful dress out to get a good look. It was stunning. I checked the size and worried at my lip when I found it to be correct. Deep plunging neckline, fitted waist, and a slit up both sides that would reach mid-thigh once the designer dress was on. It was beautiful in its simplicity.

"Looks like there's more," Bryson said, pulling my attention from the dress as he held up two pale pink slippers. Ribbon just like the one on the box was wrapped around the shoes.

"Are those ballet shoes?" I croaked.

"Maybe. Not sure what to look for." He flicked his attention to the box and reached inside. "There's a note. Says 'Looking forward to seeing you tonight.'" Tapping the end of the card against the shoes, I couldn't rip my wide eyes from them. "So, not Tallon."

"My mom," I said, though not as confident as I wanted to be. "She hates my clothes, really anything I choose for myself. This is her way of making me fit the part of her and Rich's daughter. Have to keep up appearances with all their shithead rich friends."

The label was one I recognized as a store Mom would deem appropriate.

The dress was from Mom.

The dress was from Mom.

Though, if it was, why was I convincing myself?

10

TINLEY

"Any idea who will be there tonight besides your mom and Rich?" Bryson asked as he adjusted his grip on the steering wheel. "I haven't been to one of their infamous holiday parties in years."

I snorted at the word infamous, watching the slight drizzle of rain combine to form thin rivers streaming along the tinted passenger window.

"Oh, the parties are even more pretentious now than they were back then, if that's possible. They have no less than two a year and break up the invites based on wealth and importance. Tonight's party, the first one of this holiday season, is for the most important influencers and business partners, so I expect they'll go all out. In the past, they've rented out the entire Belle Meade mansion, including the carriage house and stables, just to be extra douchey. Tonight's guest list will be comprised of business partners, their richest friends, a few dirty politicians, and maybe even a country star or two."

"That sounds terrible," he grumbled. He cast a look my way out of the corner of his eye. "I don't understand how you and Tallon turned out so... normal."

I barked a laugh and shook my head, loose waves I'd spent an hour perfecting caressing over my naked shoulders and slipping down my chest. "I wouldn't go as far as calling us normal. Tallon is neurotic on the best day with major control issues. And I'm, well, one trigger away from my ultimate demise."

"Normal to me. We all have our issues. I mean, the money, the status part, neither of you ever made me feel less because of how I grew up," he responded with a nonchalant shrug.

"Because you're not," I stated as I twisted in my seat to face him.

"Not how the rest of your family sees things. Since I wasn't raised with some nanny wiping my ass or a private school education, I'm below you and T."

Fuck, I really hated my mom. I never had the balls to say anything when she treated Bryson like shit in the past. Though tonight was different. *I* was different.

I reached out and placed a comforting hand on his thigh, getting distracted by the size and strength hidden beneath his black slacks. My fingers flexed, pushing against the hard muscle. Hell, it would take three of my hands to encircle his thigh. I glanced to my own, suddenly feeling tiny and susceptible.

"They're jerks," I said. "Always have been. Though I'm not sure why Mom tries to act like the money should matter. She grew up middle-class and fucked her way to the status she has now." The corner of my lip curled in a snarl. "Tallon was thirteen and I was three when she and Rich got married and Mom's life changed to what it is now. How she's held on to Rich this long, I have no clue."

"Tell me the truth. Why are you at odds with your mom?"

The squeak of the windshield wipers filled the otherwise silent car as I debated what and what not to tell him.

"Don't tell Tallon," I said. "It would.... He's always got along with Mom, and I don't want to disrupt that. What she and I have is.... She wouldn't ever feel the way toward Tallon as she does me."

"What if she hurts Tallon?" he mused.

My features hardened. "Then I'd rip her throat out and call you to help me bury the body."

"What the fuck?" he said with a nervous laugh.

"What? We're not at that comfort level yet? I always just assumed you'd be the one I'd call to make a body disappear after all your time undercover with that gang."

"Pretty sure the Irish mafia would be offended if they heard you call them a gang. And yeah, of course I'd help you get rid of a body. I just meant, fuck, you're hard-core." He shot me a conspiring wink. "I like it."

"She basically accused me of doing it as an attention grab."

He bristled, sitting up straighter in the seat. "It?"

"The abduction and subsequent rescue. Since I wouldn't tell anyone about what happened and it appeared to the police that I went with the guy willingly," I said in a rush. "At the hospital, when she finally came to see me after I'd been there a few days, she asked the doctors what happened since I wouldn't say. Well, there was no evidence of rape," I rasped. "My wrists, feet, and toes were the only things physically wrong with me. She took all that as evidence to conclude that I did it to make her mad, to draw Rich's attention from her. She'd always had a sick obsession of thinking I wanted her husband. Who's seventy-fucking-two."

At his silence, I continued to ramble, unable to stop now that I'd opened this can of fucking worms.

"After they had to amputate a few toes to save my feet from the infection that had set in, she said I did it all to crush her dreams. *Her* dreams. I did used to love it, though I fell in love with more contemporary dance than ballet as I grew older. So there I was, realizing I'd never dance again, had lived through hell for weeks, been forced to do things—" I cut myself off and shook my head, allowing my head to drop. "My world was crumbling around me, and she added to the destruction. Then there was you, with your simple words."

"Why not tell us?" he clipped out.

Peeking out the corner of my eye, I stared at his knuckles tightly wrapped around the steering wheel, completely void of color.

"A part of me wanted to, but then the other part just couldn't muster up the energy to add that to the mess my life was. Like I said, she'd always been snide toward me, but her accusation was a new low. I just wanted to fade away, for nothing to matter, so I kept my mouth shut."

"For six damn months." I nodded, cringing at the hurt in his tone. The tense silence that built between us had me squirming in my seat. "I didn't know."

"I know you didn't, and neither did Tallon. He has a unique relationship with Mom. He remembers living with her and our biological father, witnessing what he did, and based on those stories, it wasn't good. So I think he does what he does now to keep protecting her, having zero clue the vulnerable mom he watched get treated like shit is a vile bitch now. Money changed her in the worst possible way, and somehow I grew into a threat, assuming I wanted to compete with her, wanted the ridiculous life she lives. It's why I danced as much as I did, even though I hated it. The hours put in with the dance company and the hundreds of performances throughout the year kept me out of the house and away from her."

"Do you want me to kill her?"

My eyes widened as I stared at his profile, tracking the way his jaw ticked beneath his now neatly trimmed beard.

"You're serious," I rasped.

"It's a yes-or-no question, Tinley. Answer me."

Oh, there was that commanding voice again. That voice did so many delicious things to my insides, even though he was talking about murdering my mother. Squeezing my thighs together, I pressed a hand to my chest.

"No. I don't want that on your conscience or mine."

His returning nod was stiff. "Just so you know, my conscience already grays the line between right and wrong. Sometimes good people do bad things according to the world's standards to protect the ones they love. When it comes to family, Tinley, for you, my mom, Vic, and Tallon, there is no black-and-white. I'll do anything to keep you guys safe."

"Pull over," I whispered, my heart now slamming against my chest with the force of a sledgehammer.

"What?"

"Pull over." I motioned out the windshield toward an approaching, somewhat empty parking lot. Thankfully, that was all it took for him to obey, no doubt having heard the urgency in my voice. "Over there." I pointed toward the back corner where one of the overhead lights was out.

"Tinley—"

"Just fucking do it."

"Yes, ma'am," he said, his smile feral. Apparently, he didn't enjoy being bossed around as much as he liked to do the bossing.

The moment he slammed the gearshift into Park, I released the seat belt and shifted until my knees pressed into the seat.

"What are you doing?" he asked, alarm in his tone.

"You have no idea how your absolute urge to protect me, even from my mother, turns me on."

His brows pinched together. "Okay. Why are we here, though?"

Oh, sweet man. Had he really never had his cock sucked in the car? That made me mad at his late wife. What an ice queen. What was the purpose of getting married if you didn't put your personal cock to use at any available time?

Sweeping my hand up his thigh, I gripped his already hard dick through his slacks, giving it a squeeze, watching his reaction.

"Shit, what the hell?"

"Just let me do this," I said, slowly pumping my hand. "I need this before we go to that party full of old fuckers with their leering eyes and their wives who will eye-fuck the hell out of you."

"I'm not coming in my pants." He squeezed his eyes shut. "Again."

The corner of my lips twitched upward at that.

"Oh, sweet Bry. I never said you'd come in your pants. I have grand plans of you doing that in my mouth."

He made a sound like he'd choked on his tongue. Taking his short distraction as my opportunity, I made quick work of his belt, leaning across the console to use both hands. As stunned as he was, he still lifted enough for me to wedge his pants and boxer briefs down.

I licked my lips at the thick cock I'd gotten a glimpse of the other morning. Starting at the base, I trailed a finger up the impressive length, swirling a pad over the swollen head. I smiled at the bead of precum that coated my skin. Locking my eyes on his hooded ones, I stuck the finger in my mouth and hollowed out my cheeks, swiping the liquid along my tongue.

"Is that all you wanted?" Bryson said, his deep rumbling voice almost vibrating along my chest. "Just a taste?"

I smiled around my finger and shook my head.

"Damn, you're beautiful," he said, cupping my cheek. It was sweet, so Bryson. Though the wicked gleam that flicked in his eyes and the way his hand slipped into my hair were the complete opposite.

The slight pressure had me chuckling as he guided my lips lower. This side of him, the control and dominance he exuded, was a surprise. Not sure what I expected, but not this spanking, possessive, controlling man.

I loved it.

Pressing a forearm against his lap, I used it for balance as I circled my tongue along the head, lapping up the salty flavor. Slipping him past my lips, I sighed, savoring the full feeling and envisioning how amazing it would feel once he was finally inside me. Taking as much as I could, I swallowed, working my throat to take him even deeper.

A growled curse filled the truck's cab, his hips lifting off the seat, thrusting his cock deeper until it tapped the back of my throat. Pulling back, I slowly slid back down, bobbing up and down, completely engrossed in his flavor and zealous reactions, all because of me. Most girls hated blow jobs, but there was something heady about bringing a man to his knees, making him beg and plead all because of your mouth. It was powerful as hell.

That hand in my hair tightened, yanking at the roots. I groaned at the spark of pain that shot through my scalp and went straight to my clit. Wrapping my hand around his base, I squeezed hard while I hollowed my cheeks and moved my lips up and down his shaft.

"Fuck, your mouth is perfect. Let me feel the back of your throat again. Take it all like a good girl."

I whimpered around his dick, his dirty words making more wetness leak from my core as I shifted to take him deeper. Fisting my hair, he took control and began fucking my very willing mouth, the hand on the back of my head keeping me exactly where he wanted.

With a barked curse, hot liquid coated my tongue, slipping down my throat as I swallowed fast to make sure not a drop could escape and dirty his slacks.

Hand to his thigh, I pushed back to my side of the truck and sat back on my heels, swiping at the corners of my lips with a finger, ensuring I didn't have any on my face. I relished the way his chest heaved, the sweat on his forehead that glistened in the passing cars' beams of light. The rain chose that moment to pick up, pounding along the roof and hood, drowning out our loud breaths.

Reaching over, he slipped a hand around the back of my neck, urging me back over the console. He met me halfway and slammed his lips to mine. Like a starved man, he devoured my mouth, sucking my tongue like I'd just done to his cock.

His groan reverberated through my chest, making the tingles from earlier turn into a pleasurable burn.

"Just so I understand this correctly," he said, pulling back a fraction. "Me saying I'd kill your mom if you gave the thumbs-up turned you on and made you want to suck the life out of my cock?" My smile grew as I nodded. "Well, okay, then. Good to know. Very good to know. Except there's not a way for me to return the favor."

I patted his cheek and sat back in my seat, pulling the strap across my chest to latch the buckle. "That's okay. I didn't do it for that. I did it because I wanted to. I did it because I couldn't wait another second to feel you in my mouth and hear you come undone because of me."

Bryson shook his head in clear disbelief. He wiped a hand down his face. "Again, I've never met another woman like you, Tinley."

I narrowed my eyes. "And you never will. Because if you do, I'll call my backup body dumper to take care of her."

His brows flew up over his forehead. "You have a backup body dumper?"

"Sure. Doesn't everyone?"

"Does this person know they're your Plan B body dumper?"

"Well, no. But I'm sure Tallon will rise to the occasion if I ask. Especially if I tell him it's the body of a girl who aided in breaking my heart."

A soft look passed over his face.

Clearing my throat, I hitched a thumb behind us. "Now I'm ready to mingle with a bunch of narcissistic assholes and their desperate-for-attention wives."

Chuckling, he shifted the truck into Reverse. "Yes, ma'am."

Hmm. I was really starting to like the sound of that.

11

BRYSON

I loathed this shit. The few parties I attended as Tallon's plus-one in college were all the same. The men looked down at me because of my off-the-rack suit, and the women? Well, Tinley wasn't far off in her accusations earlier. We'd only been here an hour and I already felt dirty as fuck from their stares.

High-pitched fake laughs carried through the carriage house, somehow rising above the rain hammering against the metal roof and the occasional roll of thunder. Highball glass of whiskey in one hand, the other pressed against Tinley's lower back for reassurance, we stood behind a tall table while she munched on the three plates full of finger foods.

"Best part of enduring this," she said around a mouthful of some puff pastry. Closing her eyes, she tipped her head back and moaned. I watched with fascination at the ease at which she felt in her own body. Such a contrast to those years following the abduction. "Here."

Before I could protest, she popped a pastry past my lips, her fingers swiping along my lower lip before pulling away. I kept my gaze locked on hers as I chewed, running my tongue along every place she touched.

"Good, right?"

"Very," I said after taking a small sip of whiskey. "Though I know my dessert will be the best thing I'll eat tonight."

She shifted, eyes scanning the dessert table. "Oh yeah? What did you have your eye on? I'm thinking the apple tart, though the chocolate pastries look amazing too." When she turned back, brows raised, waiting for my answer, I just shot her a wink. Biting her lip to slow her growing smile, she nodded. "Oh. Right. You meant me."

"I did."

"I'll allow it."

Throwing my head back, I laughed so loud it drew a few strange looks. Apparently only fake fun should be had at this thing, and genuine laughter was frowned upon.

Wrapping a hand around her thin waist, I tugged her closer. "Will you now?" I muttered into her ear.

"If your mouth is as talented as your fingers, then absolutely. Though...." Keeping her movement subtle and using the table as cover, she moved my hand to her leg, slipping it beneath the material to the silky soft skin of her inner thigh. Her breath hitched when my fingers continued upward and brushed along her damp panties. "What are your thoughts on a little naughty foreplay to make this party a bit more entertaining?"

"A little?" I scoffed. Moving a finger beneath her panties, I stroked her slick slit. "Have a bit more faith in me than that, kid." Thank fuck she'd worn a pair of closed-toe heels instead of the flats that came with the dress. That extra height put us nose to nose, meaning I didn't have to bend to pet her soft pussy in a roomful of strangers. "Remind me to thank the party planner for putting these tablecloths up as privacy curtains."

She slid her legs farther apart, giving me more room to explore.

"This has to be the hottest thing I've ever done," she said breathlessly. I watched her flushed chest rise and fall. That same flush crept up her neck and cheeks. "Please don't stop," she whimpered.

Scanning the crowd to ensure no one was picking up on our naughty activity, my gaze landed on her stepbrother, Bart, who stared at Tinley from across the room with a look that seemed more lust-filled than brotherly. Without saying a word to those in the small group surrounding him, he started our way.

"Shit," I groaned. Bart was not a fan of me, nor was I of him. He was a fucking tool who thought because he was a surgeon that he was fucking god and above everyone else. "Incoming."

She whimpered when I gave her swollen nub a hard pinch before reluctantly pulling my hand away. Desperate for a taste, I stuck the two slick fingers into my mouth and sucked the sweet taste of her off the digits.

"Oh, you're going to pay for that," she hissed beside me, gaze locked on my fingers. "No more car head for you."

"Hey there, little sis."

Tinley's features hardened, all amusement and lust gone. I turned to face the prick, who studied Tinley and me with narrowed eyes.

"Bart," she remarked flippantly. Going back to her plate, Tinley picked through her food, though not as enraptured with the selection as before.

My lips turned down in a frown.

"How, pray tell, did *you* get into a party like this?" the bastard said with a vile grin aimed at me. "Maybe I should talk to security about letting the poor—"

"Shut your fucking mouth. You sound like the prick you are," Tinley snapped. "Go annoy someone else with your elitist bullshit."

That was it. I loved her. Well, loved that mouth of hers—for many reasons after earlier. There was a sliver of something I couldn't label that burned in my chest at her defending me.

Me.

I was the protector, yet here she was doing what she could to defend me.

Who was I kidding about this ending when I left to go home? This was more than a few-day fling.

"Shut the fuck up, you—"

"Watch your fucking mouth," I growled, positioning myself in front of Tinley as best I could.

"And what are you going to do about it, middle-class?"

My hands formed into tight fists.

"I'd be careful what you say, Bart," Tinley mused from beside me as she reached to drag a giant shrimp through some cocktail sauce. "I'm his body-dump person, and you know I've had a very long time to consider all the ways I could make you disappear for good."

I stilled, watching Bart's face pale. *What the fuck was that about?* I flicked a confused glance between the two.

"Right," he said, clearing his throat. "Like anyone would believe you."

Okay, clearly I was missing something.

A slender hand slipped over Bart's shoulder, the red nails digging into his tux.

"Tinley, what are you doing to upset your brother?"

Tinley snorted and took a drink of the Sprite she'd asked the bartender to put in a highball glass.

"Hello, Mother," she responded dryly after a beat. "And it's *step*brother."

I used to consider her mother pretty. Many of the features she'd passed down to Tinley, though now they looked nothing alike. With the injections and implants, I couldn't see a resemblance. Even the woman's hair was too fake blonde. Nothing like her daughter's that, when not rose gold, was beautiful with its various natural highlights, making it shimmer in any light.

Oh hell.

How long have I been cataloging her features in such detail?

"We're all one family now, dear. Though I wish you'd start acting like the polite woman I raised." Tinley's lip curled in a snarl. "And what have you done to your hair?" Bethany Parker, Tinley's mother, exclaimed with fake horror. "Please tell me that will wash out. You'll never find an acceptable husband looking like that."

"Nope," Tinley said, popping the *P*. "It's permanent. I even had it injected into my scalp to ensure it will grow this color. Guess it's a good thing I'm not looking for an acceptable anything."

I chuckled, drawing her mother's furious gaze my way.

"Pleasure to see you again, Brenton."

"Bryson," Tinley hissed. "Mom, you've met him hundreds of times. Don't be a bitch."

"Watch your language," she whispered, glancing around. "This isn't that trashy bar you work at. There are important people here, classy, well respect—"

Tinley snorted. "Right. That's why I've seen more tit tonight than I ever do at work."

Holy hell. Now I understood why Tallon asked that I accompany Tinley. *Did not know I'd need to play bouncer. Should've brought my fucking cuffs.*

Bethany's too-plump lips pursed as she gave Tinley a quick once-over. "Well, at least you dressed appropriately. Good for you."

"Yes, thank you for that. Though I chose different shoes."

Bethany's brows dipped. Well, they kind of did, as much as her frozen face would allow.

"Honey, I'd like you to meet someone." Tinley's stepfather's deep voice cut through the bubble of tension encompassing the small table. "Oh, hello, Tinley. You look beautiful." Placing a hand on her elbow, he leaned forward to place a kiss on her cheek, which she quickly pulled away from.

I flicked my gaze to Bethany, who glared at Tinley with hate in her bright blue eyes. She caught me watching and sneered.

"Who is this, honey?" she said, plastering a smile on her plastic face as she turned to her husband and the three men and two women standing behind him.

I gave the group a quick glance. The men ranged from a few inches shorter than me to my height. Two had protruding bellies while the other was thin, almost sickly so, which only made his skin seem that much pastier. His gaze lingered on Tinley with rapt fascination. I shifted closer to her, which made the woman on his arm follow the movement since she was clearly devouring me with her blatant stare.

Holy fuck, what was wrong with these people? I'd never felt like a piece of meat like this before—well, except the other night when those bartenders made it clear they only saw me for one thing. Tallon always said there was something wrong with me that I couldn't take women up on the offers that came my way. But it never felt right.

"These are the men behind the security firm we recently hired after that last attack on our client list. We're very lucky to have them work the firm into their full schedule."

The way Tinley inched backward, shifting closer, had me focused on her instead of the names he rattled off while introducing the group. She twisted, eyes searching mine.

"I think this is our cue," she whispered.

She gripped my offered elbow, but before we could fully turn from the group, one man spoke up, pausing our retreat.

"And who is everyone else?" the too-thin one asked with a tight smile.

My skin felt too tight, anger building at the disgusting way he kept focusing on Tinley. Yes, she was beautiful, but he could have some fucking decency and not stare, clearly telling those around us that he wanted to rip the damn dress off and fuck her right there in front of everyone.

Though that was the way every man in the room looked at her, including her stepbrother. Except her stepfather, who wouldn't look her way at all.

Odd.

"My son, Dr. Richard Bartholomew Parker the third, and my step-daughter, Tinley Harper." I rolled my eyes that she didn't get her full name rattled off like her stepbrother. "And friend."

I felt Tinley stiffen beside me, her black nails digging into my arm where we were still connected.

"Not just friend. Fantastic lover too."

"Fucking hell." I half laughed, half groaned. Grabbing my drink off the table, I downed the contents. *There goes the idea of sipping it slowly.*

"Now if you'll excuse us, we were on our way to find a coat closet to fuck in."

It was almost comical the way her mother's skin went pale before flushing red.

"Ah, to be young again," Rich said around an uncomfortable laugh. "We all remember our twenties."

Before any more of the awkward comments could reach my ears, Tinley pulled me toward the closest exit. Women followed us with their judging stares, leaning toward the person beside them with their lips hidden behind a raised hand, clearly whispering about our abrupt exit.

The moment the side door swung open, a gust of cold air soothed the burn in my cheeks. Rain continued to pour from the dark clouds, rushing through the gutters and pouring onto the grass-covered lawn. Thankfully, the overhang protected us from the weather, though a cold mist from the wind already coated my face.

"Well," I said to Tinley, where she leaned against the wall digging through her small purse, "that could've gone better."

"Figured it was better to get us out of there before either of us could smash a glass and stab my mom in the jugular."

I swallowed hard. That should not be hot. Though that kind of passion, that rage clearly bubbling under her skin, was fucking amazing. The emotion she bared was such a welcomed difference over Heather's cold, calculated way to handle things.

Tinley did everything fiercely.

It made my cock stir knowing she'd be a damn wildcat once I finally grew a set and fucked her. Which I would do just as soon as I knew this was more than her living out her fantasies with her childhood crush. Because if we slept together and she tossed me away, well, I wasn't sure I'd let her go as easily as she could me.

That was why this morning, even though it pained me to walk away, I did.

Her mumbled grumblings and the grind of flint pulled me from my thoughts. A billow of smoke poured through her lips after a deep inhale. She cut her eyes my way.

"My family stresses me out, okay, and I can't drink, so...." She held up the cigarette between two fingers. "Don't judge me."

"No judgment here. I'm not sure who I hate more at this point in the night. Your mother for being a fucking cunt"—that made Tinley's lips twitch upward—"your stepbrother for being creepy"—that made her lips dip—"or every other man in there who looked at you like they wanted what I'm just beginning to call mine."

A megawatt smile pulled up her lips. Touching her lower one, she ran a finger along it, watching me.

"Is that so?" she said. "Well, I'm glad you're finally catching up. Because you've been mine for a while."

Leaning against the wall beside her, I plucked the cigarette from between her fingers and pressed it to my lips. Inhaling, I slowly released the smoke, coughing like a damn fool. The barked laugh that escaped as she tossed her head back made the pain and embarrassment worth it.

"Now I remember why I quit," I said, still coughing.

Tinley studied the cigarette, spinning it between two fingers. "I only allow myself one a day. My one indulgence, though since you've been here, I haven't needed it—until tonight, that is. I guess that makes you my new indulgence."

Pride filled my chest at the strange compliment. The rain filled the comfortable silence, an occasional roar of laughter from inside breaking the peace that surrounded us. Out here alone, with the stormy weather preventing others from venturing outside, it felt private, even though anyone could walk out at any second and disrupt our slice of peace.

As if she sensed the same, Tinley shot me a mischievous look, shoved off the building, and wrapped her hand around mine. I followed as she tugged me around the corner where just a few feet of the overhang covered the area. Lights from the party inside and around the massive property gave enough illumination for me to see the desire in her ice-blue eyes.

"Here?" I asked, voice low and husky.

"Here," she confirmed, guiding my hand to her waist.

Both hands gripped her hips, the smooth material of her dress bunching beneath my palms. I advanced, forcing her to retreat until her back pressed against the building. Two fingers pinched the butt of the cigarette, extracting it from her hold before flicking it into the rain. Both hands cupped her cheeks before slipping into her hair. With a firm hold, I held her immobile as I lowered, closing the distance between us. With her lower lip between my teeth, I gave it a playful nip, using her gasp to my advantage. I covered her mouth with my own, pushing my tongue inside as a preview of what I planned to do next between her thighs.

"Please," she begged.

"Yes, ma'am." I chuckled as I skimmed my lips down the lean column of her neck. Puffs of white smoke rose in the cold air from my heated breath as I ran the tip of my tongue along her collarbone and sternum until the silky fabric halted my descent.

The damp concrete soaked through my slacks as I knelt before her, hands sliding up her long legs, bunching the dress around my wrists. Even in the dim light, there was no mistaking the damp spot along the front of her cream-colored thong. Without moving it aside, I pressed my lips to her center and pressed my tongue forward, teasing her over the material.

Her musky scent filled my nose. Done teasing us both, knowing I was running out of time before we were caught with my head up her dress, between her thighs, I tugged the scrap of material to the side. Silky arousal coated my tongue as I sucked her swollen nub between my lips, flicking the tip with my tongue.

"Oh fuck," she said above me.

A cruel smile tugged at my lips with each thrust of her hips pushing her hot center against my mouth. Blunt nails dug into my scalp, holding me in place.

Sucking at her clit in quick bursts, I plunged three fingers deep into her pussy, the digits sliding inside with ease. She whimpered above me, her hold flexing and releasing. Filthy wet noises drove me higher, my cock throbbing inside my slacks, wanting his turn at her sweet cunt.

With a garbled curse, her thighs sealed to my ears, hips bucking against my mouth as she rode out her release. Only after she sagged against the wall did I stop and slowly pull my fingers out of her, licking off the taste of her as I ducked my head out from under the silky curtain. Her dress whispered back in place, only a few wrinkles marking the front. I slowly stood, adjusting my demanding dick to hide my raging hard-on. Pressing a quick kiss to her lips, I pulled back and reached for her hand.

"You ready to go?" At her dazed nod, I chuckled and pulled her close until her front sealed against my chest.

It was official.

This beautiful woman.

My best friend's little sister.

Was mine.

Turning the corner, I stopped. Tinley slammed into my back at the abrupt pause. One man that Rich introduced earlier stood on the patio, glaring at his phone. I cleared my throat to draw his attention.

Narrowed eyes locked on mine, shifting to something dark before surprise registered on his features. With a nod, I continued toward the door and wrenched it open, ushering Tinley through with a hand to her back. The heavy weight of eyes settled on my back as I followed through the door back into the crowded room filled with slightly inebriated guests.

Despite the laughter and merry chatter, something was off, almost like a malicious undertone wafting through the air. Careful to keep Tinley close, I scanned the room, pausing on Bethany, her hate-filled glare directed at Tinley while she casually sipped from a near-empty champagne flute. Next to her, Bart also followed Tinley's every move, though the dark glint in his gaze appeared more devious than full of loathing.

My hackles rose, muscles tense.

"Get me out of here," Tinley said over her shoulder.

"Fucking gladly."

12

TINLEY

Exhausted from the night's events, we picked up a dozen donuts on the way home and vegged out on the couch. I wasn't sure how many reruns of *Friends* I missed while dozing off and on from the comfort and safety of being snuggled in his arms. That plus the heat pouring off him made fighting the pull of sleep impossible.

Blinking awake, I shifted, my drowsy gaze finding Bryson asleep behind me. Leg tossed over mine, arm draped over my waist, we were still cuddled on the couch the same way as when I drifted off. Careful to not wake him, I twisted to lie on my back and sighed, my eyes fluttering closed as his unique musky scent filled my lungs, making a sleepy smile curl my lips.

Who would've thought this would actually happen? All those childhood nights dreaming of this, fantasizing of being in his arms—of being his. And now he was mine.

His massive hand moved along my hip, pulling me tighter against him. Even in his sleep, Bryson was possessive.

Watching his face for any signs of him waking, I carefully stretched, reaching to grab the phone off the coffee table. I clicked the side button to illuminate the screen and check the time.

Three in the morning.

Beneath the clock were several missed calls and text notifications.

I frowned at the strange background. It took a few blinks for my mind to come up to speed and realize it wasn't my phone but Bryson's. Clicking the side again, I quickly scanned the names of the missed texts and phone calls. All were from his mom, none from Tallon.

I released a relieved exhale. After my comments at the party, I wasn't sure if anyone would reach out to Tallon and let him know his baby sister and best friend were together, though I knew deep down Mom wouldn't call him with the news. She'd welcome any new man into my life, as it meant I wouldn't be pandering after hers.

I rolled my eyes. Like I'd want his old saggy balls and ass. No, thank you. I liked my men slightly aged, tattooed, and dominant, with a sweet heart and a monster cock.

Though that last quality I'd tacked on only a few days ago, since I had no clue Bryson hid that thing from me the last few years. With good reason. Any woman who saw his cock would either be mesmerized and never want an average-size dick again or horrified. Thankfully, I fell into the former category.

Even if we hadn't had sex yet.

Bastard.

It was sweet, this slow thing, though I was more than ready to make him mine in every way.

The phone in my hand vibrated, his mom's name flashing on the screen.

Nerves twisted my stomach, and my pulse began to race. It was the middle of the night, and he'd already missed several calls. That couldn't mean anything good. My heart dropped before flying up into my throat.

Victoria.

Swiping the bar to answer the call, I pressed the screen to my ear.

"Hello," I said tentatively, voice cracking from the long nap.

"Um...." A whoosh of air passing the speaker filled my ear as if she pulled the phone away from her face, no doubt to check the screen and make sure she'd called the right person. "Is Bryson there?"

"Hey, Mrs. Bennett," I said as the massive man stirred behind me. "It's Tinley, Tallon's—"

"Tinley, yes. Hi there, sweetie." I fell to my back when Bryson sat up. He scrubbed a hand over his face, clearly in a fog from just waking up.

"Is everything okay?" I asked, Bryson's hazel eyes studying me.

"No, it's Victoria. She's sick, and I'm not really sure what to do with her high fever—"

Before she even finished, I ripped the phone away and held it out to Bryson. "It's your mom. Victoria is sick."

The flash of worry and panic that flicked across his face made my heart hurt.

"Mom, I'm here," he said into the phone. Standing, he paced the living room.

Tucking my knees up, I hugged my shins, watching and listening to follow along with the one-sided conversation. My heart hammered as I tried to swallow down my panic.

"Yeah, it's happened before when she had an ear infection. I'm guessing that's it if she's pulling on her ear." His lips twitched upward. "No, you do not need to take her to the ER." Bryson glanced my way, and somehow I knew. I just knew what he was asking with a single glance.

I nodded and leapt off the couch, hurrying to my bedroom. Knees pressed to the rug, I blindly searched under the bed for my old duffel. The tips of my fingers brushed against the coarse fabric handle. Tugging it free, I tossed it to the bed as I stood to dig through my disheveled drawers.

His voice, still talking to his mom, grew louder. With a quick glance over my shoulder, I found him in the doorway, something I couldn't read on his face as he studied my duffel, then me.

Shit, what if that look wasn't an invitation but more of a heads-up that he was leaving?

I shrugged and turned back to find a pair of warm leggings.

Fuck that if he thought he could leave me behind. Whether he liked it or not, I was going with him, because I had to. And not just for him. I wanted to see with my own eyes that Victoria was okay, wanted to be there when Bryson got to hold and comfort her. Why? Hell if I knew. I just knew I needed to go with him.

"Going somewhere?" he called from the door.

"Yeah, Louisville. Want to come with me?"

"Tinley—"

"Don't fucking start with that. I'm going with you. Is she okay? Should I call my family's doctor and have them drive up or get us an appointment with—"

Strong arms wrapped around me, tugging me back to a firm chest. I blew out a breath as my head hung. I felt his heart at my back, his quick breaths fanning down the column of my neck. He was worried; I could sense it. Maybe that was what drove this absolute need to go with him, to see her and make sure she was okay.

"Thank you." A chill ran down my spine at the brush of his lips along the shell of my ear. "Thank you for understanding and for offering to come with me."

"Not offering, Bry. I'm going with you."

"Yes, yes, you are, but not now." Turning me, he lifted me like the boys used to do in a performance and sat me on top of the dresser. "It's three in the morning. I'm not getting on the road at this hour." He swallowed, and I couldn't help but follow the bob of his Adam's apple. "Come on, Tinley. Think."

And I did. I really did.

Oh fuck.

"Bryson... I'm sorry. I wasn't thinking." Of course. Heather died in a car wreck going out to an early morning call, early morning like it was now. Of course he had some hesitation to getting on the road.

"I couldn't... I wouldn't survive losing someone else like that. We're waiting until sunrise. The moment those rays hit the sky, we'll be out of here. But until then, my mom has things under control. I told her how to alternate medicines to keep her fever down and help her rest comfortably. When is that therapy appointment?"

"What's today?" I really had no clue at this point since Bryson's arrival threw off all my routines in the best way.

"Monday. Too fucking early on Monday."

"Tomorrow afternoon," I said. Chewing on my lip, I reached up and traced a design on his bicep. "Do you think we could be back by then? If not, I can cancel—"

"I will have you back for that appointment, Tinley. Don't worry about that. Now come on." Wrapping his massive hands around my slim waist, he lifted me off the dresser. Fully expecting him to put me down, I was totally shocked when he kept lifting and tossed me over his shoulder. With a hysterical laugh, I slapped his ass, kind of hurting my hand, which should not have been as hot as it was.

"What the hell are you doing?" I said with a giggle.

"Getting some decent sleep for a couple hours and not on that tiny couch."

"It's a full-size couch." I laughed as we passed through the living room. Inside Tallon's bedroom, he deliberately slid me down his body inch by inch. I watched with rapt fascination as he dropped the loose sweats he wore, and then followed his boxer brief-clad ass as it bunched and flexed while crawling into the bed.

Nerves took flight in my stomach. Teeth gnawing on the inside of my cheek, I glanced at the light switch, then back to the bed. He'd want to sleep with the lights off like a normal person. Sweat slicked my now-clammy palms. Maybe I'd be okay with the lights off because he'd be close, but the thought of falling asleep in darkness and the possibility of waking up in the dark had my lungs seizing.

I shook my head and pressed a fist to my sternum, desperate to breathe.

"It's okay to leave the lights on, kid. Come on."

And just like that, like he'd always done, I felt normal. Well, not normal, but not the freak others in the past had made me feel like. I breathed a sigh of relief when his words calmed the oncoming panic attack. Shuffling along the floor to the other side of the king-size bed in my socked feet, I crawled across and snuggled beneath the covers right next to him.

One thing I never expected about this massive FBI agent was that he's a snuggler. But he so was. With a huff of annoyance, he pushed on my shoulder, manipulating my body until I lay on my side, facing away from him. I smiled at the building lights twinkling through the storm still raging outside as he draped an arm across my middle and pulled me flush against his chest.

Yep, total snuggle bug.

I hoped he knew there was no hope of him ever letting me go now. This just pushed me over the edge to pure obsession, and only death could pull me from this man.

In short, Bryson Bennett was my lobster.

BRYSON WASN'T KIDDING about wanting to leave at first light. At least I was awoken with soft kisses to my shoulder and his groggy voice whispering my name. Blinking past the sleepiness wanting to make my lids close again, I grinned against the pillow at his promise of picking up Krispy Kreme on the way if I hurried.

Rolling to my back, I smiled up at him, running a hand over his beard-covered cheek.

"Good morning," I said, voice thick. A strange look flickered over his face. My hair slid along the pillow as I tilted my head, attempting to read whatever he was thinking. "What?"

His lips pursed, clearly hesitant to respond. "Do you want to come with me to Louisville because you want to or because you're nervous to be alone after what I told you regarding the murder here? It's not a big deal, just wondering, you know?" He closed his eyes and blew out a breath. "Damn, I sound like a pussy right now."

My grin grew into a full smile. Such a sweet, sweet man. "I'm coming with you because I want to. For you and to make sure Victoria is okay. Honestly, I didn't even think about the other reason. Which is odd, considering."

"Considering what?" The way his features shifted from soft and open to stern made me chuckle. So sweet yet so protective, this one.

I loved it.

"Considering before you showed up, I was feeling more paranoid than normal."

He shoved himself up to a sitting position on the bed, tugging me up too with a firm grip on either shoulder. "What do you mean?"

I lifted a shoulder, feeling timid about what I was about to tell him. The thought of him not believing me flickered for a moment, making me debate if I should tell him the truth. But this was Bryson, not Mom. Of course, he'd believe me.

"I don't know how to describe it besides it's felt like I've had eyes on me, even in the apartment." I chewed on the corner of my lip. "That's absurd, though, right? It's probably because Tallon hasn't been home in a while, and the loneliness was making me think things happened that didn't." I furrowed my brow, remembering I hadn't told him about that strange encounter at the bar two nights ago. "Though there was that guy."

My eyes widened at the way his nostrils flared, face now flushed red. "What guy?"

I swallowed hard. Damn, he was intense when angry. "The other night at the bar, a detective came in to talk to me, and it just felt off. Everything about—"

"Detective," Bryson said like a curse. Scrubbing a hand over his beard, he closed his eyes like he was gathering all his patience. "Kid, I need you to explain everything that's felt off the last few weeks, including why you weren't surprised that a detective was coming to see you. Details. Now."

"You'll believe me?" I questioned hesitantly.

He jerked back like I'd slapped him. "Of course. Why wouldn't I?"

I nodded and blew out a breath to organize my thoughts. "Okay, well, besides the being watched feeling—"

"Which is a big thing to not tell me about until now."

I cringed. "Sorry. I'm just used to people other than my therapist telling me it's all in my head. Those first few years, I swore everyone intended to do me harm."

"Which is common after the type of trauma you went through."

"So, the being watched thing. It's here, at work, even... even last night. It feels gross, slimy almost. That's the best way to describe it."

"What about now, in this room?"

I gave that some thought. "Honestly, no. Though ever since you arrived, I haven't been as aware. I'm slightly distracted, you know, with your monster cock and all."

He didn't smile.

Right. Not the time to make jokes. Got it.

"What's this about a detective?"

Blowing out a breath, I lay back down, fluffing the pillows behind my head to get comfortable. This seemed like it would turn into a long conversation, even though we needed to get on the road.

"So that night you arrived, there was an altercation at the bar with this big meathead guy. He harassed one girl. I broke it up, and he came after me." At his curse, I shifted my gaze out the window. "Like I told you before, the bouncers are outstanding. They got to him before he could even lay a finger on me. But he said he'd be back, that we weren't done." I cleared my throat. Just saying those words out loud sent a bolt of terror through me. "Anyway, a couple nights later, the bouncer said that guy, the one they sent to the station, turned up murdered. Just a few blocks from the police station."

"Fuck," he said.

I nodded, completely agreeing with the sentiment. "Since we were the last ones to see him, the security guy said a detective might come around to ask me questions. Well, one showed up later that night. It was the timing and his persistence that had me balking. It felt off. Then you showed up, and I lost him in the crowded bar."

"I don't like this," he said after a few seconds of silence.

"But you're here and—"

"Tinley, all of this adds up to nothing good. I'm going to ask Selena—" he cut himself off at my pointed death glare and cleared his throat, "Agent Burton to look into that murder you just mentioned and get an ID on the detective." Glancing at the clock, he cursed. "We need to get on the road. I'm calling the pediatrician's office the second they open to get Vic an appointment."

Sliding off the bed, I stood and stretched my arms high over my head. I preened a little at his lust-filled stare scanning up and down my scantily clad body.

"I'll be ready in a minute. Most of my stuff is already packed."

"Sweatpants, baggy ones, a large hoodie, and a jacket. And a hat would be great," he grumbled.

Prancing over to the other side of the bed, I attempted to tackle his enormous frame to the bed. Before we hit the mattress, he spun us around, pinning me beneath his heavy bulk.

"I like your possessive and controlling side," I admitted. "It makes me feel... taken care of. Special, in a way."

"Good. Because I can guarantee that it will only get worse from here. I'll do everything in my power to keep you safe. Even if that means covering up every inch of your delectable body so I'm not constantly distracted on this road trip."

Leaning up, I pressed my lips to his. I'd planned for it to be chaste, but with a groan, he deepened the kiss, pressing me hard into the mattress. Heat sizzled in my veins, pooling between my legs as he forced my lips apart with his demanding tongue. I arched beneath him, a shiver racing along my skin at the feel of my peaked nipples brushing across his naked chest.

"You're nothing but trouble," he said as he pulled back. Standing, he adjusted himself with one hand and helped me up with the other. "Go get some clothes on. We leave in five."

Even though I expected the hard smack to my ass, I still yelped before scurrying out of the room. Rubbing my sore backside, I savored the bite of pain as I bit my lip to stop my cheerful grin. Most of the boys I'd been with needed me to take control to ensure I got what I wanted out of the brief encounter. Though it seemed it would be the opposite with Bryson.

Which was awesome.

I always wondered what it would be like to be with someone who took control and allowed me to just experience every sensation. To let go knowing I would be taken care of.

Soon.

At least I sure fucking hoped it would be soon.

The orgasm he gave me last night outside the party was soul-changing, but I wanted all of him. Every inch of his body hovering over me while he took my own. I was almost to the point of begging for it. I would right now except we had more important things to worry about than my desperate need for his cock.

Tonight, though, let the begging begin.

13

BRYSON

Monday, December 10th

"Give me a second to put my earbuds in," I muttered into the phone. After situating one into each ear, I gripped the wheel and shifted in the driver seat. "I'm good now. What's up?"

I prepared myself for him to curse my name and disown me as his friend. After Tinley's announcement last night at the party, I fully expected him to have heard about our relationship from his mom or that asshole Bart.

"You seem different," Tallon said on the other end of the line. "What's going on with you?"

I blinked, giving myself a second to contemplate my next words. He didn't sound mad or accusing. He sounded like Tallon: tired, direct, and pissed-off. Tearing my gaze off the road, I snuck a glance at the woman soundly asleep in the passenger seat, curled up like a cat, somehow fitting her entire long, lean body onto the seat.

"I'm doing okay? You good?" I responded cautiously.

"Yeah, I'm good. Now you're acting weird instead of relaxed. What the hell is going on with you?"

I leaned back against the seat, a small smile forming on my lips.

Relaxed, he said. Hell yeah, I was relaxed. I'd had two ball-draining orgasms within the same number of days that would make any man sound fucking relaxed.

"Something came up at home," I said instead of saying all that. "Victoria is sick, and my mom is struggling to handle it on her own."

"What do you need from me?" Tallon said in a rush. "I'm sure my family's doctor—"

My cheeks bunched with my wide, appreciative smile, loving that his overreaction was the same as his sister's. "I assume it's just another ear infection. We're headed up now, only about an hour outside Louisville."

"We?" he questioned. "You took Tin with you?"

The suspicion in his tone had me sitting up straighter in my seat. I wanted to tell him, tell him I was slowly falling in love with his little sister. But Tinley wanted to do it, and I needed to respect her decision despite the ache lying to my best friend caused.

"Yeah," I grumbled. "Didn't want to leave her alone. She told me something this morning before we left that worries me. She said she's felt watched over the last few weeks."

"The fuck?" he cursed. "She didn't tell me anything like that. What the actual fuck? Put her on the phone."

I shook my head although he couldn't see me. "Can't do that. It's your sister, T. You know what she's doing."

His heavy breath blew across the mouthpiece. "She's out to the world in the passenger seat, isn't she?"

I grinned. "Have you ever known her to be in the car longer than thirty minutes and not fall asleep?"

"No. Well, when she wakes up, tell her to call me. I have some words for my idiotic—"

"Watch it," I nearly growled. Clearing my throat, I tried to reel in the flash of anger his words invoked. "She was worried I wouldn't believe her. I think that had a lot to do with her not telling you or me sooner. The part that worries me, T, is she said she felt that way in the apartment too."

"What?" he replied, a mixture of horror and anger in his sharp tone.

I tapped a thumb along the steering wheel, ticking off the checklist in my head of what we needed to do next. "Can you request a locksmith to change y'all's locks? I have a tech genius friend who can help me out with examining the apartment's security feed to see if there's been security breach."

"You really think—"

"Do you want to risk her life not covering every angle?" I snapped.

"No. Fuck. Bryson, you're too fucking good to me and her. You're a good friend."

Well, stab a rusted dagger into my heart.

"Yep. Just taking care of my family. Wait," I said as a thought popped into my head. "What the hell are you doing calling this early? What's going on?"

"Fucking telemarketers," he grumbled. "I'm exhausted, but some unknown number keeps calling me. I leave my phone on in case... well, anything, and these fuckers chose today to wake me up before the damn sun."

I frowned. That was odd. Why today, the morning when Tinley and I left the apartment complex like we were going away for a few days?

"Yeah, odd," I muttered. Unease grew, making my muscles tense. "Listen, I left a message for Agent Burton—"

"Oh yeah, booty call."

"No," I said, exasperated. "Something happened at the bar where Tinley works, and the guy responsible for the altercation ended up murdered."

"That's shitty. But why does that involve us? This unsub I'm after has never killed a guy before. It would be way outside his norm."

"Because the altercation at the bar, the one that had him taken to the station, was because of your sister. He came after her." I let that sink in before continuing. "And then he ended up murdered. I don't know the specifics, but it seems like too much of a coincidence to not look into with the watching piece too."

"You're right. Fuck, I need to get home. This is all oddly revolving around her."

"I know, I feel the same. It's too damn coincidental. But she's safe. We won't be back until tomorrow for her therapy appointment. I'm sticking by her side until we get this figured out." *And longer, if she'll have me.*

"Fuck, man. I can never repay you for taking care of my little sister when I can't. I owe you big-time."

"No, you don't," I replied. "Let me know when the locksmith is confirmed. Have them leave the old lock set so we can see if someone tampered with it. I'll call my guy this afternoon and ask him to look into the security feed in the apartment lobby."

"And I'll try Burton again. I want to know the details of that case too. You have enough on your plate with what you listed and taking care of Victoria. Shoot me a text to let me know she's okay and if you need anything from me. Tell her Uncle Tal will come by soon for tea with her and those furry friends of hers."

My throat locked up with the influx of emotion. Tallon was a good man—misunderstood by many, but a good man and loyal friend. It would hurt worse than a gunshot to the balls if he walked away from our friendship because I was in love with his sister.

"Yeah, I'll tell her. That will perk her right up. She always loves her time with you."

With a clipped goodbye, I ended the call and tossed the earbuds into the cupholder. Elbow perched along the door. I scratched at my beard, lost in thought. The murder of a man who threatened Tinley, a shady detective, and the feeling of being watched over the last few weeks. Whatever was going on, it wasn't good. What it *did* add up to, I wasn't certain.

Could we tie this to the bastard who abducted Tinley ten years ago, now back and ready to make good on his promise of returning? Or was this all coincidental and had nothing in common with an unsub who got a thrill out of abusing and assaulting his victims before cutting their throats? It didn't seem plausible that these two were one and the same, even though the timing of it all seemed suspicious. If the bastard who took Tinley had that kind of rage and disgust for women, he would've treated Tinley the same as he did the new victims. But he didn't rape her during her long captivity and actually got her help when it was clear she'd die if she wasn't properly treated.

What was the connection, if there even was one?

And why did I feel in my gut that these were connected, everything circling around Tinley?

If only we had more on her case, but we didn't. We never found where he held her those three weeks. The evidence collected off her body before she was rushed into surgery to remove the infected toes and treat her hypothermia was minimal. As if she'd been washed down before she was dumped on that couple's doorstep.

The fact that we were no closer today than we were then in identifying the man responsible ate at me daily, as I knew it did Tallon. He'd carried the weight of almost losing his sister forever, thinking it was his fault she was taken. Even more recently, with having unlimited resources to find the asshole but still coming up empty, drove him to extremes. The past few years, all he focused on was work, moving from one case to the next, all revolving around crimes against women. But with each case he solved, each sick bastard he put behind bars, it drove home that he hadn't been able to do that for his sister.

I'd seen him less and less the last couple years, which was hard, but I understood why. Maybe he'd be good with me being with his little sister. That meant she'd be safe because he knew I would keep her safe or die trying.

Huffing out a laugh, I shook my head. Yeah, right. That was wishful thinking. The moment he found out about Tinley and me he'd go on a rampage, that anger and hurt directed at me. I should stock their fridge with frozen peas now just to be prepared. I wouldn't fight back. I already knew that much. If beating the shit out of me helped him work through his anger, then I'd let him.

I shot a glance at the woman still dozing beside me. *If* she allowed her brother to whip my ass would be a different scenario. She'd already proved to be just as possessive and protective as me.

With the bumper-to-bumper rush hour traffic getting into the city and nasty driving conditions from the spitting snow, it took almost two hours to make the normally one-hour drive through the city toward the north side of Louisville.

Passing the small cottage-style homes, some with their Christmas lights twinkling in the gray morning light, I worried what Tinley would think of the house. She grew up in a mansion in the Belle Meade area complete with tennis courts and a damn stable filled with well-bred horses. I didn't have any of that to offer. Which I knew deep down didn't matter, but still, nerves gnawed at my empty gut as I pulled the truck into our cracked concrete driveway.

A two-bedroom white bungalow was how the realtor described it when I first bought the place, much to Heather's chagrin. She wanted something bigger in a more affluent neighborhood like where she grew up, but not me. A smaller house was easier to fill, and not just with furniture. A small home always felt warmer to me, easier to fill with love and laughter. That was what I wanted for our daughter, not something enormous and impersonal.

A few watery snowflakes landed on the windshield, immediately melting and dripping down the glass, blurring my view of the house. Inside, the lights were already on, a steady stream of gray smoke billowed from the chimney, and the red and green lights I'd hung two weeks before shined bright along the roofline.

"You're kidding me."

I started at Tinley's voice, too lost in my head to have noticed she'd woken up. I shifted in the seat, turning my body her way. Heart in my throat, I scanned her wide eyes, which were glued on the house, seeming to take in every inch of what she could see.

"Yeah, it's not much—" I started, but she cut me off.

"Much? Bry, it's adorable. Oh, I can't wait to see the inside. Please tell me it still has some of the original features. I love the older homes in Nashville that kept the personality of the time period, like all the built-in shelves and crown molding." Her grin grew wider. "Damn, I sound so lame talking about woodwork."

Her expectant eyes turned toward me, blinking fast.

"Um, yeah," I said, trying to keep up with this odd turn in the conversation. "I kept most of the original features except the kitchen. It needed a complete redo."

Tinley nodded along as I spoke and then reached for the door. "Oh, nice. I can't wait to see the inside if it's as adorable as the outside." She lifted a single brow. "What are you waiting for?"

I chastised myself for the earlier doubts about how she would react. I was comparing Tinley to Heather, which wasn't fair to Tinley. She wasn't my late wife. No, she was so different, in the best ways. Ways that seemed to bring out the better side of me if the last few days were any sign.

When was the last time I'd laughed this much, or smiled until my cheeks were sore?

When was the last time I felt the warmth of passion or security from the one I gave my all to?

Shaking myself out of my own thoughts, I followed Tinley out of the truck, passing her by on my way to the front door as she hopped from one foot to the other, rubbing her hands together to chase away the wintery chill. Though I couldn't take my eyes off her genuine smile and how it grew as she peered through the front bay window.

"Oh my goodness, it's so perfect," I heard her gasp in an ecstatic high-pitched tone as I slipped the key into the lock and pushed the door open. "Look at how inviting the living room looks. That's a total cuddle couch, which makes sense since you're a cuddler."

"Come on," I said with a chuckle, holding my hand out to her. "Get your tiny ass inside before it freezes off."

Shooting me a quick look, she interlaced her fingers with my own, allowing me to pull her inside once I stepped across the threshold. After shutting and locking the door, I fluffed my coat out, sending tiny water droplets around the tile entry. Careful to not elbow her in the face, I stripped out of my coat before helping Tinley out of her own.

"Mom," I called out as I led Tinley through the living room.

Noises and Mom's voice in the kitchen's direction had me shifting and heading that way. We found Mom standing in front of the stove with her back to us and Victoria on her hip. The two moved and swayed as Mom danced to the soft rock station she always listened to while cooking.

"Mom."

Victoria turned first, her rosy cheeks, bedhead hair, and footed pajamas making her look younger than almost three years old. My heart ached at the sight of her. With the distractions in Nashville, I hadn't realized how much I missed her until this moment.

Her light eyes lit up the moment she saw me. "Dada," she exclaimed, those chubby hands now outstretched toward me. "Hold it."

"It" meant her. An adorable habit I absolutely had zero desire to break.

In two strides, I cleared the space between us and scooped her out of Mom's arms, pulling the too-warm child to my chest. Her arms wrapped around my neck as I held her tight. My eyes drifted shut with the deep inhale of baby powder and lavender.

"Hey, baby," I cooed in her ear. Pulling her back, I pressed my forehead to hers, checking her temperature. "I missed you, sweet thing. Missed you so much."

"I sick, Dada," she said, rubbing at her runny nose.

"I know, and we're going to get you better. We have a doctor's appointment in two hours. He'll help make you feel better."

"No owwie," she demanded, leveling me with a glare that held little weight with her sweet face. "No owwie, Dada."

"I can't promise that, but if you need a shot, we'll go get something special after. How does that sound?"

As she nodded, a wide yawn stretched her mouth open. Resting her head on my chest, I set my chin on top of her head, my eyes finding Mom leaning against the counter smiling at us.

"She had a hard time going back to sleep when I woke her up to give her medicine this morning."

"Did you use the diffuser last night with the two oils I—"

"Yes." She groaned and rolled her eyes. "But that girl just won't sleep, even when she's not sick."

"Oh," I said, remembering Tinley was behind me. The soles of my boots twisted on the tile floor. I frowned at the empty space where Tinley once was. "There's someone I want you to meet." I inclined my head toward the living room, and Mom followed while cleaning her hands with the apron tied snuggly around her waist.

I found Tinley studying the Christmas tree in the corner, running her fingers over the popcorn garland Victoria and I—mostly me while Vic watched a show—made last week.

"Hey," I said, gaining her attention. She straightened, seeing Mom at my side. "Tinley, this is my mom, Esther Bennett. Mom, this is—"

"Oh my goodness, child, you're more beautiful in person than in pictures," Mom exclaimed, already moving toward Tinley.

I suppressed a laugh at the shocked expression that overtook Tinley's face. Swiping a palm along her black leggings, she jutted it out in front of her. "Pleasure to—oomph."

My chuckle echoed through the living room when Mom moved past Tinley's offered hand to wrap her thick arms around my girl.

Victoria's head popped off my shoulder to inspect what the commotion was about.

"Um, hello," Tinley said, clearly unsure of the situation.

But Mom being Mom, she didn't give two shits about that and hugged her tighter until Tinley's muscles relaxed. After a few seconds, her arms came around Mom's back, hugging her. Ice-blue eyes found mine, giving me a glimpse at the various emotions flooding her lower lids swimming with unshed tears.

I started toward them to break Mom's hold. "Mom," I said in a rush. "You're upsetting—-"

Tinley shook her head, cutting me off before laying a cheek atop Mom's shoulder. Soft whispers filled the living room as the two women held each other tighter. Suddenly I felt like the outsider watching a too-intimate moment between them.

After a minute, Mom reluctantly released Tinley, who laughed, her smile shaky as she wiped at her now-leaking eyes.

"Sorry for the happy tears. That hug was just... *wow*," Tinley said with an amazed laugh. "Now I see where Bryson gets the cuddle gene."

Mom's smile grew wide, her slightly crooked teeth showing as she darted a knowing look between us.

"So that's Mom," I said, running a hand along my scruffy beard. The two women looked at each other and laughed. "And this little bit is Victoria." I twisted her in my arms so she could see the room better. "Vic, you met Tinley when you were just a baby—"

"My pony," Victoria exclaimed as she pointed at Tinley. "My pony."

My brows furrowed as she squirmed in my arms, demanding to be put down. The moment her footed pajama-covered feet hit the ground, she hurried toward the overflowing toy basket. I sent Tinley a shrug in response to her curious expression.

Stuffed bears of every color flew out of the basket, landing in a disheveled pile before Victoria found what she was looking for. Withdrawing her favorite *My Little Pony*, one I'd already replaced twice, she hurried over to Tinley.

"My pony," Victoria said, holding up the little soft plastic horse to Tinley. Kneeling in front of the demanding toddler, Tinley took the toy and examined it. Reaching behind Tinley, Victoria pulled a thick chunk of Tinley's rose gold ponytail and held it close to her face. "Same."

"Oh, honey," I said, finally putting two and two together. "Tinley isn't a *My Little Pony* just because their hair matches."

"My pony," Victoria stated, and crawled into Tinley's arms. "Hi, pony."

"Hi," Tinley responded with a warm smile. "Looks like we have the same taste in hair color."

Taking the offered toy back, Victoria clutched it to her chest and leaned her head on Tinley's shoulder, yawning widely.

I blinked at them as a swell of emotions I couldn't decipher filled my chest until it felt like it might burst open.

"Well, okay, then," I said, clearing my throat of whatever made my voice crack.

"Yeah." Tinley's smile grew as she rested her cheek on top of Victoria's head. Moving to the couch, she eased down onto it, adjusting Victoria in a more comfortable position once she leaned back.

Mom turned a pointed look my way, then Tinley's. A knowing toothy grin split her face.

"It's about time. So, when are you telling Tallon?" Mom questioned.

"Hmm?" I responded, playing dumb.

"Don't play me for a fool," Mom retorted in exasperation. Easing down into the armchair, she fanned out the blue checkered nightdress to cover the peek of ankle that showed. "It's obvious to everyone around you. And I know you haven't told him or that boy would've called me, demanding I package her up and ship her back to Nashville." She waved me off when I blanched, clear her words hit home. "Don't worry about him. He'll come around, Bryson. It'll take a minute, though, so expect some reaction. It's hard for siblings to come to terms with it when they know the younger one is having sex."

A sharp squeak of alarm came from the couch. Victoria's little hand came up and patted Tinley's cheek in a sweet, comforting gesture.

Holy fuck, my daughter might like my girl more than me.

How did I feel about that?

Great. I felt fucking great about that. Because today solidified the fact that Tinley wasn't going anywhere. This beautiful woman was mine, and I'd do whatever it took to keep her in our lives. Fuck my job, this house, and the comforts of the city I grew up in. If Tinley wanted to stay in Nashville, then Nashville was about to gain two new residents.

Because after this display, it was very clear Tinley wasn't just mine.

She was ours.

14

TINLEY

I paced in front of the bay window, studying the street. The sprinkle of snow from earlier now poured from the gray skies in what I classified as a class five storm. Though Bryson's mom wasn't worried at all, which should have told me to calm the fuck down, but I couldn't. Bryson and Victoria were somewhere on the road on their way back to me.

Sure, his truck had four-wheel drive, and it was really only a light dusting of snow, but still, they were out there, and I was stuck here waiting. I understood why I needed to stay home, but that didn't make the nerves and worry go away.

"Where are they?" I grumbled, checking my phone for the hundredth time in the last five minutes. I shoved it into the front pocket of my hoodie with a huff when I found no new updates on their ETA. "I mean, how far away is this doctor anyway? He should really look in to one that's closer." At Esther's chuckle, I turned to her, hands on my hips. "Am I being ridiculous?"

"Calm down, honey. They're fine. Remember, Bryson said they'd have to wait a bit at the pharmacy for the antibiotic. I'm sure he's just too busy wrangling that little bit of crazy to give you another update."

I nodded as I twisted to keep watch once again. That sounded right yet did nothing to ease the growing nausea that we were apart. "Why doesn't that make me feel better, though? I feel sick. It's dumb, but I can't help it."

"Because you love him." I whipped around, the tip of my ponytail flicking me in the face with the quick movement. "And her too. I saw it on your face when he had a difficult time extracting Vic from your arms when they had to leave."

I swallowed hard. Padding over to the armchair, I fell onto the soft cushion and sat forward, pressing both elbows onto my spread thighs. "I really love him and her. How in the heck did that happen so fast? Well, I guess not really that fast. I've always had a thing for Bry, and, well, how can you not love that little cutie?"

"Plus, she's an extension of the man you love, which means your love for him just flows over to her. It's love math, darling."

"Love math," I said with a sly grin. "I like that." Twirling the end of my ponytail, I stared at the hairs, avoiding her eyes. "Thank you. For the hug earlier." I cleared my throat of the rising emotions. "I think that was a first from a woman that wasn't forced or cold. Seeing you, knowing Bryson and the joy and love you two clearly have and give freely, it makes me jealous." I winced, knowing that made me sound like an emotional head case.

"Jealous?" she questioned.

When I dared a look her way to gauge if she was offended, I found sorrow written on her weathered face.

I shrugged and wrung my fingers together. "I grew up with the best of everything. Top-rated private school, the best dance program, on-site cooks, maids, everything, but it was just stuff. I wanted a relationship with my mother, but—"

"She's a cold-hearted bitch?"

I barked out a laugh and leaned all the way back in the chair. "Have you met her? Because that's a very accurate description."

"No, thank goodness. Not sure I'll be able to hold my tongue if we meet. I only know her from what Tallon tells me from time to time." I quirked a brow in her direction. "Just because you see them getting along doesn't mean he enjoys her company or that he's keeping a good relationship with her for himself. But that's not my story to share, it's his."

I nodded. Maybe it was time Tallon and I laid everything out on the table, really understood each other as adults, not kids. Though, if he had shared with Esther about our mom, did that mean he also talked about me and my struggles too? Unease gnawed at my stomach, wondering what this loving woman thought of me based on Tallon's stories of my fucked-up life.

"I'm doing better," I said in a rush. "I don't want you to think Bry is getting mixed up with some damaged addict who—"

"Who survived a horror that most can never comprehend, and who continues to live, smiling and opening herself to love and trust despite the odds?"

I snapped my mouth shut, my teeth clicking together. No doubt her past trauma made it so she understood me better than anyone, even my therapist.

"I just don't want you to think...." I dropped my chin to my chest. "I love him, but if my past is too much, I can try to walk away from them."

"Do you think you could?"

I peeked up through my lashes and shook my head. "But I'd try. For him. For her. I'd try to do what was best for them."

Stretching an arm out, she gestured for me to join her on the couch. Popping up, I sat in the exact spot where she patted a hand on the cushion beside her. A little too close, but no way would I turn away the opportunity for another amazing hug.

The last one earlier was literally life-changing.

A hug. From a woman who had lived through hell and could still wrap a stranger in her arms and hug the shit out of them.

"Out of all the things I've been through in my life, the most difficult was watching my caring, devoted, passionate son lose that light because the person he gave his heart to didn't reciprocate. It only got worse after Victoria, and I had to watch as two people I loved longed desperately for someone who wouldn't give them the attention and affection they needed. See, my son, and Victoria too, they need that affection and attention to feel loved. And within the couple hours that you were here, I saw you touch and laugh and love on those two more than I saw his late wife give them over the course of a month. So no, child, I don't want you to leave. Though I have to admit I'm worried about what will happen to both of them if you choose not to stay."

The hand that was patting my knee moved behind my shoulder and tugged me against her side.

"And if you hurt them, if you make them love you to where they don't see a future without you in it, and then leave, well, I have an unregistered shotgun, a shovel, and a lot of wooded Kentucky land where I could dump your body."

I should've been scared, but I was fucking impressed.

"Who's your Plan A body dump helper?"

"My best friend, Patsy, and I'm hers."

"That's cool that you've already talked about it."

"Who says we've just talked?"

That made me laugh. Laugh hard. To the point where tears streamed down my face, those same tears from earlier that I held back to not look like the emotional train wreck I was.

Her other arm came around, wrapping me in an awkward side hug.

But the funny thing was there was absolutely nothing awkward about it.

"I'm staying," I said once I quieted down, though for some reason, my tears wouldn't stop. "I want to stay so badly. He's my lobster."

"Kids these days and their strange sayings."

I chuckled at that. Sitting up straight, I wiped at my eyes. "Though I don't know if he feels the same. He wants to take the time to really feel this thing out that's happening between us."

"Moron," she spat with an eye roll.

"But if he'll have me, if he wants me even half as much as I want him, then I'll go where he goes. I have nothing holding me to Nashville, honestly. Just a crappy job and a great therapist." Who I could still see via web calls or even make the two-and-a-half-hour drive to Nashville twice a week if needed. "All he has to do is ask."

"After you tell your brother."

I cringed at that. "Yeah. After I tell Tallon and make sure he doesn't kill Bryson after."

The sound of a rumbling engine had me bolting off the couch and hurrying to the bay window. Bryson waved, a small cheerful smile on his lips as he rounded the hood, heading toward the back passenger side where I remembered Victoria's car seat was placed.

Seeing that bundled-up baby girl, the coat almost bigger than her with her sweet face peering out from beneath the fur-lined hood, did something to me. Something I'd never felt before. I'd always had this urge to protect those who needed it, but this, this was deeper than that. Even just knowing her for a short few hours, I knew deep down in my soul I'd kill or be killed for her.

Sure, what I felt for Bryson was profound, but this love for her was as if her tiny fists had wrapped around my heart and squeezed the last of the emptiness out. There was no more hollow inside me. Every inch was filled with those two.

I turned as they came through the front door.

"It's really coming down out there," he said as he awkwardly began stripping Victoria out of her puffy coat.

Stepping toward them, I helped, carefully tugging her arms free before hanging up the coat on the hooks on the wall beside the shimmery unicorn backpack.

"My pony." At her sweet voice, I turned, finding Victoria's short little arms outstretched. "Hold it."

Only a person with a heart of coal could say no to that, even if I risked getting sick myself.

Bryson looked between us, worry written on his face. "It's strep and she's contagious until—"

"It's fine," I said, tugging her from his arms. "Strep is worth it to hold her for a little while, plus I'm pretty sure that ship sailed when I held her this morning. Did they give her a shot of antibiotics too or just oral?"

Amusement crossed his features. Tossing the brown paper bag to the couch, he began tugging off his thick coat and hung it up on the free hook, then adjusted his tight black Henley. "Shot too. Her fever was high when we got there, even with the medicine."

I'd had strep several times as a kid and remembered it being terrible. The sooner she could get comfortable, the better it would be for everyone. "Good, that means she'll feel better sooner."

"You want to see if she'll lie down?" he asked, hitching his chin up the narrow stairs. "Her nursery is the first one on the right. Just look for the pink."

I smiled ear to ear. This man might cause my heart to burst with all the feels he spurred inside me.

"Well," Esther said, breaking our heated stare. We both turned, finding her tugging off the apron and laying it over the back of the couch. "You two have this covered. I'm going home to catch up on my stories."

"Thank you for not watching those with Vic." I arched a brow between the two. "I grew up with the expectation that everyone was trying to stab me in the back, seduce me, or would end up in the hospital once a week," Bryson explained.

She waved him off. "Ah, you were fine. Look at you now. I'd say it prepared you for your line of work. Always ready for anything, even the occasional possession." I laughed, making Victoria lean back to stare up at my face. "Let me know when I need to be back tomorrow," she said.

Bryson frowned, looking at the winter weather outside. "I don't want you driving on these roads, Mom."

Her fists went to her hips. "You were fine."

"And I have a truck and am younger, with better reflexes."

I hooked a thumb his way. "I can attest to that. He saved two boxes of donuts from toppling to the ground after I slammed a door in his face." I considered our options for half a second. "Bry, why don't you drive your mom home, and I'll stay here with Victoria?"

A deep line formed between his brows. "You sure?"

"Of course. We'll go upstairs and try to get some sleep." Tipping my face down, I studied her flushed cheeks. "Does that sound good to you, cutie? You want to take a nap?"

Her blonde curls bounced with her quick nod. "Night night time, my pony. I take a nap with you."

When I looked up, the shocked expression on Bryson's face confused me. "What?" I asked.

"Nothing. She's never this eager for a nap."

"Ah. Well, I'm sure the medicine is kicking in and she's finally getting comfortable. Plus, she probably knows I'm already wrapped around her finger and will hold her until she demands I put her down."

Leaning forward, Bryson pressed an awe-filled kiss to my lips before shifting to place one on top of Victoria's head.

I watched him and Esther make their way through the fluttering flakes of snow, waving when Bryson turned toward the window after helping his mom into the passenger seat.

I stood frozen as he waved back, my overwhelming emotions keeping me stock-still until he broke the moment and jogged to the driver side, then climbed inside the cab. Once the truck was gone, the street empty, I turned for the stairs.

"Okay," I said to the already drowsy Victoria. "I think I'm supposed to change your diaper before naptime. No one wants to sleep in a wet one, right?" No response. *Well, shit.* It wasn't like I'd ever done this before. "Victoria, your pony might need some help, okay? Be patient with me."

It took four tries to figure out the complexities of disposable diapers, the giggles coming from the one I was changing telling me that was three too many for any normal person. Apparently, my frustration at the cheap sticky tape meant to secure the sides was hilarious to the tiny human. Which, after it was all done, I somewhat found it all comical too. The soft gray glider molded around my back as I settled back and adjusted Victoria along my chest.

Head back, eyes closed, I zeroed my focus on every detail of this precious moment: the sweet, warm, even breaths that brushed along my neck, the lingering soft scent of baby powder mixed with the lavender from the diffuser I'd turned on the moment we walked into the nursery, and of course the little flex of fingers around my pointer finger which she refused to release.

"I don't think I ever had this," I whispered into the room, suddenly overwhelmed with conflicting emotions. "At least I don't remember ever being held by my mom. A nanny, sure, but not Mom. I think it's why I worked so hard to impress her, to win her love as I got older. I didn't want to dance, but she loved it when I did, so I kept at it. Even when my toes bled and I cried on my way to rehearsals. I did it all hoping that one day she'd... I don't know, accept me, maybe.

"But you'll never have to go through that. I'm happy for you even if I am a little sad for me. Who knows what I could've become if I'd had someone like your grandmother or your father? Maybe I'd be a doctor or a nurse or still a dancer, but for me. I can't wait to see what you'll do when you grow up." Tears gathered behind my closed lids. "And I'll see it. I'll watch you grow up. I'll be here for you no matter what happens between me and your dad. Because I want to be your person as much as I want to be his."

I swallowed down the unshed tears.

"Thank you for wanting me," I rasped. "You do not know what that meant to me. Not knowing anything about me and you just reached out. I have to take that as a sign that maybe I'm not as messed-up as everyone thinks I am. That maybe, because you see it, there's still some good left in me. I thought I lost it all, what little I had, when I was taken. It's why I tried to fade away, because what good was there in being present when only darkness filled my mind and heart, you know?" I rocked my head against the back of the glider. "Of course you don't know, and I swear on my life I will do everything in my power to ensure you never know that kind of emptiness. Maybe if your dad doesn't want me, I can be the cool aunt like Uncle Tallon is the somewhat cool—though very strict—uncle."

In the peace of the room, with her sleeping against my chest, I realized what I wanted.

To be someone's everything. I wanted to be the first thing someone thought about in the morning and the last thing on their mind before falling asleep. For them to call just because they wanted to hear my voice or make sure I was okay.

And more than anything, I wanted that someone to be Bryson. Because he was already that someone to me.

As I slipped into a light sleep, visions of a happy future starring Victoria and Bryson chased away the bad memories that always chose this time to remind me that I needed to be scared, terrified of what would happen or where I'd be when I opened my eyes. And maybe it was her sweet, even breaths or heavy weight, but those memories didn't once pierce through the happiness.

At some point, the sensation of something heavy being draped over me roused me just long enough to feel the soothing brush of lips along my cheek before I tumbled right back into the comforting darkness.

The next time I opened my eyes, they stayed that way. Having no idea how long I'd been asleep, I glanced down at the still sleeping baby in my arms, then to the heavy patchwork quilt draped over us both. A slow smile worked its way up my dry lips. Needing to see the man who'd just filled my dreams, I carefully inched my way out of the glider, my worried gaze flicking down to Victoria's face every second to make sure she stayed asleep.

Once I laid her in the crib, I carefully extracted my finger, immediately replacing it with a stuffed animal that had been discarded in the corner. I waited, watching to ensure she stayed asleep before tiptoeing out, leaving the light on because, well, I had a hunch that maybe she didn't like the dark just as much as me. The floor creaked beneath my sock-covered feet as I made my way toward the only other bedroom at the end of the hall.

That was where I found him.

Lying on top of the covers with no shirt and a pair of light gray sweatpants hugging his sexy thick legs, Bryson didn't move as I inched into the bedroom, rounding the king-size bed to his side. As if he could sense my closeness, his dark thick lashes fluttered, those amazing eyes finding me, causing a sleepy grin to pull up his lips.

"Hi," he rasped, fighting to keep his lids open.

"Hi. Can I nap with you for a bit?" I whispered. I bit back a squeal when his muscular arm snaked around my waist and hauled me over him onto the bed. Just like before, he maneuvered my body until he could curl up behind me, draping a heavy leg over both of mine as an arm wrapped around my waist, holding me tight.

Yep. Totally my lobster.

Too bad for him, he'd never get rid of me now. Even if he didn't want this, want us, he was mine, and I would never, ever let him go.

15

TINLEY

Collapsing onto the couch with a heavy sigh, I snuggled close to Bryson, wrapping an arm around his waist and laying my head on his chest to study the dancing flames warming the living room.

"And she's asleep," I said, unable to stop grinning. "That only took... an hour."

His chest trembled beneath my ear with a low chuckle. "It's a record." The tug and pull of fingers dragging through my hair had a happy hum vibrating in my throat. "You're good with her. She trusts you."

"Thanks. She really is amazing. So much like you, yet bossier."

Those fingers slipped deeper and wrapped around the back of my neck, tugging me back until we were nose to nose.

"You have no idea how bossy I can be," he said in a low voice that had my core pulsing.

"I'd like to find out," I rasped, the earlier fatigue from playing a thousand hours of *My Little Pony* and *Pretty Pretty Princess* gone.

"Would you now?" His grin turned mischievous. "Do you trust me, Tinley?"

"Yes," I said with zero hesitation. I bit my lower lip. "Please, Bry, I need you so bad."

His nostrils flared. "Strip."

I blinked, not sure if I heard him correctly. "What?"

"I said strip. Leave your bra and panties on. If I have to ask again, I'll spank that fine ass of yours until you're begging me to let you come."

I swallowed hard. *Well. When you put it like that.*

I didn't move, which made his smile only grow.

"Hmm, seems you like the sound of that, don't you, baby?" I dipped my chin in a quick nod. "That's not much of a punishment, then, is it?" *Well, fuck.* "What if I just keep denying you my cock, hmm? Teasing you until you're begging for it, then deny you altogether."

I scrambled off the couch, my fingers flying to the zipper of my hoodie, ripping the metal down and tossing the jacket to the floor. Next came my T-shirt, leaving me in a pale blue lace demi bra. Yeah, I might have hoped this would happen when dressing this morning.

Before I could start on my leggings, Bryson reached out, caressing one hard nipple with a single knuckle over the thin lace.

I shivered, my eyes fluttering closed as I blindly hooked my thumbs into the waistband of my black leggings and shimmied them down my thighs. My lids flew open at the sound of the chastising click of his tongue. I found his eyes focused between my thighs, head shaking. When I looked down, I realized my mistake. In the hurry to remove my pants, I'd slipped off my panties too.

"Sorry," I whimpered, working to separate the two. His large hand wrapped around my wrist, stopping my frantic movements. The overwhelming need for him was turning me into a bumbling mess.

"Keep going," he ordered.

Heart thundering in my chest, I finished pulling my pants all the way down, tugging them off and resituating my socks to keep my nasty feet covered. Almost completely naked, I stood before him, fighting the urge to do something with my hands. There was a thrill of him being fully clothed, clearly turned on, with his heated stare locked on my bare pussy.

He stood. My heart shot to my throat, and my breaths turned to quick pants. With a cocky smirk, he stepped around me and casually strode to the liquor cart in the corner. I watched him walk, licking my lips when he adjusted himself over his jeans while he poured a drink. He tilted his head as he examined me.

I felt more bare than just being naked. Never had I allowed someone to see me so vulnerable, so desperate and needy for them and only them. Each step was torture as he drew closer to the couch, staring at me over the rim of the highball glass with rapt attention. Setting the now-empty glass on the table, he sat in the middle of the couch, arms spread along the back.

My heavy breasts pushed against the delicate blue lace with each breath as I waited for his next instructions. This was beautiful torture. I wanted him to grab me, to push my limits of desire, yet this was just as perfect. It was slow, calculated, like him.

"Come here," he muttered.

Not giving him a second to reconsider, I climbed onto the couch and wrapped my knees around his hips, straddling his wide lap.

His eyes took in every inch of my face before tracking lower and lower. I followed his focus, a small whimper of need escaping when he stared at my spread center. Already it glistened with how wet I was.

"So beautiful," he said with a hint of reverence. Looking up through his lashes, he slipped a hand around each knee and spread them wider until my slick center pressed against his jean-covered bulge. Desperate for friction, I shifted, the rough material of his jeans brushing against my sensitive clit.

"Bry," I pleaded. What was I pleading for? Who the hell knew? I just knew he would make the painful throbbing, the emptiness that longed to be filled, go away.

He shifted his hips, pressing until his erection hard along my center. Cool air brushed against my breasts, making my already hard nipples tighten further as he tugged the tops of the lace down.

He watched me, eyes never leaving my face, as he circled each nipple with the tip of his finger. A sharp hiss slipped past my lips when that soft touch was replaced with a bite of pain as he pinched both. My hips flexed, grinding myself down on him as that pain slowly morphed to hot pleasure.

"Use me, baby," he said through clenched teeth as his fingers continue to pinch and twist my already abused tips. Death grip on the back of the couch, I rocked back and forth, grinding against him, my hooded gaze never leaving his. "That's it. Fuck, you look amazing like this."

Hand to the center of my back, I arched, shoving my breasts closer to his face. Those light lashes fanned down his cheeks as he leaned forward, engulfing one peaked tip between his lips before sucking hard and nipping with his teeth.

"Oh shit," I moaned, head thrown back, my hair cascading along my spine. "More, more, more," I begged. A whimper of pleasure and pain vibrated against my lips. A sharp bolt of desire raced through my veins, making me cry out. A palm sealed against my lips, silencing my following curses as small ripples had my body shaking.

The couch groaned as he leaned back, a cocky smile curled on his lips while I panted, barely able to catch my breath. Reaching up, he cupped my face, slowly bringing my lips down to meet his.

"Now," he whispered as he kissed the corners and along the edges, "I'm going to fuck you. Do you want that?" I whimpered, head bobbing with my eager nod. "You want me to take what we both already know is mine?"

"Yes, please, yes," I said, back to slowly grinding on him while I blindly worked his belt open. "Condom?"

"Back pocket." I leaned back, giving myself more room to work his belt and jeans loose, and arched a questioning brow. His chuckle vibrated every place we were connected. "I bought some at the store earlier."

Oh I loved that. Loved that he was thinking of me when I wasn't around, hoping we'd get this chance tonight to finally make me his. With other men, it was a release. It meant nothing. But this, knowing what we were about to do, it felt like we were sealing the deal on this relationship. This marked the start of us.

While digging into his back pocket, I grabbed a handful of his firm ass. With a growl, he ripped the foil packet from my fingers and tore it open with his teeth. With practiced ease, I rolled the condom over his throbbing cock.

Jeans open, barely lowered enough for his dick to spring free, I shivered at the sight. This was him too eager to strip or make a big deal of our first time knowing I was ready. More than ready after waiting too long for him to fill me.

Thigh muscles taut, I hovered over him, hands on his shoulders. Meeting his hazel eyes, I positioned him just outside my entrance. With restraint I didn't know I had in me, I lowered, biting my lower lip at the delicious burn as I stretched around him.

Without warning, he thrust off the couch, his hips smacking mine as he sank balls deep. My eyes sealed shut, taking in the pulses of ecstasy that radiated from my core.

"Fucking hell," he hissed, his breath brushing past my ear.

A bruising grip wrapped around my bare hips, fingers digging into my pliable flesh. The material of his shirt stretched as he easily lifted me a few inches in the air before slamming me back down, connecting us once again.

His grunts and my soft cries filled the room, overtaking the crackle of the fire and wind howling outside. Up and down he directed my movements, which was good since I was too lost in every glorious tremor as he thrust upward, our bodies colliding together over and over again.

My lower belly tightened, breath coming in short pants while sweat slicked my bare skin. I slipped one hand forward, pressing a thumb between my folds, finding my clit. My hips shuddered, rocking against him, changing the angle.

Everything exploded, stars sparking behind my closed eyes as my core tightened around him. Bryson cursed, his movements frantic as he chased his release. With a groan, head tossed back to lay along the back of the couch, mouth gaping, he sealed our bodies together while he trembled, finding his own release.

Still connected, I leaned forward, the sweaty skin of his shoulder slipping beneath my forehead as I attempted to catch my breath.

"Holy shit," he said, voice raspy as he stroked a hand along my head, raking his fingers through my long strands.

"My thoughts exactly. Except...." Using the couch, I pushed back enough to put us nose to nose. Those worried hazel eyes flicked between my own. "Can we do that again?"

The line between his brows vanished. "Yes, ma'am. Though this time, I want to watch as you lose yourself with you beneath me."

Yes. All the yeses.

With his sexual appetite as strong as my own, there was no doubt he was the only one for me.

I HELD BACK a wince from the twinge of pain as I curled my knees up toward my chest. Smiling behind the steaming coffee mug, I took a quick sip of the dark liquid as I watched Victoria play with her toys on the living room floor. My gaze drifted to the spot on the couch where we'd had our fun last night.

I squeezed my thighs together to quell the gentle ache that bloomed. Every inch of my body and heart wanted to do it all over again and again. But adulting/parenting came first. If I was to fit into their lives, I'd need to get used to not having Bryson whenever and wherever I wanted. Though it made those times when we came together that much more special.

Movement outside the bay window had me looking that way. Bryson stood just on the other side of the glass, hands on his hips, studying the ground. A frown pulled at my lips. Checking to make sure Victoria was okay—I mean, she could've grabbed scissors or started a minor fire in the thirty seconds I'd been distracted, right?—I placed my socked feet on the hardwood floors and stood.

Dread coiled in my stomach as Bryson angrily pulled a phone

from his coat pocket and pressed it to his ear. He didn't glance up, too focused on whatever was on the ground outside the window.

Cold seeped through the thin glass, making me wrap my arms around myself as I pressed closer to peer down at the snow-covered ground. Squinting through the glare coming off the glittering white, I scanned the area to see what had made him upset.

Not finding anything amiss, I turned, hurrying to the front door and flinging it open, then stepping onto the small square of concrete that was clear of snow. Bryson's head whipped my way, and I stumbled at the look of sheer rage on his face.

"Get inside," he growled, jamming a finger toward the door.

Tears welled from his harsh tone, but I lifted my chin in defiance and held my ground. "What's going on?"

"Someone was here, outside the window." I tilted my head to the side, not understanding. Except now, with this new angle, the impressions in the snow just outside the bay window were clear as fucking day. The dark brown mulch made a perfect shoe impression in the otherwise untouched snow. I followed the tracks, bits of that same mulch falling off the person's shoes as they stalked around the other side of the house.

I shook, the coffee mug in my hand trembling so badly the liquid splashed over the side onto my hand and wrist. Bryson hurried over, telling whoever was on the phone that he'd call them back, then pulled me against his chest, not caring that the mug dropped to the cement between us and shattered.

It was him. He was back, watching me from the dark—again.

I squeezed my eyes shut to not look at the window, where evidence of what he liked to do while he watched might be splattered along the glass.

"I'm working on it now, Tinley. Okay? I need you to hold it together for just a bit. Can you do that for me?"

I wanted to say yes, that I was stronger than this overwhelming fear, but I couldn't. I wasn't sure if I could hold it together. Watching. I knew exactly who liked to watch from dark corners. He followed me here.

"Please, for Victoria."

At the mention of her, I snapped out of my shocked trance, changing the course of my dark thoughts. I pushed away from him, racing inside. My erratic heart rate settled a fraction when I found her in the same spot, completely unharmed.

"He's back," I murmured at the sensation of Bryson at my back. "He's back for me."

"We don't know that for sure." Two hands settled on my shoulders and squeezed. My head dropped forward. He might not know who stood outside that window last night, but I did. "But either way, I don't like the idea of Vic and Mom staying here when we go back to Nashville later. Grab Vic and take her upstairs. Pack her a bag and grab all your stuff. By the time you're done, I'll have a plan. Can you do that?"

Oh fuck, he saw me naked. Saw me strip for Bryson, saw every intimate moment.

I smacked a hand over my mouth as bile crept up my throat. Foul, unwanted memories flooded to the forefront of my mind.

Shrugging off his hold, I stumbled to the front door and into the snow-covered yard.

The cold, wet ground seeped through the thin material of my leggings when I fell to my knees and retched. Shame and disgust fought for dominance, turning my stomach as I dry-heaved on the front lawn. Sucking down gulps of air, I swiped at my spit-covered lips with the back of my hand.

What was I going to do?

He was back, coming for me, but this time it wasn't just me in danger.

I was pathetic, bringing this to their doorstep when just yesterday I promised Victoria I'd do anything to keep her safe.

"My pony sick?" With a weary glance over my shoulder, I found Bryson making his way toward me with Victoria in his arms. "My pony, it's okay." She turned her pinched features up to Bryson. "Dada, my pony needs an owwie. She sick like me."

Smiling through the pain, I shoved off the ground and forced a smile while I dusted off my palms.

"I'm okay, cutie. I'm okay." I sensed Bryson's stare, but I couldn't meet his eyes just yet. He had no idea how someone watching would resurrect everything I'd spent years trying to push to the back corners of my mind. And now, with his innocent daughter in his arms, was not the time to tell him what that man did to me or how I'd remembered additional details over the past year.

Guilt hung around my neck like a thousand-pound weight as I took the reaching cutie from her father and held her close. I'd lost it in front of her. Fuck, I bet Bryson was pissed that I showed that kind of distress in front of Victoria. But when I finally dared a peek his way, only worry marred his tight features.

"Are you okay?" he rasped, reaching out and giving my bicep a squeeze. His hand trembled, the only sign that he was on the verge of losing it too.

"No," I said truthfully. "But let's not talk about it here, okay?" I tilted my head toward Victoria. Forcing that wide fake smile, I bounced her playfully on my hip. "We're going on an adventure! Doesn't that sound fun?"

She nodded, but her little brow was still furrowed as she studied me.

Too smart for her own good, this tiny one.

"Let's go pack, okay? You'll have to point out every toy you want to bring along." I tapped a finger against my lower lip, acting deep in thought. "Do you think *My Little Pony* should go on the adventure?"

That snapped her out of whatever she was trying to solve. As she babbled about what other toys needed to be packed, I hurried us out of the cold, stepping around the mess on the front porch from earlier, which somehow seemed like a representation of my life shattering around me, and climbed the stairs.

With the fake cheerful smile held in place, I helped Victoria pack a small bag that ended up filled with more stuffed animals and toys than clothes and diapers, all while battling to keep the raging fear inside shoved down deep.

After seeing those footprints, I knew without a doubt that my tormentor, the sick bastard who held me for three weeks almost ten years ago, was ready to make good on his promise.

He was back.

And I was certain if I was taken again, held against my will and forced to....

The outcome this time would be me as a victim instead of a survivor.

16

BRYSON

Tuesday, December 11th

Varying emotions rolled through me as I pulled away from the curb in front of Mom's best friend's house. In the passenger seat, Tinley had twisted around to watch out the back window until we turned a corner, cutting off the view of the small suburban home.

"You sure they'll be okay there?" she asked as she spun back around. "I feel like they need more security or something."

More security would be amazing, but I wasn't worried. Though the fact that she was concerned about my daughter and mom more than her own safety did strange things to my heart.

"Patsy's husband is a retired police officer with a small arsenal stashed away. I know without a doubt he'll do whatever it takes to protect the women in that home. Plus...." I blew out a breath. "This fucker isn't after them."

I hated saying it out loud, but she needed to know for two reasons. First, to not worry about Mom's and Vic's safety, which would distract her from focusing on her own. Which was the second reason. Tinley needed to know this unsub was serious. He'd crossed state lines to follow her. Which brought up a whole slew of other questions with zero answers.

The biggest two: Was the person who left those footprints outside the window the same man from ten years ago like she suspected? And how in the hell did he know where to find her if it was?

We were at my home, which wasn't connected to her in any document. So how did this sick fuck know where to go? Could he have followed my truck all the way from Nashville to Louisville? I shook my head. No damn way did I not notice a car or truck following us the entire way. Or maybe her feeling eyes on her the past few weeks was real, and this fucker knew exactly who I was from watching us together.

For several blocks, I lost myself in the three very different cases that we were working on. The murder of the female victim that happened two weeks ago, Tinley feeling watched and now literally watched last night, and the murder of the stranger from the bar where she worked.

My grip tightened on the steering wheel. He watched us. I couldn't shake the feeling that he'd seen it all. Saw her naked, watched her come apart on my lap.

"I'm sorry." Her voice cracked, snapping my attention to the passenger side.

"For what?"

"They're in danger now because of me. All of this, your life being disrupted—"

"Stop," I ordered, reaching across the center to grip her thigh.

"No. I'm a damn curse to anyone who gets near me." At a stoplight, I caught the faint trickle of tears cascading down her rosy cheeks. "You don't deserve this, and neither does she."

"This being...?" I questioned, even though I knew what her response would be.

"My shit-show life. You deserve the perfect little wife, not someone who brings some sick fucker to your doorstep. Someone who can sleep with the lights off and doesn't battle every day to keep the awful shit in their mind at bay." Wiping at her cheeks, she shook her head. "Just drop me off at the bus station. I can find my own way home. It's been fun, but this is done."

Having heard enough of this shit, I whipped into a McDonald's parking lot, causing Tinley to grab the door handle and curse. After slamming the truck into Park in an available spot, I twisted in the seat to grip the back of her neck, forcing her to meet my fierce gaze.

"First, fuck no to anything you just said. What do you think this is, some damn fling where you can just toss me to the side when shit gets difficult?"

"I'm doing it for you," she said through gritted teeth. "You don't know what we're dealing with. I do."

Oh, she was angry, but so was I. If she wanted to battle, then I'd give her a war. This talk about her leaving was not happening.

"Second of all, do you think I'm a man who will allow the woman he's fallen for to take a bus to a city where some unknown sick fuck is lying in wait for her? Give me some damn credit here, kid. I'm not going anywhere, and you're not going anywhere without me. Understood?"

Her icy blue eyes narrowed. "And if I say no to this"—she waved a hand in my direction—"of you playing protector? That I want nothing to do with you?"

My responding dark chuckle held zero humor. "Too fucking bad, kid, because I can see through your lies." Her bottom lip quivered. "I know you're saying this shit to protect me, but it won't work. I'm not going anywhere, you got that? We handle this together."

"Together," she whispered.

"Now," I said through clenched teeth, hating these next words, "if after we've caught this guy, and he's dead by my hand or your brother's, if you want me to leave, then we can discuss that then. But I'm not giving you the option now. Where you go, I go."

"I won't want that," she whispered, blue eyes pleading. "If I survive this—"

With an impatient growl, I yanked her close, meeting her halfway. I slammed my lips to her, all the worry and anger flowing through me slowly easing. A desperate whimper filled the cab, parting those luscious lips, allowing an opening to slip my tongue inside. Within seconds, her entire body relaxed, turning to putty in my grasp.

Fisting her hair at the base of her neck, I wrenched her lips from mine. "You will survive this. *We* will survive this, you hear me?"

"Yes," she cried.

"Then we talk about the future—"

"I want you. You, Victoria, and your mom. I want it all. I've wanted nothing more than a future with you. But I won't risk them. I won't be the reason any of you have the same dark spots in your mind like mine. You don't know what he's capable of, what he'll do."

Eyes sealed shut to keep my shit together, I pressed my forehead to hers. "Trust me, Tinley. Just trust me that this time we *will* get this bastard. And after we do, we'll plan out what our future looks like. Just don't push me away now, not because you're afraid of what's coming. I want to be here for you, be the one you hold when you're scared and not sure who to trust. Because we will get through this. I won't allow any other outcome."

The long pause between us had worry twisting in my stomach.

"I might..." she croaked and then cleared her throat. Pulling out of my grasp, she leaned against the door. "I might help this time."

I tilted my head, not understanding. "What do you mean?"

She blew out a breath and pulled her thick ponytail over her shoulder to play with the end.

"My therapist is helping me recall details of those few weeks I was held captive that I didn't remember. She thinks getting the details out of my head and out into the world, talking to someone who believes me, would help in my healing. And it has." Her eyes flicked to stare out the windshield. "I know I wasn't helpful ten years ago by not talking about it all, keeping the details hidden. It made Tallon's search for the guy harder than it needed to be, but I just wasn't in the right mindset to talk about it." The look she shot me out of the corner of her eye put me on alert. "The watching, like he did with us last night." Her throat bobbed with a hard swallow. "That was his thing. He liked to watch me, and...." She shook her head, bringing both palms up and pressing them to her ears. "Sometimes I think I can still hear him."

I sat completely still, not wanting to startle her now that she was opening up, but inside, a storm raged, ready to destroy this sick motherfucker.

"I've remembered things he'd say or do." Her shoulders shook with a full-body shiver, and all color drained from her face. Pitching forward, her back curved as her head went between her legs. Short wheezing breaths cut through the silence.

With ease, I hooked an arm beneath her legs and waist and hauled her over the console onto my lap. "Tinley," I pleaded. Forehead to her shoulder, I held her tighter, wishing there was something I could do to make the panic attack stop. How had she lived her life like this for the last ten years with no one close to hold her? After a minute, the wheezing soothed to deep gasping inhales and then slowly returned to normal. "Would it be easier if you were in a safe space?" Her chin dipped in agreement. "Then that's what we'll do. We're already going to see your therapist today. How about we talk about what you remember then? I think those details could help us catch him, even if it's the smallest thing like a smell or accent or description."

"Yeah," she rasped. "Yeah, that sounds good. That would be better," she said with a rushed breath as she slumped against me. "Sorry for the freak-out. Talking about what happened... I don't know, it makes it real. And I don't want it to be."

Finger beneath her chin, I tipped her face up to meet mine and smiled. "Now for the big decisions. Are you ready for this?"

Apprehension crossed her face, but still she nodded.

"Do you want the breakfast platter or an Egg McMuffin?" The tight lines on her face melted away into a bright smile. "The breakfast platter has pancakes, so it's a tough call."

"Hmm, that's a tough choice. Can I have my pancake and eat it too?"

Chuckling, I cupped her cheek, swiping a thumb along her cheekbone. "Yeah, kid, you can. You absolutely can."

TEN MINUTES after she finished both breakfast meals, Tinley passed
out cold in the passenger seat. I couldn't help but smirk at her long,
lean frame crammed into a tiny ball to fit in the seat. Heaving a
worry-filled sigh, I popped both earbuds in, then pressed the first
number in my missed call log.

Time to get to work and figure out what in the hell was going on.

"Is everyone okay? How's Tinley?"

My smirk grew into a happy grin at the worried female voice on
the other end of the line. "Hey, Rhyan," I said, shifting in the seat to
get comfortable for the long drive to Nashville. "Guess that jackass
man of yours caught you up on why I called."

"Um, yeah. Why else would I be answering his phone?" she said
slowly, like she was answering the dumbest question she'd ever
heard. "I get that a lot is going on, but when do we get to meet her?"

"Whenever. It would be good to see you two."

"We could come now, take the BSU jet if you need us on the
ground to offer our help. Seriously, anything you need, Bryson."

I leaned my head back against the headrest, rolling it against the
leather with my slow shake. "You'd be a huge help, but the next
time I see you two, I want it to be for fun, not because of a serial
killer."

Her responding laugh sounded tired. "Well, that's kind of our life,
so...."

"Speaking of which, I'd love a profile of this fucker. She seems to
think it's the same unsub who abducted her ten years ago. Later this
afternoon, I'll have more details I can send on top of what's in the
original file. How long would that take, you think?"

"A few hours for you."

I swallowed down the lump forming in my throat. "Thank you,
Rhyan."

"Of course. Anything for the guy who *literally* saved my life. Okay,
here's Charlie." The two exchanged a few muffled words on the other
end of the line.

"Hey, stop talking to my girl," Charlie's gruff voice cut in. "I need her to keep believing that I'm a good guy."

A huffed laugh escaped me. A good guy, he said, completely covered in tattoos and piercings. He was by far the most unconventional FBI agent and looked the bad guy part but absolutely wasn't. Especially when it came to Rhyan or anyone he considered family. Like me.

"I saw I missed your call. Sorry, it's been a long morning. Did you find anything?"

Charlie's hum of agreement vibrated in my ear. "I inspected the surveillance feed for the apartment complex like you asked. It took me a while, but I found something." I sucked in a full breath, expecting the news to sucker-punch me in the balls. "Whoever this fucker is, he's good."

"Better than you?" I somehow got out around my clenched jaw.

"Fuck that. Don't insult me. Of course not. Most would've skimmed over this one section of code. It looked like the rest of the programming, but this allowed the installer of the code to transmit the live video feed anytime they wanted access. There's more. Something about this code looks familiar."

I sat up straight. This could be it, our break to finally find this bastard and bring Tinley some justice. "Familiar how?"

"I've seen the unique syntax before in another case I worked on. I've racked my damn brain, gone through recent case files, but it was months ago, and I can't remember which case. But I'll find it. Just need to run that section of code through a few of my tracking software scouring my files."

I released a slow breath. "Okay, let me know when you figure it out. Maybe this can tie other cases with more leads to Tinley's. Did you shut down access to the feed?"

"Yep, and their access at the bar where your girl works."

"What?" I hissed. My breathing sped up, and heat coursed through my veins as fiery anger boiled inside my chest, only for it to turn to ice when I remembered where else she felt watched. "Charlie, she said she felt eyes on her inside the apartment too."

A string of curses filled my ears. "Fuck, that's not good consid-ering she was spot-on with the other places." *My thoughts exactly.* "I can't do much from here. If there *are* cameras in her apartment, the signal would be transmitted differently than the security feed in the lobby. You need someone on-site."

Panic seized my chest. Releasing the wheel, I rubbed a tight fist to my sternum. "Can you get here?"

"Of course, but it wouldn't be until tomorrow, and you need someone now. Plus, I don't want to pull my attention from the computer side of this case. I have a feeling we'll need me in front of my computers. I know someone who is local to Nashville and might be free to help."

"You trust them with this?" I swallowed to shove down the desper-ation in my voice. "Nothing can happen to Tinley, Charlie. I can't survive losing someone else."

"I wouldn't suggest Remington if I didn't trust her with my own life. Let me call her and see if she's available."

"Sounds good. Thank you, Charlie." My throat closed up, unable to get another word around the lump of emotion in my throat.

"Of course. I'll hit you back when I know more."

I stared out the windshield, the miles flying by. Lost in thought, I was startled when the phone ringing nearly blew out my eardrums. Thumb to the screen, I swiped across it to answer Tallon's call.

"Where are you?" he barked. "What the actual fuck is going on?"

"We're in the truck on our way back to Nashville. Guess you got the message I left this morning."

"Yes," he growled, sounding nearly feral. "You're telling me you think this fucker from ten years ago is back and followed you two to Louisville?"

"She seems to think it's connected, and I agree." Especially after she opened up about his preference to watching her. I gritted my teeth to keep my head level. Getting raging mad would do no one any good right now. I had to think clearly for her.

"That's extreme, which we both know from our jobs mean's he's upping his game. What the fuck do we do now?" I hated the hope-lessness in his low tone.

"Stay calm. That's the first thing we're going to do," I said evenly to help keep us both cool. "She's scared and more worried about us being in danger than herself."

"Typical Tinley," he huffed, though I heard the smile in his voice.

I couldn't help but grin a little at that too, only for it to fall with my next words. "Listen, she mentioned the new therapist has helped recover details she repressed from those three weeks held captive. We're going there this afternoon, and I hope she can assist Tinley in remembering more that can help us with the case. I'll document her answers and ask questions to help pinpoint details that can help."

"Sounds good. The video feed. Did you hear from your guy?"

"Yep." I sighed. "She was right about feeling watched. Someone tampered with the security feed at the apartment and bar where she works."

"Fuck," he snapped.

"Agreed. Charlie, my computer guy, wants to have someone he knows to help us on-site to search the apartment for hidden wireless cameras. He'll let me know as soon as he hears from her. What did you find out from Selena about the murder of the guy from the bar?"

A heavy pause filled the line, making me tense. "She hasn't called me back, so I reached out to a detective. He'll meet us at the apart-ment tomorrow morning to discuss the details with us. He needed time to get the files together since it's another detective's case."

Worry gnawed at my gut. "You trust this guy?"

Another weighted pause. "Yeah, we go way back." His tone shifted, signaling he was holding something back. My gaze flicked to the phone resting in the cupholder. "I'm headed to the airport now. I land later tonight. I'll try Selena again. It's not like her to not call back, especially when she has a lady boner for you and knows we're friends."

"Fucking sick," I said with a laugh. Leave it to this guy to make me laugh when tensions were high. "When we see her, don't push that idea of us getting together." I shot a weary glance to Tinley. "I'm not into her like that. Smart agent, but not for me."

"Whatever," he snarked. "I still say you need to get laid. After all this, obviously."

"I love how you're fixated on my sex life when I know it's been a while for you too, asshole."

He grumbled something incoherent, making me grin. Tallon changed after Tinley's abduction. His dating life was the most obvious. I never asked why, but the playboy I knew altered overnight to this now stoic, stick-up-his-ass version when it came to dating and going out. There was never time for a personal life; all work and no play for Tallon.

"Did you ever have time to talk to that one victim's family? I know a lot has happened since then."

Nice diversion instead of having to answer. Typical Tallon.

"No," I admitted, allowing some of my exhaustion to bleed through my voice. "Fuck, that seems like a lifetime ago. I don't think I can get it done today, but once you're in town, I can leave Tinley with you and schedule an interview."

"I'll cover it. Two suspicious murders and this fucker following Tinley. There are a lot of moving pieces right now. I just don't want anything to fall through the cracks. I can't have another victim just because my focus was only on this sick bastard after my sister."

"You can't do it all," I stated, worried my best friend was spreading himself too thin.

"I know. I'm not. I have you looking over my sister, ensuring no one will hurt her. That's a tremendous weight off my shoulders with you there taking care of her."

Like I'd eaten something sour, my features pulled into a grimace. When we told him about our relationship, he was going to lose it. Not that it mattered. I'd endure his wrath for even a minute more with her.

Though I hoped that minute would turn into forever.

Even in just the barely twenty-four hours we were in Louisville, I witnessed how perfectly she fit into our lives. We just had to get through this first.

We had to find the asshole whose threat hung over all our heads for the last ten years. I wouldn't rest or leave her side until the fucker had a bullet between his brows. No one messed with the ones I loved and lived. I'd break the law, break bones, and spill blood to ensure Tinley was safe now and forever.

I guessed what they said was true. All was fair in love and war.

This war.

And this fucker better be ready to face my wrath for all he'd done.

17

BRYSON

After having the best damn cup of coffee at a dog-themed coffeehouse in Hillsboro Village and talking for a few hours about everything but the case, we made our way through the back streets for the therapist's office. Keeping her hand clasped in one hand, the other close to my side arm, we walked along the sidewalk, Tinley talking animatedly about the cottages that lined the street.

With a smile shot over her shoulder, Tinley led me up the pristine walkway and into one of the houses that doubled as a business. The door clicked shut behind me, warm air immediately soothing the bite of winter from my cheeks and fingers. Surveying the area, I found a small waiting room to the right, completely empty. The slow trickle of water close by and the soft calming scents had some of the insistent tension draining away.

With me hot on her heels, Tinley weaved through the waiting room chairs toward a closed door and rapped a single knuckle against the white painted wood.

"We don't have to do this." I watched her fidget with her hair and chew on the corner of her lower lip, both tells of hers that she was uncomfortable. "If this is too much—"

"No." The end of her ponytail slipped from her fingers to swish side to side with the shake of her head. "I want to do this. Some details I've remembered might help us. Me being uncomfortable for a little while is totally worth it if anything I say does. Plus, well, there are other things in my past I think you should know about before we do this."

"Too late for that," I said, pulling her closer to press my lips against the shell of her ear. "When you came on my cock last night, we sealed the deal. You're mine, no matter what you have to tell me. Understood?"

She nodded. "Still, I just... I want someone to know. And I need to know that you believe me, that I'm not making any of this up for attention or—"

"Never. I'll always believe you, Tinley. I'm on your side no matter what's going on."

She swallowed, gaze falling to the floor. "I've made so many bad choices the last ten years, but if each one, if getting through every hard day got me to this point, here with you, then I'm thankful. I'm stronger, strong for you. For you and Victoria."

Before I could respond, the click of a lock put me on alert, instinctively reaching for my gun and positioning Tinley behind my back as the door swung open. The older Asian woman's serene face morphed into one of shock, her slender hand coming up to press on her chest.

"Can I help you?" she said, doing her best to sound calm though her slim fingers trembled.

"Hey, Dr. Sarah," Tinley said at my back. Her head popped around me, slim fingers wiggling in a tiny wave. "It's just me. Don't worry about this guy. He's here with me."

The doctor's intelligent regard slid from Tinley to me.

"I'm here for support," I clarified. "She asked me to come, said there were some things she'd like for me to know. And I hope you can help us with something too while we're here."

With a clipped nod, she stepped deeper into the office, opening the door wider and gesturing for us to enter. Her office was what I'd expect for a therapist, the walls painted a soft blue, the calming scents and soothing water feature sounds even stronger than in the waiting room. Two stiff-back chairs sat in front of a massive dark-stained wooden desk. To the right, grouped together in a small sitting area, were a couch with a matching armchair, a glass coffee table, and another cozy chair that appeared well worn with a side table beside it, a black notebook and pen resting on top.

The doctor motioned toward the sitting area, which Tinley had already started toward. I frowned at the love seat that would barely hold someone of my size, much less me and another comfortably. Instead of crowding Tinley, I shifted into the armchair, positioning it to face the door and the two women.

"Dr. Shue, this is Special Agent Bryson Bennett. The Bryson Bennett, Tallon's best friend. Bryson, this is Dr. Shue, but she's asked me to call her Dr. Sarah."

The therapist's thin brows shot up her otherwise smooth fore-head. "Ah, I see. This makes sense now. Welcome to the session, Bryson. I'm thrilled Tinley has brought someone into a session. This is amazing for those in therapy, having someone they care about hear what they've buried deep. It causes more harm when those things we don't want anyone to know stay festering inside us. Thank you for being here. Though you mentioned me helping you as well? Please explain before we get started."

Leaning forward, I clasped my hands, exhaling a heavy breath. "Not sure where to start, honestly." For the next several minutes, I explained everything that had happened since I arrived, what we knew to this point from the surveillance to him following her to Louisville.

"So what do you need from me?" she asked, clearly shaken by my words. "How can I help?"

"Earlier this morning, Tinley mentioned you've helped her uncover additional details from her time in captivity. I'm hoping some of those memories might help us catch the bastard. Though she had a panic attack when she tried to tell me."

Dr. Sarah's eyes cut to Tinley, who nodded. "I can't do it without you, Dr. Sarah. It was too much, but I want to help the investigation in any way I can. Can you help me, guide me through my memories in a safe space?"

Dr. Sarah pressed both palms to the armrests to stand and then strode to the desk, picking up the black office phone. She smiled at my intense stare. "It takes a while for her to slip into the relaxed state we need her in to keep her calm as she recalls those memories. I'm notifying my next patient that we'll need to reschedule to make sure we have enough time."

"Thank you," I stated after she hung up the phone, standing as she approached the sitting area. "Let me know how much, and I'll compensate you for that canceled session."

Tinley's eyes narrowed as she glared up at me. "No, I will."

"No, I will," Dr. Sarah said with a smirk. "Thank you for the offer, Bryson, but I'm more than happy to cover the cost to help with this investigation." Her calm brown eyes focused on me. "Tinley is a wonderful young woman who has an amazing life in front of her. I want to do what I can to ensure she sees it to fruition. Now, please sit, and we'll get started."

The edges of the chair brushed against my hips as I sat, my curious gaze bouncing between the two, who seemed to have a silent conversation.

Dr. Sarah nodded as if they'd agreed on something. "Before we get started on resurrecting those old memories, Tinley has some things from her past she'd like to share that she feels are important for you to know. And I agree, seeing as you two are clearly in a romantic relationship."

Jaw slack, I struggled to find the right way to respond to her correct assumption.

"Please give me some credit," she said with a laugh. "I'm well aware of how Tinley feels about you. You've been a topic of conversation a few times." My cheeks warmed with embarrassment. "And from the way I've witnessed you act around her, well, that look in your eye tells me the attraction is mutual."

Didn't realize how I felt about Tinley was that obvious, or maybe it was from her being a trained people reader. Though I knew that wasn't it, as I felt my gaze soften when I looked at Tinley. There would be no hiding my love and attraction to her from anyone in the same room as us. Which did not bode well for tonight when Tallon came home. We'd need to tell him the moment he walked in the door or he'd figure it out for himself.

"You need to know this stuff, Bry," Tinley said, drawing my attention to where she sat on the couch. Kicking off her shoes, she pulled her feet up to rest on the edge of the couch and wrapped her arms around her shins. "I feel you need to know why I am the way I am with some things, understand the reason behind some of my triggers." Her clear blue eyes lifted from the interior design magazines splayed across the coffee table to the therapist. "I need him to understand why believing me when I open up about things is important to my healing."

Dr. Sarah's brows furrowed. "Has he ever doubted you in the past, something that's driving this urge to explain the why?"

Tinley shook her head. Reaching back, she yanked the hair tie out, her thick rose gold hair cascading around her shoulders. Fingers scrubbing over her scalp, she messed up the roots and blew out a heavy sigh.

"No, he's never not believed me. The opposite, in fact. He believes in me more than anyone I've ever met. It's just that I want to make sure he understands why it's so important. I want this to work between us, and him understanding my triggers will help him maneuver around my messed-up brain."

"Tinley," I growled and inched to the edge of my seat. "There is nothing wrong with you. Never has been and never will be."

"Well said, Bryson. Tinley, you know we don't allow that kind of negative talk in this room." There was no missing the chastisement in Dr. Sarah's stern tone.

"Yeah, I know. It's just, what normal person needs to bring their boyfriend—" She cut herself off and scrunched her nose while sending me an apologetic look. "Sorry, just gave you that title.

Surprise." I chuckled at her forced enthusiasm. "Who has to bring their partner to their therapy sessions? Someone who's super fucked-up, that's who."

"More than you would think bring their significant other or spouse," Dr. Sarah replied before I could. Tinley blinked at the doctor, speechless. "You act like the memories you've repressed are uncommon. Sure, your time in captivity was unique, but you'd be surprised what others have gone through that they need help to work past. Abusive relationships, childhood abuse from someone in an authority position or family member. Everyone's trauma is different, but we all have it in some way or another."

"Okay," Tinley said, her voice soft, as if the response was automatic. "You're right." Blowing a raspberry, she twisted on the couch to rest her head along the armrest, her sock-covered feet hanging off the other. "I don't remember the exact age I was the first time Mom accused me of lying. There was a dance instructor who I didn't like, not because of how difficult he made practice but how he made me feel. At the time, I was too young to understand that creepy emotion, just that it was there and I didn't like it."

I swallowed hard, my hands tightening into white-knuckled fists. It didn't take a genius to know where this was headed, and I wasn't sure if I was strong enough to hear it.

"When the uncomfortable feeling turned to lingering touches, slips of the hands to inappropriate areas during a hold, offering massages when my muscles were sore, that's when I said something. I knew something was off about his actions, but he was an adult and a well-known dance instructor, so I kept those thoughts to myself until one day I refused to go to practice."

Tinley sealed her eyes shut and placed her folded hands over her stomach.

"I went searching for Mom and found her lying by the pool like she typically was on warm days, always with a glass of wine in hand. It took every ounce of courage I could muster to tell her what was going on, since we'd never really had a close relationship. Cold would be a better word for it, so I was nervous. When I explained what he was doing to me, to the other girls, described his actions and how they made me feel"—Tinley's eyes squeezed shut as if she were attempting to block out the memories—"dirty, she blew it off, saying I was mistaken, that he was doing no such thing, only helping me become a better dancer. When I showed her where he touched me, she grabbed my wrist so tight my knees dropped to the pool deck from the pain. There was nothing but sheer anger and hate in her eyes as she accused me of creating the lies all to get attention."

"I'm going to kill that fucking cunt," I gritted through clenched teeth. Shoving out of the chair, I started for the door. "Right now. With my bare fucking—"

"Agent Bennett," the therapist snapped, stopping me short.

I snarled over my shoulder at the upset doc before swinging my blazing gaze to Tinley, who stared my way with wide eyes. A war raged inside my head. Half of me needed vengeance, to hunt her mother down and strangle the life out of her, enjoying the feel of taking her life and seeing her fear. Though the other half urged me to close the distance between Tinley and me, to wrap her in my arms and squeeze her so tight that nothing and no one else could ever hurt her again.

"I'm not done," Tinley said hesitantly.

Oh fuck. I ran a hand along my jaw, focusing on the scrape of the coarse hair along my palm. Could I take it? Could I hear more?

Grinding my back teeth, jaw muscle throbbing, I gave a clipped nod and returned to my seat. Sitting forward, I draped my clasped hands between my spread thighs, elbows pressed to the tops of my jean-clad thighs.

"Did it stop?" I rasped. "Please tell me someone made it stop."

"It did, eventually. The other girls told their moms, who actually believed them, and he was arrested. The authorities interviewed all of his students, but Mom made me deny anything happened to me. Said I didn't have proof, that I was making it all up and that I shouldn't drag the family through that kind of drama for a bunch of lies. So I did. I lied and told them I wasn't one of his victims—"

"Is he alive?" I asked, my voice cold to even my own ears.

"No, I read he was killed in prison."

My blunt nails dug into the curved wooden armrest. "I seriously hope he died from someone fucking him in the ass with a dull shank after they sliced off his damn—"

"Agent," Dr. Sarah snapped again. I turned my icy stare at her. A look of shock washed over her features before turning blank. "This is not a space where we cast judgment—"

"Then I shouldn't be here, because I can't sit here and listen to what happened to her, which no one believed, and not be so angry I can't fucking see straight."

"What's in the past is in the past. Tinley is moving on—"

"Well, I'll move on when I find his grave and piss all over it."

A barked laugh broke our stare-off. Tinley sat up straight, her hand pressed over her open mouth, eyes twinkling with laughter.

"Bryson," she said, the word muffled. "I'll drive you to the cemetery myself."

Still brimming with fury, I shot her a wink. "Thank you. I'm thinking we were made for each other, kid."

"Well, yeah. You're my lobster."

A loud rumbling laugh shook my chest, chasing away the serenity Dr. Sarah tried to achieve in the room. The poor woman tried to keep up with our back-and-forth, her eyes volleying as she studied the odd interaction.

"Do you want to continue, Tinley?" she said after we both quieted down.

"There's more?" I groaned and pinched the bridge of my nose. My hand fell to my lap at seeing the sadness in Tinley's ice-blue eyes before they shifted to the table. "Hey, it's okay. You can tell me. I want to know it all, know everything about you, though I can't promise that those who have hurt you won't die a miserable death by my hand." I cut my eyes to the therapist. "Hypothetically speaking, of course."

"Of course," Tinley offered. "You're a man of the law. You'd never break it."

"Exactly."

Dr. Sarah blinked, clearly knowing we were covering my ass for when bodies started dropping.

"I'm not sure if this overprotective behavior is good for her healing," she offered after a minute.

"It's exactly what she needs," I said in return. "She needs to know someone will fight for her, demand vengeance for what they did to her, and keep her safe in the future. I'd burn down this town to deliver the revenge she's due. I might not have a fancy degree, but I know what she needs, and that's me."

Shoving out of the too-small chair, I maneuvered around the coffee table, plopped down on the couch beside Tinley, and tossed an arm over her shoulders.

Dr. Sarah stared at Tinley as she shifted even closer to my side. "That's maybe what you need, Bryson, but what about Tinley?"

"I want him," Tinley blurted. "No, I need him. He's right. I want someone who will fight for me. Fight for what was taken and lost, fight for my healing, and share that undying anger that still burns inside me."

The therapist pursed her lips, clearly not happy with the turn of events. Too fucking bad, because there was nothing she could do about it. I was the one with the gun, after all, though pointing that out felt like a bad call considering I did still need her help for the case.

Gripping Tinley's chin between two fingers, I spun her face to me, my hazel eyes searching her blue ones.

"What else?" I prompted. "You said the first time your mom didn't believe you. When was the second?"

Tinley's throat worked as she continued to stare into my patient gaze.

"I was eleven." The grip on her chin tightened at the quiver in her soft voice. Knowing I might lose it, potentially hurting her, I dropped my hand to her thigh and gave it a comforting squeeze. "When I told her what was going on, she didn't believe me, said I was just looking for attention again with my lies. When I told her I was going to the police, she smacked me so hard across the face her diamond ring sliced through my lip. I'd never seen her that angry as she bent over where I'd fallen to the floor, holding my bleeding face, completely in shock that my mother had hit me, and told me if I went to the police or said anything to anyone, she'd...." Tinley stopped and turned pleading eyes up to me. "Please, please do not tell Tallon. He'll lose it."

My brows furrowed. "Tell Tallon what?"

"My mom threatened to pull Tallon's college funding. You guys only had a couple years left, and I couldn't do that to him. He loved school, and—"

Tugging her closer, I planted a kiss on the crown of her head. "Shh, it's okay, Tinley. This is your past to tell, not mine."

Her lean body relaxed against me, chest falling with her heavy sigh. "Thank you. She said I didn't have proof and people would see me for the attention-hungry girl I was."

"What was it, Tinley?" I asked gently. "What did you tell your mom that she didn't believe?" I shot a glance at the therapist to ensure it was okay to press her on this.

"My stepbrother." I sucked in a gasped breath and held it, centering on the burn rather than the icy rage that flowed through my veins. "It's one reason I don't like the dark," Tinley whispered. "All bad things happen in the dark. Even though my mother said she didn't believe me, that I made it all up, the next week, Bart was sent to boarding school, and I was pulled from private school. It was under the ruse of needing to spend more time practicing and less time at school, but I knew she didn't want to risk me telling someone else. So she cut me off from everyone but my tutors and instructors. And that was how it was until... until I was taken."

Guilt weighed in my heart. Turning her head toward me, I pressed a kiss to her lips, desperate for her forgiveness.

"I had no idea," I rasped. "I would've—"

"You and Tallon were in school and then figuring out your careers after. I put on a smiling face when y'all were around because I didn't want to weigh Tallon down with his little sister's shit life. So I kept it all inside. Every day, my misery grew, leaving me more and more vacant. Honestly, the only time I felt free of all that ugly weight was when you and Tallon came to visit."

"You were under that roof, stuck in that house—" I snapped my mouth shut.

"It's why I threw myself into dance. I hated it, but it was also my escape from that house. I tried out for every performance, went to every camp or specialty training I could find. All to get away from her, to get away from everything."

Not caring about propriety, I easily lifted her off the couch and onto my lap, wrapping both arms around her waist, pressing my forehead to her shoulder. For several seconds, we simply sat there, completely silent and still.

"I'm so, so sorry," I whispered.

"I wasn't looking forward to leaving for the American Ballet Academy because of the opportunity, but to get away from her. To start fresh somewhere. I could taste my freedom even if it came with strings attached. I was weeks away from being free."

My hold on her tightened. Weeks from being free from that cunt, but then she was taken. Plucked off the street in the middle of the night before her freedom could ever start.

I hated myself, hated Tallon for not seeing it, but most of all, I really wanted to murder her mother. And now her stepbrother. And possibly her stepfather, because how could he not know his wife was a royal cunt to her young, innocent daughter?

"I think that's a good place to start." I peered over Tinley's shoulder to the doctor, who stood on the other side of the coffee table holding a pillow and a blanket in her arms. "This might be easier with you here, Bryson. We need Tinley to feel safe as I coax her into a meditative trance to access those memories we need and keep from triggering a panic attack."

Accepting the offered items, I tossed the small pillow to my abandoned chair and fluffed out the blanket. I assumed she usually lay on this couch, snuggled tight in a blanket, but not today. There was no way I could let this beautiful woman out of my arms anytime soon. Instead of shifting off the couch, I wrapped the blanket around us both, tucking the sides around my thighs and then her shoulders.

With a gentle urge, she leaned her head back against my shoulder, every inch of her long body pressed against my own.

"There," I said, meeting Dr. Sarah's somewhat amused gaze. "Now she's ready."

18

TINLEY

Oh, this was much better than the couch, not nearly as soft with tense muscles and the snug hold on me, but I loved it all the same. Heat soaked through his chest to my back, and the earlier tension drained from my stiff muscles, leaving me limp.

Shutting off my anxious thoughts, I inhaled and slowly released the breath through pursed lips.

There was a lightness in my chest now that someone besides Dr. Sarah knew my past and believed me. How different would my life had been if—

I mentally slapped myself to stop that line of thinking. I couldn't change what happened in the past, couldn't change my family, but I could alter my future for the better by not allowing the past to affect how I moved on.

Everything I was about to disclose to Bryson happened. It all happened, even if no one knew about it. Now it was time to get this heavy weight off my heart by telling my story to him.

"All right, Tinley. Are you ready?" My head slid along his shoulder with my slight nod. "Great. Let's get started by feeling how safe you are right now. No one can hurt you. Now, we'll start with your feet first, like we always do. Focus on each toe, willing the tension and stress to evaporate from the muscle."

Each second that ticked by, listening to her soft, even voice, pushed me deeper into a relaxed state, my mind going blank. With each rise and fall of Bryson's chest against my back, the slow, calm breaths brushing against my ear, I slipped deeper into myself.

In this relaxed state, I was aware of my surroundings, could hear her voice, feel Bryson beneath me, yet I wasn't alert. Peace engulfed me like a warm hug.

I heard Dr. Sarah instructing me to think back to the night I was taken. To recall the way the night air felt, the scents floating through the downtown streets, to immerse myself into that sunken memory. And because I knew, wrapped in Bryson's arms, that I was safe, I dove down into that rabbit hole, placing myself back in the night my life forever changed.

"It was winter, close to Christmas, so they played carols in the dressing rooms." My lips moved, voice carrying through the office, yet it felt like someone else talking, relaying the memories I could see playing out in front of me like a movie. "The Christmas performances are almost done. We only have two left. I'm relieved knowing next month I'll be away from it all. They made the announcement tonight that I won't return after the Christmas program. Those who knew me clapped in the audience, shouting their congratulations at the news that I'm leaving to attend the American Ballet Academy in January instead of finishing out school here. Tallon isn't here, which he said he would be, but I'm not disappointed, though I was looking forward to some time with him before having to get home. I take my time changing after the performance into a pair of my softest sweats, prepared for the cold walk to my car. I'm the last one out the side door."

"What time is it?" Bryson's deep voice cuts through the foggy memory.

I focused on everything around me, trying to figure it out.

"I don't know. Late. It's super cold the second I open the side door and step onto the sidewalk. The freezing wind cuts through my sweats. It's why I have my coat wrapped close, the collar popped to protect my bare neck. I'm focused on the sidewalk, headed for my car when..." I paused, mentally scanning the area. "Something feels off. I don't like it. Like, it's how I feel on stage—watched."

"You're safe, kid. I'm here."

"I'm almost to my car. It's parked close, but it looks funny. I've parked under a light since my BMW was broken into last month. But tonight it's doused in darkness." My heart raced, breathing growing short. I didn't want to remember what happened next, the moment I was taken. "Bryson," I whimpered, desperate for his support.

The arms curled around me tightened. "I'm here. I won't let anyone hurt you."

"I hear someone call my name." Bryson stiffened behind me. "It's why... it's why I pause at my passenger side door. But when I turn, no one is there. My stomach feels funny, like it knows something bad is about to happen. I try to hurry, ready to get out of there. I'm opening the passenger side door to toss my bag inside, but something clamps over my mouth. I'm too shocked to react. I don't know what's going on. I'm so confused. I should fight, but everything gets foggy. I can't see." I feel my heart pound against my chest. "It smells funny. A chemical smell on the thing shoved against my nose and mouth. Then... then nothing."

I shake my head. I didn't want to do any more, but it was important. If this information could help us catch the asshole after me, then I would recall the horrid memories that haunted my every thought.

"What's it like when you wake up?" Dr. Sarah's soft voice cut through my internal debate.

"Dark," I whimpered. "I can't see anything. It's so dark, and I... I can't move. If I do, it hurts, like a knife against my wrists." My brows furrowed. "I'm cold. No longer wearing my jacket or sweats I left TPAC in. But I'm wearing something. It feels like my leotard and leggings but tighter, too tight because it's not mine. The clothes are too small." I turned my memories down to my feet. "My toes, they hurt like they do when I'm wearing my pointe shoes, except like the outfit, they're too small. My feet are throbbing."

"I know it's dark, but is there anything you can see?" Bryson said into my ear.

"No, it's just dark."

"Try for me, Tinley," he encouraged. "Look around for anything. A shape, a shadow, something on the wall."

Holding a breath, I placed myself back on the lumpy surface and did as Bryson asked. I saw nothing, just like I remembered. Zero light filtered into the room.

Except....

"A dot. A red dot in what I know is a corner. It's the corner where he'll sit and watch. I hate it when he watches." Warm tears leaked down my face. "It hurts. My toes, my feet. They hurt so bad."

"Why, Tinley? Why do they hurt so bad?"

"Because all I do is dance in the too-small toe shoes while he watches from the dark corner. I feel his eyes on me. Hear his voice telling me what do to." Bile rose up my throat. "He makes me dance just for him, he says. He likes the one dance I did last month in the special performance put on by my dance company. My feet are bleeding and numb, but still he makes me do it over and over again while he watches. I can hear him. Hear him telling me how good I'm doing, how I'm only his while he makes those noises. A high-pitched noise while he.... I can't see his face. Never his face, but I see his hand moving, his pants around his ankles." I choked down a sob. "But it's better than when he touches me. I'm so tired and hungry. I'm so hungry, and everything hurts."

"What kind of food does he bring you?" Bryson asked.

I scrunched my eyes tight together to remember that random detail. "It's always the same. Peanut butter and jelly on white bread. It's not enough. I'm always hungry."

"What happens when you're not dancing, Tinley?" That time the question came from Dr. Sarah.

I swallowed hard. "He talks and touches me while I'm on the bed. But I can't move."

"We need to stop this," I heard Bryson say, but I shook my head. "It's not worth it, baby."

"Yes, it is," I hissed. "He was near her."

"Her?"

"Victoria."

"Tinley." Heartache filled his voice, but I shoved it aside and sank back into my memories.

"His touch always feels funny. Not skin. Like soft rubber, maybe. Never skin on skin and only super soft, nothing that would cause me pain. And he'd talk. Tell me how I was always meant to be his. Born to be his forever." One time, when he stood over me in the pitch-dark, caressing my skin, popped forward in my mind. "He calls me his other half. His pretty puppet. He says... he says I'm just like her."

"Do you recognize the voice?" Bryson questioned, his voice gentle in my ear.

"No."

"What about an accent?"

"No."

"Does he sound educated?"

I gave that one a second, focusing on what was said and the pronunciation. "Yes."

"Old or young?" Bryson whispered along the hot skin of my neck.

"Not sure."

"Do you ever see his face?"

"No."

"You said you saw his hand." I jerked in Bryson's hold, hating that memory of seeing his disgusting dick and his thin white hand wrapped around it.

"White. He's white. And thin. His hand looks thin and smooth, not old and wrinkled."

"You're doing great, Tinley," Dr. Sarah whispered. "What else can you remember?"

"The mattress is old. And smells. The place smells because I never leave. I smell."

"Is he always there?" Bryson asked, his voice strained.

I furrowed my brow, concentrating. "No. He leaves for what feels like hours, maybe a whole day. But when he is there, he stays for hours. That red light in the corner is always on, though. And I feel him watching me, even when he's not there." I swallowed. "He says I'm special. Sometimes, in the dark, while he's touching me, I hear him touching himself. I hate it. I don't want to be here."

"You get free, Tinley. You come back to me."

"My whole body hurts, but this is different. Not from the dancing or cold but an ache. I can't stop shivering, but I'm sweating. He's panicked. I hear him pacing in his dark corner, but that bright light pointed at me keeps me from seeing him while he's in the room. When it's on, that's all I can see."

"What about when he drops you off on the couple's doorstep? Can you remember that?" Bryson asked while rubbing his hands up and down my arms.

I focused on those last few minutes, those minutes when I assumed he was dumping my nearly lifeless body.

"I'm in a car. It's dark outside the windows."

"Are you in the back seat or trunk?"

Mentally I stretched my senses out, trying to feel what I was lying on, desperate to give him some details. "A back seat, I think. It's leather, soft leather beneath my fingertips. I'm not bound, but my body is so heavy I can't move even if I want to. Every breath takes work, and I debate just stopping altogether to make it all end. I'm so tired."

"I know you are, kid. I know. Just a bit longer and you're free. Almost free."

The strain and worry in his voice almost pulled me out of the somewhat trance, the need to comfort him overwhelming.

"He carries me. Like everything else, he's gentle. He tells me over and over that we're not done, that he'll be back for me. He says I'm his special puppet."

"What about after he lays you down?" Dr. Sarah asked. "Do you remember hearing a car drive off or a truck?"

I squeezed my eyes, focusing on the sounds, but all I could hear was the steady thrum of my brain beating against my skull from the fever. I shook my head. Forcing myself deeper into that moment, I focused on the feel of the cold concrete beneath my bare skin, the bite of the winter wind against my too-hot face. A shadow shifted above me, making me peek my eye open a sliver. Vision too blurry to make out any features, but I could see him leaning over me.

"He knocks," I whispered. "He knocks on the door, or maybe rings the doorbell? Then he's gone. But I'm not alone for long, only a few seconds before the door opens."

"You did great, Tinley," Dr. Sarah said. "I think that's all for today. Why don't you get some sleep? You're safe in my office with Agent Bennett."

"A nap sounds great," I mumbled, my body and mind already almost out to the world.

"I'm here," Bryson said against my ear. "Sleep, baby. No one will touch you in my arms."

With a heavy sigh, I slipped the rest of the way into the comfort of darkness, knowing my dreams would be sweet after falling asleep in his powerful arms.

THE SOUND of Bryson's muffled, deep voice tugged me awake. Blinking away the sleep coating my eyes, I squinted against the late afternoon sun's rays blazing through the window.

"Yeah, that's what I was thinking too. He called her name, took her the night they announced she was leaving. He knew her, wanted only her. After this, I'm 100 percent certain the security feed hack was this bastard. He's back for her. We need to interview that couple again, ask them if they remember seeing a car drive off or someone walking down the street. It was an odd hour for anyone else to be taking a midnight stroll." I kept still against Bryson to not alert him that I was spying on his phone conversation. "We'll find him, T. This new information can help us. Did the locksmith get things handled at the apartment?" A pause. "Good. My buddy's tech guru said she would come by tonight. Once Tinley's awake, we'll head that way."

"She's awake," I rasped, pushing off his thigh. The muscle tensed beneath my palm as I placed my sock-covered feet on the floor. I scanned the small room, a frown pulling at my lips. "Where's Dr. Sarah?"

Bryson reached out, grasping the back of my neck, and gave it a squeeze. "Yeah, she's up. We'll head to the apartment now. I sent the CliffsNotes of today's session to my profiler friend. She'll get something worked up for us ASAP. It might not be much, but I feel like we're missing something here. Hopefully the profile will give us some insight into what that is."

"Before it's too late."

That was what I heard tacked on to the end of that sentence.

Turning away, I ran my nails over my scalp, tossing my hair, hoping that would erase the last bit of fog clinging to my brain after that nap.

"She stepped out for a bit. Dr. Sarah, that is. How are you feeling?"

I debated lying, saying I was fine, but I couldn't do it. Not with Bryson. "Drained. Tired. Gross."

"Gross?"

I lifted a single shoulder and picked at some invisible lint on my leggings. "I always feel that way after I remember... that." I cut my eyes his way. "And now you know exactly what he did. I can't imagine what you think—"

"It changes nothing." I offered him a sad smile. I wanted to believe him, but really, how could it not change the way he saw me? Now he saw how damaged I was inside and out. "What can I do to bring you back to center? To feel un-gross?"

I scanned his features for any sign that he was uncomfortable or weirded out. "How about a hug?" I suggested tentatively. "A hug would be really great."

He wrapped his thick arms around my shoulders and pulled me to him. My lids fluttered closed as I inhaled against his neck, that masculine scent grounding me to the here and now. My arms went around him, sealing me tighter against his barrel chest until there wasn't enough room for air between us.

"There is nothing gross about you," he said into my hair.

I wished that were true. But even if I let no one see the emotional scars, the physical damage to my feet, the missing toes and deformities from years of dance were most certainly gross. Though unless I became a stripper—which double nope for many reasons, but the main one was not dancing for others' entertainment—I could always keep that physical reminder of my past hidden.

After a few moments of silence, I untangled myself from his hold and planted a kiss on his bearded cheek.

"Thank you. For everything you're doing."

His large hands engulfed my face. "Always, kid." Drawing me closer, he planted a delicate kiss on my forehead. "If you're ready, we need to get going."

Was I ready? Absolutely not. My stomach churned with unease as we stood and headed for the front door, hands locked together.

Something told me that the moment we walked out the front door, this new nightmare, being hunted and stalked by the man who already took so much from me, would be a thousand times worse than when we'd entered the office several hours ago.

And there was absolutely nothing I could do to stop it.

19

TINLEY

Frozen in place, my feet refused to take another step inside the apartment, leaving me stuck just inside the doorway with the closed door at my back. Which was fine since Bryson demanded I stay in this spot while he scoured the apartment, gun in hand, inspecting every room for threats.

That was exactly where he found me a minute later as he emerged from my room, holstering his gun. He stopped short, eyeing me with concern.

"Something is different," I said cautiously. My hair slid along my back as I surveyed every inch of the apartment I could see. I inhaled deep, fighting to pinpoint what was different today than it was yesterday morning when we left for Louisville.

"The locksmith was in here," Bryson offered, inspecting the room just as I was. "Maybe that's what you feel?"

I wrapped both arms around myself and rubbed my palms up and down my arms. "It feels... colder than that. I can't explain it."

Bryson stepped forward and planted his hands on both my shoulders. "Maybe you're still feeling watched." Sliding them down my arms, he held my hands and walked backward, guiding me toward the couch. "The tech person is on her way up to check for hidden cameras."

I closed my eyes and rolled my shoulders, stretching my neck one way, then the other in an effort to calm my frantic nerves. "It doesn't feel the same as before. I don't know. All I know is it's different." I tilted my head to the side, my lids fluttering open. "It feels... ominous almost."

"Sounds promising," Bryson joked with a tight smile. His lips parted, ready to say something else when a fist pounded against the door. In a flash, he was between me and the door, gun in hand before I could even blink.

"Wow," I gasped, waves of lust rolling through my veins as he stalked toward the door. His dark-wash jeans tightened around his thighs and ass as he moved, those thick arms flexing, causing the black material of his long-sleeve T-shirt to stretch to its max. I swallowed, mostly to ensure my tongue was inside my mouth. "That's so hot. When does Tallon get back? Please tell me later, much, much later, so I can have my way with you before he comes home."

Bryson pulled up short and shot an amused look over his shoulder. "Tonight. Late."

"Oh goodie," I rasped, blatantly staring at his ass.

"But first." He tilted his head toward the door. "We need to sweep the apartment for cameras. Then we can play."

"With toys?" I questioned with a hopeful lilt to my voice I didn't even try to cover.

His responding dark chuckle sent tingles along my skin. "Whatever you want, baby." He laughed again at my widening grin. "What am I going to do with you?"

I raised a single brow in challenge. "Anything you want."

"Wow." He laughed.

"That's what I said."

"I can hear you two through the door," said an amused feminine voice from the hallway.

I tensed when Bryson swung open the door, his large frame

blocking me from seeing who stood on the other side. I shifted to the edge of the couch, trying to look around him.

"Thank you for coming on short notice." With a sweeping hand, he gestured into the apartment and stepped aside. "Come on in. Any friend of Bekham's is a friend of mine."

My eyes went wide as I took in the unique woman who strode through the door. There was an air about her, a "gives no fucks" attitude that made me immediately want to know everything about her. And oh my, she was small, though I had an inkling that if I told her so, I'd be on her shit list. By the look on Bryson's face, he too was surprised by the woman's appearance. As she passed by, the top of her head barely came to the middle of his chest, and that was with—

Hold the fuck on.

"Are those the new furry Doc Martens?" I squealed and leaped off the couch, hands outstretched like I might rip them off her tiny feet. "I've been looking for those everywhere."

The woman blinked as I squatted in front of her to get a better look at the boots I'd wanted for months. A small smirk curled at the corners of her full lips. "It helps when you have feet the size of a toddler's. And have a friend who works there who gives you a heads up on upcoming shipments."

"Super jealous right now for so many reasons."

Adjusting her heavy-looking black Jansport backpack, she held out her small hand to me. "Remington Dotson."

I stared at the black sparkles along her short nails as I gripped it, allowing her to help me up off the floor. "Tinley Harper." Inclining my head toward Bryson, I introduced him before dropping her hand. "So you're the computer guru here to tell me if I'm crazy or not?"

"Tinley," Bryson growled, but I waved him off, keeping my expectant gaze on her.

"Charlie gave me a brief rundown of what you're needing, but why don't you tell me in your own words so I don't miss anything?" As she spoke, Remington walked toward the kitchen, her eyes flicking around the room, seeming to take in every detail. At the island, she set her backpack on top of the granite and slid out a fancy-looking laptop.

I started to tell her how I'd felt watched and detailed out which rooms, but the words dried up in my throat, all thoughts fading when she shrugged off her long puffy coat. Remington might have been a tiny thing, but with the way her inked muscles flexed as she set up her computer, she was fit and strong. I lost myself checking out her tattoos. One sleeve was all color, the designs flowing together with so much detail that I couldn't make out where one picture stopped and the other began. The other arm was all black lines and shading that looked like clouds mixed in with other designs, a complete contrast.

My gaze slid to the white sugar skulls dotting her black tights that disappeared beneath a short, tight leather skirt. A white V-neck T-shirt was tucked into the waist, a black bra beneath completing her outfit.

I loved it. If I wasn't so obsessed with nineties trends, I'd totally raid her closet. Not that anything of hers would fit. I was a good six inches taller than her, and where I was built like a pole, she was curvy, filling out every inch of her outfit in a way that made her sexy as hell.

The petite features on her heart-shaped face scowled, snapping me out of my blatant observation.

"Sorry, what was your question?" I asked, heat building beneath my cheeks.

A comforting hand settled on my shoulder, relaxing me instantly.

"She's felt watched in the apartment. We know the stalker hacked into the building security feed, but Charlie said we needed someone here to look inside the apartment." The woman's stick-straight black hair shifted as she nodded, focused on her computer while she listened to Bryson. "That's where we stand. What do you need from us?"

"Nothing. Bekham sent over the line of code he found, so I'll use that when searching the available Wi-Fi signals close enough to reach this apartment." Her brilliant green eyes flicked to the fridge. "What are the odds you have anything to drink? The drive from

Franklin was a bitch at this time of night. I swear people need to stop moving into this city. It's already popping at the seams as it is."

"Sorry, all I have to offer is water or chocolate milk," I said sheepishly. Ugh, she was so cool, and here I was with chocolate milk. There was some liquor stored above the fridge, but I didn't have the key, nor did I want to know where it was. Sometimes the temptation was too much to pour a drink and chase my dark memories away for just a little while. Not knowing how to get into that cabinet saved me a few times. Though if you looked closely enough, there were a few dents along the edges of the hinges where I'd tried to pry it open one desperate night.

Remington grimaced but kept typing. "Anything stronger?"

I opened my mouth to say no, but Bryson answered before I could.

"Bourbon or vodka? Her brother has both in the cabinet. I had a glass of bourbon the other night. It's the good stuff."

Her eyes lit up as she nodded, her hair seeming to shimmer in the light with the movement. "Hell yes. Bourbon, please."

With a tight grip to my chin, Bryson turned my face up to his. "Watch her while I get the key, okay?"

I planted my butt on the stool across from Remington, facing the stove and dark wood cabinets. Her narrowed eyes flicked between me and the direction Bryson had disappeared. "What the hell was that about? The key, as in he keeps shit locked away from you? Are you in some kind of abusive relationship? Do I need to kick his ass?"

A chuckle bubbled in my throat, though it dissipated at the steely glare she had locked over my shoulder. I tilted my head as I considered her assumption. Why would she automatically think he was a controlling, abusive asshole unless she knew the signs to look for— perhaps *personally* knew what to look for?

"No, nothing like that," I blurted, holding out both hands. "I was —*am* an addict. I *asked* my brother, Special Agent Harper, to hide the key to the liquor cabinet. That's what Bryson is getting, and he didn't want me to look and possibly have the temptation later to go find the key in a moment of weakness. Bryson is a good guy. The best," I said with a clear lovesick tone. Resting my elbows on the counter, I placed my chin in my palm. "He's only protecting me from myself."

A flicker of sadness flashed across her face before she schooled her features and turned back to the humming laptop. "Good. Because I wasn't sure if I could take that fucker if you asked me to. Is he part giant or something?"

I almost said "only his cock" but held my tongue. Wouldn't want to make the poor woman jealous that I had a hot boyfriend *and* he came with a monster cock. That would be rude, and I really wanted this cool chick to be my friend.

"How do you know Charlie?" I startled at Bryson's voice at my back.

"He helped me out a long time ago and we've stayed friends since," Remington said absentmindedly as she studied the screen. "I'm running a search, but I'm not picking up any abnormal signals radiating from the apartment." Her eyes found me and flicked across my face. "You said you felt watched." I dipped my chin, actively avoiding watching Bryson pour their two drinks. "Which room or rooms?"

I sucked in a breath. There weren't any abnormal signals. What if I was wrong about this whole thing? Would she accuse me of making it all up, thinking I was doing this for attention? My heart raced, causing heat to build within me and sweat to slick my palms. Bryson said he would believe me, but if there wasn't proof, how could he?

"Tinley." I jumped, nearly toppling backward off the stool at Bryson's shout near my ear. "Stop it."

"Hey," Remington snapped, causing both Bryson's head and mine to whip in her direction. She pointed a black nail at his chest. "Don't yell at her."

With an embarrassed groan, I buried my face in my palms. Shit, I'd gotten lost in my head again. It happened more frequently lately. It had to be the stress of sensing he was back and watching me from the shadows.

"He's fine," I grumbled, my words muffled by my palms pressed to my lips. "He's trying to help again." Sitting up straight, I avoided her confused stare. "The living room and my room." I paused, thinking back to the last few weeks and where I felt the most uncomfortable. "And my bathroom."

"She mentioned once that she didn't feel watched in her brother's room."

A half-full highball glass filled with ice cubes and dark liquid slid across the bar top. Remington wrapped her short fingers around it and raised it to her lips. Before taking a sip, she stared into the glass.

"Will this...?" The ice clinked against the glass as she shook it for emphasis. "Are you okay with us drinking around you?"

Bryson dragged another stool closer, his own highball glass in hand.

"Oh yeah, for sure. I even work at a bar. It's more that I crave the escape, not the alcohol, if that makes sense. It's more about the relief than the actual vice."

She tilted her head to the side, her sleek, long bob shifting along her neck. "That's very self-aware."

I preened at her compliment. "Thank you. It's taken a while to get to this point, but the work is paying off."

After taking a quick sip, Remington stepped away from the laptop, glass in hand, and stalked around the living room, keeping close to the walls. Bryson and I twisted around on the stools to monitor her movements.

"Not to freak you out or anything," she said from across the room, "but just because I didn't find a signal now doesn't mean there wasn't one before."

"What are you thinking?" Bryson questioned before I could.

"Well, if this guy is as good as we think he is—"

"Why do you assume that?" I asked.

The clink of the ice filled the quiet as she took another long sip. "You were right. This is the good stuff. So, the line of code Bekham found in the main security feed that allowed instant access whenever he wanted was complex. The way a few sequences were tied together made it almost invisible to anyone." She shot a wicked grin over her shoulder. "But thank goodness for you, Bekham isn't just anyone.

What it tells us is he has training." Turning back to the wall, she tilted her chin up, searching the ceiling. "Could even be his job. That would make sense, wouldn't it?" At this point, it seemed she was talking more to herself than us. "Though not a developer. What he created to have the access and keep the code hidden was too complex for a simple coder."

Having come around back to the kitchen, she shook her head and finished the last few sips of her drink in one big swallow.

"I see nothing in here. Sorry." She sighed. "I wish I could help, but I'm not finding shit."

I turned my eyes down, studying the granite. "Yeah, it could've all been in my head, right? I mean, how would he have gotten into my apartment in the first place? I'm just being paranoid. Thank you for driving all the way here. Sorry it was for nothing."

"You okay?" Bryson asked.

I sighed, worried how he'd react to not finding any evidence. "Yeah, I just—"

"Not you, Tinley. Remington?"

I snapped my head up at the urgency in his voice.

Face pale, features slack, she blinked slowly. "I... I don't know. I feel... I feel funny." She swayed on her feet before stumbling to the side of the island, gripping the edge so she didn't crash to the floor.

I shot off the stool, causing it to topple to the floor, and wrapped an arm around her shoulders as she teetered again. Panic shot through me. I turned wide, pleading eyes to Bryson, who seemed frozen in shock.

"What the fuck was in that drink?" she slurred.

Bryson opened his mouth but snapped it shut. His untouched glass hovered in the air beneath his nose. "I don't smell anything."

"I might be small," she said, her eyes fluttering closed before slowly opening again, "but I'm no lightweight."

With a heavy sigh, she gave up the fight of standing and slumped against me. A grunt escaped as I adjusted my hold to keep her upright. Bryson rounded the island, scooped her up into his arms, and strode to the couch.

Chewing on the corner of my lower lip, I studied her relaxed features as Bryson laid her down gently before pressing two fingers to the side of her neck.

"What's going on?" I murmured.

"I don't know what the hell just happened. Her pulse is strong, so whatever it is—" He stood up so fast that I stumbled backward in surprise, catching myself on the edge of the couch. Determination filled his face as he stormed into the kitchen and stopped in front of the fridge, head tilted as he examined the cabinet that held all the liquor in the house.

Focus half on Bryson as he studied the lock with the flashlight on his phone, I blindly tugged a blanket off the back of the couch and draped it over Remington. Guilt burned in my chest. Whatever just happened to her was because of me. I was a damn curse to anyone who even looked my way. The woman did nothing but offer to help see if I was right about feeling watched inside the apartment.

"Fuck." I jumped at Bryson's loud roar. He slammed his fist into the front of the fridge, leaving behind a sizable dent. "Pack a fucking bag, Tinley."

"Why? What's going on?" I asked.

"There are tool marks, as if someone tampered with this lock."

"Tampered with the lock," I repeated, my voice hollow. I blinked, though it didn't make my vision any clearer. My breaths turned to short wheezes as I stood frozen. Somewhere in the distance, Bryson called for an ambulance before calling Tallon. "Why is he doing this? Why me? Why can't he be obsessed with someone else?"

Tears slicked down my cheeks, but I couldn't move to wipe them away.

"I want it to stop," I whispered. "I want all this to stop. I can't—"

"You can." Calloused palms scraped along my cheeks, applying pressure until I snapped my gaze upward. "You can and you will. I'll be with you each step, okay?" I tried to nod but couldn't make myself knowing my agreement would be a lie. "An ambulance is on the way for Remington. With how fast the drug took hold, I'm assuming a roofie or something similar."

"Why?" I whimpered. "Why do that?"

His features tightened.

"Tell me," I grated through clenched teeth.

"I think you're missing the point, Tinley."

"Then tell me what I'm missing, Bryson," I snapped.

"How about how? How about when?"

My thoughts froze, the world stilling as my breathing kicked into high gear, coming in short, wheezing gasps. Light-headed, I swayed on my feet. "He was in my apartment."

"It looks that way. When, who knows, but I had that bourbon the other night and was fine after." I searched his hazel eyes, pleading for him to help me make sense of what was going on. His eyes softened. "If I had to guess, he was here while we were gone. That's why it felt different in here and maybe why we can't find the cameras. He took them, cleaning up any evidence of his stalking. He knew the moment Charlie cut his feed to the lobby that we were on to him. How he did all this *and* came up to Louisville, I don't know, but it all makes sense."

A resigned look fell over his face, lips pressed in a tight line. With a firm, comforting squeeze, he dropped his hands from my shoulders to turn for the couch. Two fingers to her neck, Bryson monitored Remington's pulse again and held a hand beneath her nose. After a minute, he stood, gently gripped my elbow, and led me toward my bedroom.

I balked at the entryway, the sensation I'd felt earlier in the apartment coming back with force.

"What's wrong?" Bryson's clipped tone was deadly serious as he moved a hand closer to his gun, eyes taking in every inch of the room.

Unable to respond, I pressed a fist to my sternum to keep my heart from beating right out of my chest. Steps slow and cautious, I moved around the small bedroom, checking every shadowed corner and crevice. Frustration mounted with every second I came up empty-handed. Shoulders slumped in defeat, I stepped in front of the dresser to pack.

A frown tugged at my lips, brows furrowing as I dug through my underwear drawer. Sorting through the mass of boy shorts, I rummaged for my regular, everyday lace thongs.

Except there were none.

It nagged at the back of my mind, but instead of dwelling on that, I shoved the oddity aside, assuming they were all dirty from not doing laundry since Bryson arrived. When I moved to the next drawer, my fingers hovered over the neatly folded and stacked leggings that normally were a jumbled mess. Understanding dawned on me like a punch to the gut.

Someone went through my things.

The dresser shook from the force of me slamming the drawer shut and using the furniture to propel myself toward the other side of the room. Confused shouts and quick footsteps sounded at my back. I didn't take a second to explain as I hurried into the closet.

My hand visibly trembled as I reached it high into the air, stretching for a flimsy cardboard box I used to store mementos. The tip of a single finger brushed the edge, inching it off the shelf before it tipped, falling straight for my face. Before it could hit me, the cardboard was snatched midair and slowly placed at my feet.

"Tell me what's going on, Tinley," he demanded, though his voice was tense with worry.

Ignoring him, I yanked open the flaps. Stomach lodged in my throat, I tipped the box to see inside. Silently, I prayed to anyone who would listen that all my old dance gear—leotards, shoes, tights, and tutus—were still stuffed inside.

A pitiful whimper vibrated in my throat, choking me when the bottom of the box was all I found.

Nothing. It was all gone.

"No," I shouted, desperately ripping apart the cardboard to make the illusion of an empty box disappear. "It's gone. It's all gone."

A firm grip took hold of my chin, forcing my face up to his. "What's gone? Talk to me," he demanded.

"My dance gear. All my old—" The words dried up in my throat. I couldn't breathe, my lungs desperate for air but refusing to work. The impact of my knees slamming into the hardwood didn't resonate as I slumped to the walk-in closet's floor. Black dots littered my vision, growing larger.

Knees to my chest, I curled into a tight ball and buried my face between my thighs, desperate to make the reality of the situation somehow not real.

But it was.

Not only was the monster back, but he was prepared for my return.

20

BRYSON

I forced down another grumble of annoyance at the paramedic squatting in front of us and the bright pencil light he continued to scan across her unblinking eyes. Though she didn't flinch, I knew it wasn't comfortable. With a resigned sigh, the guy clicked off the light and held her wrist, checking her pulse again.

Cocooned in several blankets, Tinley still shivered on my lap.

The kid in front of me labeled it as shock, though I felt it was too simple a word for what she was going through. Her unresponsiveness and slack face shredded my soul every second she remained despondent. It killed me knowing I was helpless, useless to her in this moment. All I could do was hold her tight and continue to whisper in her ear that she was safe, that I was there to protect her.

My attention flicked to the two other medics rolling the stretcher with a still unconscious Remington out into the hall, an ambulance waiting downstairs to rush her to Vanderbilt. After describing what happened, medics agreed with my assumption that the drug she ingested only knocked her unconscious, not affecting her heart or breathing.

"I'd like to get her to the hospital."

My gaze snapped back to the worried EMT, his concern clear from the deep lines along his forehead.

Tinley tensed in my arms. "No," she rasped, finally speaking though she still stared at the wall, not acknowledging anything visually.

"Ma'am, I—"

"She said no," I growled and tightened my hold around her waist. I dared him with my glare to take her from me. "I'll ensure she stays hydrated and rests. She's not leaving my side."

The paramedic shook his head. "Fine. But if anything changes, get her immediately to the hospital. I don't like how she's not responding. We might need to assess her mental—"

"Out," I roared, making him stumble backward at the sheer rage in my bellow. "Leave. Now."

The remaining EMTs in the room stared, jaws slack and faces growing paler by the second. Annoyance, anger, and fear for her continued to rage inside me. Not only were the idiots contaminating the scene, but their hovering presence was irritating as fuck. Now that Remington was safe, I had to focus on the woman in my arms. I knew what she needed, and it wasn't her being carted to the damn hospital, causing more trauma.

As the last person filed out, a blur of a black suit raced inside. A person hot on Tallon's heels clipped the EMT as he too entered the apartment. I held Tinley tighter against my chest, ready to protect her with my life against this unknown male.

Chest heaving, nostrils flaring with each quick breath, Tallon fell to his knees in front of the couch, grasping for his sister.

"Who is he?" I hissed, my jaw tight as I glared at the stranger.

The tall, thin fucker wore a gray suit with the collar of his white dress shirt undone, well-worn dress shoes, and a "don't fuck with me attitude." He didn't give off bad vibes, but I couldn't stop myself from snarling his direction as he studied me and Tinley.

"What the hell happened, Bryson?" Tallon snapped, dragging my glare to him. "Fuck, you want introductions now? That's the local detective I reached out to for more information on that male victim's murder. Jameson Bend, Special Agent Bryson Bennett. Bryson, Jameson. There, fucking happy, B?"

Knowing the man wasn't a threat and having Tallon there, some of the tension eased from my tight muscles. Only to return with a vengeance when Tinley pressed back, refusing to be taken from my arms. With a quick headshake, she ducked her head beneath my chin.

Tallon's lips pursed in a tight line as he studied her, then me, cataloging each place we touched. Fuck. This was not the time for him to find out. Tinley did not need that added stress.

"She's in shock," I said, adjusting my hold on the bundled-up woman. "We need to get ahead of this, T. I feel like we're ten steps behind this fucker. He was here, in this apartment."

Tallon eased from the floor to perch on the edge of the coffee table. He ran a hand through his short blond hair, his exhausted gaze lingering on Tinley.

"You have no idea how right you are." Shooting me a look, he hitched his chin toward his sister. "She should go in her room while we talk about this."

"No," Tinley and I said in unison, my voice strong and forceful, hers weak and shaking with fear.

Inhaling through my nose, I struggled to calm my rising irritation. Today wasn't even over and I was already at max capacity. From seeing those footprints outside the window in the snow to the revelations Tinley disclosed in therapy to the shit show in the last hour. I was torn between getting her as far away from this place as possible, yet the agent in me knew that wouldn't solve anything. If we wanted this to end, we had to stay here, decipher clues, and find the motherfucker who stalked what was mine.

"The bastard was in her room." Tinley shivered along my lap at the reminder. "He was in this apartment. I'm not letting her out of my sight."

"I get that," Tallon snapped. "But what we need to talk about is too much for her—"

"I've lived through hell, Tal," Tinley said, her voice stronger than moments ago, "and survived. I'm fine hearing whatever you have to discuss."

Sadness flooded Tallon's features, his bright blue eyes somehow dimming with her words. "Tin, I'm just trying to protect—"

"No, you're trying to put me in a little glass box, shutting me out for your own peace of mind. Not mine." Pride welled in my chest at her rising indignation. Anger was better than that blank, emotionless state. "This is my life. I have a right to know."

"I am trying to protect you," Tallon retorted. "From this bastard and yourself."

"Oh, because you know so much about what triggers me?" Twisting, she sat up straight, angling toward her brother. "Don't start that shit of protecting me from myself. I'm doing that all on my own. I'm working through my shit to get better. I'm doing that work, not you. So you don't get to walk in here after saying it's to protect me, after I haven't seen you for more than a few hours in months. Say whatever you need to say, Tal. I'm not a fragile kid anymore."

"Get off his lap," Tallon hissed, glaring at my arms wrapped around her waist. "I can't fucking focus with you there."

"No," she said, squaring her shoulders. The blanket fell a little, slipping off her shoulders. Before I knew what I was doing, I'd adjusted it back around her to keep her warm.

Tallon's calculating stare tracked the movement.

"I talked to all the detectives who could've been involved with the male victim's case," the Jameson guy said, cutting through the rising tension. I released a breath when his distraction worked, Tallon's attention moving from me to him. "None of them went to that bar to question Tallon's sister. One planned to stop by and ask the manager for security footage, but he hadn't even gotten around to doing that yet."

"What does that mean?" Tinley asked.

"It means whoever approached you that night at the bar wasn't FBI or the Davidson County police force." Jameson moved to lean a shoulder against the wall. "My guess, based on how Tallon said you felt, he was pushing to get you out of there. It was the bastard who's behind all this."

"I agree," I stated, hating the words. "We confirmed there was a security breach in their surveillance footage, so he'd know that guy threatened Tinley, which is why he ended up dead."

"Not only dead, B," Tallon said, back to stewing over Tinley's body curled on my lap. "His throat was slashed, with a jagged tool."

"And they cut his dick off," Tinley added. "Right?"

Every male in the room cringed. If Tinley wasn't sitting on my lap, I'd cover my crotch just at the mention of it being severed from my body.

"Yes," Jameson confirmed with a grimace.

A beat of silence filled the apartment as we all got lost in thought.

"What's with the significance of the throat slash?" Tinley asked.

"It's the same signature as the bastard I've spent the last year hunting," Tallon said, slumping forward. "Though none of it makes sense. Two victims here in Nashville with the same cause of death: one female like this unsub's other victims, the other a male, which we assume is because of Tinley. None of the other cases I've worked have anything to do with my sister. Besides the captivity piece, nothing suggests these cases are tied together, yet now this."

I started to respond when my phone vibrated along the couch cushion. After checking the screen, I hitched my chin toward the device and swiped the screen to answer the call, then pressed the Speaker button.

"Charlie. You're on speaker with—"

"What the fuck happened to Remington?" Charlie's bellowing voice rattled through the phone. "Drugged? What the actual fuck, Bryson?"

"We're trying to figure that out now," I said, keeping my tone even despite the guilt eating at me. "The medics just took her to the hospital. They'll monitor her while—"

"What? She's not there with you?" The shift from anger to fear in his tone had me sitting up straighter.

"No, they just left—"

"Get fucking officers to that hospital right now. People you trust, agents if you can. She needs twenty-four-hour protection until we catch this guy."

"Charlie," I barked. "What the hell are you talking about?"

"I've got this," Jameson muttered, his phone already sealed to his ear. "What's her last name?"

"Dotson. Remington Dotson." Charlie's voice cracked. "She's already been through hell once—"

"Bekham," I snapped, pulling the phone closer to my mouth. "Explain what the hell is going on. Now."

"I figured out where I saw that line of code." I sucked in a breath. *Fuck.* This couldn't be good. Tinley looked at me at the same time I glanced down at her. "Did Remington clear the room of any cameras before...?"

"Yeah, she said there were no unusual signals coming from the apartment."

"Good. So I found—"

"Bryson," Rhyan's panicked voice cut Charlie off. "Is she with you?"

"Remington—"

"No, Tinley," she corrected.

"How does this woman know my sister?" Tallon asked.

"Later." I sighed. *Fuck, this is a shit show.* "Rhyan, yes, Tinley is here with me, her brother, and a detective. We're all carrying, so she's safe with us."

"That's good, really good, but I'm not sure it will be enough. I think you need to get her into protective custody." The room froze at her words, the air seeming to be sucked out. "I've worked on the profile all day, and I couldn't figure out a few inconsistencies, but then Charlie told me what he found. It's worse than I thought. The unsub after Tinley is brilliant, with significant resources at his disposal. He's more than a stalker. He's obsessed with her. It revolves around a female he fixated on before her, and he's now considering Tinley as that female's replacement. Which, Tinley, are you in the room?"

"Yes," she whispered toward the phone.

"I need you to think back on something. Bryson already gave me the CliffsNotes of you recounting your time in captivity, and one thing stuck out that could help with the profile."

"Okay." My heart lurched at the tremble in her voice. "What do you need?"

"You said he only gave you peanut butter and jelly sandwiches on white bread to eat." With a soft curse, Tallon stood and disappeared from view, clearly upset at hearing these details. "I need to know if you remember him *saying* anything about the food. About *you* preferring that kind of food."

I studied Tinley's face as she sealed her eyes closed. Snaking a hand beneath the blankets, I interlaced her fingers with my own and gave them a gentle squeeze. Suddenly her eyes flung open, surprise alight in them.

"He said it was my favorite. That he knew it was my favorite, and that's why he made it for me."

"But it's not, is it?" Rhyan prompted.

"No," Tinley responded with a quick shake of her head. "I don't like grape jelly. I've always preferred strawberry."

"That's what I thought."

"What, Rhyan?" I nearly begged. "What does all this mean?"

"Tinley recounted that the dance shoes and clothes were too small, like they weren't hers. Add in the childlike food, and him saying Tinley reminded him of her, I'm thinking.... Him seeing Tinley triggered something he'd long kept hidden because she reminded him of his first victim." I dipped my head, pressing it against the back of Tinley's. "And I'm assuming she was young, maybe around Tinley's age at the time she was taken. That will help us narrow down the suspect pool once we have a list based on the profile. We can look into a suspect's background, searching for the catalyst of his voyeurism and obsession. Maybe even ID who she was, which will lead us to him."

"Was?" Jameson asked, having moved closer to the couch, his focus on the phone.

"I have to assume with the unsub dressing Tinley in those clothes and the tender care he took with her during captivity, his first victim is most likely dead. By his hand or natural causes, I'm not sure, but this means he will go to any lengths to get her back. If he gets his hands on Tinley this time, we won't get her back now that he's prepared. Basic profile: mid-forties, white male, with the loss of a female in his past—I'm thinking a sister or close relative. When he took Tinley before, it was out of desperation. He was disorganized and unprepared for providing for a long-term captive. But now he's had time to perfect his long game and experience."

I squeezed my eyes shut. "The announcement that she was leaving for school."

"That was his trigger to act instead of just watch from the audience. Which means he was in the crowd often. That can help us narrow down a suspect pool. I'll have Charlie run a search of who all purchased multiple tickets at TPAC during the time Tinley performed," Rhyan said.

"Experience?" Tinley probed, eyes glued to the phone screen. "You said time and experience. What do you mean? Has he held others?"

"Not exactly," Rhyan hedged.

"That's where I come in," Charlie cut in, his voice echoing through the living room. "That line of code. I knew I'd seen it before. Last year, the cybercrimes division of the FBI asked for my help on a dark web case involving live torture feeds and bidding in a group chat. Every time we'd get a hint of where to find the hidden chat room and feeds, they'd go underground, only to pop up again under our radar. Whoever created these rooms is good, and I hate to say this, but maybe even better than me."

"What do you mean, bidding?" Tallon asked from somewhere in the kitchen.

"Those with access to the chat rooms can bid on what happens next to the women in the live feed. It's demented, the shit they come up with, but the fucker is making significant cash, which means it's worth the risk. Various forms of torture are available to bid on. And that's not the worst part. When the victim is past their usefulness, the fucker adds an alternative to the bidding selection." We all leaned closer to the phone, the anticipation palpable in the room. "They turned the last video into a live snuff film."

I felt Tallon's approach before I heard his voice directly at my back. "Were they held captive for extended periods while they were tortured?"

"Yes," Charlie confirmed.

"When they were murdered on film, how did he do it? Was it always the same?"

"He slashed their throats on film. We've only uncovered three victims so far, but with the efficiency of the torture and complexity of the chat rooms, I have to assume there are more victims out there. But with no way to know where the films were recorded, it always came to a dead end."

No one spoke, too in shock to even respond.

"Which is where I come back in," Rhyan said. "With the connection of the code on the security feed at the apartment and with the dark web chat rooms, we have to assume these two are working together."

"Two?" I rasped.

"The technical unsub, the one who's stalking Tinley, is the voyeur. He's setting up the chat rooms, the secure video feeds, and payments for the bids. And considering he's a voyeur, I assume he's also the one choosing the victims."

"But he didn't hurt me," Tinley said. "He just... he just watched, barely even touched me."

"Which is why I believe the one doing the torture, the hands-on aspect of these crimes, is his partner," Rhyan explained. "Somehow they met, maybe on a similar dark site that led them to partner up, each getting what they wanted. The one gets to watch, the other dealing out the torture and murder while making money. A lot of money."

"Why did you suggest protective custody?" Tallon asked. "If

Tinley is special to him, reminds him of someone he lost, he doesn't want to hurt her."

"I'm assuming this next part won't be in my official profile," Rhyan said carefully. "But the way he treated her before, no harsh touch or sexual assault, and talked about her being so sweet and innocent, he was warming her up to him, hoping she'd return his longing. Maybe he forced himself too soon on his first victim, and that made her pull away or leave. This time, I'm concerned he's angry because of what Bryson told me he potentially saw on the cameras in the apartment and witnessed standing outside his house. Seeing her intimate with another man could push him to punish or rush Tinley to love him back if he gets his hands on her."

"What do you mean, what he witnessed?" Tallon questioned. "Intimate...."

My lids fluttered closed, a resigned sigh escaping as I carefully lifted Tinley off my lap and sat her on the couch. I knew what was coming next. There was no way to avoid it now.

Pushing to my feet, I turned, shoving my hands into the front pockets of my jeans, and leveled a guilty stare at my best friend.

"He saw me and Tinley."

"You and my baby sister," he said through gritted teeth. As all the pieces snapped together, hurt registered on his face before morphing to pure rage. "You fucked my sister," he roared, storming around the couch, hand clenched into tight fists at his side.

As I knew I would, I stood as still as a statue as his fist flew toward my face, knowing full well it would hurt like hell. Though nothing could hurt worse than the glare of pure betrayal that seemed to sear through to my soul. I deserved his anger and pain for not telling him, for him having to find out like this. Though later I would correct him.

I didn't just fuck his sister.

I made love to the woman who owned my heart.

The woman I'd die to protect.

An amazing lady who I desperately wanted to be more than a girlfriend.

Knuckles cracked across my jaw, pain immediately flaring at the point of impact. The force and zero deflection sent me stumbling back a step to stay upright. Stars danced in my woozy vision, keeping me from seeing his follow-up gut shot. A pain-filled hiss whistled through my teeth as all the air expelled from my lungs.

Fuck, he wasn't holding back. Another well-placed punch landed against the side of my face, making me spin. Blood and spit flew from my parted lips.

All right, that's enough. It was one thing to understand his anger, but I wasn't about to let him beat me to shit, resulting in me being unable to protect Tinley.

I blocked the next swing, my forearm colliding against his, and used the force to shove him to the side, catching him off-balance.

Cheeks flushed red, sweat glistening on his forehead, he glared at me with pure hatred. A part of me cried out at what I was witnessing. Years of friendship deteriorating right before my eyes, all because I fell in love with his sister. Was this when I'd lose my best friend?

"Stop!" Tinley shouted as she placed herself between us. "The fuck are you doing, Tal?"

Hunched over, hands on his knees as he sucked down deep breaths, Tallon jabbed a finger at me. "He took advantage—"

With more force than I expected, she slapped his hand and shoved his shoulders. "No, he didn't, and don't you fucking dare accuse him of something like that. You know Bryson. He's your best fucking friend. You know he wouldn't do that to me. I was the one who came on to him—"

"And he should've said no," Tallon roared, eyes wild.

"Why? Because I'm too broken for your friend?" she shouted, stopping him short when he attempted to advance a step.

His mouth gaped, eyes went wide. "What? No."

"Is it because I'm not good enough for him?"

"The fuck, Tin? Of course you're good enough for him."

"Then why? Why is us being together not okay? Sure, you're finding out at a shit moment, and yeah, the timing of me telling Bryson how I feel wasn't ideal, but fuck, you know him." She jabbed a finger my way. Tallon's slightly softer gaze flicked to me before going back to his sister. "You know he's a good man, an amazing father, someone who would die to protect me." Her voice softened with each word. After a glance over her shoulder, she stepped closer to her brother and gripped his shoulders. "So tell me why, Tal. Why would something between me and him be such a bad thing? Do you... do you not trust me?"

My heart cracked at the desperation in her voice, at those vulnerable words laid out for her brother. If he fucked this up, I would beat the shit out of him. She needed his support now more than ever.

In a quick move, he tugged her close and wrapped her in a tight hug. For several seconds, he just held her. Finally, his eyes opened, regret shining through them as he met my own.

"Of course I trust you, Tin. I only want the best for you, for you to be happy. Safe and happy."

"Then that's Bry," she whispered just loud enough for me to hear. I chanced a glance at Jameson. He watched the two of them, face completely unreadable. "If that's what you truly want for me, then be happy for me. Be happy that I finally had the courage to tell him how I feel, how I've always felt. This isn't a fling, Tallon. I love him."

21

TINLEY

Welp, that timing was utter shit.

W I groaned and buried my face in my hands, shaking my head at my dumb ass.

Who says they love someone for the first time not to the person they actually love but in the middle of a fight with their brother?

This girl.

Fuck, that could be another toxic trait: poor timing.

Perched on the edge of Tallon's bed, I studied the closed door, hoping that could help unmuffle the words from the other side.

"So, you and Tallon's friend."

"Yeah. You can see how well that went over. Fuck," I whimpered, smacking the heel of my hand against my forehead.

I shot Detective Jameson a side-eyed glare when he chuckled at my misery. They'd delegated him to keep an eye on me from at least five feet away—that order came from Bryson—while the two friends worked through their "issues." Though it had been long enough now, I wondered if they'd made up and transitioned to talking about the details of the case.

A few minutes of silence settled between us before it grew too uncomfortable for me to stay quiet. "So, how do you know my brother?"

When he didn't reply, I twisted on the bed to face where he leaned against the window, focusing on the Nashville skyline.

"We've known each other for a while."

I cocked my head to the side, trying to understand his hesitant tone.

"And..." I drawled, motioning with my hand that I wanted more details.

His light brown eyes cut my way. "And I guess you could say we were friends before."

"But not now."

"Not for a while," he muttered under his breath. He used the window as leverage to push off. In two strides, he paused at the door and inched it open. His tall, lean body blocked my view of the living room despite my attempts to see around him. "You two dipshits done in there? We have bigger damn issues than you hugging it out."

I huffed out a laugh at his words and gruff tone. Jameson seemed nice, intense, but in a way that rivaled Tallon, which said something. Like those two could go toe-to-toe and both be left standing. Wonder if he had a stick up his ass like my brother or if he was more easy-going when not stuck in a shit storm chasing two depraved men.

I swallowed hard.

Two.

And I thought it was bad when I just had to watch out for one. Now with this other guy who that profiler Rhyan was almost sure was in the mix, it seemed I needed to be scared, terrified. Now I not only had to worry about the sick voyeur bastard but also the one who enjoyed torturing his victims before killing them on camera.

Would all this stop, no more women turned to victims, if they had me? I shook my head. No, only catching them would make the two sickos stop.

A loud crash from the living room sent me shooting off the bed. Maneuvering beneath Jameson's arm, I pushed the door open wider, stepped into the living room, and skidded to a stop. Glass littered the floor beneath the overturned metal frame that used to be the coffee table.

I gaped at the mess before turning to Bryson and Tallon. Bryson stood in the kitchen, his eyes clenched shut in what appeared to be utter agony. I started toward him, but a pitiful cry to my right had me drawing up short at finding my brother, my big, strong nothing-ever-fazed him brother on the floor, back against the wall, devastation written on his face.

I jerked one way, then the other, not sure who to go to first.

"What's going on?" Jameson said right behind me. When neither answered, he started toward Tallon.

"Charlie," Bryson croaked. The pain in his voice jolted me into action. I stumbled over my own feet in my desperation to get to him. I wrapped my arms around him, burying my face against his shoulder. "A video was just sent to him."

"Of me?" I said, my lips brushing again the fabric of his shirt.

"No." Breaking out of my hold, his arms engulfed me, squeezing so tight I almost couldn't breathe.

"Selena." Tallon's crackling voice had me twisting to see him. Jameson crouched beside him, a hand on Tallon's shoulder. "He had Selena."

Had?

My stomach dropped to my feet while what little I'd had to eat that day made its way up my throat. "What do you mean, had?" I rasped.

Neither responded. Bryson just squeezed me even tighter. The laptop open in front of us, the screen blank, caught my attention. I glanced up, finding Bryson's eyes still squeezed shut, head shaking. All that should've told me I shouldn't do what I was about to do. But what could I say? I was brilliant at being self-destructive.

Toxic trait number one hundred and forty-three?

My fingers trembled as I slowly reached out to tap the spacebar, bringing the blank screen to life. A section of the screen was blacked out with a Play icon in the middle, calling to me to push it. Maneuvering the small arrow to the center of the video display, I clicked on it.

No one moved or shouted as the video played, everyone too over-whelmed to pay any attention to me. The black screen flickered, and then a bright light illuminated a single naked female restricted to a metal chair.

A familiar female.

Special Agent Burton.

I hugged Bryson tighter, eyes glued to the screen, unable to look away.

Gagged, dark liquid coated her skin, drawing attention to long lacerations along her legs and arms, the light glinting off the blood. Her once beautiful face was swollen, gashed, yet the expression of sheer terror was still clear as day as she watched something or someone off-screen.

My heart raced, and sweat slicked my skin, making my hair stick to my forehead and the back of my neck. Agent Burton struggled in the chair, mouth now open, appearing to be screaming, though no sound poured through the speakers. A man walked across the screen, his back to the camera, but a flash of his profile, that long, dark hair, tugged at a memory.

"I know him," I rasped.

Before I could blink, the screen slammed shut with so much force that I flinched, eyes squeezing shut.

"What the hell are you doing?" Bryson yanked me away from his side and held me at arm's length. Desperation and fear swirled in his hazel eyes, face lacking its normal color. "You don't need to see that. What the hell—"

"What do you mean, know him?" Jameson said, now standing on the other side of the island.

With a growl, Bryson yanked me close, slamming my chest to his and twisting, putting his bulky frame between me and the detective.

"I think... I think that was the man who came to the bar, the fake detective."

"How do you know?" Something inside me wept at Tallon's emotionless tone.

I shrugged. "I'm not positive, but I remembered the guy being attractive but... off. If that makes sense." I chewed on the corner of my lip. "But I need to see it again to be sure."

"No," Tallon and Bryson barked in unison.

"It makes sense," Jameson said.

Tallon reached out, grabbing him by the front of his shirt and shoved him hard.

"She's not watching that." He jabbed a finger in the laptop's direction. "It's a fucking snuff film of someone we know, someone we worked with."

All the color drained from Jameson's face. He swallowed hard and nodded while adjusting his shirt from Tallon's manhandling.

"What do I do now?" I asked no one in particular. "Where can I go?" Tears filled my lower lids as I stared at my sock-covered feet. "Where can I go where he won't follow me and kill anyone associated with me?" Each breath became harder to take. "When will it stop? What if he takes you—"

Bryson whirled me around and held my face between his hands.

"Stop. Breathe."

I tried, I really tried, but each rasp felt like ice slicing down my throat and lungs. With a quick look over my shoulder, he turned back to me, a look of determination in his eyes before sealing his lips on mine.

Tugging me closer, he slipped a hand into my hair and yanked, a bite of pain erupting along my scalp. I gasped, giving him the opportunity to devour me with pure desperation. I kissed him back, fisting his shirt as he pulled me from the edge of a panic attack with each sweep of his tongue. Moving back, he held me in place with the hand in my hair, forcing me to meet his intense gaze.

"We will figure this out and keep you safe. There is no 'I,' you hear me? You are not doing this alone, and you won't try to play the hero by putting yourself in danger. This will not end with you. This only ends with us working together and putting this motherfucker six feet below ground. Do you understand?" I licked my lips, the heat beneath my skin now fueled by lust, then panic. "I said," he gritted out, tugging even harder on my hair, "do you understand?"

"Yes, yes, I understand," I rasped. When his hold relaxed, I slumped forward, my forehead hitting his shoulder. "But what now? I don't... I can't stay here."

With my eyes shut, I could almost feel the three men having a silent conversation.

Tallon was the first to speak up. "There's one place that's secure that we could go. Our parents' estate—"

"Fuck. No." Bryson said before I could. "Not happening."

"Why not?"

"Because if I get anywhere near your mother, I'll either snap her neck or shove her off the balcony. The answer is no. She's not allowed to be within six feet of Tinley or else I will not be responsible for my actions."

"What am I missing?" Tallon questioned, his earlier surprise gone now, exhaustion in his low tone.

I twisted in Bryson's arms to face my brother. "Later. I'll explain later why he's reacting this way."

Tallon sighed and gave a reluctant nod while rubbing a hand over his short blond hair. There was so much sorrow and worry behind his eyes, pulling at my heart. With more effort than I expected, I extracted myself out of Bryson's hold as the need to comfort my big brother mounted. Free from Bryson, I hurried around the island and wrapped my arms around Tallon.

It only took a second before his brawny arms moved around my back and squeezed.

"We need to report the video to the local FBI office and update my task force with the profile and two-suspect angle," he said. "The more people focused on this case, the faster we can catch these two bastards. Can that Charlie guy forward the link to the Nashville director? And see if he can analyze the video for anything we could use to connect the cases or show where he's doing all this."

"Of course, but what about Tinley?" Bryson asked. "We can't stay here."

"I called in a CSI team when I first got here," Jameson added. "They should be here soon to lift prints off the liquor bottle. Though the rest of the apartment is compromised between us and the medics."

"Our only choice is a hotel." Tallon's chest vibrated beneath my cheek with each word. "It's not ideal, but that's our only option at this hour. I'll see if we can get a safe house set up for her if we need a long-term solution."

Stepping back, I wiped my clammy palms down my thighs and nodded. "I'll go pack." But as I stared at my bedroom, I couldn't force my feet to move. "Bryson? Will you come with me?" I hated the weakness in my trembling voice.

With zero hesitation, he gripped my hand and led me across the living room. Guiding me to the bed, he urged me to sit on the edge. His knees popped and he groaned as he squatted to put us at the same level. Despite the shit evening, I smirked, my lips quirking at the edges.

He shot me a dangerous look. "Don't even say it."

An almost smile pulled at my lips. "Whatever you say, old man."

Some of the tightness around the edges of his eyes softened. "You must be okay if you're able to crack jokes."

My shoulders lifted in a small shrug. "Not really okay, but I'm functioning, so I'll take that as a win." Turning my gaze to my fingers, I inhaled deeply. "Is she dead?"

"Yes," he croaked.

"Are you sure? You know videos can be manipulated—"

"I'm sure."

My fingers curled into tight fists. "It's my fault."

"No, it's not. If it's anyone's, it's mine because I brought her here."

"When did she go missing?" I understood uncovering the why wouldn't change the outcome. Agent Burton was dead, but if her death wasn't because of her association with me, it would be a little easier to process.

"I'm not sure if anyone knew she was missing. I'll reach out to her supervisor and ask. Now." He stood and stretched his arms high over his head. "What do you want me to pack for you?"

I chewed on my lip, staring at the dresser drawer I knew he'd rifled through. "He went through my things," I whispered. "He touched my clothes. I don't want to wear anything he touched." A full-body shiver had me hugging myself.

Bryson grunted in what I assumed was agreement. To my surprise, he grabbed my hand again, helping me off the bed. The two other men paid us no attention, too engrossed in whatever conversation they were having, as we moved from my bedroom to Tallon's. Inside, Bryson ripped open various drawers, tossing sweatpants, undershirts, and a few pairs of boxers onto the bed.

"There," he said, staring at the pile of clothes. "That should work until we can order you some new ones."

My heart sank at that thought. I didn't have the money to replace my wardrobe. Maybe I was being dramatic and should get over the thought of wearing clothes that man touched.

"Hey," Bryson said. I blinked, finding him standing in front of me, his lips tugged down in a frown. "We'll get this guy and figure all this out, okay?" I nodded, but he kept going. "You're not doing this alone."

"I know," I whispered. "I just.... For ten years, I worried that this day would come. And now that it's here, I don't know what to do. There are so many moving pieces, and I don't know how we'll catch him this time when we couldn't before."

The bed jostled as he sat beside me. "We have more information this time. You remembered more, which will help. I know you don't know my buddy Charlie, but he's good. If there's anything tying this guy to you, he'll find it. He and Rhyan are on our side, and with those two, I know we can catch this bastard."

A commotion in the living room had us shifting our attention to the doorway just as Jameson raced into the bedroom.

Fuck, what now?

"The station just called. Officers were at the hospital to intercept the ambulance and protect that woman inside, but it never arrived."

"What does that mean?" My voice trembled.

"They turned on the ambulance's tracker and are on their way there now. I've instructed them to proceed with caution."

All I could do was blink at the detective, my mind completely blank.

"He either thought Tinley was in the ambulance or—" Bryson cut himself off with a curse.

"Or?" I croaked.

"Thought it was me. If he was watching the apartment, he knew that was the alcohol I liked. But now that it's her and not me, he might use her as leverage. He's lost the element of surprise. Charlie warned me that the moment he shut off the fucker's feed to the apartment's security footage, he'd know we were on to him. This might be his attempt to gain the upper hand again."

"And that video was an example of what will happen to my sister if we allow that to happen," Tallon said from where he filled the doorway, arms crossed over his chest. I almost rolled my eyes at the arrogant look on his face. "I want Tinley in witness protection. And your mom and Victoria."

A pitiful squeak came from my chest at the thought of those two being in harm's way because of me.

Bryson scrubbed a hand over his face. "This fucking day will not end. Let's find somewhere for tonight. All of us. We four stay together, me and Tinley in one room, you two in the other. Then we decide what to do from there. We need all the information before making a call like that. Maybe the first step is a safe house, then witness protection if we need to get that far. I'll reach out to the family who's housing my mom and Vic, warn them of what's going on so they can be prepared."

"Bryson," I whispered. "I don't…. Nothing can happen to her. I promised her. I promised Victoria I'd do what I had to do to keep her safe."

His features softened. Leaning in, he kissed the side of my head. "And you are by sticking with me." I chanced a look at Tallon, whose eyes were focused on each place Bryson and I touched. But there wasn't anger there. Confusion, longing, or maybe even relief. Any of those I'd take over what I witnessed earlier with him at Bryson's throat. "If you're by my side, then I can focus on keeping her safe by staying one step ahead of this fucker. All of us can think clearer with you within sight."

I nodded, even if it didn't feel right. It felt like if I just gave myself up to this guy, then all the people I loved—or hell, even associated with—would stop dying. But I trusted him. Trusted my brother. If they said this was the right way to do things, then that was what I'd do.

Though deep down in my gut, I knew.

No matter what we did or where I went, he'd find me.

It was a matter of when, not if.

I just hoped that when that time came and I was gone, Bryson and Victoria would be safe, unharmed by the evil shadow that haunted me my entire life.

With all the darkness in my life, maybe this was inevitable.

A fitting end for me.

22

TINLEY

Cold seeped from the tinted window into my shoulder as I stared out into the cloudy night brightened by the blinking downtown Nashville lights. Both arms wrapped around my chest, I hugged myself tight, hoping to calm my nerves.

It didn't work.

Bryson, Jameson, and Tallon worked to secure both rooms: mine and Bryson's the one I was currently standing in, Jameson and Tallon bunking in the adjoining room. The fast food cheeseburger and fries we picked up on the way to the hotel sat heavy in my stomach as the burden of the day—hell, the last ten years—settled, and the reality of my fucked-up situation, of Remington's abduction, and Agent Burton's death hit me square in the chest.

A tight fist circling over my sternum, I willed the increasing tightness to ease.

Four more deaths all because of me. Those medics and the ambulance driver were dead because they stumbled into the darkness encompassing me. Now Remington was missing, and a massive hunt was on to find Agent Burton's body. It was too much to process in such a short time frame.

Chin to my shoulder, I watched Bryson type furiously on his

phone from where he sat on the single king bed. Tallon and Jameson were nowhere to be seen. Their side of the door was closed, no doubt to debate our next move in private. Or possibly work out whatever tension simmered between the two men.

Almost like he could feel my stare, Bryson's gaze flicked from the screen to me.

"Hey, sorry, let me get a couple things in place." With a sad smile, he turned back to his phone, brows pulled tight.

"It's okay. I know this is a lot to coordinate and handle all at once." My heavy sigh fogged the window when I turned back toward the dark night. "What else can happen today?" I grumbled to my disheveled reflection. Messy, slightly greasy hair pulled up in a haphazard bun. Wrinkled clothes that hung limp off my lean frame from the all-day wear. "Will this ever end?"

Warmth soaked into my back a second before arms wrapped around me, tugging my back against a firm chest. "Yes. It will end. We'll find this bastard. I promise, Tinley."

"And what then? What will happen to us?" I asked, my unfocused gaze stuck on the building's lights across the street. "What will happen when all this is over?"

"What do you want to happen?" he asked, tone hesitant.

Twisting around, I wrapped my arms around his chest and sighed at the sense of safety that enveloped me. "I want you. I want you and Victoria and your mom. I want that cute house to be my own. But I have nothing to bring to the table, Bry. I'm broke, broken, and—"

A hard slap to my ass had my next words clogging in my throat, a yelp of surprise escaping instead.

"What have I told you about talking like that?" he snapped. "Get on the bed."

Before I could process the sudden turn of events, I was dragged to the bed and urged to sit on the edge. Eyes wide, heart hammering from anticipation, I watched as he moved about the room, first locking our side of the connecting room door, then stripping off his gun and resting it on the dresser. His heated gaze never left mine.

Hip pressed to the edge of the dresser, Bryson gave me a slow once-over.

"Strip." I slow-blinked, the single word, the casual command short-circuiting my exhausted brain. "Do you really want to know what happens if I have to tell you again?" He arched a brow in challenge and smirked.

I swallowed hard and cleared my throat. Every cell in my body screamed, *"Yes, I want to know what happens if I disobey."* Fingers grasping the edge of my hoodie, the soft material molding beneath my tight hold, I pulled it over my head in a somewhat awkward motion when one arm got stuck in a sleeve and the neck snagged on my thick bun. Tendrils of my pinkish hair escaped the hair tie, falling alongside my face and tickling the back of my neck.

Heat sizzled beneath my skin, dampness pooling between my thighs as I continued to strip the layers of clothing until all that remained were my socks, underwear, and sports bra.

Bryson trailed his hazel eyes along my bare skin, frowning when he came to the remaining clothing.

"All of it."

Shifting side to side, I wrangled myself out of the snug sports bra, my breasts already heavy and nipples pebbled, desperate for his mouth and teeth. The musky scent of my arousal wafted through the air as I slid my damp panties down my thighs and kicked them to the growing pile of discarded clothes.

A flash of panic surged when I stared at my socks. He'd said everything, but I hated my feet, hated how ugly they were from years of dance and damage from those weeks in captivity.

Sensing my hesitation, he shoved off the dresser and closed the short distance between us. His hold was soft yet unyielding as he wrapped a hand around my neck, thumb beneath my chin, tipping my face upward. Searching eyes scanned my face before his head dipped in a clipped nod.

"Every part of you is beautiful, Tinley. Don't hide anything from me." Squatting, he held up one foot and slowly stripped off the warm, thick sock. Meeting my worried gaze, he held up the ugliest part of me, the part I hid at all costs, and kissed the arch. My heart swelled as he moved to the next foot, repeating the process. Setting both bare feet on the thin hotel room carpet, he pressed his hands into the mattress beside me, jostling me. Face an inch from mine, he brushed a gentle kiss along my lips. "Yes, you have something to bring to my life, to Victoria's life. You. You bring you, and that's everything I never knew I needed, but now that I have it, I never want to live without."

Shoving off the bed, he stood at full height, chin dipped as he stared down at me.

"Now. You need a distraction, don't you?" I nodded. Fuck yes, I needed a distraction from this day, from this life. His smirk turned savage. "Well?" He flicked his gaze to his crotch, where his hard cock tented the front of his jeans. My fingers curled, gathering handfuls of the comforter in my hold. I licked my dry lips. "You want it, then you know what to do. Take out my cock, Tinley."

That deep voice, those filthy words caused a shiver of pleasure to race through me, and a new rush of arousal slipped from my core. My fingers shook as I worked his belt and popped the top button of his jeans. A tug drew down the waist band an inch, revealing the swollen head. Peering up through my lashes, I eased forward. With the tip of my tongue, I licked the drop of precum from his slit, a cruel smile forming when he tossed his head back in pure bliss.

A harsh hiss followed by a moaned curse filled the room. Thick fingers wove into my hair, tightening at the base.

"Cock teases don't get a reward," he rasped, his hooded gaze now solely focused on me.

I was naked, dripping wet, no doubt leaving evidence of my arousal on the bedspread. I should care, but all I wanted was his thick cock in my mouth. To hear him let go because of me and for me to use him to help push the events of the day out of my mind.

The grind of his zipper filled my ears as I slowly worked it lower. A hand cupping each firm ass cheek, I pressed the material low on his hips, allowing his hard cock to pop free from the confines of his boxer briefs. With a tight grip around him, I pumped my hand. His hips flexed, thrusting harder. Pressure against the back of my head urged me closer until my lips brushed against him. Lips parted, I enveloped the soft head and swirled my tongue before sliding down his shaft.

"Fuck, your mouth is heaven. Touch yourself." Bryson's strained voice had a groan vibrating in my throat. "Yes," he hissed.

Not giving myself a chance to reconsider, I glided a hand between my thighs, slipping a single finger between my wet folds. The moment my finger pressed against my swollen clit, I gasped, jaw widening to take his dick deeper until it bumped the back of my throat. Up and down I slid my lips along his cock in time with the tight circles I drew with the pad of my finger against myself.

Another hand slipped into my hair, holding me still with an unrelenting grip. My leg muscles spasmed as my finger sped up to match Bryson's thrusts, slowly fucking my mouth, going deeper with each plunge.

Tears leaked from my eyes, thighs trembling with the need to close but restricted with him standing between my spread legs as I climbed higher and higher, chasing my release as he did his own.

"Damn, you have the perfect mouth," he said. "Look at me."

Forcing my eyes open, I peered up at him through my wet lashes.

"Watch me as I fuck this beautiful mouth." I whimpered at his dirty words. The effect hitched me higher, my finger speeding up. "Finger-fuck yourself, baby." Pulling all the way out, he stared down between my legs where my other hand had slipped off his thigh and between my own. "Now," he growled.

A pitiful whine carried through the room as I plunged three fingers deep inside my pussy. My breath hitched, hips moving as I thrust my fingers in and out, inching me toward release.

"Stop," he commanded.

I ignored him, too lost in chasing my release to care about the consequences. A solid grip on my wrist wrenched my hand free, a cry escaping at the sudden loss.

Taking the fingers I'd just had deep inside me, he wiped the slickness along his cock. I watched as the evidence of my arousal glistened along the silky smooth skin. Stretching my hand higher, he stuck those three fingers between his lips while his other hand forced my mouth back open and he thrust his hips forward, filling me.

The musky taste of him mixed with me had my eyes fluttering closed. Bryson's tongue swirled along my fingers, teeth scraping at the skin as he sucked every drop before pulling them free of his lips and stepping back. I followed the movement, desperate to keep that connection between us, but he gripped my head, forcing my face to the ceiling, holding me in place.

A gentle yet dominant tug pulled me to the mattress, the cool comforter a shock to the overheated skin along my back. Fingers wrapped tight around my ankles and wrenched upward. Without warning, he spread my raised legs wide and thrust forward, sinking balls deep in one powerful thrust. Mouth open, no sound escaping, I arched off the bed, hands grappling for purchase on the comforter to keep me in place. Releasing my ankles, allowing them to rest on his shoulders, he pressed forward, almost bending me in two.

A dull burn heated my muscles with the intense stretch and pressure, but the pleasure from this new angle shoved the discomfort to the background. Teeth sunk deep into my lower lip, I squeezed both lids shut as a body-trembling release shot through me while he continued to pound my pussy. Tears leaked from the corners of my eyes as pleasure raced through every cell and nerve.

"Fuck," he grunted. "You're squeezing the life from my cock, baby. Don't fucking stop."

I couldn't even if I tried. He filled every inch of me, each thrust creating additional ripples of pleasure.

"Pinch your nipples," he commanded, his darkened gaze on my bouncing tits.

With zero hesitation, I cupped both full breasts, pinching both nipples between my fingers until the bite of pain forced a hiss from my clenched teeth.

"That's it, baby. Damn, you're perfect. Perfect pussy, perfect tits, perfect woman inside and out."

"Just fuck me," I groaned. I didn't want the sweet right now. I needed that anger and frustration back that forced me to swallow his dick.

"Yes, ma'am." He chuckled. "Let's see how flexible you still are."

"Yes," I cried out as he spread my legs wide, hands slipping down the inside of each one as they spread wider and wider. "Farther," I ordered when he stopped at the first hint of my muscles resisting.

He kept pushing with my encouragement until I was in a full split, legs spread as wide as they could go.

"Holy fuck," he groaned.

"Imagine this while you fuck my ass." Just the vision of the future dirty scene had me crying out a second time, his own barked curse signaling his release. Warmth filled me, making me realize we didn't use a condom. Not that I gave two fucks. I trusted him to not endanger my health, and I'd had an IUD for years, preventing pregnancy until I was ready.

Releasing my legs, he fell forward, collapsing on top of me. All the air rushed from my lungs at the delicious weight. But instead of forcing him off, I curled my arms around his back, the T-shirt damp beneath my fingers, and wrapped my legs around his waist.

"I think I'm dead," he mumbled into the bed beside my ear.

I didn't stop my wide smile. "Don't be dead. I need us to do that a few more times before bed."

"You'll be the death of me, woman."

"But what a way to go, right?"

Pushing up, he pressed his lips to mine in a searing kiss. Not breaking our connection, Bryson pushed off the bed and stood with me wrapped around him. Clutching his head, I kissed him with every ounce of emotion in my heart.

"I meant what I said," I told him, pulling back an inch as we moved through the small room. "I love you, Bryson. I love you, all of you." I winced when the harsh bathroom light flashed on.

"I don't know how it's possible," he said, slowly lowering me to the floor. The cold tile bit into the too-hot skin of my bare feet. "For someone like you to love a man like me. All I know is that this between us is beyond anything I've ever felt. When you're not around, you're all I think about. You're in my dreams and somehow my reality too. I'd say I love you too, but I can't." I sucked in a breath as hurt radiated through me. "Because this is too strong for such a simple word. You're the fresh air I've long been suffocating for. Every smile, every look makes me want to fall on my knees and worship you for the amazing woman you are. How can this be love when it feels like so much more here?" He rested his hand over his heart.

Tears welled and leaked freely from the corners of my eyes.

"I have little to offer you, Tinley, but I can tell you I'll love you until my last breath. My every thought and breath will be for you and Victoria. I will spend every day making sure you know how much you mean to me and how your presence gives me life. This isn't a marriage proposal. I wouldn't do that in a cheap hotel room amid everything we're going through. It's a commitment to you that I'm yours. Where you go, I'll go, because I don't want this life without you in it."

My shoulders shook as I held back a happy sob. Reaching up, I cupped his beard-covered cheeks between my palms and pulled his lips down to meet mine. This kiss was soft, a sealing of our commitments to each other. The taste of salt hit my tongue as my tears made their way over our lips.

"Now to survive this. Then we make plans for the future," I said after pulling back.

Bryson nodded, and a shy smile tugged at his swollen lips. "Plan our forever." Sounded perfect to me. "Now." His slap to my ass rang out in the small bathroom. "Let's get in the shower. When my girl says she needs more of me to sleep, then more of me is what she'll get."

I bit my lip, chancing a glance down, finding his cock back to half-mast. Gripping the hem of his shirt, I tugged it upward, revealing the row of taut ab muscles. As he finished stripping the T-shirt off, I trailed my short nails down his stomach, digging in ever so slightly to leave red streaks along his tan skin. Continuing lower, I gripped the waistband of his jeans and tugged them and his boxer briefs down until they pooled around his boots.

He toed off one worn boot, then the other, and I helped him step out of his jeans before he tugged off his socks. Kneeling in front of him, I ran my palms up his thick thighs, gripping the taut muscles and reveling in their strength.

"Damn, I love the way you look at me," he said, voice rough.

"You're amazing," I whispered. "You have no idea how many nights I imagined this. Fantasized about what you'd look like naked and wanting me. I should be embarrassed of how many times I played with myself with you on my mind, but"—I tipped my chin up and met his hooded stare—"I'm not."

Looping both hands beneath my arms, he raised me until I had both feet beneath me.

"I have no clue why," he said, eyes searching mine.

"One day, I'll get you to see just what an amazing man you are. Not only to me but a great friend to my brother, a dedicated man to putting the evil around us behind bars, and what makes you one in a million is the father you are to that adorable little girl. She will always know her worth because you're beside her, telling her she's even more than she believes. Your smoking-hot body is enough to make any woman want you, Bryson, but it's you, the man you are, who made me fall for you before you ever knew my heart was yours."

When he opened his eyes, raw emotion poured through, lashes wet from his unshed tears.

"Thank you," he rasped.

"I promise not to take you or your amazing heart for granted. Ever." Interlacing our fingers, I pulled him toward the glass-encased shower.

Moving me aside, he reached in and twisted the handle to the right, taking the initial blast of cold water instead of me.

Well, there you go. A hot, sweet man exists in the world.

Bryson Bennett might be the only one ever created, and I for fucking sure was not sharing this unicorn with anyone else. No, I'd stab the woman who tried to take him away from me and feel zero remorse after.

Stepping into the now-warm spray, I sighed as the heat relaxed my tight muscles. A moan vibrated past parted lips as powerful hands wrapped around my shoulders and began kneading, pressing in all the right spots.

Rough calluses scraped down my wet skin, stopping to grip my hips.

"Were you serious?" he asked, slick lips brushing against the shell of my ear.

"About what?" Leaning back, I grabbed one of his hands and moved it toward the apex of my thighs. My breath hitched as I pushed his fingers between my folds.

His other hand grabbed a handful of my ass, squeezing hard enough to no doubt leave a bruise. "Letting me take this ass one day." He slipped his fingers between my cheeks to press on my tight hole.

"Yes," I gasped. "But not today unless you packed some lube."

His dark chuckle sent a shiver down my spine. "Soon, then."

"Yes, please." Internally, I chastised myself for forgetting all my fun toys. Shower sex was way more fun with teasing at every erogenous zone.

I wasn't always this sexual, my teen years more dedicated to dance than finding a partner who knew what he was doing. The years after my abduction, while trying to find anything that would fill the gaping hole in my dark soul and keep me busy, out of my head, were when I realized how much fun sex could be—with the right person. However, none of my past exploits compared to this. I was safe with Bryson. I could relax and completely let go, knowing he was there to catch me.

"Good thing that's not the only place I can fuck." His hard cock slid between my ass cheeks, sliding up and down as his finger plunged into my wet center. "I want to fuck those tits tonight, but first let's see if I can make you scream just like this."

And holy fuck.

He did.

Twice.

23

BRYSON

Wednesday, December 12th

Watching her sleep was fucking creepy, but I couldn't bring myself to care enough to stop. Long pinkish-blonde hair, somehow still damp from the shower before bed, splayed out along the white pillow. Lips I loved to kiss parted, the sheet covering her naked chest rising and falling with each of her deep breaths.

Beautiful was too mundane a word to describe Tinley.

A sliver of guilt wove its way into my gut, making me shift my attention to the dark TV sitting on the dresser across from the bed.

Had I ever done this with Heather? Was I ever completely in awe, enamored by her beauty and heart? I racked my brain to remember the early stages of us dating, but only our wild sexcapades around the office, keeping our relationship hidden, came to mind.

I loved my late wife.

Didn't I?

Rubbing a palm along my beard, the scrape of the coarse hair filled my ears.

Maybe there were different versions of love. That was what made what I felt for Heather and what I now felt toward Tinley so opposite. With Tinley, I was almost obsessed, her presence imprinted on every cell in my body. With Heather, it was easy, cold at times, but routine. There was nothing routine about Tinley, which I loved. Her passion and ever-changing mood were fascinating and entertaining.

Not that I'd ever tell her that. I wasn't that great with women, but telling her I found her shifting moods entertaining would no doubt keep me sex deprived and suffering from blue balls for a month.

Even now, I didn't view those years spent with Heather as a mistake. There were positives mixed with the bad. Of course, the best part of that marriage was Victoria. Knowing I'd have her at the end of it all, I'd do it all over again. Even knowing my heart would hurt for years after Heather's death, and even before that from her constant neglect and coldness.

Tinley stirred beside me, snuggling closer and wrapping an arm around my bare chest.

The corners of my lips tweaked upward.

Tinley made me feel wanted, desired—loved. I never knew a relationship could be this way. When both people were open with their feelings, carefree with their needs and desires, touching just because they could.

A knock on the door beside the bed had me groaning and shifting out of Tinley's hold. To not be a prick and rub my relationship with his sister in his face, I slipped on a pair of sweats before opening the adjoining room door. Tallon glared at my bare chest.

"What?" I grumbled, crossing both arms and widening my stance. If he wanted to fight again, I sure as hell wouldn't give him another free shot. My temple and jaw still ached from yesterday.

He eyed the brightly lit room behind me. "She still can't sleep in the dark?"

"Nope."

"That bother you?"

"Nope."

He sighed. "You didn't tell me you got new ink," he muttered, hitching his chin toward my decorated arms. "I like it."

We stood in awkward silence for a beat. I wasn't sure what to say, which really sucked dirty dick since Tallon was my best friend. I hated this awkwardness my relationship with his sister had wedged between us. It would take time, time away from this shit tornado we were stuck in the middle of, but hopefully he'd revert to the Tallon I called my best friend.

"You want my guy's number?" I asked, arching a brow. This was a running joke between us. There was no way Tallon would allow anyone to permanently mark his skin.

He snorted and shook his head. "Well, I can't say my suggestion didn't help your fucking grumpy ass. Just wish the solution wasn't with my sister."

My lips twitched. "Can't say I'm sorry it happened, but I am sorry you found out the way you did."

"Yeah, that was a punch to the balls."

"You know I won't let anything happen to her."

Tallon's tight features softened. "I know, and I know you're good for her. Just give me longer than twenty-four hours to stop busting your balls about it."

My chest rumbled with a low laugh. "Deal. Now, what do you want if it's not to bust my chops about dating your sister?"

"We need to discuss our next moves. We can't stay here forever, and I want to put this fucker behind bars ASA-fucking-P."

"Any updates on Agent Burton?" I didn't need to finish the thought. Tallon knew what I was asking. Had her body been recovered?

Tallon shook his head and looked back into his room. Tilting to the side, I saw the Nashville detective walking around the hotel room, a small white towel wrapped around his waist.

"He's going to the station to handle things from the local level. We have jurisdiction because of the tie between these murders and the bastard my task force is after." He inhaled deep and shook his head. "Two of these nasty fuckers. Who would've thought?"

"Makes you wonder how they met. Is there some kind of app for that shit?"

"Let's fucking hope not. Can you imagine if the bastards we hunt all teamed up with a partner? They'd be that much harder to identify and catch." We both gave that thought a heavy beat of silence. "My last count was thirty-two women across the country. Thirty-two women who went through hell before they died. What if... what if there are more? What if I can't catch them before—"

I shoved his shoulder, making his bright blue eyes snap to me and narrow. "It's not just you, it's we. We are a team working together to catch these two. You're not doing this alone. We have the full force of the FBI at our beck and call, and Charlie and Rhyan are the best. We will catch these two."

He started to say something, but a vibration had me stretching for my cell phone moving on top of the nightstand. I glanced at the screen.

"It's Charlie."

"Hmm" came a half sigh, half grumble from the bed. Her ice-blue eyes blinked open and found me, a small smile tugging her lips upward only for it to fall when she glanced over my shoulder to where I felt Tallon standing. "What's wrong?"

"Not sure." Knee to the bed, I leaned forward and kissed the top of her head. I twisted toward Tallon. "Give her a second to get dressed. Then we'll come to your room. I'm not leaving her alone for a second."

"Good idea," he said instead of giving me hell. Then he spun on his heels, disappearing through the open doorway.

"Let me call you back," I said into the phone instead of a greeting.

"No. We talk now. We have a strong suspect," Charlie said instead.

I immediately popped off the bed. Digging through my bag, I tossed a pair of sweats, her sports bra from yesterday, and my FBI sweatshirt over my shoulder toward the bed.

"Get dressed," I said. "Charlie and Rhyan have something."

Her eyes widened, all signs of lingering drowsiness gone. In the next blink, she slid off the bed, the sheet puddling around her narrow waist, leaving her full bare breasts fully exposed. They held my rapt attention, the peaked nipples begging for my lips and teeth.

"Hey," she said, snapping her fingers. "Killer. Stalker. Missing friend. Get out of your tit trance."

I shook my head. A low laugh rumbled through the other end of the line, telling me Charlie heard her words.

"Shut the fuck up," I grumbled, snagging a T-shirt for myself out of my bag and holding it tight in my fist.

"Hey, man, I get it," Charlie said, humor in his tone. "But time and place, man."

"Tell that to my dick."

"I'm not talking to your dick. That's strange even for me, and I'm into some kinky-ass shit. The other night, Rhyan and I—" A chuckle shook my chest at the following barked curse and mumbled apologies. "Sorry, baby. You're right, he doesn't need to hear the details. He'll just get jealous about—oof. Stop hitting me."

The moment Tinley was fully dressed, I pressed a hand to her lower back, guiding her across the room toward the adjoining one. Thankfully, Jameson had ditched the towel and was finishing buttoning up his dress shirt from the day before, now fully covered in wrinkled slacks.

Tinley stood awkwardly to the side as Tallon's and Jameson's eyes both zeroed in on me.

Pulling the phone from my ear, I flipped it to Speaker.

"We're all here. Go ahead, Charlie."

"Based on the profile Rhyan gave me and some search parameters, I gathered a rather long list of names from those who purchased tickets to the ballet performances Tinley performed in during that last year. Then I narrowed that down to those who bought more than once. Then we added in some details from the other case—"

"I figured with the two very different personalities, even if Unsub One wasn't the one torturing and killing, he'd want to be a part of the selection process for their victims," Rhyan cut in. "So I asked Charlie to run the names on that long list against anyone who'd traveled to the cities where the bodies Agent Harper was investigating appeared. That brought us down to three names."

"Three," Tallon stated, awe in his almost reverent tone. "That's amazing."

"Thank you," the two said in unison.

"But there's more," Charlie said, clearly excited about this additional revelation. "I looked deeper into the three, and guess what I found?"

We shifted closer to the phone lying atop of the unmade bed.

"What?" Tinley asked.

"One, a Mr. Drew Trent Vincent, lived right next door to the house Tinley was deposited in front of ten years ago."

"It's him," I said, excitement thrumming through my veins.

"That name sounds familiar," Tinley said beside me.

The second she said it, I nodded because it did sound familiar.

"Probably because he's a partner in the firm that's running the cybersecurity for Tinley's stepfather's investment firm."

"What are we waiting for?" Tallon snapped. "Let's go bring that fucker—"

"Don't," Rhyan said, almost panicked. "You can't."

"Why the fuck not?" I said through gritted teeth.

"It's circumstantial evidence," Jameson said with a heavy exhale. "There's nothing really tying him to either Tinley's case ten years ago or the murders."

"He's right, whoever that unfamiliar voice is," Rhyan agreed. "Charlie can't even tie the line of code he found to Vincent. Everything we have is circumstantial at best. A judge would never grant a warrant for his arrest or even a search warrant of his home based on this information. We need more."

Silence filled the room.

"Remington?" Tinley asked, coming to sit right beside the phone. "Have we heard about Remington?" Tallon placed a comforting hand on her shoulder. "Anything?"

"No," Charlie rasped. Fuck, he was torn up about this as much as us. He'd sent her to me, and shit went south. My friend no doubt felt responsible for her abduction. "The techs processed the ambulance but couldn't find anything that would tell us where she was taken. They sent scent dogs to the scene but came up empty-handed...or empty pawed?"

"Pawed," Rhyan said. "They don't have hands."

"I can't just sit here with a name, the name of the bastard tracking Tinley and who—" I snapped my mouth shut and squeezed my eyes closed, tilting my face to the ceiling. "I can't just sit on my ass doing nothing while he's out there."

A ding of another cell phone pierced the air. Jameson pulled his out, blanching at whatever he read on the screen.

"They found a body just outside of downtown. They think it's the female FBI agent."

I swallowed hard to keep my pain and anger shoved down deep. Tallon roared and spun, slamming a fist into the drywall, sending bits of plaster crumbling to the floor. Tinley buried her face into her palms, quiet sobs leaking through her fingers.

"I can go—"

I held up a hand, cutting Jameson off. "This might be a way to split us up, singling us out to make a grab at another person close to Tinley."

"I agree," Rhyan said.

Different scenarios ran through my mind about what to do next.

"Would there be any harm in going over to Vincent's residence, seeing if we can get him to slip up about an alibi or something?" It was a stretch, but hell, I was desperate to nail this fucker. If I couldn't get him behind bars the legal way, I was prepared to take a less-than-legal route. Anything to protect the woman I loved.

"No, but it will tip him off that we have our suspect pool narrowed down to him," Charlie said. "He already knows I'm on to him because I've cut off his camera access around town, and he sent that link with the video directly to me."

"Can we tie him to the video that way?" Tallon asked. "That was a fucking snuff film with an FBI agent. We can prosecute—"

"Already tried," Charlie said, sounding utterly exhausted. Fuck, he and Rhyan must have stayed up all night working on this for us. "He bounced the signal between servers, different countries, different IP addresses. There's no way for me to track it to him specifically."

"What if we seized his computers?" Jameson asked.

"He's smart enough to cover his tracks. If there's even a hint of someone digging, he'll have a backdoor switch ready to wipe his systems if triggered."

"Thanks, Charlie," I said. "I'm sure you're beat. Send me over everything you have on this Vincent guy and—"

"Wait," Tinley called out in a rush. Chewing on her lip, she looked from me to the phone and back again. "Can I talk to Agent Rhyan?"

"I'm here," Rhyan's soft voice poured through the speaker.

I nodded, but Tinley shook her head. "Not in here. I want to talk to her alone."

I paused at that, my worried gaze slipping over to Tallon, who studied his sister, just as concerned.

"Of course," Rhyan said before I could respond. "Take me off speakerphone."

Immediately, Tinley snatched the phone and touched the audio button, switching it so they could have a private conversation. But when she maneuvered around me, heading toward the other room, I gripped her elbow and tugged her to a stop.

I tilted my head toward Tallon and Jameson's bathroom. "In there." I pursed my lips at her frown. "I can't risk you being out of sight like that. Please don't ask me to." I would beg if needed. There was no way I could give her the privacy she clearly wanted with her in another room, alone and vulnerable.

Her features softened. Standing tall, she pressed a kiss to my cheek before twisting on her sock-covered feet and hurrying to the bathroom. When the door closed with a soft click, I turned to the other two.

"What's that about?" Tallon asked, stepping to stand beside me.

"No clue," I muttered. "Maybe she needed a female's perspective on this? A serial killer took Rhyan, almost killed her, but I don't think Tinley knows that. At least I haven't told her."

"We need a plan," Jameson said, snapping me out of my thoughts.

"Tallon can stay here with Tinley," I said, staring at my bare feet while I plotted our next steps. "I'll go with you, identify the body, and help with the investigation. Then you and I are going by this fucker's home and see if we can rattle his cage a bit. We need him off-tilt. Up to this point, he's had a plan, and we've been on the defense. If we can catch him off guard, maybe he'll slip up, make a mistake we can actually arrest him on."

With an agreeing grunt from both men, we shifted into action. While getting dressed, I fought the urge to tell Tallon to go in my stead, that I'd be the one who stayed behind with Tinley. But I knew this was the best option for everyone. Tallon wouldn't be distracted by her fuckable lips and long legs that felt amazing wrapped around my waist while I sank deep into her center...

Fuck.

I gave myself a hard slap, the sting snapping my mind back to what was important. This was not the time for my dick to be the head thinking. If we wanted to catch this guy, find some evidence we could use to prosecute him, then I needed to focus, not think about the woman I loved with all my heart and each inch of my soul.

She needed me to be strong for her. To go out there and get shit done.

And that was exactly what I planned to do.

A STEADY THROB pulsed along my jaw from keeping it clenched it all day. Seeing Selena's beaten, tortured body almost pushed me over the edge of my control. I'd seen bodies with worse treatment, sure, but this was someone I knew. Someone who, days before, was so full of life and didn't deserve any of what happened to her. How they subdued an agent was something none of us could solve. The unsub had to have had the element of surprise on his side, but even then,

Selena was a fighter. She had hours and hours of self-defense and combat training.

So how? How did he get the drop on her?

From what Tinley said in the therapy session, it sounded like the fucker Vincent used chloroform when he attacked, yet there were no burns or redness around Selena's nose and mouth which would indicate the use of chloroform on a rag pressed tight.

So what did he use? The same drug he put in those bottles at the apartment to knock out Remington so fast? We needed to know what was in the bourbon. The seat groaned as I leaned back to reach deep into my front pocket and extract my phone. Pressing a number I'd already called twice today, I held the phone to my ear.

"Davidson County—"

"CSI department please. This is Special Agent Bryson Bennett with the—" Without another word, the line went silent. Tapping my fingers along the door, I watched the downtown streets fly by the window. Thankfully, the snow didn't hit this far south, which made the driving easier than it had been in Louisville.

"Criminal Science—"

"This is Special Agent Bryson Bennett. I need to know what you found in the liquor bottles in Agent Harper's residence. Have those been processed?"

"Agent, I need approval before I release the details of an active investigation—"

"Fuck the red tape. I need to know now. There's a young woman's life on the line. Don't let those higher-ranking assholes' rules get in the way of us finding her before she's killed." Sure, I laid it on thick, but I needed answers. Now.

"I drew samples from all the bottles and ran them through the mass spectrometer. All the samples came back with high levels of one drug: ketamine."

After thanking the CSI tech, I tossed the phone to my lap. "Ketamine," I said out loud, looking to the driver seat. Jameson's brows shot up his forehead. "That makes sense with how fast it acted. Though how did he get that in liquid form?"

"It's unfortunately not that difficult to get a hold of. Special K is a drug anyone can purchase if they know the right dealer. It's become somewhat of an issue in the Nashville area as of late," Jameson mumbled into his hand as he rubbed it along his lips. "None of which we could trace."

Great. Just fucking great.

24

TINLEY

Still dressed in Bryson's oversized clothes, I leaned against the window, surveying the pedestrians walking along the sidewalks. Annoyance and jealousy grew as I observed them living carefree. No one stalked them. No one died because of proximity or association. How nice would that be, a life without constantly looking over your shoulder or darkness lurking in the corners of your mind?

Tallon's deep voice had me turning his direction. Still on his phone, coordinating a safe house for me to stay until they caught this guy. Not that any of us had a clue when that would happen.

The sun's afternoon rays heated the glass pane, soaking warmth into my forehead as I bobbed it back and forth, running the conversation with Agent Rhyan from earlier over again in my mind. She was certain this guy wouldn't stop until he had me or was dead. Based on the conversation between the guys and Charlie, it sounded like arresting him was out of the question unless he slipped up. Which, according to Rhyan, probably wouldn't happen unless they forced him to abandon his well-thought-out plan for me and improvise.

How we could disrupt his plan, get ahead of him for once, was the mystery she and Charlie were working nonstop to figure out. The main reason I wanted to talk to her alone was for information. Not specifically on this Drew guy but some insight into what to do if he abducted me again.

According to Rhyan, though, it wasn't an *if* but when.

When he abducted me again.

It was unsettling to know my previous thoughts were right, but strangely comforting. This way I could plan—or rather we, Rhyan and I—for when that time came. Prepared with her profile, what to say and how to direct the conversation to keep me alive and unharmed until the guys could find me, it made me feel... powerful. Having the knowledge to beat the bastard at his own game, even if he won at kidnapping me, was amazing.

I couldn't remember the last time I felt this strong on my own. Sure, with Bryson, I felt invincible, but by myself, not so much until now.

And that strength, the knowledge that I could overcome whatever was thrown at me, was remarkable. It felt like a piece of me, a piece that bastard stole ten years ago, shifted back into place. I now looked forward to a future, actually *saw* a future—a bright one.

When I was caught, held by the same man who'd destroyed my future, took the freedom I'd looked forward to, I could fight back.

I would win.

"You okay?"

I startled at the closeness of Tallon's voice. Shifting to lie back against the window, I tucked a pinkish lock behind my ear. "Yeah, just thinking."

"Ready to share what you and Agent Rhyan talked about?" The back of my head rolled along the tinted glass as I slowly shook it. "Fine," he grumbled.

Shoving his hands into the side pocket of his sweats, he came to stand beside me, taking in the downtown view. After a few minutes of tense silence, I couldn't take it anymore.

"What's with you and Jameson?" I asked in a rush. "You two seem...." I tilted my head one way, then the other. "Familiar but awkward."

Tallon cleared his throat and shook his head. "We were friends, I guess you could say."

"Wait. Are you gay?" I blurted before immediately covering my mouth. "Sorry."

He shot me a side-eyed glare. "Would that bother you?"

"Are you kidding me?" I dropped my hands to my side, jaw slack. "Fuck no, it wouldn't bother me. It would bother me if you didn't feel you could tell me, if you were hiding something from me. You know I love you no matter what."

He raised a blond brow. "Interesting. If you feel that way about me, why would you not think I feel the same way about you, Tin? Why didn't you ever tell me you were into my best friend?"

"You're avoiding the question," I retorted, not liking how he'd diverted the conversation back to me.

"So are you," Tallon countered with a knowing smirk.

"You first," I encouraged, jabbing him in the chest with a single finger for emphasis.

"No, I'm not gay. Jameson and I... we had a complicated friendship. One that"—he brought two fingers up to pinch the bridge of his nose, squeezing both eyes shut—"ended."

"Why?" I pressed. Shifting closer, I laid my head against his shoulder.

"Because things happened."

"Cryptic," I muttered, earning me a huffed laugh from Tallon. "For what it's worth, he seems like a nice guy. I can see why y'all would be good friends."

"Why do you ask?"

I lifted a shoulder. "I want you to have more than just me and Bryson, more than work to fill your day. It would be nice to know when I move to Louisville that you have someone here." I scrunched my nose. "I kind of feel stingy taking your only friend."

"You're really going to do it? Move in with him?"

"Well, yeah. It's not like I have anything holding me to Nashville." He flinched like I'd threatened to slap him across the face with a dildo. "Don't take that personally. You're always gone, Tal. I get it, you're trying to prevent other women from going through what I did, so you pour yourself into your job. I don't resent you. But this is my chance to move on, and I'm taking it."

Turning on his heels, he moved to the desk chair and fell into the seat. "I don't want to see either of you hurt. I can't—" His voice cracked. "When he lost Heather, I almost lost him. And every time you fall back into the same habits, same routines, I almost lose you." The sheer worry in his tight eyes made my heart hurt. "I love you both, and I want you both to be happy. I really do. I just can't lose either of you if this doesn't work out."

I curled my fingers into a tight fist. "Stop waiting for the other shoe to drop," I snapped. "I'm doing better. I'm better with him. And I'd never do nothing to endanger that sweet little girl."

"I know you wouldn't, and I can see that you're doing better. I'm happy for you. I just...." He groaned and squeezed the back of his neck until his knuckles went white. "I'll always be waiting for the shoe to drop because then I won't be caught unaware again." I sucked in a breath. This was the first time he'd ever admitted to why he waited for me to fail. "At least if I expect it, expect that call to come, it won't hurt as much. If I'm prepared, then...." He released a breath. "Then maybe I won't drown in this fucking guilt I can't seem to escape. I wasn't there for you the night you were taken. I was supposed to be there, remember? I was supposed to come watch your performance."

"Yeah," I stated, not understanding where he was going with that statement. "You would always come when you could." Back then, Bryson was just coming off his undercover stint as a junior agent, and Tallon was moving up the ranks at the Nashville FBI field office. When he could make it work, he came to a performance, which I loved, but when he couldn't, he didn't, and I thought nothing about it.

Until now.

"I should've been there. I should've been there that night and maybe the fucker would've seen me and known I'd rip him limb from limb if he got near you. If I wouldn't have been so fucking selfish that night, if I would've left—" He cut himself off. "That call from your dance company the next day asking if I knew where you were gutted me. And I've been free-falling since."

I sucked in a breath at the pain in his voice. Hurrying over, I wrapped my arms around his neck and squeezed.

"I'm sorry. I always expect the worst. It has nothing to do with you, Tinley. Nothing. Do you hear me?" Moving my arms, he pushed me back so I could look him in the face. "It has everything to do with me trying like hell to make sure I'm never caught off guard again. I fucked up that night, and I'm doing everything I can to make up for it now."

"Tal," I croaked. "There is nothing to make up for. It happened. Even if you would've been there that night, who's to say he wouldn't have hurt you to get to me? I'm glad you weren't there. I'm glad you were somewhere safe far away from me."

Something like awe flashed across his face. "I'm pretty damn lucky to have a sister like you."

"I agree," I said with a watery smile. Shrugging out of his hold, I moved to perch on the edge of the bed. "And waiting for the other shoe to drop isn't a way to live, Tal. Live for you. Not me, not your job, but for you. What do you want?"

He grimaced.

Well, that didn't seem good.

Obviously I didn't know the full story of his "friendship" with Jameson but I wouldn't pry. He would tell me on his own time.

"I know it seems fast," I said, breaking the silence of his non-response. "With me and Bry—"

He laughed and interlaced his fingers behind his head. "But it's not. You've known him for over a decade. Though I wish you would've told me you harbored a crush on my best friend."

I rolled my eyes. "Right, because you've always been so understanding with my boyfriends."

His smile grew. "That guy deserved it."

"You broke his nose," I said, fighting a smile.

"He shouldn't have made you cry."

I tapped a finger against my lips, acting deep in thought. "Very true. I'll allow it."

His laugh warmed my heart. This was us. The carefree back-and-forth. Though most of the time, Bryson was with us. Just thinking about him made me miss him.

"I have it bad," I said, rubbing the heel of my hand against my sternum. "I really love him. I've always liked him, liked how easy everything was between us. But now there's this added tug. It's hard to explain, but I know it's the real deal."

"If it were any other guy, I would've beaten their ass for sneaking around. But it's Bryson." Tallon shot me a worried look. "Just don't overshare like you always do—"

"You mean like talk about his monster cock?"

Tallon groaned and slipped his hands to the side of his head, pressing both palms to his ears. "I can't hear you."

"Or how he does this thing with his—"

"Nope. Nope. Nope," he repeated over and over, almost shouting the word.

My laugh kept me from going on about anything and everything that would make my brother uncomfortable. Movement out of the corner of my eye had me popping off the bed, twisting toward the door.

A forearm sealed to my collarbone, gently pushing me back until I stood behind him. I blinked in amazement at the gun that materialized in his hand.

"Where did that come from?" Instead of answering, he just shot me a wink over my shoulder. "Ew. I hope you used lube. No one wants things up their ass—"

"Fucking hell. Stop. It was an ankle holster. What the...?" He groaned and shook his head. "What am I going to do with you, Tin?" His tone was chastising, but the small smile he shot me ruined the effect.

Not waiting for a response, he stalked toward the door, gun tightly clutched between his hands. For a man of his size, he moved swiftly and on silent feet.

"Do they teach you guys that at FBI school? The silent walk thing?"

"The academy?"

"Yeah. Though that makes it sound like it's a prep school and everyone wears plaid skirts and navy jackets."

He drew up short and shot a glare over his shoulder. I just held up both hands in an innocent shrug. Sighing loudly—a little too dramatically, if you asked me—he turned back to the door and bent forward, picking up the folded piece of white paper.

As much as I was trying to ease the tension from the moment with random humor, my heart thundered against my chest, threatening to beat right out as he unfolded the single page. The held breath burned in my lungs, but I didn't move a muscle as I waited for Tallon to speak up.

"The hell?" When his shoulders dropped, the tension clearly fleeing his tense stance, I stumbled closer. His bright blue eyes flicked over the paper to me, then back to whatever was written. "It's the bill saying they hope we enjoyed our stay and a laundry list of food we didn't order."

"You checked us out?" I mumbled as I slid the paper from his pinched fingers to inspect it closer. "Um, who ate the double cheeseburger and milkshake? I'm pissed I wasn't invited to your little midnight picnic—"

"Did you hear me? It wasn't ours." Grumbling a string of curses, he stomped to the hotel phone and yanked the receiver off the base, jamming his finger onto the keypad.

I arched a brow but continued reading the laundry list of food orders and...

"Ew. You two watched porn together?"

"What? No."

"I mean, if that's your thing...."

"What?" Phone still pressed to his ear, he stared at me.

"What, what?"

"If that's my thing? What were you going to say?"

Huh. Odd thing to pick up on.

"Um, I guess, good for you? Though I would question your answer from earlier about not being gay. Unless you two just yanked your dicks in separate beds, no touchy-touchy—"

"Fucking hell. Sorry I asked."

"But you did," I crooned.

"Never mind. They aren't fucking picking up. Typical. I'll need to go down to the front desk and figure this shit out. We can't check out today. The safe house isn't ready, so we'll need at least another night here. I'm guessing it's fraud or they mixed up room numbers."

"Or it's that Vincent guy trying to separate us. You leaving me up in the room while you take care of this?"

Tallon's features hardened. "You're right. Fuck, why didn't I think of that?"

"Because you're a male and heard the word 'porn,' which meant all your brain cells stopped functioning correctly."

"I'm an FBI agent—"

"And still a male."

I preened as his jaw tightened, clearly annoyed. What could I say? Little sister habits die hard. I still enjoyed pestering him to the point of fuming annoyance. *Shit, what number is this now? Toxic trait number seven hundred and twenty-three?*

"We'll go down together," he said after a few calming breaths. He'd done that since we were little, never wanting to show me the simmering aggression that clearly boiled under his skin. "This way, you don't leave my side."

"For now," I muttered.

"What do you mean?"

"I mean for now, Tal. You and Bryson can't be at my side every second for the rest of my life. Don't you feel like we're just postponing the inevitable? If this isn't his plan to get us apart, then what's next? Fire alarm? Catching one of us when we go out to grab food since we're not trusting room service?" I shook my head. "Forget I said anything. I'm just being super negative."

Tallon reached for the door but drew up short. After eyeing me quickly, he stepped around me and dug into the black duffel lying by the perfectly made bed. Still squatting in front of the opened bag, he shoved an object into the air.

"Here. Take this."

I plucked it from his fingers and held it close, inspecting the small folding knife. "What about a gun?"

"You gone to the shooting range while I've been away, like I told you to?"

I rolled my eyes and flicked the blade open.

"Careful with that. I keep it sharp." Twisting around, he showed me how to fold it back into the handle and pressed it into my palm. "If anything happens—"

"We're just going down to the lobby and right back up," I grumbled.

"Right, but like I said before, if you plan for the worst, then you're never caught off guard. If anything happens to me and you get around this guy, you fucking kill him." Reaching up, he wrapped a hand around my shoulder and squeezed—hard. "You hear me? You use that knife and gut him open like the pig he is."

"Tallon," I whispered, a sudden flash of panic stealing the strength in my voice.

"Kill him and don't think twice. It's either you or him. You understand that?"

"Yeah. Yeah, okay."

"Say it, Tinley. Say you understand it's you or him."

"You're scaring me, Tal," I whimpered.

Tugging me hard, he drew me to his chest and squeezed so tight I couldn't breathe. "I know, Tin. I know, but I need to know if something happens, you'll fight and win. You're all I have. You're all that means anything to me."

A sob broke from my chest. "It's me or him."

After a few uncomfortable pats to my back that made me feel like he was trying to burp me instead of provide comfort, he held my shoulders and pushed me out to arm's length.

"Hide it somewhere that if you're searched, he won't find it. I've dealt with sick bastards like this. He won't stop, and I need to know you can take care of yourself if something happens to me."

I searched his face. A face I'd seen my whole life but now had a hint of something I never wanted to see again.

Fear.

25

BRYSON

Jameson whistled as we eased along the quiet streets of the upscale neighborhood. This area of Nashville was known for new money, which meant large houses to prove to everyone how important and wealthy the homeowners were. The stone and brick monstrosities made my little home back in Louisville look like a dilapidated shack.

"I clearly am in the wrong profession," Jameson said as he flicked on his blinker, slowing to make a right turn. "I'm not lining up at the soup kitchen by any means, but I sure as hell couldn't afford to even rent a room from these people."

I hummed my agreement but kept my mouth shut. Sure, the houses were amazing, the streets clear of debris and families out playing in the soggy yards without a care in the world, but I knew what lurked behind the fancy facade. Knowing what I now knew about Tinley's life and what I'd pieced together about Tallon's, I'd take my small home and decent paycheck any day of the week.

At least my home, as small as it was, was filled with love and laughter. Not anger, resentment, and parents walking the fine line between social drinker and alcoholic. And I was proud of what I could offer Victoria and Tinley. Her reaction to my home was every-thing. What I offered was enough for someone like her.

She'd been given everything in life, yet so much was taken from her too.

The hand resting on top of my thigh curled into a fist.

I might not be able to give her the luxurious things she grew up with, but with me, Tinley would be loved, safe, and free. She thought she brought nothing to the table, but that amazing woman did not know how wrong she was.

Tinley completed me in a way I didn't know was missing until she filled that vacant gap in my heart. And she'd taught me something these last few days.

That I deserved to be happy and to be loved with the same fierce-ness I gave to others. That my overbearing self in the bedroom was wanted, enjoyed by the right person who could turn right around and do the same, not be scared to tell me exactly what she wanted and when. That to be friends and lovers at the same time, to like and love my partner, could be a reality.

True happiness, soul-smothering love, was real.

With her, at least.

Despite our age difference, pasts, and baggage, we were perfect for each other.

"This is it," Jameson said, breaking me out of my trance.

The town car came to a complete stop in front of a large colonial-style home. Just like the others lining the street, the yard was kept up, the trees trimmed, with winter flowers blooming along the pristine beds lining the walkway to the front door. But that was where the warmth stopped. Maybe it was because I knew what type of evil lurked behind those windows, but the darkness pouring through the panes seemed to ooze malice.

"You sure about this? Are we smart to tip our hand, letting this fucker know we're on to him?"

I rubbed my jaw, debating how to respond. "What other options do we have? We need to get him off-balance so he makes a mistake. This could push him to do just that."

"And if that mistake ends up with one of us dead?"

I cut him a side-eyed glare. "It won't."

"What about that computer chick? What if he just kills her to tie up loose ends?"

"I don't think he will," I said, more to myself. Jameson was right. Going to this Vincent guy's house and showing our hand was a risk. "He needs her for leverage over Tinley—unless he gets his hands on one of us, that is. If he's watched Tinley like the profiler said he has, then he knows she's extremely protective of others. She'll do just about anything, even put herself in the line of fire, to make sure others are safe."

"Doesn't bode well for us keeping *her* safe," Jameson said, voice tight.

"I know." Fuck, did I know. "Which is why we have to do this. The sooner we get this guy off-balance, the sooner he'll make a mistake and give us something we can use to arrest his ass."

Jameson nodded and opened his door, me following suit. My boots squelched on the soggy ground when I stepped out of the car, leaving large footprints in the saturated grass. Fanning out my North Face coat, I reached back, double-checking that my gun was covered.

Unease built in my gut as we marched up the front walk toward the large red door. Jameson adjusted his suit jacket, grumbling under his breath about his wrinkled clothes. Rolling my eyes, I reached around him and pressed the doorbell.

Clasping both hands in front of me, I stared at the bright red paint and waited.

And waited.

With the sun setting behind the house, shadows doused the front of the porch. A chill crept beneath my skin, and the hairs on the back of my neck stood on end. Keeping my movements casual, I positioned my right hand close to my gun, to be ready for anything, and checked over one shoulder, then the other, scanning the streets and neighbors' yards for threats.

A happy melody of bells echoed from the other side of the door again. With his finger pressed to the round doorbell, Jameson pushed it as soon as the chimes stopped ringing.

I shot an incredulous glance between him and where he continued to trigger the doorbell.

Not relenting, he shrugged. "What?"

"Seriously?"

A small mischievous smile curled on his lips. "It's fun—"

"What are you, ten?"

"Thirty-two, and it's annoying as hell if anyone is inside the house trying to avoid coming to the door. If someone *is* home, the insistent noise is driving them insane, forcing them to come out and stop me," he explained while continuing to hit the button over and over.

I rolled my eyes and leaned back to see up and down the front of the house. "How do you and Tallon know each other again?" I asked, studying the plantation shutters for any signs of movement.

The ringing stopped. Jameson's hand fell to his side. That smirk vanished. "We met through mutual friends. You want to go check around back?" he said before I could dig further into his response.

"Nah, if no one came to the door after that—" I stopped at the roar of a large engine drawing closer. A shiny black Escalade whipped into the driveway, idling halfway to the garage. I squinted to see through the dark tint.

"What's our next move?" Jameson asked, having turned to watch the SUV.

The engine cut off, dousing the area in still quiet, and the driver door swung open. I released a breath when a black pump appeared beneath the open door, followed by another. A short woman with perfectly styled brown hair peered around the black metal.

The wife. In the report Charlie sent me, it stated the two had been married for a few years and only recently moved to Nashville for the job he currently held.

"Can I help you?" she asked, nose in the air, scanning us with a coldness only extreme money could buy.

Grumbling under his breath about his clothes, Jameson held out his badge as I withdrew my papers from my back pocket, holding it out in front of me.

"This is Detective Bend," I said, tilting my head in his direction. "And I'm Special Agent Bennett with the FBI."

"Detective? FBI?" Her eyes widened as she glanced between us. Movement across the street had Jameson and me tensing as we looked in that direction. The neighbor now stood on the front porch, curiously observing our interaction.

"Can we talk inside?" Jameson questioned, his tone firm but gentle, brokering no room for disagreement.

She nodded but turned to reach back inside the SUV. I stiffened, hand moving toward my gun.

"You need help to bring anything inside?" Jameson called out to her while firing me a condemning look.

"No, I've got it. Just need my keys."

Right, that made sense. Flexing my fingers, I eased my hand to my side.

The door slammed shut, only a purse held tight in her grasp as she strode toward us, chin raised. Breezing past us, she unlocked the door and stepped inside.

A series of consistent beeps echoed around the front entryway as Jameson and I stepped over the threshold, closing the door behind us, followed by three quicker beeps signaling the alarm system was disarmed.

She rounded the corner from down the long hall and crossed both arms over her chest. "You won't get any information from me."

Jameson and I shared a look. He was the first one to respond. "Ma'am, we're here—"

"You don't seem surprised," I mused as I took in her defiant stance. "And what information do you think we're after?"

She huffed, the impatient sound raising my hackles. "I'm not surprised. Drew prepared me for someone to possibly come by asking questions. He instructed me to direct you to our attorney."

My brows inched up over my forehead. "Drew Vincent, your

husband, prepared you with a response in case a detective and FBI agent showed up at your door?"

Her smile was anything but friendly. "Yes. He said something happened with one of his clients, and you're attempting to pin the blame on the firm." Those red lips sealed shut as if she'd already said too much. "He's a good man and excellent at his job. That is all I have to say. You should leave. Now."

The uncertainty in her voice caught my attention, and by the way Jameson studied her, he heard it too. But was it because she didn't believe his lie or because she was helping cover for him, having known what type of evil he was capable of?

"We're not here about a cyberattack or anything company related. He lied to you, and I think you know that. We're here for him and him alone because we believe he's involved in the abduction, torture, and murder of at least thirty-two women." Her brown eyes went so wide it was almost cartoonish. So she didn't know. That settled a bit of the urge to wring her tiny neck. "Ten years ago, he abducted a seventeen-year-old girl and held her captive for over three weeks."

"You're lying," she stated, tone not nearly as haughty as it was just moments ago. "I know that's a lie." An emotionless mask fell across her features, washing away the shock. "Get out."

I tilted my head as I dissected my previous words to understand what the fuck I just said that made her wavering conviction now resolute. At first it seemed like she believed me, but not now. Jameson figured it out before I could.

"You don't believe him because all the abduction and time in captivity would require him touching someone." The woman's throat worked as she swallowed hard, but she remained silent. "You know he wouldn't do that. Because he doesn't touch you, can't touch you. Skin-to-skin contact is abhorrent to him."

"I don't know what you're talking about," she said, her voice quivering. "We're married."

"And have you consummated that marriage?" Jameson asked, pity in his soft tone.

"Get the fuck out," she screeched. Her frantic eyes scanned the surrounding area, landing on a decorative vase sitting on a nearby table. Jameson and I left as that vase sailed through the air, shattering against the closed front door.

I studied the streams of water that dripped down the wood. "He might not touch you, but he does like to watch you. He says that's all he needs. Your husband is a voyeur."

She pressed a trembling hand to her chest. Wetness shined in her lower lids.

"We need your help—"

"Get out," she rasped. "Get out of my house."

"Ma'am—"

"Fine," she said, glaring at me. "Show me some evidence that my husband of three years is the monster you claim. We might have an unconventional marriage, but that doesn't make him what you're accusing him of."

My lips sealed shut as hers curled in a snarl.

"That's what I thought. Get out, or I'm calling the police to force-fully remove you from my residence."

As I turned, a picture above the fireplace in the adjoining sitting room caught my eye. Disgust had my stomach churning.

"Does he ever make you dance for him?" With my attention on the portrait above the mantel of a blonde ballet dancer with features that closely resembled the woman I loved, I only heard her gasp. "Put on a ballerina costume? Make you dance while he watches from the corner pleasuring himself?"

"How—"

I lasered my stony gaze her way, and she blanched at whatever she saw written across my face. "Because that's what he made the young girl do for those three weeks."

She swallowed, her hand around her neck. "Was she blonde?"

My nod was stiff.

"Oh my—" A hand flew up and covered her gaping mouth. "I'm going to be sick."

The quick click of her heels on the shiny hardwood floors echoed as she rushed out of view. I started to follow, but Jameson placed an arm across my chest keeping me in place.

"Give her a second," he muttered. "We just told her she's lived with a monster the last three years."

I ground my teeth, casting a glance in the direction she'd vanished. We didn't have time to wait for her to have a second. It was cold of me to demand she tell us everything she knew after exposing her husband, but we were wasting time.

Time Tinley didn't have.

26

TINLEY

"Ridiculous woman," Tallon grumbled under his breath as we lingered in front of the elevator.

A woman standing close side-eyed him over her shoulder as I hid my smirk behind a fist that was encased in the ultra-long sleeves of Bryson's FBI sweatshirt.

"She was just flirting with you, not asking for a marriage proposal," I joked.

"Unprofessional." Jabbing his finger against the Up button several more times, he huffed and crossed his arms in impatience. "At least we got the bill worked out. I sure as hell am not paying for porn I didn't watch."

I lost it, no longer able to restrain my laughter at all the glares now directed our way. Grabbing his shoulder, I gave him a shake. "Calm down, Tal. I think you need to eat. You get hangry when you're hungry."

"Do not," he grumbled. "But yeah, I could eat."

"Same," I agreed. "How about that old-school diner we used to go to around here? It's close by, isn't it?"

"Fuck yes." His blue eyes met mine and lit up with excitement. Leave it to my brother to be excited about food and not the hot young thing at the front desk who literally threw herself at him. I had to give the girl props. She faked that trip like a damn Oscar-winning actress. "A greasy burger and milkshake sound amazing."

"And pie," I added.

"Then Krispy Kreme?"

I pressed a hand on my chest. "Brother, you know the way to my heart."

"Always have," he stated with a pleased grin.

A ding dragged our attention to the arriving elevator, the doors slowly opening. I stepped inside along with another woman and three men while Tallon held the door open before following. A chorus of voices called out various numbers, Tallon pushing the corresponding button after each.

I sucked in a breath as the elevator jolted, my stomach somersaulting. Tallon shot me a comforting smile when I gripped his elbow and shuffled between him and the elevator wall.

The elevator slowed at the first floor, a ding echoing the arrival before the doors whooshed open. The woman and one man weaved their way through the small crowd, leaving us and two other occupants.

At the next floor, the two men exited, one hitting Tallon's shoulder with his own as he passed, casting a muffled apology over his shoulder. Tallon stepped to the side, pushing me tighter against the wall. A sharp hiss whistled through his teeth, and my eyes snapped to his face.

"What's wrong?" I questioned.

"I must have slept weird last night or something." He rolled his shoulder as if trying to work out the tightness.

Just as the doors began to close, a hand jutted between them, forcing them back open. One man who'd just stepped off boarded the elevator again, mumbling under his breath about being an idiot and getting off on the wrong floor.

Wearing a black baseball hat and a thick coat, he maneuvered to the opposite corner, keeping to himself. Still holding on to Tallon while he massaged his shoulder blade, I studied the man out of the corner of my eye. Not sure what I expected, maybe a gun or knife wielded our way? Apparently the last few days had riled my imagination, making me think everyone was after me.

When nothing nefarious happened and the doors closed with no incident, I released a calm breath, relaxing back against the elevator wall. At least until Tallon's body lurched forward. His palm slammed into the shiny closed doors before he could fall to the floor.

"Tal?" I rasped, heart in my throat.

"I don't feel so great," he said, though the words were slightly slurred.

Dipping beneath his outstretched arm, I shoved a shoulder under his armpit to help him stand. A small cry of relief slipped out when the ding echoed, signaling our floor, and the doors slid open. Teeth clenched, I strained beneath his heavy weight and hauled him into the hall with an arm wrapped around his waist.

Five doors. That was all I had to walk until we were in the safety of our room.

"Tin," he slurred, drawing my worried gaze down to his upturned face. Glassy blue eyes met mine. The panic behind them sent my heart racing. "Run."

"Here, let me help you." Tallon's massive weight lifted as the man from the elevator wrapped my brother's other arm around his own shoulders, easing some of the burden. "Too much to drink?"

"No, he just... I don't know what happened."

"You can call 911 from the room." Mind frozen in panic, I could only nod and keep up with his quick pace. As we approached our door, a bolt of awareness had my heels digging into the ugly hall carpet. The man turned, frowning. "Everything okay?"

"I can take it from here." My voice shook with the fear lacing through my veins.

Fuck.

Fuck.

Fuck!

This didn't feel right. *He* didn't feel right.

My entire body trembled as I stared the man down.

"I'll help you to your room, Tinley."

My mouth went dry, lungs freezing.

"How do you know my name?" I whispered. With a sudden wave of terror-inducing strength, I threw my weight to the side, hoping to dislodge his hold around Tallon. The moment his arm slipped, I slammed into the wall, pain shooting along my shoulder and head as it bounced off the drywall.

A desperate plea escaped as Tallon slipped from my grasp and slumped to the ground, completely unconscious. I dropped to my knees beside my brother, tears streaming down my numb cheeks as I shook his shoulder.

"Tallon," I cried. "Tallon, wake up. Tal." A sob seized my lungs. Movement had me glancing up through the tears. I didn't even react at the sight of the gun pointed at my head.

No, not mine. With the back of both hands, I wiped the wetness away to see clearly. I shook my head in desperate disbelief at the sight of the gun barrel pointed at the helpless Tallon.

"Please," I whimpered. "Please don't hurt him."

"What happens next is completely up to you, Puppet."

I couldn't help it. That soft voice, that horrid name.... Wetness soaked my panties and through the sweatpants, no doubt puddling on the floor. Not giving two shits about my urine-soaked garments, I flung myself on top of Tallon, ensuring if the gun fired, the bullet would hit me first.

"Get up." I shook my head against his command. "If he doesn't get medical attention soon, he will die, Puppet." I buried my face in Tallon's back, muffling my desperate sobs. "His life is in your hands, Tinley. Your choice."

"What choice?" I rasped, still unable to look up at the man who haunted my nightmares.

"Your life for his."

27

BRYSON

The tissue rasped against the side as Mrs. Vincent ripped it from the indented square tissue box clutched in her opposite hand. After folding it carefully, she dabbed at her swollen, red-rimmed eyes and swiped it under her dripping nose. Utter grief had prevented her from giving us anything we could use. Jameson and I alternated asking questions, hoping she'd give us something we could take to a judge to get an arrest warrant. But with every second that passed with only more circumstantial evidence, my hope diminished.

Yes, he was a fucked-up guy in the bedroom.

Yes, he traveled a lot for work.

Yes, they'd just moved to Nashville.

Yes, he lived here ten years ago.

None of what she gave us was solid evidence, yet from my perspective, each sliver of information confirmed he was our guy, evidence or not. Now I had to decide where I would draw my moral line in the sand.

Wait to gain evidence which gave this sick bastard more time to vanish, or worse, grab Tinley?

Or take matters into my own hands and deal out the judgment I knew was warranted?

"What am I supposed to do now?" she cried. "My life, or marriage, was a sham. And now, now I'll be tied to him. My name.... I'll be ruined."

"That's what you're worried about?" I snapped and stood from where I sat tense as fuck on the too-stiff couch. "How this will affect you?"

Her eyes met mine and narrowed.

"Do something right by the victims, the women he made money off with their torture and murder that afforded you this house." She flinched. I didn't feel guilty about my words or sharp tone. "Show us his office. Give us his computers. Help us find something that will point to where he and his partner are keeping a woman right now. Save a life instead of grieving over the fucking irrelevant status you lost."

Her throat worked as she swallowed.

"Up the stairs, but I need to call our attorneys. There's confidential information on those computers from his clients. You accessing his computer could break his—"

"Did you not hear me?" I yelled. "There is a woman held captive *right now*, and you have a chance to help save her life. And you're here worried about that fucking company? We don't fucking care about them. All we care about is getting the information we need to save her."

"Right," she whispered, gaze dropping to her lap. "Up the stairs. Take whatever you need." Pushing on the armrests of the high-back chair, she swayed a bit when she stood. "I need a moment to myself. Let me know if you need anything else." Without looking up, she stumbled out of the room, using the wall for support.

"That was—"

"Don't even say it," I snapped at Jameson.

"I was going to say brilliant. I couldn't sit there and listen to her pity party for one more second. She didn't give two shits about those women or how she could help, just her fancy life being uprooted."

I grunted in agreement. We started toward the stairs when my phone vibrated in my jeans pocket. Pulling it free, I immediately swiped the screen, answering the call.

"T," I greeted. "What's going on? Everything okay—"

"Bry." My stomach dropped at Tinley's shaking voice on the other end of the line instead of Tallon's.

"Tinley, what's going on? Where is your brother?"

Jameson paused halfway up the stairs and turned, brows pulled inward.

"I'm calling to tell you that... that this isn't for me."

"What? What are you talking—"

"Please let me talk." I sealed my lips shut. Flipping it to speaker-phone, I held it out between me and Jameson. "I've been lying to you and everyone else. It's time I came clean. Ten years ago, I lied about being abducted. I went willingly. Just like now."

My mouth opened, but nothing came out.

"I can't lie to myself anymore. I'm in love with someone else." My back crashed against the wall from the radiating pain growing in my chest. "And I'm leaving to be with him. Don't look for me. Don't try to find me. Just let me go." The tightness in her voice was evidence of her holding back unshed tears. "And when Tallon wakes up, tell him the same." A pause. "You are not who I want to spend my forever with. Goodbye, Bry."

The last half second of the call was her soul-wrenching sobs echoing through the line.

Then nothing.

I stared at the phone in my hand.

"Please tell me you read through all that," Jameson said cautiously.

"Yeah," I rasped. The word was almost too difficult to get out through the emotions strangling my throat and chest. "I know what that means."

The fucker had my girl.

"I'm sending officers to the hotel now." When I glanced up, I found Jameson staring right back at me with a phone pressed to his ear. "She said *when* Tallon woke up. Hopefully that means...."

"Yeah, hopefully."

Flipping to my recent call log, I pressed Charlie's number.

"Any word on Remington?" he asked in way of greeting.

"He has Tinley." The words were a struggle to get out. Though the silence on the other end of the phone didn't sit well. "Bekham, did you hear me?"

"Yeah, I heard you." He sighed.

My body shook with restrained anger. "You don't sound surprised."

"That's because of me," came Rhyan's voice. "I told him, and Tinley, that this outcome was nearly inevitable."

"What?" I growled, clutching the phone so tight the edges cut into my palm and fingers.

"He wouldn't stop until he had her, Bryson. She knew that too. It's why she asked to talk to me earlier."

Betrayal and gratitude mixed, making me unsure of how I felt about this new revelation. "What did you tell her, Rhyan?"

"Everything she needs to know in order to stay alive until you can find her." My legs gave out. I slid down the stairwell wall until I awkwardly perched on the edge of a wooden stair. "She's a smart woman, Bryson. She can do this, but you have to do your part and find her. What I gave her will only work for a short while before he—"

"Stop," I pleaded. Never had I called myself fragile, but at that moment, that was exactly what I was. If I heard what she suspected he wanted from Tinley, I would fracture, leaving me utterly useless to find her.

"Get your shit together," Charlie barked into the phone, the sound of fingers hitting keys filling the background silence. Déjà vu hit me, the scene eerily familiar to one month ago when Charlie was debilitated from not knowing Rhyan's location. "We can do this. We can find her together. Give me something, anything we don't already know."

"Officers are on their way to the hotel. We'll know soon about

Tallon." I glanced up at Jameson, who stood on the step just above the one I sat on. "What the fuck are you doing just sitting there?"

"What?" I snarled.

"Because from where I stand," he said in disgust, "it looks like you're just giving up on finding your girl. Letting that bastard win."

"Fuck you," I snapped and shoved off the wooden stair to stand tall, putting us eye to eye.

"Only if you ask nicely," he retorted with a sharp, malice-filled smile. "Now come on. Hopefully your buddy on the other end of that phone can find something useful on the bastard's computer."

"You're near his computers?" Charlie said, excitement clear in his high-pitched tone. "Get me the IP address and let me work my magic. If there's anything in there that can lead us to her, I'll find it without triggering the system to wipe itself."

"And we still need evidence," Rhyan added from somewhere in the background.

"Baby," Charlie scoffed. "We're way past needing evidence to wrap up this case. Isn't that right, Bryson?"

The promise of violence against this guy had a slow grin pulling up my cheeks. Jameson's eyes widened, and he took a cautious step back, tripping on the stair.

"Abso-fucking-lutely. That fucker's ass is mine to put in a shallow grave."

"Good thing this call isn't recorded," Rhyan muttered.

Taking the steps two at a time, I moved past Jameson, shoving open one door after another in search of the office. At the last door at the end of the hall, I twisted the doorknob and pushed, but it didn't budge.

"It's locked," I said into the phone pressed between my ear and shoulder. "Three deadbolts too. This has to be the one."

"So?" Charlie laughed. "You're a big, ex-college tight end. I'm sure you can figure—"

Not waiting for him to finish, I shoved the phone into my back pocket. Putting a foot between me and the door, I lunged, ramming a shoulder to the center of the door. The crack of wood sounded down the hall. Deep breath in, I channeled all my anger, all the fear and worry for Tinley, and sailed toward the door, my shoulder breaking through, splinters of wood carving through my shirt into my skin.

More skin shredded when I jerked free of the jagged edges surrounding the shoulder-size hole. Warm liquid leaked down my bicep, some soaked up by the remaining pieces of my long-sleeve cotton T-shirt, the dark fabric hiding the evidence of the minor injury. Before I could get my hand through the newly made hole, Jameson stuck his leaner arm through.

The thunk of the deadbolts sounded above the blood thundering in my ears.

Careful to not trample over him, I waited until Jameson was clear of the door before rushing into the office. A chill skated across my exposed skin, goose bumps pebbled along my arms, and hairs stood straight along the back of my neck, none of which had anything to do with the distinct temperature difference from the hallway.

Taking in the bank of computers, I sucked in a deep breath, the chilled air seeming to slice down my dry throat, and said a silent prayer that we'd find her in time. That she'd be unharmed and the future we were just starting to plan would come to fruition.

Fisting my hands, I shoved aside all the doubt and worry, focusing on the anger and determination to find Tinley. There was no other option.

And after she was home, safe...

Then I'd release this rage on the fucker who dared to touch my girl.

28

TINLEY

Tallon's life for my cooperation. It was a simple decision.

So when I assisted in dumping Tallon's body in our hotel room, I didn't fight him.

When he changed me out of my soiled pants and underwear, I didn't fight him.

When he walked me out of the hotel, knowing I was heading to my fate, I didn't fight him.

I did exactly what he asked, swallowing down my screams of anguish and cries of fear, all for Tallon's life to be spared. True to his word, which shocked the hell out of me, the moment I was bound and lying on the back seat's floorboard of his BMW, he called in an anonymous tip that an officer was down in the hotel and gave the 911 operator the correct room number.

Now, as I lay awkwardly along the floorboard, hands bound behind my back and feet secured, I studied what little I could see out the window from my odd angle. I could only make out a few fast food signs as we careened down the highway. Twice I caught large green signs with white lettering signaling upcoming exits, but the words were too blurred for me to read.

All-consuming fear had absorbed the earlier debilitating panic, leaving me numb and unresponsive. Or maybe the numbness was from the sound of Bryson's heart breaking that now ran on a loop in my mind, reminding me of his pain. There was no doubt he knew what was going on. He knew my feelings for him would never waver like I told him they did. No, the heartbreak I heard on the phone was because he knew.

He knew because he knew me.

I gave myself to save another.

And even though I was currently being driven to a fate I'd feared and dreaded the last ten years, I'd give myself up again and again to keep those I loved safe. With this fucker hearing me end things with Bryson, now, hopefully, he'd forget about the adorable, innocent two-year-old he could use as leverage, and even Bryson himself. Though I doubted he'd ever allow himself to be caught.

Except I believed the same about Tallon.

I chewed on my dry lip, peeling back a layer of skin with my teeth. Was what happened with Tallon my fault? Had all my jokes and teasing eased him into a false sense of security? Had Tallon's guard been down because of me?

Unshed tears clogged my throat, a salty taste lingering on the back of my tongue. All I wanted to do was give up, lie back, and scurry into the dark spot in my mind where I could escape it all. Except I wasn't done yet. I couldn't give in to the mounting emotions that would leave me vulnerable just yet. I still had one more life to save.

"Thank you," I rasped around the lump in my throat, the foul words making my stomach sour. I watched what I could see of his profile for any signs that he heard me. "Thank you for getting me before he did. I was scared."

This was a risk.

Earlier, Rhyan explained that I was special to this monster and he had the urge to take care of me. I could use that now, if this half-brained idea didn't backfire and end with us all dead.

"Who, Puppet?"

I swallowed the bile rising in my throat that his nasally voice incited. "That guy, your partner. He scares me."

Another bit of information Rhyan drove into my brain during the short yet extremely informative call. I could use the obsession against him, make him think I felt safe around him and wanted to be with him. Feeding into his fantasy could shift the leverage in my favor.

Could being the operative word.

A smile stretched across his thin face, somehow making him look even more sinister. I watched in horror as a slender, pale hand extended into the back. Blood seeped from my lower lip, coating the tip of my tongue from where I bit down, fighting the urge to shy away. The hand settled along my thigh, covered in the pair of sweatpants I'd found on the floor in our room, which still held Bryson's lingering scent. That comforting smell tethered me to the present, not allowing me to slip into the dark recess of my mind to avoid feeling any of this.

"He knows better than to come near you. You're my special puppet. Just for me."

"Then why did he come after me?" There was no faking the tremble in my voice as his fingers kneaded my tense muscle.

"You were never in danger. I only instructed him to take care of those who hurt you. That man had no right to threaten you, and the female... well, I couldn't hear what she said to you, but the face you made told me all I needed to know. Both needed to be taken care of, my present to you."

Each sharp inhale was like ice slicing down my dry throat and lungs. Those deaths, their murders, were a gift to me.

Before I could spiral down into guilt-filled oblivion, his words triggered a curious thought.

"Then why send him to the bar?"

Silence.

The longer he remained unresponsive, the more my mind cleared, the hope of my plan actually working dimming my mind's need to let go.

Fight or give up.

"It's either you or him."

Tallon's words from just an hour before rang in my head.

Me or him.

Me or him.

If everyone else was safe and I had the opportunity, I would choose myself.

But first—save Remington.

"He never went to your place of work, Puppet. You're mistaken."

I adjusted along the floorboard to ease the numbness spreading through my arms and the ache in my neck.

"Oh yeah, maybe." I wasn't wrong, though. "It was this one strange guy is all. You're right, you wouldn't do anything that would put me in harm's way. I'm sorry, I just assumed that man who came to the bar that night and tried forcing me outside to talk about that mean man's murder was your partner."

Silence again.

Please let this work.

Please let this work.

I had to save Remington.

If I lived through this—and that was a big if—I wouldn't survive the weight of her death resting on my shoulders. Two was already too much; I couldn't live with three.

"What man?" I sucked my lip between my teeth, debating my next words. "What man, Puppet?" he insisted.

What I said next could be my salvation or death sentence.

Only one way to find out.

"Oh, um, he said he was a detective, but they didn't send anyone out to interview me. It was late, at the bar. He was handsome, really good-looking but scary. Is that who makes the videos?"

I held a breath, lungs burning as I awaited his reply.

The hand still around my thigh squeezed before pulling away and grasping the wheel. I could almost feel the tension rising in the car.

"He was creepy," I said after a few seconds. "I'm afraid he'll come after me next. He said he would. He said I'd be his special girl too."

That was a lie, but this monster didn't know that. I was trying to save Remington, and I'd lie through my damned teeth to make that happen. Now to blindly lead him toward the outcome I wanted.

"If only there was a way to make sure he couldn't come after me when you're away from me." Yeah, I was assuming he'd leave for long stretches like before, but hopefully I was right. "But to make sure I'm safe forever, he'd need to be caught or dead."

Something told me he would choose the first option over killing his partner. The monster driving was thin, short for a man—weak, almost sickly looking. There was no way he'd best the guy I met at the bar that night. If this creep wanted me to be his and only his, he'd need to ensure his partner was behind bars. Good thing I had somewhat of a plan to toss out for him to consider.

"If the FBI caught him *with* a living victim who could identify him, they'd pin everything on him," I rushed. "And... and I'd be really grateful if you could save my friend Remington. She was nice to me." More silence. Fuck. I needed to get him talking. A chatty killer was good, per Rhyan. "I still don't understand. Why did you have him take her? All the others had hurt me, but she didn't."

"It wasn't supposed to be her," he gritted out, both hands tightening on the wheel. "But leverage is leverage, isn't it? And tell me, Puppet, how grateful would you be if I saved your friend?" A part of me shriveled up inside and hid to protect myself. Similar to how I'd slip to a special place in my mind when Bart snuck into my room those nights before I told Mom. "How grateful would you be if I lead the FBI to his doorstep, saving her if he hasn't killed her already?"

"Oh." I licked my lips, eyes franticly shifting back and forth. "That... that would be great. But what about you?" I pushed as much concern as I could muster into my frail voice. "He'd tell them about you, and then I'd be alone."

A dark chuckle filled the car, sending a terror-filled shiver down my spine. If there would've been anything in my bladder, I would've peed my pants again.

"He could try, but there's nothing tying our mutually beneficial partnership together. The fool doesn't understand that my side of the partnership is untraceable. We've never met in person, and everything communicated online erases the moment we read the message. Yes, yes, this sounds like a perfect opportunity to end it all now that I have you. Plus, the films have made me enough money to keep us comfortable without having to work for the rest of our lives."

I choked on a sob. "Wow, you're so smart," I somehow got out around my clenched teeth. "How will you do it?"

I was laying it on thick. At some point he would catch on that I was playing him, but hopefully not before I saved Remington. Though Rhyan said he was delusional, reality lost on his desire to have me all to himself again.

"I know what you're doing, Puppet." *Well, shit.* "I'm the puppet master here, not you. Though you bring up a great opportunity to kill two birds with one stone."

"Please save her," I cried, no longer caring if he heard the fear and sadness in my panicked voice. "I'll do anything."

He shot a wink over his shoulder and chuckled. "Oh, Puppet, I already know you will do everything I want with or without me saving her. You have other weaknesses I could leverage."

My shoulders trembled with my sobs as tears dripped down my cheeks. After several minutes of being lost in hysteria, my body slumped along the floor, all my fight and energy gone.

"Where are we going?" The emotionless voice that carried through the car sounded as dead as I felt inside.

"Somewhere they will never find you. Tell me, Puppet, are you ready to finish what we started?"

29

BRYSON

"Anything?" I asked for the hundredth time in the last five minutes. The chair bounced beneath me with the up-and-down motion of my jittery legs.

"For fuck's sake. No one can work like this," Charlie grumbled. "And my response is the same now as it was last time. I've got shit."

A low groan emitted from the soft leather as I leaned back in the office chair, heels digging into the floor as I rolled back and forth, studying the ceiling.

"Tell us what we know about this guy again," Jameson said. Disheveled more now than he looked before, he was slumped against the wall in the same position he'd been since we got the call that Tallon was alive and en route to the hospital for monitoring. The medics were already there when the officers arrived. An anonymous 911 call directed them to a Ketamine OD.

We all knew who the call came from and the reason Tallon was alive.

Tinley.

Tallon would be pissed when he found out she gave up her life for him. But it was too late to do anything about it except find her. Which wasn't going well.

"Born in Henderson, Tennessee," Rhyan started, "to Lori and Ben Vincent, who both passed when he was eighteen in a murder-suicide in their home. That home has since been bought and sold several times, currently occupied by a young family who I spoke to at length, confirming there were no other structures on the property."

I nodded along, ticking off everything we'd already been over, making a checklist in case she said something I didn't already know.

"Vincent was his high school valedictorian and did his undergrad and graduate school out of state."

"I've gone through anyone who had contact with him while he attended both, and no one has a connection to Nashville," Charlie added. "I'm keeping that list running in the background in case we come up with something to narrow down the suspects on this fucker's partner."

"Good," I said. "But that fucker isn't our goal, unless you think this Vincent guy will take Tinley to wherever the partner is holding Remington."

"No, this guy will want to be alone with Tinley," Rhyan said. "He won't share."

"Fuck." I groaned.

"He had a sister, one year younger than him, who died when she was sixteen and he was seventeen. Her death record lists cause of death as inconclusive, no foul play. Though knowing what we know about Vincent and his obsession with Tinley, it's safe to assume he killed her. Based on the autopsy results Charlie dug up, it looks like she suffocated, though there were no signs of a struggle or ligature marks."

"Okay," Jameson said, brows furrowed as he studied the floor. "Let's get in this guy's head. He loved his sister, probably a little too much based on what we've put together. She did something, and he killed her. Then he randomly saw Tallon's sister dance one night, and she reminded him so much of his sister that he fixated on her."

"Yes, exactly," Rhyan said. "A voyeur always has these tendencies, something from their childhood usually, so we can assume he watched his sister without her knowing. He probably killed her for betraying him, maybe betraying his trust."

My stomach twisted into knots. "Like how he feels Tinley did to him after he watched us through my front window."

No one responded, confirming my statement.

"Okay, we assume he nabbed Tallon's sister in a rush the first time, right?" I nodded at Jameson, not really knowing where he was going with that line of thought. "Because she was about to leave for some dance academy. This time he's had time to plan, to find a place to keep her where we won't find her until he's done with her."

I narrowed my eyes at him.

He shook his head. "I'm just working different angles here."

"I know," I snapped. "Doesn't make it any fucking easier."

"What if this additional time, him watching her the past few weeks, building up to taking her, gave him time to find a place that meant something to him? To them?" Jameson sighed and tossed his head back. "Fuck, I don't know."

"Him and Tinley?" I questioned.

"No, him and his sister. If all this started because of his younger sister, doesn't it make sense that it's where it would end too? Somewhere they shared, or he at least perceived they shared, an emotional location. Tallon's sister said the clothes and shoes were too small when he held her captive ten years ago, and now it's obvious those were his sister's. Wouldn't the location for all this to end be just as important to him?"

For this to end.

To end.

Fuck, please no.

"Guys," Charlie shouted. I leaped out of the chair, pressing both hands to the desk as I leaned over the phone. "I just got something... odd."

"Odd how?" I barked.

"Coordinates odd."

"Where do they lead?" Jameson asked, shoving off the wall to pace the small space not occupied by the desk covered in monitors.

"Give me a second. Okay, it looks like a house, but the exact coordinates are for out on the back side of the property covered in trees. I'm pulling up an aerial view, but I can't see anything."

I ran the possibilities over in my mind. "Who did it come from?"

"Based on the similarities in the code and how it was sent... our least-favorite voyeur."

"Could be a trap," I countered.

"Or it could be where he's holding that Remington woman," Jameson added. I shot him a questioning look. "Well, if we're still in this guy's mindset, he has what he wants. There's no need for the loose ends a partner would add. Maybe this is him not only trying to divert us from him while he gets farther away with Tallon's sister but also tying up that partnership either by him being arrested or dead by shootout."

I considered the options.

"It's too much of a risk to not take the coordinates seriously, but I agree it could be a way to divert our attention from locating him." I hitched my chin toward the phone in Jameson's hand. "Call SWAT. Make sure they're aware of every detail before sending them to the location. They need to proceed with caution, as the unsub has a hostage/victim on the premises. We'll stay here and work Tinley's case."

He gave a clipped nod, focus already on his phone as he exited the room.

In the quiet, the situation weighed heavily, like an elephant sitting on my chest. I rubbed a fist against my sternum to ease the ache.

"You still there?" I asked over the phone.

"Yeah, we're still here," Charlie responded.

"What are we missing?" I thought back to Jameson's line of thinking. "Let's say he has a place in mind, somewhere special to him that reminds him of his sister that he wants to take Tinley. What about where they grew up?"

"Let me look." The clicking of keys filled the office. "Looks like the hospital records for his birth were sent to an apartment complex. Same with his sister."

I fell back into the chair and scrubbed a hand over my face. Outside, the last of the brilliant sunset had disappeared.

"What about other hospital records?" Rhyan asked. "For him and his sister."

"What are you thinking?" I questioned.

"Maybe this Vincent character wasn't the only mentally fucked-up person in their house. Usually mental disorders like this are triggered from an abusive parent or one who shared the same preferences."

My lip curled in disgust. "We all know the stats of murder-suicides stemming from abusive relationships."

"Exactly. So if the two kids were ever sent to the hospital, maybe a different address was listed. Check the wife too. If he wasn't abusing the kids, she could've been the target of his anger."

Scenes from my childhood flooded to the forefront of my mind, assaulting me with memories I'd done a damn good job of forgetting. I sucked in a breath and squeezed my eyes shut, trying to stop the onslaught.

"Nothing on the hospital records side, for anyone. If he was abusive, he kept it one level below needing medical attention. And you know what else is odd now that I'm really looking into his childhood? The school records for both. It seems they were home-schooled. The principal was listed as their father. Looks like Vincent's first time in public school was when he finished his senior year, after his sister's death, at a local high school before getting a full academic scholarship for his undergrad."

"What does any of that mean?" I asked no one in particular.

"It means they were trapped in that house with either a physically or sexually abusive parent with no way out," Rhyan retorted.

"And the sister had two people abusing their authority. One parent and her older brother," I added.

"What if it was mutual?" Rhyan stated, almost as if she were asking herself instead of us. "In cases like this where it's just immediate family members, no outside human interactions, incest happens."

My stomach churned. "That's fucking sick."

"I didn't say it was right. I'm saying there are case studies showing it happens when siblings are that close in age and secluded from society."

"I don't know which is worse," Charlie added, "her being abused by her brother or her willingly engaging in an intimate relationship with him."

"It doesn't change the fact that he has Tinley now and is using her as a stand-in for his dead sister," I grated, jaw so tight I wouldn't be surprised if the muscle snapped.

"Right." Rhyan sighed, sounding as exhausted and worried as Charlie. I felt bad making these two work as hard as they were on a case that wasn't theirs to solve. But I knew my two friends wouldn't back down knowing what was on the line. Plus, I'd saved Rhyan's life, so this made us even.

Something clicked.

"Wait, you said they were taken to an apartment after they were born, but if they were secluded from society—"

"They would've needed a secluded location away from the prying eyes of social services," Charlie said. "Huh."

"That doesn't sound good." I groaned.

"It's just that there's a gap in his records." Charlie cursed under his breath, causing me to sit up straight. "That means he's digitally removed every bit of evidence on where they were between the ages of three and sixteen. After that, they lived in the house where the murders occurred."

"How do we find it, then?" There was no covering my panic. This was the lead we needed. I could feel it.

"Giving me more than thirty seconds would be a good start." Excitement poured through his rushed words. This was his element, and I needed to trust him to find the answers I couldn't.

"I know, sorry. I'm just—"

"I get it. You know how much I get it. You kept me in line, kept us on task with a clear head when Rhyan—" Charlie cut himself off and cleared his throat. "Now it's my turn to return the favor. I'll find something for us to use."

My head whipped up when Jameson reentered the room.

"SWAT is headed that way. We'll know soon. What did we learn while I was out there handling the tactical assault team?"

"Nothing that will help us find her," I said, voice low.

"Yet," Rhyan added. "Nothing that will help us find her yet. Hey, you. That detective."

Jameson arched a brow at the phone. "Yeah."

"I like the way you think. We should talk. Ever thought about joining the FBI and becoming a profiler?"

Jameson's jaw dropped, leaving him gaping.

I chuckled. Standing, I stretched my arms high overhead and twisted, cracking my back with the movement. "I'm going to get some water while we wait. You good?"

He nodded and went back to talking rapidly with Rhyan.

Leaving the room, my only connection to possibly getting a lead on where Tinley was held, proved more difficult than I expected. Halfway down the hall, I leaned back against the wall and closed my eyes.

All I could do was wait.

Wait to find out her fate, which was now tied to my own.

30

TINLEY

With the adrenaline crash and sobbing, it was enough for my body to succumb to exhaustion despite the danger surrounding me. The change from smooth roadway to the crunch of gravel under the car's tires snapped me awake. My lids fluttered as I attempted to remember where the hell I was and why my body hurt. Smooth cream leather and upholstery on all sides snapped me back to the reality of my situation.

Even though I felt better, more clearheaded than the terror-consuming fog from earlier, I chastised myself for passing out. I had zero clue as to how long we'd driven or in what direction. How long did I sleep? At what point in the drive did I succumb to the emotional exhaustion?

Fuck. This wasn't good.

The car slowed, my restrained body rocking forward when it came to a complete stop. My heart rammed against my chest, my pulse thundering in my ears, almost drowned out by the sound of the engine stopping. A slight shake and the sudden burst of fresh cold air were the only indication a door had opened.

I struggled along the floorboard, hoping for a view of what waited for me outside the car, but it was too dark to see anything. *Damnit.* It was still daytime when I passed out, but now it looked well into the night based on the depth of darkness outside.

A shriek lodged in my throat when the door above my head swung open. The interior lights blazed down, assaulting my sensitive eyes. Before I could get my bearings, two hands gripped under my armpits and pulled.

"Somebody help me," I cried out as I thrashed along the floorboard to dislodge his hold. "Help! Help!" I screamed, voice cracking.

The hands disappeared, only to reappear wearing opaque latex gloves. Eyes wide, I sucked in a deep breath, ready to scream like my life depended on it—which it did—but a glove-covered hand smacked across my mouth, muffling the sound.

"You said you'd be good," he snapped, leaning into the car to hover over me. "Who else needs to die because of you?"

The fight immediately drained from me, and his smile turned malicious.

"That's a good girl. Now, I'm going to help you out of the car, loosen the bindings around your feet, and you're going to walk inside, on your own free will, without a fight. Aren't you?"

I nodded even if I was screaming, *No*, inside my head.

This was it. I could feel it. An ominous finality hung in the air as he grunted, pulling my dead weight from the car. I cried out, immediately stopping myself when my ass and thighs smacked the gravel-covered ground, the sharp edges jutting through the sweatpants and piercing my skin.

Continuing without a care, a knife appeared in his hand and glided over the plastic tie securing my feet.

I gaped at the knife.

A knife.

A whimper bubbled in my chest. Shifting my shoulders and chest, I maneuvered to feel the knife Tallon gave me earlier, which I'd hid inside my sports bra. The sensation of metal and plastic digging into the underside of my right breast sent a wave of hope and relief through me, giving me renewed energy.

Sure, I had a weapon, but could I muster up the courage to slip it out without being detected and stab this man to death, or at least enough to give me time to hide?

Death seemed like a much more permanent punishment I'd like to dish out.

This man ruined my life, turned me into this—though I'd had a bit of a start with the lurking darkness from the incidents in my childhood. This man stole weeks of my life—no, years. All those years I used alcohol and sex and painkillers to dull the pain, that pain caused by him.

"Up you go," my captor said with an upward motion.

I shifted so he would see my hands still bound behind my back. With the faint light from the still-open door, I noticed his furrowed brow. "I can't stand up on my own bound like this. Can you either cut me free or help me up?"

He considered me for a long moment with an emotionless mask that had my insides quivering from fear. I sucked in a breath when he held up the steel blade, any hope of being free dimming when he flicked the knife closed and shoved it into his back pocket. Gloved hands grasped both shoulders and helped haul me upright. Well, kind of. He stumbled backward, barely able to help me stand before releasing me.

A flame of hope burned brighter.

This asshole was weak, nothing like my Bry or Tallon.

I could take him if it came to a physical fight. Plus, I had the advantage of the hidden weapon.

I swallowed and whipped my head left and right, trying to make out anything in the inky darkness. Could I actually do this all on my own? Or should I do what Rhyan prepared me for, get him talking long enough for the boys to find me?

All on my own, I'd worked to save myself this past year, done all the hard work with therapy and keeping my vices at bay. This was the same—sure, maybe a little more violent—but I could save myself.

A hiss rushed through my clenched teeth at his tight grip around my bicep. My stomach churned, the urge to vomit almost too much to stop when he touched me.

He marched up a set of rotten wooden steps, hauling me behind him. Afraid the boards would give under our combined weight, I stepped with light toes, hurrying to keep up. On the porch, I took in the area from this new vantage point. Paint peeled off the boards, exposing the rotten wood that made up the long porch. At one end, a wooden swing hung haphazardly from one chain, and two rocking chairs that appeared weaker than the stairs creaked with the gusting wind.

I shivered at the creepy-as-hell house that looked like the perfect backdrop for the next remake of *Texas Chainsaw Massacre*. A high-pitched creak of the metal hinges drew my attention to the now-open door. Not stepping over the threshold, I took in what I could see of the inside, which looked a shit ton better than the outside. There was still the "no doubt this place is haunted" sense, but not nearly as desolate. Allowing him to pull me along, I stepped into the small entry. The overpowering scent of furniture polish, bleach, and a strong floral smell assaulted my nose, making it crinkle.

"You cleaned for me," I stated, keeping my tone soft, faking awe. "It's beautiful."

Buying that load of shit like the crazy-ass he was, the fucker preened at my compliment.

"Wait until you see your old room."

I swallowed hard.

Fuck. Fuck. Fuck.

My *old room?*

Shuffling down the hall, he switched his hold to grip one of my bound hands.

Dated wallpaper peeled from the wall while dark sconces with dust-covered bulbs dotted along our way to the last bedroom. Hand resting on the doorknob, he turned to me, smiling.

A creepy-ass smile that immediately stole my breath.

"I wanted to bring you here before." *Damn, the freak is blushing.* "But I panicked when I learned you were leaving me." That smile dipped into a frown. "But this time I'm prepared. No one knows about this place. I've taken care of that. Now we can be together without interruption in my childhood home."

He continued to ramble to himself, but all I could focus on was what he said about not knowing about this place. And with his technical ability that had even stumped Bryson's friend Charlie a few times, I had no doubt he meant those words.

The wooden door groaned as he shoved it open and guided me inside.

Musty air filled my lungs as I sucked in a breath and forced a wide, fake smile. Internally, I screamed at the injustice of it all, of this disturbing fate I was destined for.

Wallpaper peeled from the walls, too faded and damaged to tell what design it once had. A single twin bed, beside it a single nightstand with a lamp on top, casting the only light in the room.

Though the house was old, the wooden bed had a sheen that made it appear new, along with the pristine white comforter and pillows that rested on top.

"My sister loved her dollhouse." Everything in me screamed to not turn and see what he was talking about. Shallow breath held, I slowly turned to where he stared. Ice raced through my veins as I took in the creepy two-story Victorian dollhouse that sat in the corner. "And I loved it because it was big enough to hide behind, so I could watch through the tiny windows. She liked it when I watched. It made her feel less alone."

My stomach cramped with the flood of terror and disgust that washed over me.

"Watch what?" My voice trembled, giving away the fear I had no hope of hiding.

He shook his head like he was trying to dislodge whatever played in his sick head. Those eyes were dead, completely vacant of any warmth when they locked on mine. "Her and Father."

Bile surged up my throat with such force that there was no keeping it down. Doubled over, I emptied my stomach onto the clean hardwood floor, which ended up being just spit and stomach acid.

He jumped back, releasing my hand with a barked curse. Yelling about the mess, he stormed out of the room. The sound of stomping footsteps faded, but my mind still whirled at his revelation, too distracted to act on my sudden freedom before he came back inside. A rag dropped to the floor, a cleaning chemical spray bottle following.

"Clean it up," he barked. A hard shove to my shoulder sent me stumbling to the side. Legs unstable, I crumpled to the floor, pain reverberating where my knees caught my fall. "Now."

Sobs racked my body; only quick pants of air filled my lungs. Careful to keep my movements slow, I lifted my bound hands as far as I could at my back, keeping my eyes downcast. "I can't."

With a frustrated sigh and a comment about my incompetence, he withdrew the knife from earlier, sliced through the bindings on my hands, and tossed the scrap of useless plastic across the room. Blood rushed to my numb fingers, sending painful tingles along both hands.

"Now." His bellow made the room shudder.

Afraid of his rage at the mess, I curled into myself, cowering from his anger.

Impatient stomps shook the floor. The toe of two black shoes paused just inside my line of sight. "This place better be clean for me or you will get it when I come home."

"Come home?"

Fingers tangled in my hair and yanked my face up to the ceiling. A pitiful, cracked scream raced out of my throat.

"Are you hard of hearing, boy? I said clean."

"Boy?"

Oh snap. This is bad. Oh, so bad.

As I stretched for the rag, my hair pulling at the roots from his unrelenting hold, I turned pleading eyes up to meet his wild ones.

"I'm Tinley, remember? Tinley." I swallowed. "Your special puppet."

I stopped breathing at the snarl that curled his lip. With a hard push, he released me, my elbows catching my upper body before I could face-plant into the small puddle of vomit.

"You were special," he hissed. Turning, he strode over to the bed and sat on the edge. His dark eyes narrowed at my still hands.

Not wanting to anger him further, I grappled for the cleaner and rag. After spraying the area plus some, I began wiping up the floor.

"All those gifts. This house just for you, all for nothing but a damn dirty whore."

I winced. "Gifts?"

"The dress looked beautiful on you, just like I knew it would." I swallowed down a whimper. When I chanced a look his way, I found him smiling. "Though you liked my first one better. I'm so glad you used it as much as you did." I froze, staring unblinking at the evil incarnate man. "Especially out in the open. How many times did you and I find release at the same moment? I couldn't get enough of your legs spread, hand between your thighs—"

"Stop," I rasped. Fuck, I was going to be sick all over again. "You watched me?"

His dark, humorless chuckle sent a shiver of warning down my spine. "Oh, Puppet, I've watched you for a long time. Our first encounter was cut short, but it gave me time to perfect this. It felt right for you to be here."

I still couldn't breathe properly. That sex toy, the one I loved so much. I gagged but swallowed it down to not upset him with another mess. I'd received the toy in the mail, saying I'd won it in some Instagram giveaway that I didn't remember entering, but hey, it was a free sex toy.

"This was your house," I somehow got out.

He looked around the room, his features softening. "Yes. I knew I'd always find my way back to you, and I needed a place for us. When I checked on it, I found the house and surrounding forty-five acres in foreclosure." When he looked back at me, he pointed at the floor. "You missed a spot. Everything has to be spotless," he roared.

I flinched back but somehow kept scrubbing.

"Tell me about your sister," I said between silent sobs.

"Keep him talking, Tinley. That's your best bet for survival."

I repeated Rhyan's words like a mantra.

"Beth was...." He sighed. Legit happily sighed. Disgust coated my skin like a second layer. "Perfect. Though our father didn't think so about either of us. Our punishments were different when we inevitably screwed something up. Mine came with a belt to the back and thighs. Hers... hers came at night when he thought no one was watching."

"But you were."

His eyes shifted to the dollhouse. There was no way it was the original, the entire thing looking too new, but that didn't seem to matter to him.

"Yes, I was always watching." Reaching down, he adjusted himself over his slacks. "Father never knew I hid in her room and waited. I liked it."

"What... what happened to her?"

His brows drew together. "I thought she was ready, that she was mine. I'd watched over her. She'd been my entire world, and then she ruined it." The last words were more of a hiss. "She screamed. Screamed when I crawled in her bed, ready to finally act out every-thing I'd watched. I didn't mean to hold the pillow down so long. I just wanted her to stop screaming."

I swayed, falling forward and catching myself on both hands. A ringing sounded in my ears, the world around me hazy.

"She loved to dance. To lock herself in her room and pretend she was a ballet star." Prima ballerina, but I sure as shit wasn't about to correct him. "I'd watch through the window, watch how those moments made her smile." That far-off look shifted, and he focused on me. "When I saw you that first time, dancing on stage and looking just like her, I knew."

"Knew what?" I said, gulping down as much air as I could to keep from passing out. The fumes of the potent chemical burned in my lungs, but I didn't care.

"Knew you were my chance to make it right. A second chance with Beth, to have our forever."

I shook my head back and forth, my limp ponytail snapping side to side.

A vile grin split his lean face. "Oh yes, Puppet. Even though you're no longer special, spoiled by that bastard who dared touch my puppet, you're still mine. Now," he said with finality as he slapped the top of his thighs, "before I make us your favorite, peanut butter and jelly, I think it's time to show me just how grateful you are."

"Grateful? For... for what?"

He cocked his head to the side. "For sending that FBI hacker—who is damn good, might I add. Maybe when I get to the office on Monday, I'll look him up and try to bring him on board with our firm. Anyway, for sending him the coordinates to your friend's location. Now, I will not be held responsible if my ex-partner harmed her before they get there. It also depends on if they took my information seriously."

I slumped back against the wall and hung my head. New, happier tears lined my lower lids. I did it. I gave Remington the best chance at survival, for being found in time. That made all this bearable.

"Get on the bed, Puppet." I didn't move, couldn't. Somewhere in the room, a drawer opened and slammed shut. "You won't like what will happen if I have to ask twice."

Pushing off the rough hardwood floor, I stood, my palm smacking the wall—almost going straight through it—to keep from falling over.

"I need food," I said. "Water."

The room spun when I turned, searching for him. Movement behind the dollhouse snapped my eyes back that way. Two beady eyes peered through the other side of the tiny windows, half of his body sticking out the side, completely visible.

Careful to not fall, I shuffled forward slowly, making my way toward the bed. I stared at the dingy bubblegum-pink leotard, my gaze snagging on a familiar red rose-shaped toy sitting right beside it.

It was too much. My knees gave out, the mattress springs creaking under my collapsed weight.

"Put it on like a good little puppet. This is a show I've waited a long time to see in person."

That was when I heard it. The slick of skin against skin, his high-pitched keening sound that he made when he'd jacked off while watching me those three weeks he held me captive.

I couldn't do this, couldn't go through this again. Sealing both palms over my ears, I curled into the fetal position on top of the bed. Releasing all the despair I'd held at bay since Tallon collapsed, I sobbed for his innocent sister who lived a life of terror, and cried for me, who seemed destined to the same.

But more than anything, the heaviest tears that fell were for the future with Bryson I'd just allowed myself to hope for that now would never happen. Fingers dipping beneath the oversized FBI sweatshirt, I dug beneath the tight band of my sports bra and wrapped my palm around the metal handle.

Goose bumps erupted in its wake as I slid it down to my stomach. Palm slick with sweat, fingers trembling, it took three failed attempts before the blade flicked open. The razor-sharp edge sliced into my skin, the pain barely registering from the numbness slowly devouring my body.

I couldn't give any hints to the monster watching from across the room about what I planned to do. Peace settled over me, calming my thundering heart and easing my mind.

Tallon was right all along. I had a choice.

Him or me.

Tonight would be the end of my ten-year torment and his decade-long wait for my return.

Because one of us wasn't leaving this room alive.

Him or me.

Only time would tell which.

31

BRYSON

Thursday, December 13th

"The woman abducted from the ambulance is safe." I bolted out of the uncomfortable hospital waiting room chair at Jameson's announcement. "Beat to hell. She apparently put up one hell of a fight. They didn't locate the unsub."

My short nails dug into my palms from my tight fists. "And Tinley?" I'd held on to a sliver of hope that she would be there too.

Jameson's features softened as he shook his head.

"Fuck," I roared, making everyone in the waiting room glare in our direction.

"Where are we with the potential location search?" he asked as he sat in the plastic seat opposite me.

"Charlie is still working on it. What do you mean, the unsub wasn't on-site? How did they let him get away?"

Jameson clasped his hands together. The picture of calm, though I knew he felt anything but that. "I won't know the full details until I get down to the station." He twisted to look past the doors where a few doctors and nurses had disappeared through. "But I need to be here."

As did I. Tallon was my best friend. He deserved to hear the news about Tinley from me. Maybe then I could keep his ass in bed instead of discharging himself and running out into the streets butt-ass naked to look for her.

He was still out cold per the doctors who'd come out every once in a while to update me, after a bit of persuasion. Being my build had its perks when needing to strong-arm someone into giving you information.

"At least she's safe," I said with an exhausted sigh. Leaning forward, I balanced my elbows on top of my thighs. I glanced at the clock along the wall across from the waiting room.

Midnight.

At this point, Tinley had been missing for ten hours if we assumed she was taken the moment she called me. Jameson put an APB out on Vincent's BMW, but nothing was reported around the Nashville area, which made us all assume Tinley was no longer inside the city limits. That left us with the burning question we were fighting to find the answer to.

Where was she?

"We'll find her," Jameson said. I glanced up without lifting my hanging head. "Don't give up on her. If she's anything like her brother, she's a fighter."

"I just feel so helpless," I admitted. "All we've done is wait. I'm ready for action, ready to take the fucker who took Tinley down."

"Who we assume took Tallon's sister," Jameson corrected. "We still haven't found any concrete evidence that he's a part of this." I rolled my eyes. "Yeah, I agree that he's the guy. But we have nothing to tie him to this case, and even less to prove he abducted her today."

He was right. Of course, the cameras at the hotel and in the adjoining parking garage were disabled, and not a single person recognized Vincent or Tinley based on the photos officers showed around the lobby and to the front desk workers.

"But we know he did," I stated adamantly. "And we know she's in danger. Based on Rhyan's profile, we don't have long before—" I swallowed down my next words. "I've never met anyone like her." Fuck knew why I was opening up about my feelings, exposing my shredded heart, but I couldn't stop. "I have to find her. She's everything. Hell, maybe she's always been everything, and I was too dumb to recognize my other half until now."

"Or maybe the timing was off," he said offhandedly. "She's younger than you and Tallon. Plus, I have to assume she's gone through her own rebuilding after what happened ten years ago." I nodded. "The question now is are you willing to be there when she has to rebuild again?"

I sat up straight. "If I could take her pain, take the work to help her heal, I'd do it. I'd rip myself apart to keep her from having to rebuild what she's accomplished to move on. No, moving on is too easy of a term. She's forged through an incident that would've drowned most others. She's a fighter. I want to help her to keep fighting." I stared at my hands, studying the thin white scars I'd amassed through the years. "I want to walk beside her through the darkness that I know will come after so we can live in the light together after all the hard work is done."

At Jameson's sharp whistle, I shot him a withering look.

He raised both hands in surrender. "Sorry, man. I didn't expect Tallon's best friend to be a philosopher."

My lips quirked at the corners. "Just speaking the truth. I've lost someone I loved before, but this time it's different. I can affect this outcome if only I had—"

The ringing of my phone cut me off. Stretching across three seats, I yanked the charger from the wall, leaving the cell phone with a long white tail. Charlie's name on the screen sent my pulse racing.

I clutched the phone tight and said a silent prayer that we had a lead.

"What do you have?" I said as calmly as I could, even though it felt like a live wire was shooting electricity through my veins.

"A lead."

I sucked in a sharp breath. "How?"

"Because this guy is good, but I'm fucking better."

"Not the time," Rhyan snapped somewhere in the background on the other end of the line.

"It took a lot of digging, but what no one in the family knew was the mother was taking antidepressants on the side. After assuming what was going on in that house, I can understand why."

"Charlie," I hissed, the phone's edges biting into my palm with my tightening hold. "Get to the point."

"She didn't go through insurance, so I assumed she paid cash each visit, but I found one receipt where she paid with a check." I bounced on the balls of my feet, all exhaustion gone. "I was able to locate an image of the check she used, and guess what was listed up in the left-hand corner?"

"An address," I said in a rush. Motioning to Jameson, who stood opposite me, staring at the phone in my hand like he could hear the other side of the conversation, I started for the exit. The automatic double doors slid open as I approached, sending a gust of bitter winter wind inside, soothing my warm cheeks.

Horns honked and tires screeched as drivers slammed on their brakes to not hit us as we raced across the street toward the parking garage. Charlie continued to talk, saying he sent me the address.

"How far?" I asked, slightly breathless from the run and cold air.

"An hour, maybe an hour and a half."

I relayed the information to Jameson. He shot me a smirk over the roof of the town car. "Challenge accepted."

I returned his grin with one of my own.

Hold on, kid.

Hold on for me.

AFTER A HEATED DISCUSSION, we decided to not inform the local authorities. One, because if we were wrong, we'd all be in deep shit, and two, because if we were right, well, I still had my mind set on ending this nightmare on my own terms. Fuck the judicial system and the damn oath I swore.

This man's death was mine.

Bloodlust thrummed through my veins, heating me to the point of boiling. Too hot, I stripped off my jacket and tossed it into the back seat. Sweat beaded along my forehead, dripping down my temples. Reaching toward the knobs on the dash, I twisted the AC all the way to the left, deflating at finding it already as low as it could go.

"The county give you this shit car?" I asked, glancing around it with more scrutiny than before.

"All the money goes to hiring more cops, more detectives." He shifted in his seat and leaned an elbow along the driver side door. The wheel trembled beneath his hold as we flew down the interstate, blue lights flashing, no doubt going close to one hundred. Though with his relaxed posture, you'd think it was a slow Sunday drive. "I'm fine with it."

Pulling my gun out of its holster, I checked the clip and slammed it back into place, just needing something to do with my hands. *Damn this nervous energy.*

"What about Agent Rhyan's offer to join the BSU?"

He shot me a glance out of the corner of his eye. "Thinking about it. Can't say I'm not intrigued."

"She's building a new team from scratch in Texas. From what I know about her, I'd jump on that opportunity if I were you. She'd be a good boss, and you'd learn a lot. Plus, her asking you is a hell of a compliment. She's no doubt putting together a superstar group."

"Maybe," he mused.

"How long have you and Tallon been friends?" I shifted in the seat again, earning me the stink-eye from Jameson.

"Sit fucking still. You're making me nervous. And, well, we were friends for a few years, met through some mutual friends, but then when his sister went missing, it changed everything. He was career focused before that, but after her abduction, it supercharged this need for him to spend all his time saving lives. After that, we drifted apart. I have a demanding job here, and he threw himself into each case he was given, not giving two shits about himself or what he was leaving behind."

Jameson's lips dipped into a frown.

Interesting. There was definitely more there between the two than either let on. But what... well, I could figure that out later. Now my focus was on the plan for once we arrived at our destination.

"How do you want to play this out since we're without backup?" I asked. Unable to help it, I shifted in the seat, trying to find a more comfortable position. "Charlie said it looked like a medium-size home stuck in the middle of some acreage. A home means lots of entry and exit points."

"Honestly, with this fucker, assuming he has Tallon's sister, we can't use any of our past tactics. We have to be smarter than him, which means going with our instincts, not a detailed plan."

"So just show up," I said, slowly mulling over the idea. "Read the scene and go from there."

"Exactly."

"I can get on board with that. As long as we're clear on one thing."

"The bastard is yours. Yeah, I know."

"Damn straight." The headlights reflected off the yellow stripe separating the two-lane country road we'd turned onto. "I feel bad for her," I said, staring out into the dark watching the trees pass by.

"Tallon's sister?"

"Why don't you call her Tinley?" I questioned.

He shrugged. "Too intimate when I didn't know her before all this. Doesn't feel right to just start calling her by her first name when she's never introduced herself."

Well, that was oddly considerate of him and open-minded.

"But no, not Tinley. This asshole's sister. She never had a chance." I returned my unseeing stare out the windshield. "Maybe neither of them did."

"A philosopher and empathetic. I think you're a rare breed, Agent Bennett. Most men would just be raging at the situation, yet you're thinking through all sides." He smiled. "I see why you're his best friend. Tallon doesn't handle shallow fools well."

I barked a laugh. "You can say that again. The dude has a short fuse when it comes to someone not thinking things through and considering all options before making an informed decision. Maybe a little too much." My phone dinged, signaling an upcoming turn. "There's a long driveway coming up in one mile on your left. And I'm not justifying this fucker's actions."

"Of course not. I know what you're saying, and I agree. Though we've all been through something in our lives that could've changed us, turned us into monsters like this Vincent guy. It's part of life, but how we let it mold us into who we become is what differentiates us."

"Good to know I'm not the only philosopher in the car." A soft chuckle rattled in my chest at his grumbled response as he turned the car down a darkened drive.

The crunch of gravel beneath the tires filled the car, silencing our conversation. Sitting up, I squinted to see farther ahead, only finding more trees. After a sharp bend in the drive, the headlights illuminated a one-story house that could be the set of any slasher film.

Before I could tell him to cut the lights—no need to announce our approach—Jameson flicked them off, dousing us in inky darkness, and eased the car to a stop.

The passenger door opened without a sound, the grinding of gravel beneath my boots joining the chorus of nocturnal animals. I turned, catching Jameson retreating toward the back of the car out of the corner of my eye. The trunk opened, the faint light enough for me to see him strapping on his bulletproof vest. Worry wove its way through my chest at the reminder that I didn't have one of my own. Going into the unknown situation without a vest was reckless behavior totally outside my norm, considering I had Vic waiting for me to come home. Even if Jameson had a spare, with his leaner build, there was no way it would cover my barrel chest.

I'd just need to be extra cautious, which wasn't ideal considering I already wanted to run into that house guns drawn and ready to fire. Not bothering to lower the trunk and risk the sound signaling our arrival, Jameson stepped to my side, still working on the Velcro straps for a snug fit.

Palm slick with sweat, I adjusted my hold along the coarse grip of my Glock. A quick hitch of my chin toward the house sent us both into motion. Mirroring the other's stride, we crept on silent feet, our guns at the ready, full focus on the front porch steps. The restraint to not rush our approach had my breaths coming in quick pants. Despite the cold night, anxious energy had sweat dripping down my spine, soaking the back of my dark shirt.

I held up a fist, stopping several feet from the steps leading to the porch. Brows furrowed, I studied the fresh tire tracks. Gun secured in one hand, I pointed at the clear indentions, signaling to Jameson where a car had been there recently. Worry grew in my gut that we were too late, but I forced it down to maintain the focus needed to keep us safe. Adjusting my grip on the gun to center my thoughts, I started for the stairs only to freeze.

I couldn't move as I stared at the crimson marring the rotten wood.

Blood.

Heart slamming inside my chest, my pulse thrummed in my ears, muting the outside world and whatever Jameson was whispering. Careful to not step in the odd bloodstain, I inched up the steps, each board groaning under my weight, then Jameson's. Two more odd designs glistened in the light pouring through the open front door from the inside of the house.

Two fingers raised, I indicated inside the house. Jameson nodded in understanding that we were entering together. Rage and trepidation surged through me. My hands shook with the flood of nervous energy.

Squeezing the grip of the gun, I stepped over the threshold. The overpowering stench of cleaning products mixed with the unmistakable coppery scent of blood assaulted my nostrils as I stalked through the house, following the bloody prints down a short hall, eyes scanning every dark corner for threats.

Throat dry from each rapid breath, I swallowed to breathe through my mouth as we neared the end of the hall where the stench of blood was the strongest. I chanced a look over my shoulder at a tense Jameson. Face tight, nostrils flaring, he gave a clipped nod. We both knew what the clues meant. We were too late.

A cry of anguish filled my chest as grief tried to stab its icy claws into me.

"Means nothing," Jameson whispered. "Don't give up on her."

Chest rising and falling, I nodded. He was right. I couldn't give up until I saw her with my own eyes. Taking five seconds to get my shit together, I blew out a heavy breath and turned to continue our search.

Back sealed to the hall wall, bits of the stiff paper flaking off, I placed one foot in front of the other moving deeper into the darkened hall. The prints were thicker, almost pools of blood now, all coming from the last room. At the edge of the dark wood doorframe, I paused and peered around the molding to get a glimpse inside.

A shocked breath caught in my throat at the blood spray covering the room in red. Splatter dotted the walls, more on the ceiling, with a large puddle, still glistening bright red, coating the hardwood floors on the other side of the single twin bed. Holding my breath, I advanced into the room. Gun gripped with both hands, I cleared the area of threats while avoiding the droplets of blood.

Jameson's gasp and low curse followed by a prayer cut through the quiet as he entered the room, but I paid him no attention.

My sole focus now that the room was safe was to uncover who the puddle of blood belonged to. Who all this blood belonged to.

Steeling myself for the worst, I pitched forward to look on the other side of the bed.

My heart stopped.

The world around me ceased to exist.

A lean body lay faceup on the floor surrounded by a thick crimson puddle. The vacant eyes wide open in what looked to be surprise were not my Tinley's.

They were his.

Drew Vincent.

I released the held breath burning my lungs, nearly slumping to the side in relief. Giving up on not disturbing the crime scene, I moved around the bed and squatted low. I held two fingers to his neck, his skin cool to the touch, verifying what I already knew.

A crack came from my old knees as I stood to full height. Holding up those two fingers, I stared at the ruby red liquid coating my fingertips.

"This just happened," Jameson said, gun still in hand but not nearly as tense as seconds ago. His head moved on a swivel as he took in the room in its entirety. "That's a fucking creepy-ass dollhouse."

I twisted and frowned. Turning back to the body, I used the toe of my boot to nudge his shoulder, the one place that wasn't coated with blood. His once blue dress shirt was soaked through, small gashes littering the front across the chest, stomach, and lower.

"Those footprints...."

I nodded without looking up at Jameson. "Were hers. And I'm assuming she stole his car too. That's why it was missing from the front."

"There's a shit ton of blood. Do you think she's injured?"

My heart clenched at the thought. "I don't... I don't know. It doesn't matter. She's on the run. No doubt freaking the fuck out. She just murdered someone. Fuck," I yelled, scanning the room. "There's so much fucking evidence."

"Some that could point to her."

"I can't think about that right now. I have to find her," I rasped. "She's got to be scared."

"First you have to help her by taking care of this," Jameson said with so much conviction that I snapped my head up, eyes wide. "Don't look at me like that. She's innocent, even if that damn body on the ground says otherwise, but a jury won't see it that way. Even if she claims self-defense, could she handle being put on trial? No, scratch that. Do you want her to stand trial for a murder you were more than willing to commit yourself?"

I took in the room, and something snapped into place. "That's why the footprints looked off. She's no doubt wearing socks." Her missing toes and slipping along the wood made the prints hard to disguise before.

"Meaning they can prove she fled the scene of a murder that she committed in cold blood."

It only took half a second to pick up what he was suggesting we do.

"What are the odds that the gas in the kitchen works?" I mused, holstering my gun.

I bristled at the mischievous smile that pulled up on Jameson's face. "You go find your girl. I can take care of this." He dipped his hand into the pocket of his slacks and pulled out the car keys.

I caught them midstride as I raced for the door.

He didn't have to tell me twice.

As I sprinted through the house of horrors, one question ran on a loop.

Where would Tinley feel safe to go at one in the morning?

I'd just wrapped my hand around the driver-side door handle when the answer smacked me in the face.

Smiling to myself, I yanked the door open and slid behind the wheel.

I knew exactly where she'd go.

32

TINLEY

Situated in the last spot in the very back of the small parking lot near the dumpsters, I studied my bloody hands, twisting them in the faint light. Somehow I'd had the clarity to back into the parking spot, putting the license plate to the concrete block wall. There was no doubt that Bryson had every cop in the state and maybe the next out searching for this car, knowing Vincent had me.

He had me. Until... until he didn't.

I tried to swallow only to find my mouth too dry, my tacky tongue sticking to the roof. I'd murdered someone in cold blood. Well, the first stab wound was sort of an accident when he hovered over me to force me into that disgusting leotard.

The other fifty times that blade sliced into his chest while I screamed and cried, well, that was just sheer rage and 100 percent not accidental. When his eyes had widened with surprise at the knife's handle jutting out of his chest, I acted. A dam of restrained emotions broke, flooding me with everything I'd held back the last ten years. I wanted to deal him the same hurt and pain, the same fear I'd lived. Once those floodgates opened, there was no shutting them off until sheer exhaustion and the inability to lift my arm one more time stopped me from inflicting more gruesome wounds to his already dead body.

Glassy gaze shifting over the steering wheel, I stared at the glowing red sign that informed drivers of the hot, delicious goodness that awaited inside those glass doors. Back of my hands resting on the tops of my thighs, I studied the dried blood coating the palms. Thankfully the sweatshirt was black, hiding the visual evidence of what I'd done, but from the thick and sticky feel of the fabric, it was no doubt saturated in that man's blood.

That man who was now dead because of me.

Maybe I was sick. Disturbed. But that thought made a slow grin spread up my blood-splattered cheeks.

Running a nail along the coagulated line of blood along one palm, I scraped off the sticky substance and rubbed it on my pants. Maybe I should've showered before I ran from the house, but the panic from what had almost happened, combined with what I'd done, kept me from thinking clearly. The image of the cops, FBI, and anyone else with a badge barging through the door and finding me on top of the body covered in blood, holding the murder weapon, had me racing out of there.

Thankfully, I had enough clarity in my shocked state to grab the keys to the car. Based on the surrounding trees I saw when he led me into the house, there was no escaping on foot. Digging into the pocket of his open pants was repulsive, but impaling his limp dick and balls with the knife had made me feel better about the act. Then I just left covered in blood with zero plan. Nowhere to go and out in the middle of fucking nowhere.

It had taken a while to find my way back to the interstate. As soon as I had my bearings, I white-knuckled the wheel and steered the car toward the one place I could always count on, my safe haven.

Krispy Kreme.

But what to do now was the question at hand. I sat in the car I'd stolen from the man I'd murdered, covered in his blood. No shoes. No change of clothes, just blood-soaked socks and sweats. Zero food or water and no money, though it wasn't like I could go inside anywhere like this. Hell, with my hands covered in flaking blood and blood soaking my cuticles, I couldn't even use a drive-through.

And worst of all, I had no one to call.

Deep in my heart, I knew Bryson wouldn't judge me for what I did in self-defense, but I didn't want to make him choose between me and his job. I murdered someone. Pretty sure he took an oath that required him to arrest me, even if he did more than love me. And the biggest reason I couldn't reach out to him was I had zero clue how to do so without my phone, where his number was saved in the favorites list.

Mulling over my options, I curled an arm around my growling stomach and hugged myself.

All in all, considering the last twenty-four hours, I was holding it together pretty well. A trickle of guilt said I was evil for not being more upset or traumatized by what I did. But the reality was I didn't feel bad at all. I found myself more relieved than anything else. It was over. The constant need to look over my shoulder, waiting for the other ball to drop, was done. I shouldn't feel relieved while his blood still coated my hands and body, but I did. Not sure what that made me, but I wasn't sad about taking a life.

Though I felt alone and really, really hungry and beyond thirsty. With all the tears I'd cried over the last twelve hours plus lack of water, I was clearly dehydrated. I was past even having enough saliva to swallow to soothe my parched throat.

Maybe I'd die here of starvation and thirst. They'd find me weeks from now, a husk of myself still sitting in this same car, still covered in blood. Or I could turn myself in, get that part out of the way, and then ask Rich to hire me an excellent lawyer.

Headlights flashed through the windshield as an older-model black car skidded into the parking lot. The thick cotton bunched along my back as I slunk down the soft leather to watch through the gap between the steering wheel and dash as the car slowed to a crawl, heading what felt like straight toward me.

The brakes squeaked as it pulled to a stop directly in front of the BMW, blocking me in place.

My breath sped up, chest moving up and down in quick succession.

I was trapped.

But when familiar broad shoulders exited the car, then turned, giving me a glimpse at a face filled with worry mixed with relief, all the tight tension in my chest loosened. I tracked his quick movements as he rounded the hood, jogging toward the BMW's driver side. Jerking forward, I fumbled with the multitude of buttons along the door until I hit the right one, unlocking all the locks.

Cold winter air burst through as the door flung open. Between blinks, Bryson went from standing to on his knees, hands reaching for me. Searing, calloused palms encased my cheeks, his worry-filled eyes searching every inch of my face.

"Tinley," he rasped. I opened my mouth, but nothing came out. "Are you hurt?" I shook my head but lifted my shoulder at the same time. "What does that mean? Do you need to go to the hospital?"

One hand slipped from my face, falling to my lap, and gripped the hem of the oversized sweatshirt. I placed one blood-coated hand on his before he could raise it higher than an inch.

"I'm okay. No hospital." I worried at the edge of my lip. "Bryson —" My voice cracked, unable to tell him what I'd done.

Sympathy washed over his face, easing some of the lines. "I know, I know. I was there. I saw."

I choked on a dry sob. "How did you find me?"

Amusement lit in his eyes as they flicked to the glowing red sign before settling back on me. "When you weren't there, plus the missing car, I asked myself where you would go. Where would Tinley Harper, scared and hungry, go at this hour?"

Despite it all, I felt my lips tug upward in an almost smile.

Flipping his hand over, he gripped my own and held it up higher, allowing the light from the storefront to highlight the blood covering my skin.

"We need to get you clean." His lips pursed in a thin line as he shifted to inspect the inside of the car. "And get rid of all this evidence."

"Get rid of the.... You can't be serious."

"Very. Come on. I'm sure you're tired, but we need to get moving. We have very little time." Sliding both hands beneath my armpits, he easily hauled me out of the car and stood, shifting me around to carry me bridal style. "Are the keys still in the ignition?" I nodded, still unsure about what the hell was going on. "Good girl."

He started to slip me into the passenger seat, but I stiffened. "I'm covered in blood." I nodded toward the dingy cloth seats of the town car.

Bryson studied the car like he was solving some kind of math equation. With a clipped nod, which I assumed was for himself, he opened the back door. "Grab my jacket." I stretched out, the soft shell creasing under my pinched fingers. The fewer places I touched, the better. "Drape it across the passenger seat so you can sit on it. If you could pretzel yourself like you always do, that would be great."

"Pretzel myself?"

"Yeah, tuck your knees up. I guess more like accordion your body."

I held back an inappropriate laugh and nodded in understanding. After spreading out the large jacket to cover the seat, he sat me down in the middle. Not touching the floorboard, I pulled both feet up to the seat. In a quick motion, Bryson pulled off his shirt and wrapped the arms around the headrest, the main part of the black T-shirt now covering the back so I could relax against the seat.

With Bryson close and the weight of the day hitting me full force, my lids were already drooping when he opened the driver door. I jumped, eyes flying open, when his door slammed shut.

Worry lurked behind his gaze as he glanced across the seat and reached out, cupping my jaw. "Sleep, baby. You're safe now. I'll take care of everything from here."

Like a command I couldn't ignore, my body went slack, lids fully closing, and the first full breath of the night escaped my softly parted lips. With his hand squeezing mine, the comfort of his presence, oblivion swept in before the car even left the parking lot.

I woke with a jolt, heart racing, but I wasn't sure why. Beside me, the driver seat was empty, door closed. Panicked, I bolted up straight in the seat, scanning out the windshield for Bryson. A blinking neon sign off in the distance drew my attention. The flicker of something had me turning to look out my window. Standing inside a small glass enclosure, Bryson was in front of a desk talking with a questionable-looking man who stood on the other side. Almost like he could feel my stare, Bryson checked over his shoulder, hazel eyes locking on me. Single finger raised in the air, he turned back to the man behind the counter.

Only slightly relaxing now that I knew he was close, I surveyed the area outside the car. Rough-looking cars, motel room doors facing the outside, and what looked to be a run-down pool sat in the middle of the chain-link fence surrounding it filled with holes and missing sections.

The driver door opened, allowing Bryson to slip inside.

"It's not much, but places like this don't ask questions." Fingers wrapped around the key, he started the car and inched forward, weaving through the parking lot before pulling into a vacant space. "Let me carry you again. Here's the key." A single key with a plastic room number keychain fell into my outstretched hand. My face must have scrunched in confusion, making him laugh. "Nothing high-tech for places that rent by the hour. "

Sealing me against his bare chest, he carried me into the room. Once inside, he juggled me to pull the key free and closed the door behind us with a hard kick. Covered in blood, I fully expected him to drop me on the bed, ready to get away from any evidence that could tie him to the murder, but he strode right for the tiny bathroom. The light over the sink struggled to click on, flickering a few times before the hum of the fluorescent bulb carried through the bathroom.

"I'm going to set you down inside the bathtub. I need you to strip off everything." Turning, he reached for the trash can and pulled out the small clear bag. "Stuff it all in here. I'll go grab another trash bag from the other room."

The cotton stuck to my skin, parts of the sweatshirt stiff from the dried blood. Naked, I stuffed the soiled clothes into the two bags, which Bryson took and tied closed. I cranked the shower knob all the way to the right, and a rush of freezing cold water sprayed my toes from the tub spout.

"Once that's warm, turn on the shower and start scrubbing. Don't stop until I get back."

Panic hit me square in the chest. I shot my hand out, grabbing for his arm before I could stop. "Where are you going?"

Those tight lines around his eyes and along his forehead smoothed. "To get us both some clothes that can't tie us to the crime scene. Do not open the door for anyone but me." Pulling out his phone, he placed it on the edge of the sink. "If you get scared or something happens, call Jameson. His name is in my favorites. I shouldn't be gone over thirty minutes. There's a Walmart right next door."

I chewed on the corner of my lip. "Can you get me some food?"

"Of course, baby. Clean clothes, food, and water. Then we talk."

I hung my head. "Okay."

"Hey, don't worry, Tinley. I mean talk as in making sure you're okay. I'm not judging you for what you did at that house." I tipped my head up, peering at Bryson through my tear-crusted lashes. "I'm so damn proud of you, but I have to do all this first to keep you safe. I can't have anything pointing to you for that fucker's death."

"What about the house?"

"Jameson is taking care of it. That's all I know. The water should be warm now. Clean up. I'll be back soon."

Warm lips pressed to my forehead, lingering for a moment before he turned and left the bathroom.

Exhaustion rolled through me, making me sway on my feet. Careful to use the grimy tile for support to not fall, I wrapped two fingers around the metal pin and pulled, switching the water flow to the showerhead.

Instead of unwrapping the small bar of soap resting on the dish or turning to soak my hair, I sank to the questionably clean tub and curled both knees to my chest. Warm water cascaded over my head, drenching my hair, still partially contained by a hair tie. Pink water ran off my skin, rushing toward the open drain. With a heavy sigh, I pressed my forehead to my knees and shut both eyes.

I had no clue how long I sat there, allowing the falling water to clean my skin, unable to muster the energy to start scrubbing. The water had shifted to barely warm when gentle hands began kneading the top of my head, fingers trailing through my hair. There was no need to look up and see who was washing my hair, so I stayed curled in my tight ball, hoping that was enough to keep the reality of what I'd done at bay.

Hair clean, he pulled one hand free, scrubbing every inch with the small bar of soap all the way up to my shoulder before moving to the next.

"I need you to stand for me." Bryson's voice was soft, like he knew how fragile I felt.

My muscles protested as I uncurled my stiff body and took his hand to help me stand. With quick, efficient movements, he scrubbed the rest of my body clean, all the way down to my toes, though I couldn't bring myself to care about my ugly feet, numbness from emotional overload officially overtaking me.

Water still running, he helped me out of the tub, wrapped me in a small scratchy towel, and stripped out of his own clothes. I clutched the towel to my chest as he quickly scrubbed himself down in the now-cold water.

Turning off the shower, he slung a towel around his waist, the ends barely meeting.

"There are clothes, socks, food, and water in the room." I nodded and turned. "Hey, Tinley?" My wet hair clung to my back and shoulders as I paused, twisting to meet his imploring hazel eyes. "We'll get through this. You and me. Everything will be okay."

I forced a smile to help ease his worry and headed into the bedroom. No underwear, not that I minded. I pulled on the women's basic pink matching sweats and used the saturated towel to finish drying my hair while Bryson dressed in a similar outfit, though his sweats were light gray.

He cringed at my fluorescent pink outfit that would no doubt glow in the dark. "Sorry, that was all they had in your size."

"It's fine. It's clean and warm. That's what matters." Digging into the McDonald's bag, I pulled out a hamburger and practically shredded the orange wrapper to get to the deliciousness inside. A half cry, half moan of pleasure escaped as I bit into the Quarter Pounder with cheese, the grease and salt exploding on my taste buds. Mouth still full, I took a long sip of the large Coke.

Bryson laughed, watching as he pulled out his own burger, digging in with much the same desperate fashion. Cramming a handful of fries past my lips, I smiled, this one real, the food helping my outlook more than I expected.

"Thank you." I was past caring about talking with my mouth full. "For everything tonight. Though won't you get in trouble? Pretty sure I'm a fugitive."

Bryson laughed, covering his mouth with a loose fist so food didn't fly out. "You're not a fugitive. And yeah, maybe I'm dabbling in the gray area of justice right now, but I don't care. There's no way I'll allow you to be charged for killing that fucker. He deserved it. I know that and you know that, but without evidence, no one else would've seen it that way. You did what needed to be done."

Tallon's face flashed in my mind, making me choke on the sip of drink I'd just downed. "Oh my goodness," I said around my coughing. "I'm the worst sister ever, only thinking about me—"

"Pretty sure you've had your plate full tonight."

I fake-scowled and pointed a limp fry at his face. "Are Tallon and Remington okay?"

Bryson took his sweet time taking a long drink, clearly not hearing the desperation in my raspy voice. "Both are fine. Tallon is awake and should be discharged from the hospital tomorrow. Remington took some hits, but she'll be fine." He shoved a fry into his mouth and arched a brow in my direction. "I'm assuming they both owe their lives to you." I broke off his stern stare. "You're amazing, Tinley Harper. Fucking amazing."

I swallowed down a too-large bite. "I had to. All this was my fault."

"Tinley." The intensity in his tone snapped my attention back his way. "You know that's not true. None of this was your fault. None of it."

Sure, deep down, I knew that. All I did was dance one night, and bam, that bastard had me in his sights. But still, I felt guilty about all the death and hurt that happened because of me.

"I know." I tapped a fry against the top of my drink lid. "He was disturbed, not right in the head." I swallowed hard and shifted on the bed. "It was him or me. I had to do it."

"I know."

"He used to watch his sister be raped by their father and did nothing about it." Unable to stomach eating while recounting what he'd told me, I shoved the remaining food back in the bag. Drink cup held in both hands, I leaned back against the headboard, studying the floral-patterned flat comforter. "He killed her. She tried to stop him when he attempted to assault her, and he killed her for it. He was a terrible, evil human." When Bryson tried to talk, I held up a hand. "I know I should feel guilty, but I don't. I'm relieved that it's over, that he won't hurt anyone else. I'm glad I took his life. I'm glad it was me who did it and that he's not getting a chance at a trial. What does that say about me that I don't feel bad? That I'm happy?"

"Nothing. It means nothing, Tinley, you hear me? My only regret is that I wasn't there to see the life seep from his eyes, to see the sheer defeat he must have felt when you stabbed him. Me being happy that he's gone doesn't make me a bad person. You ending the string of death he left in his wake doesn't make you a bad person either."

I mulled over Bryson's words as he cleaned up, moving the brown to-go bags, wrappers, and drinks to the two-person round table near the door.

"What happens now?" I asked.

"Now"—he stripped back the stiff duvet and climbed beneath the paper-soft sheet—"we sleep for a few hours. Then we go back to life as it was before forty-eight hours ago."

I gaped at him. "That's it?"

"That's it. I've taken care of that fucker's car—"

"How?"

A menacing smirk tugged at his lips as he punched the deflated pillow. "I still have some connections in the world's underbelly who loved the tip of a BMW just waiting to be taken and stripped for parts." He pulled me toward him and maneuvered my limp body until I was beneath the sheet and curled against his chest. "Does that bother you?"

My barked laugh snuck out before I even knew I was laughing. "Bother me? That you know car thieves when I just murdered someone? No, Bry, it doesn't bother me. Kind of hot, actually."

I was almost asleep when his lips brushed against the shell of my ear.

"I was so worried that I'd never see you again, that I'd be too late to save you. Then you went and saved yourself. You're an amazing woman, and I can't wait until the day when I can officially make you mine."

A radiant smile spread across my cheeks as I drifted off, knowing tonight I'd sleep soundly even in the dark. Partly because of the man beside me, but more because I'd done something not even the fairy tales could conjure.

I slayed my villain, and that was the perfect ending to start my future.

33

TINLEY

Sunday, December 16th

Snuggled against Bryson's chest, I inhaled deep and then slowly released it through soft lips, allowing my body to relax. He tipped his face down, his attention straying from the conversation with Jameson and Tallon, and grinned. Leaning forward, he sealed a kiss to my temple then turned back to the two men.

"I still can't believe you blew up a house for my sister," Tallon said, shaking his head, a disbelieving smile stretched across his face. The slightly pale tint of his normally tan skin and the dark circles under his bright eyes were the only signs that anything had happened three days ago. Tears swelled in my lower lids, heart heavy at almost losing him to the monster who'd tried to take everything from me. Almost like he felt my attention and mind going down a dark path, Tallon shot a wink over his shoulder.

"I have no idea what you're talking about," Jameson answered from across the living room. He sat relaxed, one foot propped up on the opposite knee in one of the chairs, grinning ear to ear like the cat who ate the canary. "As I told the local police who arrived on the scene after I called in my location, the reason I waited outside in the first place was because I smelled gas wafting out the open front door. I didn't even get to investigate the tip that our potential suspect was inside before it exploded. With the debris and fire, there was no way to truly know what happened inside that house."

"And they bought that?" Bryson laughed, the deep rumble from his chest tickling my ear.

"Of course they did. I told them we had a tip about a potential suspect's hideout, though when we arrived, you had to leave to check on another lead. Speaking of, where is that fucker's car?" Jameson's foot dropped to the floor as he sat forward, pressing his forearms to the tops of his thighs. His gaze met mine for a brief second. A smile twitched at the corner of his lips before he directed his attention back to Bryson, waiting on his answer.

"Probably scattered around the state by now. The guy I called works fast. It's how he's evaded the cops for so long."

"What kind of people have you surrounded yourself with?" Tallon asked, faking shock.

"No one new," Bryson said with a shrug. I grumbled at the movement. "Just old... acquaintances who don't know my real name."

Smart, sexy, and dangerous. My happy smile grew, a dull burn rising in my bunched cheeks from all the smiling I'd done the last few hours. I was in love with a brilliant man. Everyone was safe. Tallon, Bryson, Remington, and me. We made it through. There was a string of bodies left in that man's wake, which made my heart hurt if I thought too hard on it, but deep down, I knew it wasn't my fault.

None of it was my fault. That was the bit of truth I grasped on to anytime I felt bad about it all. I had to remind myself that I was the victim, the survivor, the innocent girl caught in his morbid fascination. There would be tough days ahead, that I was certain of, but Bryson promised to be there by my side. To walk through the dark with me.

And that made it all seem less daunting.

Doable.

Because we could get through it together.

Today was the day I started my new life. With him.

"You all packed?" Bryson asked, lips against my hair. "Or do you want to buy everything new?"

I shook my head. As revolting as the idea of that bastard touching my clothes was, knowing he was dead erased the ick factor of wearing them again. Plus, I wasn't in a financial position to drop a few hundred dollars on new clothes, and I liked my carefully collected items I'd selected through the years from thrift stores and Goodwill.

"I'll pack in a few. Is that okay? Right now I just want to savor this." I gestured around the room.

"This?" Tallon said, twisting on the couch, back pressed against the opposite end's armrest.

"Hanging out, not talking about murder or stalkers. It's...." I let out a loud sigh. "Nice knowing no one is out there plotting to hurt me."

Tallon's eyes shot to the side, sharing a look with Jameson.

"What?" Both men sealed their lips in a flat line. "What?" I demanded as I pushed off Bryson's thigh to sit up straight.

Tallon scrubbed a hand over his short blond hair. "When SWAT raided the location where they found that woman, Remington, there was no one else there. The bastard evaded the team and disappeared." I held a breath and swallowed, slowly shaking my head in disbelief. Tallon's brows dipped, worry shining through his pleading eyes. The couch groaned as he pitched forward and gripped my knee. "Don't worry, Tin. I'll find the fucker. You're safe. We have no reason to believe he'd come after you. With my task force already in place looking for this guy—"

"And me," Jameson cut in. "Now that I'm in on this, plus with the two murders here in Nashville we assume were done by him, I have local jurisdiction to assist on the case."

"And Jameson," Tallon said, clearing his throat. "Plus the profile Agent Rhyan gave us on this guy. I know we'll find him fast. Before, there was conflicting evidence because there were two people involved. Now we only have one to hunt down."

I searched his eyes, looking for any signs. "Okay, I trust you, Tal, but I need you to keep Bry updated if things change and you think

I'm on his radar. I'll be in Louisville with Victoria, and I won't risk her being in danger because of me."

Bryson's arm snaked around my waist, tugging me back. Soft lips brushed against my temple.

"When do you two plan to leave?" Tallon asked, face pinched like he'd eaten something sour.

"Soon," Bryson responded. "I'd like to be home by supper."

I couldn't help the grin that once again spread up my cheeks.

Home.

After checking the time on my phone, I reluctantly peeled away from Bryson. It was almost time to get packing. Arms stretched high to the ceiling, I savored the dull ache from our previous evening's activities.

When I was halfway to the bedroom, a knock on the door sounded through the apartment.

All three men leaped from their seats, attention zeroed on the door. Bryson beat the other two, his gun clutched in his grip as he twisted the doorknob. Unable to see past his thick frame, I moved to find a beaten and bruised Remington standing in the hall. She rolled her eyes at the gun now hanging by Bryson's side.

"Seriously?" She scoffed. "Is this how you always greet visitors?"

Bryson chuckled as he holstered the gun and opened the door wider for her to step into the apartment.

"What happened to your face?" I asked, weaving through the other two men standing as still as statues. Hands on her shoulders, I pulled her into a tight hug. A sharp hiss whistled through her teeth, making me immediately drop my hold and move back a step to give her some room. When I started to apologize, the words froze in my throat, finding her green eyes wide with what looked like horror or surprise, her gaze trained over my shoulder.

Twisting to see what scared her, I frowned. Both Tallon and Jameson still stood in the same place, similar looks of shock on their combined slack faces. Beside me, Bryson's head whipped back and forth, looking from Remington to the two men, clearly picking up on the oddness of the situation too.

"You?" she squeaked. "What are you two doing here?"

My brows dipped. "That's my brother Special Agent Tallon Harper," I said hooking a thumb in his direction. "And detective Jameson Bend. I'm confused. What"

"Remy?" Tallon and Jameson said in unison cutting me off, their voices sharing the same disbelieving tone.

Before I could ask what the hell was going on, Remington turned on the heels of her Doc Martens and started for the door.

"Obviously this is a bad time. Good to see you again, Tinley, and good luck," she called over her shoulder before disappearing down the hall.

Tallon and Jameson shared a look, faces morphing from shock to determination before racing after her. Their loud voices calling out for her to stop echoed down the hall.

"What the hell was that about?" I asked, blinking at the place where the two of them were just standing. "Remy?"

"Not sure, kid, but I'm sure we'll find out soon enough. Now"—he popped his hand against my ass, sliding me forward an inch from the force—"go pack. It's time."

Rubbing my abused cheek, I met his soft gaze. "Time for what?"

"To start our forever."

EPILOGUE
TINLEY

One week later

The hot mug warmed my chilled palms as I gripped it tightly in both hands. Avoiding Tallon's penetrating gaze, I shifted my attention around the coffee shop, taking small sips of the delicious coffee just to have something to do with this nervous energy that was desperate to explode out of me.

"I'm at a loss for words, Tin." I nodded, agreeing with him because I sure as shit didn't know what to say. He'd just heard every dark secret I'd spent most of my life keeping hidden from him during the two-hour therapy session with Dr. Sarah. "I'm sad that you felt like I wouldn't believe you or would look at you differently. I'm your big brother. It's my job to protect you." He snorted. "Now the recent sexual harassment and malpractice investigation into our fucked-up stepbrother makes sense. I'm sure Bryson and that Charlie guy had something to do with that. Though jail isn't enough punishment for that sick bastard."

"I'm sorry—" I started, but he wrapped his hand around my wrist, stopping me.

"Don't you dare say you're sorry. You have nothing to be sorry for.

Maybe if... maybe if I would've been honest with you, you would've felt you could be the same with me."

My pinkish hair slipped over my shoulder as I tilted my head, not understanding. "What haven't you been honest with me about? You're like the perfect son—per Mom, anyway. She always wanted me to live up to your standards," I grumbled.

His grip on my wrist tightened.

"She's manipulated us both for far too long, Tin." At his forceful exhale, I peeked up through my lashes. Staring out the window behind my shoulder, he looked lost in thought. "But today, because of you being brave and inviting me to that session, I'm going to do the same."

I straightened on the wooden bench. Forgetting about the coffee, I wrapped both my hands around his and tried for an encouraging smile. My heart hammered as I waited.

Was this it? The moment he and I put it all on the table and moved past whatever wedged between us years ago? I hoped so. I missed my brother. Not the overworked, stick-in-the-mud jackass he'd been the last ten years but the one who would joke around with me, see the good in the world, and had fun. Maybe he needed this just as much as I did today.

"You don't have to, Tal," I whispered. His bright blue eyes met mine, and he shook his head. "Don't feel forced because of what I told you today. This isn't a competition on whose trauma is worse," I said, trying to lighten the mood.

It didn't work.

"It happened in college." My jaw snapped shut, and I sealed my lips to keep from interrupting. "When I found out my...." His eyes flicked to the ceiling as if he was searching for the right word. "Kink. I think that's what kids are calling it nowadays."

My huffed laugh made one corner of his lips twitch upward.

"And what did kids call it back then?" I asked.

"We didn't. There was a stigma back then on this kind of thing. It happened one night at a party. Me and the other two were drunk as shit. One thing led to another, and it was fun. More than fun."

"You and...."

"Me, a guy, and a girl."

I nodded, letting him know I was now tracking. I mean, he could've been talking about a reverse harem for all I knew.

"And that's how you knew you were into being a furry."

His blond brows shot up his forehead. "What the hell? What's a furry?"

"When you like to get dressed up as an animal and have sex," I said, barely refraining from adding the "duh" at the end.

"I don't even want to know how you know about that, but fuck no. I'm not into being a Furby—"

"Furry."

"Whatever."

"So, just you and another guy and a girl."

"Yes."

"A ménage."

Tallon cringed. "Yes."

"Oh, cool. Okay, well, keep going now that I know we're not talking about you wearing a bear costume."

His features softened. "You don't seem offended that your big brother likes to fuck a woman with another guy."

I shrugged. "I mean, if that's your thing and everyone is consenting adults, then sure. Have at it."

A lightness I hadn't seen in years seemed to radiate from his smile and happy eyes. With a relieved sigh, he relaxed back against the booth.

"I always pictured this going differently. Mom said—"

"She's a fucking cunt."

At Tallon's barked laugh, a few heads turned our way. He shook his head as he watched me. "Somehow she found out and held it over me, said she'd tell you how disgusting I was and you'd never want to see me again. Looking back, it was absurd, but you were so young, and I couldn't risk losing you. So I kept it from you, from Bryson even, knowing everyone would look down on me if they found out."

"She blackmailed you," I gritted out. "She blackmailed her own son. For what?"

"Anything. Mostly she just enjoyed holding it over my head, and then—" He stopped and cleared his throat. "The night you were taken, I was with two people. I'd already felt guilty over my kink, but then you were taken while I was taking part in it, and—"

"You felt somehow accountable."

He nodded.

"Tal," I whispered. "You living your life didn't affect how that night turned out. It wouldn't have mattered if you were there or with nine people." It hit me like a ton of bricks, making me slump backward. "She told you I'd blame you."

Tallon nodded. "Remember, Tin, I blamed myself already. Then there was Mom, whether she knew or just assumed, saying I did this to you because I was fucked-up. I've carried that mistake on my shoulders ever sense. I ended all those relationships, stopped going to the bars where we'd meet up."

"And stopped living in the process, Tal."

His returning nod was stiff. Silence stretched between us.

"Is that it?" I asked.

"Yeah, well...." He closed his eyes and blew out a breath. "That woman, the computer one."

"Remington."

"Well, there's a story that—" The sharp ring of his cell phone cut him off. Picking it up off the table, he narrowed his eyes at the screen. "Speaking of Mom...." After hitting the Decline button, he set it back down, only for it to ring again.

"Get it. See what the witch wants, because I need this uninterrupted story of Remy like yesterday."

After hitting the green button, he flicked it over to speakerphone.

"Mom," he said in greeting, though his tone was ice cold.

"Tallon, there's been a development, and I'll need to stay with you for a little while."

Tallon's eyes were surely as wide as mine as we exchanged a look.

"What's going on?" he asked.

She huffed, clearly annoyed. "Someone sent photoshopped pictures of me and Jessie, our pool boy. As if I would fuck the help."

Photoshopped. Right. The fact that she'd kept her afternoon delight time with the ever-rotating door of pool boys from Rich all these years was astonishing. Either Rich was naïve or just didn't want to deal with the fallout of calling her out on her affairs.

"And he's kicked you out," Tallon said, putting it all together before I did.

Clasping a hand over my mouth to stifle a laugh, I leaned forward to not miss a second of her new misfortune.

"Which is why I'm headed to your apartment. You will meet me there to let me in, and I will need a key. Also—"

"No," Tallon said, more like a curse than a reply. "You're not staying with me."

"WHAT DO you think your sister will say when she finds out you were out fucking around while she was taken?" I could almost hear her malicious grin through the phone. All my humor faded, replaced with anger at the bitch. *How dare she treat us this way, pit us against each other all these years and still have the audacity to ask for more?* "You know she blames you for what happened that night—"

"Oh hell no," I hissed. Grabbing the phone, I took it off speaker and pressed the smooth glass to my ear. "You listen, and you listen good. We're done with you. You will not contact us again. There are no more calls, texts, or favors. You are a vile human, and I don't want you around me or my brother."

"Give me that," Tallon said just as he yanked the phone from my hand. After clearing his throat, he leveled a look my way and then pressed it to his ear. "What she said."

Hitting the End button, he tossed the phone to the wooden table between us and heaved a heavy sigh.

I knew I should wait to allow him a few seconds to process what all just went down, but that bitch didn't deserve any more of our time.

"So," I said, wrapping my hands around my gray mug. "Tell me the story about Remy."

A slow smile crept up his cheeks.

And just like that, my brother, the real Tallon, was back.

What are Tallon, Jameson, and Remington hiding?

**Find out in Tallon's story, *Mine to Love*, releasing June 27th!
Preorder today.**

Keep reading for a BONUS epilogue!

BONUS EPILOGUE
TINLEY

December of the following year.

Humming along to the *Mickey Mouse Clubhouse* theme song playing in the living room, I swayed back and forth to the beat, Victoria singing her version from where she sat straddling my hip. At her favorite part, I ditched the spoon, allowing it to rest along the side of the pot, and grabbed her raised chubby hand to dip our hands up and down in the strange dance we'd created the last thousand times we'd done this.

"My pony," Victoria exclaimed. I hummed in acknowledgment, not taking my eyes off the steaming pot of chili. "My pony, my mommy."

Eyes going round, I held a breath, forcing a smile as I turned to her smiling face. Reaching up, I swiped at the corner of her cheek to wipe away the traces of her lunch. This wasn't the first time she'd called me that, and each time, I wasn't sure if I was elated or sad. It felt greedy to encourage her to call me that when Bryson and I weren't married. Not that I was going anywhere, but nevertheless, if something happened between us, I didn't want to cause Victoria any pain or confusion by allowing her to call me mommy and then leaving.

Pinching her cheeks together to make her lips pucker like a fish, I morphed my own in the same shape and gave her a fish kiss.

"I'm your pony now and forever, sweet girl," I said. Grabbing a rogue curl that fell from her pigtails, I tucked it behind her ear. "And I will always, always be there for you."

"I kind of like the sound of that."

I whirled around on the balls of my feet, a wide grin spreading across my cheeks. Bryson leaned against the entryway, still dressed in a suit, having just gotten home from work. It had been a few days since I'd last seen him, as he'd been working on an intense case. A happy squeal erupted from both me and Victoria.

Bryson's face lit up as he shoved off the doorframe and strode into the kitchen, enveloping us both in a tight hug.

"I missed you," he said into my ear. The hand at my waist slipped lower to grab a handful of my ass and squeeze—hard. I bit my tongue to contain my responding groan.

Victoria's warm body was lifted away, leaving me cold and vacant. Bryson tossed her in the air, Victoria's giggles sounding through the kitchen.

"And how have my favorite three girls been while I've been away?" Holding Victoria tight to his chest, Bryson stole a quick kiss while rubbing my somewhat rounded belly. "You feeling okay?"

I rolled my eyes in fake annoyance. "Yep, same as when you asked me this morning when you called."

"Just making sure." His smile grew as he turned to the also beaming Victoria.

"What?" I said, eyeing the pair. "What are you two up to?" Hands on my hips, I leveled them with my most stern stare, though all it did was make them both laugh.

"I have a confession to make," Bryson said while adjusting his hold to keep the squirming Victoria in place. "I'm tired of calling you my girlfriend, and clearly the boss of the house"—he bounced Victoria around for emphasis—"is done calling you her pony."

"My pony is my mommy," Victoria said, sounding almost exasperated.

Oh, we were going to have our hands full with her. I just knew it.

"Is that so?" I hedged, biting the corner of my lip to hold back my growing smile. My heart soared with hope while my stomach fluttered with nerves. I placed a hand over my five-months-along belly to ease the sensation.

It didn't take Bryson or me long to decide one sweet child wasn't enough. Little did we know it would only take a month after I removed my IUD to get pregnant, though neither of us minded. My eyes still filled with tears thinking about his sheer joy when I told him I was pregnant. We still didn't know the sex, though Bryson was sticking to his assumption that it was a girl.

"It is, which is why Victoria and I have a very important question for you, Tinley."

I sucked in a breath, knowing what was coming. I'd hoped for this day, longed for it for months, and now that it was here, the joyful anticipation was more than I could've ever imagined.

"I'm listening," I rasped.

Victoria looked at Bryson at the same time he looked at her. He widened his eyes and inclined his head my way.

"This is your part, little bit," he whispered loud enough for me to hear.

I pressed a hand to my lips, hiding my spreading grin. Victoria's smile fell to a serious expression that only made me want to laugh even more.

"My pony will be my mommy." She pointed to herself, then to Bryson, almost jabbing him in the eye. "And Daddy's mommy."

"Wife," he corrected. Turning sheepish eyes to me, he withdrew his hand from the side pocket of his slacks. He held his upturned palm between us, and I couldn't look away from the black velvet box resting on top. "What she's trying to say is we love you." The building tears broke free at that point, cascading down my bunched cheeks. "We love you so much, and we want to make you ours forever. I know it won't be easy, that there will be more hard days than easy ones, but

I want all those days with you. You're the heart of this family, Tinley, the love, passion, and joy that only you can give."

Hand cupped around my mouth and nose, I continued to nod while blinking back tears.

"So," he said before lowering to one knee. At his stifled groan, I burst out laughing, earning me a playful smack to my backside. "Tinley Rebecca Harper, will you make us, me and Victoria, the happiest two people on this earth and become my wife and Victoria's mommy?"

"Yes," I whispered, nodding so hard my blonde hair bounced. "Yes, yes, yes. I want you both so much. Yes, I will marry you," I said, cupping Bryson's cheeks and kissing his lips with the same fierce emotion running through me. Turning to Victoria, I squished her lips like I did earlier and did the same to mine before popping a kiss to her fish lips. "And, sweet girl, nothing would make me happier than to be your mommy. Forever."

"Forever," Bryson said with a happy sigh.

Now to start my new life.

With them.

Happy. Safe. Loved.

Forever.

Preorder Mine to Love coming June 2022!

ALSO BY KENNEDY L. MITCHELL

In Clear Sight: A Small Town, WITSEC Interconnected Standalone Series

Guarded (Coming September 2022)

Cherished (Coming October 2022)

Saved (Coming December 2022)

Hidden (Coming February 2023)

Protection Series: A Dark Romantic Thriller Interconnected Standalone Series

Mine to Protect

Mine to Save

Mine to Guard

Mine to Keep

Mine to Hold

Mine to Love (Coming June 2022)

SEALs and CIA Series: A Navy SEAL Interconnected Standalone Series

Covert Affair

Covert Vengeance

More Than a Threat Series: A Connected Bodyguard Romantic Suspense Series

More Than a Threat

More Than a Risk

More Than a Hope

Power Play Series: A Protector Romantic Suspense Connected Series

Power Games

Power Twist

Power Switch

Power Surge

Power Term

Standalones:

Finding Fate - Dark, Captive Romantic Suspense

Memories of Us - Contemporary, Small Town Romance

ACKNOWLEDGMENTS

Wow. Another book done. I hope you enjoyed it! I had so much fun writing these two. They story just flowed from the moment I sat down and started writing. Their chemistry and back stories were ones I've worked on for a while. The part about Bryson's past with his mother comes from how I was raised. There were several in my church that believed that there was no need for consent when married, it was the man's right to take what he wanted since they were married. Obvi I 100% disagree with that but it was a belief by some.

I loved writing Tinley saving herself. Being smart and strong made me love her a thousand times more. I could have easily had Bryson come in and save the day but that's not what Tinley needed. She needed to slay her own dragons to prove to herself and everyone else that chapter of her life was closed. Now she can move on with a love filled life with Bryson and Victoria.

OMG Victoria what a sweetie am I right!

Lots of long hours, many- MANY- text go into polishing a story. I might have characters and a plot in mind but that only gets you so far. My alpha readers are who really make this story make sense. Thank you to Kristin who reads nightly and always responds to my planning texts even when she's in the middle of a tennis match! And of course Em and Chris who have been with me from the start. With out you three I wouldn't want to do this.

Darlene, thank you so much for beta reading! I had no idea I needed to tie up some loose ends until you pointed that out. You're amazing and I can't thank you enough for helping me put out a polished story.

Then there is my ARC team who help me promote and give honest feedback to the story before it's even released. You guys are beyond amazing. Thank you so much for all that you do to help get my books out there. I love our little close nit group.

And last but not least... thank YOU. Thank you for reading. For picking up my book and giving me a chance. I couldn't do this with out you. Every comment, review, and email is read. Thank you for giving me a sliver of your time.

Until next time.

Happy reading friends.

ABOUT THE AUTHOR

Kennedy L. Mitchell lives outside Dallas with her husband, son and two very large goldendoodles. She began writing in 2016 and has no plans of stopping.

She would love to hear from you via any of the platforms below or her website www.kennedylmitchell.com You can also stay up to date on future releases through her newsletter or by joining her Facebook readers group - Kennedy's Book Boyfriend Support Group.

Thank you for reading.

Made in the USA
Columbia, SC
25 May 2022

60928352R00214